HARVEST IN TRANSLATION

Also by Orhan Pamuk

THE WHITE CASTLE

Orhan Pamuk

THE BLACK BOOK

Translated by Güneli Gün

A HARVEST BOOK
HARCOURT BRACE & COMPANY
SAN DIEGO   NEW YORK   LONDON

To Aylın

According to what Ibn Arabi relates as an accomplished fact, a
sainted friend of his, whom spirits elevated up to the heavens,
on one occasion arrived on Mount Kaf, which circumscribes the
world, and observed that the mountain itself was circumscribed
by a serpent. Now, it is a well-known fact that there is no such
mountain which circumscribes the earth, nor such a serpent.

—THE ENCYCLOPEDIA OF ISLAM

Translation copyright © 1994 by Güneli Gün
Originally published in Turkish as *Kara Kitap*
by Can Yayinlavi Ltd. Sti, © 1990 by Orhan Pamuk

Requests for permission to make copies of any part of this book should be
mailed to: Permissions Department, Farrar, Straus & Giroux, Inc.,
19 Union Square West, New York, New York 10003.

Grateful acknowledgment is made for permission to excerpt from the following:
Madame Bovary by Gustave Flaubert, translated by Alan Russell, © 1950 by
Alan Russell, by permission of Penguin Books Ltd. *The Conference of the Birds*
by Farid ud-Din Attar, translated by Afkham Darbandi and Dick Davis, © 1984
by Afkham Darbandi and Dick Davis, by permission of Penguin Books Ltd.
Dante's Inferno by Dante Alighieri, translation by Mark Musa, © 1971 by
Indiana University Press. *Seven Gothic Tales* by Isak Dinesen, © 1980 by
Random House, Inc. *Remembrance of Things Past* by Marcel Proust, translated
by C. K. Scott-Moncrieff and Terence Kilmartin, © 1982 by Random House, Inc.

Library of Congress Cataloging-in-Publication Data
Pamuk, Orhan, 1952–
   [Kara kitap. English]
   The black book/Orhan Pamuk: translated by Güneli Gün.—1st Harvest ed.
   p. cm.—(A Harvest book)
   ISBN 0-15-600329-5
   I. Gün, Güneli. II. Title.
PL248.P34K3713 1996
894'.3533—dc20   96-5281

Printed in the United States of America
First Harvest edition 1996
E D

Contents

PART ONE

1	The First Time Galip Saw Rüya	3
2	*The Day the Bosphorus Dries Up*	14
3	Give My Regards to Rüya	19
4	*Aladdin's Store*	35
5	Perfectly Childish	42
6	*Master Bedii's Children*	52
7	The Letters in Mount Kaf	58
8	*The Three Musketeers*	72
9	Somebody's Following Me	80
10	*The Eye*	96
11	We Lost Our Memories at the Movies	105
12	*The Kiss*	115
13	Look Who's Here!	121
14	*We Are All Waiting for Him*	131
15	Love Tales on a Snowy Night	139
16	*I Must Be Myself*	155
17	Do You Remember Me?	161

18   *The Dark Void*   179
19   Signs of the City   184

PART TWO

20   The Phantom Abode   205
21   *Are You Unable to Sleep?*   215
22   Who Killed Shams of Tabriz?   219
23   *The Story of Those Who Cannot Tell Stories*   233
24   Riddles in Faces   236
25   *The Executioner and the Weeping Face*   248
26   Mystery of Letters and Loss of Mystery   256
27   *A Lengthy Chess Game*   268
28   The Discovery of the Mystery   276
29   *I Turned Out to Be the Hero*   291
30   Brother Mine   295
31   *The Story Goes through the Looking Glass*   319
32   I Am Not a Mental Case, Just One of Your Loyal Readers   325
33   *Mysterious Paintings*   345
34   Not the Storyteller, the Story   350
35   *The Story of the Prince*   363
36   But I Who Write   380

Part One

Chapter One

THE FIRST TIME GALIP
SAW RÜYA

Do not use epigraphs; they will only kill the mystery in the piece! —ADLI

Go ahead, kill the mystery; kill the false prophet too who pushes mystery!
—BAHTI

Rüya slept on her stomach in the sweet and warm darkness under the blue-checkered quilt which covered the entire bed with its undulating, shadowy valleys and soft blue hills. The first sounds of the winter morning penetrated the room: carts passing by sporadically and old buses, the salep maker, who was in cahoots with the pastry man, banging his copper jugs up and down on the sidewalk, the whistle of the shill at the *dolmuş* stop. The navy-blue drapes leached out the leaden winter light that came into the room. Galip, languid with sleep, studied his wife's head which poked out of the quilt: Rüya's chin was buried in the down pillow. In the curve of her brow there was something surreal that brought on anxious curiosity about the wondrous events that took place inside her head. "Memory," Jelal had written in one of his columns, "is a garden." Then Galip had thought: Gardens of Rüya, Gardens of Dreaming. Don't think, don't think! If you do, you will suffer jealousy. But Galip couldn't help thinking as he studied his wife's brow.

He wanted to explore in full sunlight the willows, the acacias, the climbing roses in the enclosed garden of Rüya's tranquil sleep. Shamefully apprehensive of the faces he met there: You here too? Well, then hello! Along with the unsavory memories he expected, registering with curiosity and anguish the unexpected male shadows: Beg your pardon, fella, but just when and where did you meet my wife? Why, three years ago at your place; in the pages of a foreign fashion magazine bought at Aladdin's store; at the middle school you both attended; at the foyer of the movie theater where you two stood holding hands . . . No, no, perhaps Rüya's head was not this crowded and this cruel; perhaps, in the only sunny corner of her dark garden of memory, Rüya and Galip might have, just now, embarked on a boatride.

A few months after Rüya's folks moved to Istanbul, Galip and Rüya had both come down with the mumps. In those days either Galip's mom, or Rüya's beautiful mother Aunt Suzan, or both, leading Galip and Rüya by the hand, would take them on buses that jiggled along the cobbled streets to Bebek or to Tarabya where they'd go on boatrides. Those days, it was the germs that were redoubtable, not the medications; it was believed that clean Bosphorus air could alleviate the mumps. Mornings, the water was calm, the rowboat white, the boatman always the same and matey. Mothers or aunts would always sit astern and Rüya and Galip side-by-side in the bow, hiding behind the boatman whose back rose and fell as he rowed. Under their thin ankles and feet that looked alike stuck out over the water, the sea flowed by slowly—the seaweed, rainbows of spilled diesel oil, semitransparent pebbles, and the still legible pieces of newspaper which they checked out for Jelal's column.

The first time Galip saw Rüya, a few months before getting the mumps, he was sitting on a stool placed on the dining table for the barber to cut his hair. Those days, the tall barber with the Douglas Fairbanks mustache used to come to the house five days a week to shave Grandpa. That was at the time when the lines for coffee got longer in front of both the Arab's and Aladdin's store, when nylons were sold by traffickers, when Chevvies slowly began to proliferate in Istanbul, and when Galip started grade school and carefully read Jelal's column which he wrote under the pseudonym of "Selım Kaçmaz" on the second page of *Milliyet* five times a week, but not the time when he first learned to read; Grandma had taught him to read two years before all that. They sat at one corner of the dining table and Grandma, blowing the smoke of the Bafra cigarette that was never absent from her lips, making her grandson's eyes water, hoarsely divulged the great magic of how letters joined up with each other, and the unusually large horse in the alphabet book became bluer and more lifelike. The horse under which it said HORSE was larger than the bony horses that belonged to the lame watercarrier's and thievish ragman's horse carts. Galip used to wish he could pour a magic potion on this healthy alphabet-book horse that would bring it alive, but later, when he wasn't allowed to start school at the second-grade level but had to go through again the same alphabet book with the horse, he realized it was a silly wish.

Had Grandpa really been able to go out and get the magic potion he promised to bring in a pomegranate-colored vial, Galip would've poured the liquid on the dusty copies of *L'Illustration* full of First World War zeppelins, mortars, and muddy corpses, on the postcards Uncle Melih sent from Paris and Algiers, on the picture of the orangutan nursing its baby that Vasıf had cut out of *Dünya*, and on the faces of the weird people Jelal clipped out of the papers. But Grandpa didn't go out anymore, not even to the barber's. He was home all day. Even so, he dressed up just as he did in those days when he had gone out to the store: his old English jacket with wide lapels which was gray like the stubble that grew on his face on Sundays, drop trousers, cuff links, and a narrow tie that Dad called "the bureaucrat's cravat." Mom said *"cravate,"* never "cravat": her family had been better off than his in the old days. Then Mom and Dad would talk about Grandpa as if they were talking about those old, peeling wood-frame houses another one of which collapsed daily; and later, forgetting about Grandpa, if their voices rose up against each other, they'd turn to Galip: "You go upstairs and play now." "Shall I take the elevator?" "Don't let him take the elevator by himself!" "Don't take the elevator by yourself!" "Shall I play with Vasıf?" "No, he gets mad!"

Actually, he didn't get mad at all. Vasıf was deaf and mute, but he understood that I was only playing "Secret Passage," and not making fun of him, as I crept on the floor dragging myself under the beds to the end of the cave, as if to reach the depth of darkness in the apartment building, like a soldier who proceeds with feline caution in the tunnel he's dug into the enemy trenches; but all the others, aside from Rüya who arrived later, had no notion of how it was. Sometimes Vasıf and I stood at the window together watching the streetcar tracks. One window in the concrete bay of the concrete apartment building looked on the mosque which was one end of the earth, the other window on the girls' lycée which was the other end; in between were the police station, the large chestnut tree, the streetcorner, and Aladdin's store which buzzed with business. As we watched the customers go in and out of the store, pointing out cars to each other, Vasıf could get excited and produce a fearsome snarling noise as if he were fighting the devil in his sleep, plunging me into abject terror. Then, just behind us, seated in his gimpy armchair across from Grandma where they both smoked like a couple of chimneys, Grandpa would comment to Grandma who didn't listen, "Vasıf scared the devil out of Galip again," and then, more out of habit than curiosity, he'd ask us: "So, how many cars did you count?" But neither paid any attention to the detailed account I gave on the numbers of Dodges, the Packards, the DeSotos, and the new Chevrolets.

Grandma and Grandpa talked right through the Turkish and Western music, the news, the commercials for banks, cologne, and the state lottery, as they listened to the radio which was on from morning to night, and on top of which slept the figurine of a thick-coated and self-confident dog that didn't look like a Turkish dog. Often they complained about the cigarettes between their fingers as if talking about a toothache they'd become accustomed to because it never ceased, blaming each other for their failure to quit; and if one commenced to cough as if drowning, the other proclaimed being in the right, first with victory and merriment, then with anxiety and anger. But sooner or later, one of them would get good and mad: "Lay off, for God's sake! My cigarettes are the only pleasure I've got!" Then, something read in the paper would get dragged in: "Apparently, they're good for the nerves." Then maybe they would fall silent for a bit, but the silence during which the tick-tock of the wall clock in the hallway could be heard never lasted very long. While they rustled the newspaper in their hands and played bezique in the afternoon, they kept right on talking; and when the others in the building showed up for dinner and to listen to the radio together, having finished reading Jelal's column, Grandpa would say, "Maybe if he were allowed to sign his own name to his column, he'd pull his wits together." "A grown man too!" Grandma would sigh and with a sincere expression of curiosity on her face as if she were asking for the first time the same question she always asked: "So, does he write so badly because they won't let him sign his name to his column? Or is it because he writes so badly that they won't let him sign his name?" "At least, very few people know it's us that he's disgracing," Grandpa would say, opting for the consolation they both resorted to from time to time, "since he isn't allowed to sign his own name." "Nobody's any the wiser," Grandma would respond with a demeanor the sincerity of which didn't convince Galip. "Who says he's talking about us in those columns anyway?" Later—when Jelal received hundreds of letters from his readers every week and republished the earlier columns, this time under his own illustrious name, having changed the pieces only a little here and there because, according to some claims, his imagination had dried up, or because he couldn't find time from womanizing and politics, or because of simple laziness—Grandpa would repeat the same sentence he'd repeated hundreds of times before, affecting the boredom and the somewhat obvious pretensions of a two-bit stage actor, "Just who doesn't know, for God's sake? Everybody and his brother knows that the bit about the apartment building is all about this place!" and Grandma would shut up.

It was about then that Grandpa was beginning to mention his dream, which recurred more often as time went on. The dream he recounted, his eyes flashing as they did when he told the stories they repeated to each other all day long, was blue; in the navy-blue rain of the dream, his hair and beard grew and grew. After listening to the dream patiently, Grandma would say, "The barber is due to arrive soon," but Grandpa wasn't cheered by the talk about the barber. "Talks too much, asks too many questions!" After the discussions of the blue dream and the barber, Galip had heard Grandpa mutter weakly under his breath a couple of times: "Should've built it somewhere else, a different building. Turns out, this place is jinxed."

Much later, after they moved out of the Heart-of-the-City Apartments which they sold off flat by flat, and, just as in other buildings of the same type in the area, the little boutiques, gynecologists who performed abortions on the sly, and insurance offices moved in, every time Galip passed by Aladdin's store he wondered, while he studied the building's dark and mean façade, just what Grandpa had meant by saying the place was jinxed. Even when he was young, having noticed that the barber always inquired, more out of habit than curiosity, about Uncle Melih whom it took years to return first from Europe and Africa and then from Izmir to Istanbul and the apartment compound (So, tell me sir, when is the oldest boy coming back from Africa?), and being aware that Grandpa enjoyed neither the question nor the topic, Galip had sensed that the jinx in Grandpa's mind had more to do with his oldest and oddest son leaving his wife and firstborn boy to go out of the country and then his return, when he did return, with a new wife and new daughter (Rüya).

As Jelal related to Galip years later, Uncle Melih was here when they started building the apartment compound. They couldn't compete with Hacı Bekir's sweetshop and his *lokums*, but they knew they could peddle Grandma's quince, fig, and sour-cherry preserves in the jars they lined up on the shelves. At the building site in Nişantaşı, Uncle Melih would meet his dad and brothers, some of whom arrived from the candy shop in Sirkeci (which they first converted into a cake shop and later into a restaurant) and the others from the White Pharmacy at Karaköy. Uncle Melih, who wasn't yet thirty then, would take the afternoons off from his law offices where he spent his time either quarreling or drawing pictures of ships and deserted islands on the pages of old lawsuits rather than practicing law, arrived at the site in Nişantaşı, took off his coat and tie, rolled up his sleeves, and got going just to egg on the construction workers who slacked up as the time to quit approached. It was then that Uncle Melih began to pontificate about the necessity of learning European confiture, ordering gilt wrappers for the chestnut candy, starting up a colorful bubble-bath mill in partnership with a French concern, acquiring the machinery from companies in America and Europe which kept going bankrupt in epidemic proportions, finessing a grand piano for Aunt Halé on the cheap, having someone take Vasıf to an acclaimed ear and brain specialist either in France or Germany. Two years later, when Vasıf and Uncle Melih left for Marseilles on a Romanian ship (the *Tristina*) the rose-scented photograph of which Galip first saw in one of Grandma's boxes, and eight years later when he read the bit among Vasıf's newspaper clippings about the ship's hitting a floating mine and sinking on the Black Sea, the apartments had been built but not yet inhabited. A year after when Vasıf returned alone to the Sirkeci train station, he was still deaf and dumb "naturally" (this last word, the secret or the reason for the accentuation of which had never become clear to Galip, had been spoken by Aunt Halé when the subject came up), but in his lap he clasped an aquarium full of Japanese goldfish the sight of which he couldn't bear to leave at first, which he watched at times as if his breath would stop, at times with tears running out of his eyes, and whose great-great-great-grandchildren, fifty years later, he would still be watching. At that time Jelal and his mother were living in the third-floor apartment (which was in later years sold to an Armenian) but since it was necessary to send Uncle Melih the money to continue his commercial research in the streets of Paris, they moved up into that small attic apartment on the roof (which was at first used as storage room and then converted into a semiflat) so that their own apartment could be rented out. His mother had already been thinking of taking Jelal and returning home when the letters Uncle Melih sent from Paris containing recipes of candied fruit and cakes, formulas of soap and cologne, photos of movie stars and ballerinas who ate or used them, and the packages out of which came minty toothpastes, marrons glacées, samples of liqueur-filled chocolates, and toy fireman's or sailor's hats began to dwindle. For them to come to the decision to move out of the flat and return home to the wood-frame house in Aksaray, which belonged to her mother and father who had a small post in the charitable foundations administration, it took the Second World War to break out and Uncle Melih to send them a postcard from Benghazi on which could be seen a strange sort of minaret and an airplane. Following this brown-and-white postcard, which bore the information that the route back home had been mined, he'd sent other black-and-white postcards from Morocco where he went after the war. A handpainted postcard, showing the colonial hotel where an American movie was filmed later in which both the arms dealers and the spies fall for the same nightclub dames, was how Grandma and Grandpa found out that Uncle Melih had married a Turkish girl he met in Marrakesh, that the bride was a descendant of Muhammad, that is, she was a Sayyide, a Chieftain, and that she was extremely beautiful. (Much later, when Galip took another look at that postcard, years later when he was able to identify the nationalities of the flags waving on the second-story balconies, and thinking in the style Jelal used in the stories he called "The Bandits of Beyoğlu," he'd decided that "the seed of Rüya had been sown" in one of the rooms of this hotel that looked like a wedding cake.) They didn't believe Uncle Melih himself had sent the next postcard that arrived from Izmir six months later, since they'd been convinced that he would never return home. There'd been some gossip that he and his new wife had converted to Christianity, joined up with some missionaries on their way to Kenya, to a valley where the lions hunted deer with three antlers, and established the church of a new religious sect that brought together the Crescent and the Cross. Some curiosity seeker who knew the bride's family in Izmir brought the news that, as a result of the shady enterprises Uncle Melih undertook in North Africa (like arms dealing and bribing a king), he had become a millionaire, and succumbed to the whims of his wife, whose beauty was on everyone's lips, whom he intended to take to Hollywood and make famous, already the bride's photos were supposed to be all over French and Arab magazines, etc. In reality, on the postcards that had gone around and around in the apartment building, getting scratched and ill-treated like money suspected of being counterfeit, Uncle Melih had written that the reason they were coming home was that he'd been so homesick, he'd taken to his bed. But they felt better "now" that he'd taken in hand, with a new and modern understanding, the business concerns of his father-in-law who was in tobacco and figs. On the next card the message appeared more tangled than nappy hair and the contents were interpreted differently on every floor perhaps because of the inheritance problems that would eventually push the family into a silent war. But later, as Galip read for himself, all Uncle Melih had written, in not too overwrought a style, was that he'd like to return to Istanbul soon and that he had a baby daughter he hadn't decided what to name yet.

Galip had read Rüya's name for the first time on one of the postcards that Grandma stuck into the frame of the mirror on the buffet where the liqueur sets were kept. It hadn't surprised him that Rüya meant "dream"; but later, when they began figuring out the secondary meanings of names, they were astonished to find in a dictionary of Ottoman Turkish that Galip meant "victor" and Jelal "fury." But that Rüya meant "dream" was so commonplace, it wasn't surprising in the least. What was uncommon was the way Rüya's baby and childhood pictures were placed among the row of images which went around the large mirror like a second frame (and which angered Grandpa from time to time) of churches, bridges, oceans, towers, ships, mosques, deserts, pyramids, hotels, parks, and animals. In those days, rather than being interested in his uncle's daughter (called a "cousin" in the new usage) who was supposed to be the same age as him, Galip was more interested in his "Chieftain" Aunt Suzan who looked into the camera sadly as she parted the black-and-white cave of the mosquito netting to expose her daughter Rüya sleeping inside the scary, sleepy cave that stirred the imagination. He had understood later that it was this beauty, as Rüya's photographs went around the apartments, that momentarily silenced the women in the compound as well as the men. Back then, most of the discussions centered around just when Uncle Melih and family would return to Istanbul and on which floor they'd live. For one thing, heeding Grandma's entreaties, Jelal had returned to the compound and moved back into the attic apartment when he could no longer abide living in the spider-filled house in Aksaray after the untimely death of his mother who'd remarried a lawyer and died of some disease each doctor called by a different name. On behalf of the newspaper for which he came to write columns under an assumed name, he'd report on soccer games with the intent of ferreting out fixed matches, describe extravagantly the mysterious and well-crafted murders perpetrated by the thugs in the bars, nightclubs, and whorehouses in the backstreets of Beyoğlu, devise crossword puzzles in which the number of black squares always exceeded the white, take over the serial on wrestlers because the real writer who was stoned on opium wine couldn't come up with the next installment; and from time to time, he would write columns like "Discerning Your Personality through Your Handwriting," "Interpreting Your Dreams," "Your Face, Your Personality," "Your Horoscope Today" (according to friends and relations he'd first started sending encoded messages when he sent them to his sweethearts through these horoscope columns), do stacks of the "Believe It or Not" series and film criticism on new American movies which he took in free on his own time. Given his industriousness, and if he continued living in the attic apartment by himself, it was thought he'd even save enough of the money he made as a journalist to get himself married. Later, when Galip observed one morning that the timeless pavement stones between the tram tracks had been covered under some senseless asphalt, he thought the jinx Grandpa talked about was connected to this odd congestion in the apartment compound, or to being out of place, or something else similarly indefinite and frightening. So when Uncle Melih, as if to demonstrate his resentment at his not being taken seriously, suddenly showed up in Istanbul with his beautiful wife and beautiful daughter, he moved, of course, right into his son Jelal's apartment.

When Galip was late to school on the spring morning after Uncle Melih and his new family arrived, he had dreamed that he was late to school. He and a beautiful girl with blue hair, whose identity he couldn't make out, were riding on a public bus which took them away from school where the last pages of the alphabet book were to be studied. When he woke up, he realized not only was he late, his dad was also late for work. And at the breakfast table, on which an hour's sunlight fell and whose blue-and-white cloth reminded him of a chessboard, Mom and Dad were discussing the people who moved into the attic apartment as if talking about the mice that commandeered the compound's air shaft or about the ghosts and jinns who hung out with Mrs. Esma, the maid. Galip, who was ashamed to go to school now that he was late, didn't want to think why he was late any more than to wonder who the people were who moved in upstairs. He went up to Grandma and Grandpa's flat where everything was repeated all the time, but the barber was already asking about the people up in the attic while he shaved Grandpa, who looked none too happy. The postcards which were usually stuck in the frame of the mirror were now scattered, odd and foreign articles had appeared here and there—and a new scent to which he'd eventually become addicted. Suddenly he felt a faintness, an apprehension, and a longing: What was it like, living in the countries he saw on tinted postcards? What was it like, knowing the beautiful aunt whose pictures he'd seen? He longed to grow up and become a man! When he announced he wanted his hair cut, Grandma was pleased, but the barber, being insensitive like most blabbermouths, sat him on a stool he placed on the dining table rather than in Grandpa's armchair. On top of that, the blue-and-white checkered cloth which he took off Grandpa and tied around Galip's neck was so big that, as if it weren't enough that it almost choked him, it fell below his kneecaps much like a skirt on a girl.

Much later after their first meeting, 19 years 19 months and 19 days after (according to Galip's calculations), looking at his wife's head buried in the pillow some mornings, Galip would register that the blue quilt on Rüya and the blue cloth the barber took off Grandpa and tied around Galip's neck gave him the same willies; yet he never mentioned anything about it to his wife, perhaps because he knew Rüya would not have the quilt recovered for a reason so vague.

Thinking the morning paper might have already been slipped under the door, Galip rose out of the bed with his habitually careful, feather-light movements, but rather than go to the door, his feet took him first to the bathroom and then to the kitchen. The teakettle was neither in the kitchen nor in the living room. Given that the copper ashtray was full to the rim with cigarette stubs, Rüya must've been up all night reading or not reading a new detective novel. He found the teakettle in the bathroom: there just wasn't enough water pressure to run that scary contraption called a "*chauffe-bain,*" so bath water was heated in the same teakettle, a second one not having managed to get itself purchased. Before making love, much like Grandma and Grandpa, and like Mom and Dad, they too sometimes heated water, quietly and impatiently.

Grandma, who'd been charged with ingratitude after one of those fights that began with "quit smoking," had once reminded Grandpa that she had never gotten out of bed after him, not once. Vasıf had stared. Galip listened, wondering what Grandma meant. Later, Jelal had pronounced on the subject also, but not in the same sense as Grandma: "Women not allowing the sun to rise on them," he'd written, "as well as getting out of bed before the men, is customary among peasant folk." After reading the conclusion of the column in which Grandma and Grandpa's morning routines had been described pretty factually (the ashes on the quilt, the toothbrushes in the same glass of water as the false teeth, the habitual quick perusal of the obituaries), Grandma had said, "So, now we're peasant folk!" "Should've made him eat lentil soup for breakfast so he'd know what it is to be a peasant!" Grandpa had responded.

As Galip rinsed the cups, looked for clean knives, forks, and plates, took out of the fridge that smelled of spiced pastrami the cheese and olives which looked like plastic food, and shaved with the water he heated in the teakettle, he contemplated making a noise loud enough to wake Rüya, but he didn't manage to. So he read the sleepy contents of the ink-scented paper which he pulled out from under the door and spread out next to his plate. He thought of other things as he drank his unsteeped tea and ate the stale bread and the thyme-flavored olives: This evening he'd either go to Jelal's or to the movies at the Palace Theater. He glanced at Jelal's column, decided to read it when he got back from the movies that night, but at the insistence of his eye he couldn't help reading one sentence; he rose from the table leaving the paper spread out, put on his coat, was at the door but went back inside. Hands stuck in his pockets full of tobacco, change, and used tickets, for a while he watched his wife carefully, respectfully, quietly. He turned, pulled the door lightly behind him, and left.

The stairs, mopped in the morning, smelled of wet dust and dirt. Outside, it was a cold and muddy day darkened by the coal and fuel-oil clouds that billowed out of the chimneys in Nişantaşı. Breathing puffs of damp vapor into the cold air, he walked by piles of garbage on the ground and got into the long line at the *dolmuş* stop.

On the opposite sidewalk some old guy who wore his jacket for an overcoat with the collar pulled up was choosing his pastry at the vendor's cart, sep- arating the meat buns from the cheese. Galip suddenly got out of the line and ran. He turned the corner, picked up a copy of *Milliyet* for which he paid the news vendor who'd set himself up in a doorway, folded and tucked it under his arm. Once he'd heard Jelal mimic derisively an older female reader: "Ah, Jelal Bey, we love your columns so much, sometimes Muharrem and I get too impatient and end up buying two copies of *Milliyet*." Then they all laughed at the impersonation together, Galip, Rüya, and Jelal. After a long wait, having been soaked in the dirty rain that began as a drizzle, having gotten on the *dolmuş* push and shove, and having satisfied himself that no conversation would ensue on the *dolmuş*, which smelled of wet cloth and cigarettes, Galip folded the newspaper down to the size of the column on the second page with the care and pleasure of a true addict, glanced out of the window momentarily, and began reading Jelal's column for that day.

Chapter Two

THE DAY THE BOSPHORUS
DRIES UP

Nothing can be as astounding as life—except writing. —IBN ZERHANI

Are you aware that the Bosphorus is regressing? I doubt that you are. These days, when we're so busy murdering each other with the insouciant boisterousness of children on a lark, which one amongst us reads anything informative about the world? We give even our columnists half-hearted readings as we elbow each other on ferryboat landings, fall into each other's laps on bus platforms, or as we sit on *dolmuşes* where the newsprint shivers uncontrollably. I got wind of the news in a French geological journal.

The Black Sea is warming up, it turns out, as the Mediterranean cools down. That's why sea water has begun to flood into the immense caves that gape open on the ocean floor and, as a result of similar tectonic movements, the basins of the Gibraltar, the Dardanelles, and the Bosphorus are rising. A fisherman we last interviewed on the shores of the Bosphorus, after describing how his boat went aground in the same deep waters where he once set anchor, put to us this question: Does our prime minister give a damn?

I don't know. All I know is the implications of this fast developing situation for the near future. Obviously, a short time from now, the paradise we call the Bosphorus will turn into a pitch-black swamp in which the mud-caked skeletons of galleons will gleam like the luminous teeth of ghosts. It isn't hard to imagine that this swamp, after a hot summer, will dry up in places and turn mucky like the bed of a modest stream that irrigates a small town, or even that the slopes of the basin fed abundantly by gurgling sewage that flows through thousands of huge tiles will go to daisies and weeds. A new life will begin in this deep and wild valley in which the Tower of Leander will jut out like an actual and terrifying tower on the rock where it stands.

I am talking about new districts which will be built, under the noses of the municipal cops rushing about with citation books in their hands, on the mire of the lacuna once called "The Bosphorus": about shantytowns, stalls, bars, cabarets, pleasure palaces, amusement parks with merry-go-rounds, casinos, about mosques, dervish tekkes and nests of Marxist factions, about fly-by-night plastics workshops and sweatshops that manufacture nylon stockings. Observed in the midst of the apocalyptic chaos will be carcasses of ships that remain from the old Municipal Goodworks Lines listing on their sides, and fields of jellyfish and soda-pop caps. On the last day when the waters suddenly recede, among the American transatlantics gone to ground and Ionic columns covered with seaweed, there will be Celtic and Ligurian skeletons open-mouthed in supplication to gods whose identities are no longer known. Amidst mussel-encrusted Byzantine treasures, forks and knives made of silver and tin, thousand-year-old barrels of wine, soda-pop bottles, carcasses of pointy-prowed galleys, I can image a civilization whose energy needs for their antiquated stoves and lights will be derived from a dilapidated Romanian tanker propelled into a mire-pit. But what we must prepare ourselves for in this accursed pit fed by the waterfalls of all of Istanbul's green sewage is a new kind of plague that will break out thanks to hordes of rats who will have discovered a paradise among the gurgling prehistoric underground gases, dried-up bogs, the carcasses of dolphins, the turbot, and the swordfish. Be forewarned about what I know: the catastrophes that happen in this pestilent place quarantined behind barbed wire will affect us all.

On the balconies where we once watched the moonlight that made the silken waters of the Bosphorus shimmer like silver, we will henceforth watch the glow of the bluish smoke of burning corpses which could not get buried. Sitting at the tables where we once drank *rakı*, breathing the overpowering cool of the flowering Judas trees and the honeysuckle bushes that grow on the shores of the Bosphorus, we will taste the acrid and moldy smell of rotting corpses burning in our gullets. No longer shall we hear the songs of the spring birds and the fast flowing waters of the Bosphorus where fishermen line up on the wharves, now it will be the screams of those who, fearing death, go at each other with the swords, knives, rusty scimitars, handguns, and shotguns that they've got hold of, weapons dumped into the water to frustrate a thousand years of unwarranted searches and seizures. Natives of Istanbul who live in boroughs that were once by the seaside will no longer open their bus windows wide to breathe in the smell of seaweed as they return home dog weary; on the contrary, to prevent the smell of mud and rotten corpses from seeping in, they'll be stuffing rags and newspapers around the municipal bus windows through which they watch the horrible darkness below that is lit by flames. At the seaside cafés where we get together along with vendors of balloons and wafer *helva*, henceforth we will not be watching naval illuminations but the blood-red glimmer of naval mines blowing up in the hands of curious children. Beachcombers who earn their livelihood collecting tin cans and Byzantine coins that stormy seas belch up on the sand will now have to pick up coffee grinders that floods once pulled out of wooden houses along the boroughs on the waterfront and dumped in the depths of the Bosphorus, cuckoo clocks in which the cuckoos are covered with moss, and black pianos encrusted with mussels. And that's when, one day, I shall sneak through the barbed wire into this new hell in order to locate a certain Black Cadillac.

The Black Cadillac was the trophy car of a Beyoğlu hood (I can't bring myself to call him a "gangster") whose adventures I followed thirty years ago when I was a cub reporter, and who was the patron of the den of iniquity in the foyer of which were the two paintings of Istanbul. I greatly admired. There were only two other cars just like it in Istanbul, one belonged to Dağdelen of the railroad fortune and the other to the tobacco king, Maruf. Our hood (who was made into a legend by us newsmen, and the story of whose last hours we serialized for an entire week), having been cornered by the police at midnight, drove the Cadillac and his moll into the dark waters of the Bosphorus at Undertow Point because, according to some, he was high on hash, or else he did it on purpose like a desperado riding his horse over a precipice. I can already figure out the location of the Black Cadillac which the divers couldn't find despite the search that went on for a week, and which the papers and the readers soon forgot.

It should be there, in the deepest part of the new valley once called the Bosphorus, below a muddy precipice marked by seven-hundred-year-old shoes and boots, their pairs missing, in which crabs have made their nests, and camel bones, and bottles containing love letters written to unknown lovers; back behind slopes covered with forests of sponge and mussels among which gleam diamonds, earrings, soda-pop caps, and golden bracelets; a little way past the heroin lab quickly installed in the dead hull of a boat, beyond the sandbar where oysters and whelks are fed by pails and pails of blood from nags and asses that have been ground into contraband sausages.

As I search for the car in the stillness of this noxious darkness, listening to the horns of the cars that go by on what used to be called the Shoreway but which is now more like a mountain road, I shall meet up with palace intriguers who are still doubled up in the sacks within which they were drowned, the skeletons of Orthodox priests still hanging onto their crosses and staffs and wearing balls and chains on their ankles. When I see the bluish smoke that comes out of the periscope being used as a stovepipe on the British submarine (which was supposed to torpedo the SS *Gülcemal* carrying our troops from Tophane harbor to the Dardanelles, but instead itself sank to the bottom, diving into moss-covered rocks, its propeller tangled in some fishing nets), I shall understand that it's our citizens now who are comfortable in their new home (built in the shipyards of Liverpool), drinking their evening tea out of China cups, sitting in the velvet officer's chairs once occupied by bleached English skeletons gulping for air. In the gloaming, a little way off, there will be the rusty anchor of a battleship that belonged to Kaiser Wilhelm, and a pearlized television screen will wink at me. I shall observe the remnants of a looted Genoan treasure, a short-barreled cannon stuffed with mud, the idols and images of fallen and forgotten states and peoples, a brass chandelier with blown-out bulbs standing on its tip. Descending further down, sloughing through the mire and rocks, I shall see the skeletons of galley-slaves sitting patiently chained at their oars as they observe the stars. Maybe I won't pay enough attention to the necklaces, the eyeglasses, and the umbrellas that droop from trees of seaweed, but for a moment I shall look assiduously and fearfully at the Crusader knights mounted with all their arms, armor, and equipment on magnificent skeletons of horses that are still stubbornly standing. And I shall register with fear that the barnacle-covered skeletons of the Crusaders, replete with their emblems and their armament, are guarding the Black Cadillac.

Slowly and cautiously, as if asking for the Crusaders' permission, I shall respectfully approach the Black Cadillac, barely lit from time to time by a phosphorescent light the source of which is not distinguishable. I shall try the handles on the doors of the Cadillac but the vehicle, covered entirely with mussels and sea urchins, won't permit me entrance; the greenish windows will be too stuck to move. That's when, taking my ballpoint pen out of my pocket, using the butt end, I shall slowly scrape off the pistachio-green layer of moss that covers one of the windows.

At midnight, when I strike a match in this horrific and spellbinding darkness, I shall observe the embracing skeletons of the hood and his moll kissing in the front seat, her braceleted slim arms and ringed fingers around his, in the metallic light of the gorgeous steering wheel that still shines like the Crusaders' armor, and the meters, dials, and clocks dripping with chrome. Not only will their jaws be clasped together, their skulls, too, will have welded together in an eternal kiss.

Then, not striking another match, as I turn back toward the city lights, thinking that this is the best possible way to meet death at the moment of disaster, I will call out in pain to an absent lover: My soul, my beauty, my dolorous one, the day of disaster is at hand, come to me no matter where you are, mayhap in an office thick with cigarette smoke, or in the onion-scented kitchen of a house redolent with the smell of laundry, or in a messy blue bedroom, no matter where you are, it's time, come to me; now is the time for us to wait for death, embracing each other with all our might in the stillness of a dark room where the curtains are closed, hoping to lose sight of the awesome catastrophe that is fast approaching.

Chapter Three

GIVE MY REGARDS
TO RÜYA

My grandfather had named them "the family." —RAINER MARIA RILKE

On the morning of the day his wife was to leave him, Galip climbed the steps that went up to the building where his office was located on Babıali in the old city, the paper he'd been reading tucked under his arm, thinking of the green ballpoint pen that he dropped into the depths of the Bosphorus years ago during one of those boating excursions their mothers took them on when he and Rüya had the mumps. That night he realized, as he examined the farewell letter Rüya left for him, that the green ballpoint on the table with which the letter had been written was identical to the one that fell in the water. Twenty-six years ago Jelal had loaned him the pen that slipped away, noticing how Galip hankered after it. On learning of the pen's loss, and after asking and hearing where it fell out of the boat into the sea, Jelal had said, "It can't really be considered lost because we know what part of the Bosphorus it fell into." Galip was astonished that Jelal hadn't brought up this lost pen when he wrote of taking a ballpoint pen out of his pocket to scrape away the pistachio-colored moss off the windows of the

Black Cadillac, in his column about the Day of Disaster, the details of which Galip had been reading just before he entered his office. After all, the coincidence of details dating back years ago, centuries ago—like his imagining the Byzantine coins stamped with Olympus and the caps of Olympus soda-pop bottles in the mire of the Valley of Bosphorus—was the sort of observation which delighted Jelal and which he worked into his column every chance he got. Of course, that is, if his memory hadn't deteriorated as he claimed during one of their last interviews. "As the garden of memory grows arid," Jelal had said on one of the last evenings they were together, "a man dotes on the last trees and roses that remain. Just so they won't wither away, I water and take care of them all day long. I remember, I remember so that I won't forget."

Galip had heard from Jelal how, the year after Uncle Melih went to Paris, when Vasıf turned up with an aquarium in his arms, Father and Grandfather had gone to Uncle Melih's law offices on Babıali and trudged up to Nişantaşı all his files and furniture on a horse cart and stored everything in the attic. Years later, after Uncle Melih and his beautiful new wife and Rüya had returned from Morocco, after bankrupting the dried fig venture he went into with his father-in-law in Izmir, after getting barred from the drug and the confectionery stores so that he wouldn't ruin family businesses as well, and after he decided to get back into law, he had the same furniture moved to his new offices, hoping to impress his clientele. Later still, one night when Jelal was remembering things past, alternating between anger and laughter, he told Galip and Rüya that one of the porters who'd carried the furniture up to the attic twenty-two years ago had been the same one who had later moved the refrigerator and the piano, having developed expertise in moving tricky articles in the intervening years, which had only managed to turn him bald.

Twenty-one years after Vasıf had carefully studied the same porter to whom he'd given a glass of water, the reason why the office and the old furniture had gone to Galip was explained differently: according to Galip's father, Uncle Melih grappled not with the opponents of his clients but with the clients themselves; according to Galip's mother, having become paralyzed and senile, Uncle Melih couldn't tell his court records and law briefs from restaurant menus and ferryboat schedules; according to Rüya, her darling dad had already guessed what would happen between his daughter and his nephew, and that was why he'd been willing to hand over his law offices to Galip, who was still only his nephew, not yet his son-in-law. So now Galip had the naked-pated portraits of some Western jurisprudents whose fames as well as their names had long been forgotten, the fezzed pictures of teachers who had taught at the law school half a century ago, and the dossiers of lawsuits where the judges, the plaintiffs, and the defendants were long dead, the desk where Jelal studied in the evenings and where his mother traced dress patterns in the morning, and on one corner of this desk, the husky black telephone which, more than a tool of communication, looked like an unwieldy and feckless contraption of war.

The bell on the phone, which sometimes rang of its own accord, was startling. The pitch-dark receiver was as heavy as a little dumbbell and when dialed, it grumbled with the squeaky melody of the old turnstiles at the Karaköy–Kadıköy ferryboat dock. Sometimes it connected with numbers at random, rather than the numbers dialed.

When he dialed his home number and Rüya actually answered, he was surprised: "Are you awake?" He was pleased that Rüya no longer roamed in the enclosed garden of her own memory but in a world known to everyone. He visualized the table on which the phone stood, the messy room, Rüya's stance. "Have you read the paper I left on the table? Jelal seems to have written some fun stuff." "I haven't," Rüya said. "What time is it?" "You went to bed late, didn't you?" Galip said. "You got your own breakfast," Rüya said. "I couldn't bear to wake you," said Galip. "Whatever were you dreaming?" "I saw a cockroach in the hallway late at night," Rüya said with the flat voice of a radio announcer warning sailors of a loose mine sighted in the Black Sea, but she then went on anxiously: "Between the kitchen door and the radiator in the hallway . . . at two o'clock . . . a big one." Silence. "Shall I hop in a taxi and come home?" Galip said. "The house is scarier when the drapes are closed," said Rüya. "Want to go to the movies tonight," Galip said, "at the Palace? We could stop by at Jelal's on the way back." Rüya yawned. "I'm sleepy." "Go to sleep," said Galip. They both fell silent. Galip heard Rüya yawn faintly once more before he hung up.

In the days that followed, when Galip had to remember this phone conversation again and again, he couldn't decide how much of their verbal exchange he had actually heard. Let alone the faint yawn. Seeing how he remembered with suspicion the revised versions of what Rüya had said, "It was as if it weren't Rüya I was speaking to but someone else," he thought and imagined that this someone had duped him. Later on, he came to think that Rüya had said what he heard, but after that phone conversation, it wasn't Rüya but he himself who had slowly begun to turn into someone else. He kept reconstructing what he thought he heard or remembered through his new persona. In those days when he listened even to his own voice as if it were someone else's, Galip understood very well how two persons on two ends of a phone line speaking to each other could turn into two entirely different persons. But at first, going for a simpler explanation, he'd blamed it all on the old telephone: all day, the clumsy thing had kept ringing, making him pick up the receiver.

After speaking to Rüya, Galip had first called a tenant who had brought a lawsuit against his landlord. Then he got a wrong number. In the time before İskender called, he got two other wrong numbers. Then he reached someone who knew he was "related to Jelal Bey" and asked for Jelal's phone number. After the calls from a father who wanted to save his son who was in jail for political reasons and an ironmonger who wanted to know why the judge had to be bribed before the verdict, İskender called because he, too, wanted to reach Jelal.

İskender hadn't spoken to Galip since they were classmates in high school, and he quickly ran through all that had happened in the intervening fifteen years, congratulating him on his marriage to Rüya, maintaining like many others that he too had known "that's what would happen in the end." Now he was the producer for an advertising agency. He wanted to put Jelal in touch with people from the BBC who were doing a program on Turkey. "They want to do a live interview with a columnist like Jelal who, for thirty years, has been involved with what goes on in Turkey." He explained in unnecessary detail how the TV crew had already talked to politicians, businessmen, and labor organizers, but insisted on seeing Jelal whom they found most interesting. "Not to worry," Galip said, "I'll get him for you in no time." He was pleased to have found a reason for calling Jelal. "I think the people at the newspaper have been putting me off for the last couple of days," said İskender; "that's why I resorted to calling you. For the last two days Jelal hasn't been at the paper. Something must be going on." It was a known fact that Jelal would sometimes disappear for several days into one of his hideouts in Istanbul, the locations and phone numbers of which he kept from everyone, but Galip had no doubt that he'd get hold of him. "Not to worry," he said again. "I'll get him for you in no time."

He was unable to get him. All day, every time he called the apartment or the *Milliyet* newspaper offices, he fantasized changing his voice and talking to Jelal under someone else's guise. (He had planned to say, using the same voice from the radio plays, as on those evenings when Rüya, Jelal, and Galip sat around, imitating readers and admirers: "Of course, I'm on to you, brother!") But each time he called the paper, the same secretary gave him the same answer, "Jelal Bey isn't in yet." As he grappled with the phone all day, Galip had the pleasure of hearing his voice fool someone just once.

Late in the afternoon he called Aunt Halé thinking she would know Jelal's whereabouts, and she invited him to dinner. "Galip and Rüya are coming too," she said, again mistaking Galip's voice for Jelal's. "What's the difference?" Aunt Halé said when she realized her mistake. "You are all my negligent kids, the lot of you are the same. I was about to call you too." After chewing him out for his failure to keep in touch, using the same tone of voice as when she scolded her cat Coals for scratching the furniture, she told him to stop at Aladdin's store on his way to dinner and pick up some food for Vasıf's goldfish: the fish wouldn't eat anything but food imported from Europe, and Aladdin would sell the stuff only to steady customers.

"Did you read his column today?" Galip asked.

"Whose, Aladdin's?" his aunt said with her habitual obduracy. "Nah! We buy *Milliyet* so that your uncle can do the crosswords and Vasıf might cut out articles to amuse himself. Not to read Jelal's column and rue the condition to which our nephew has sunk."

"In that case you might call and invite Rüya yourself," Galip said. "I really don't have the time."

"Don't you forget now!" Aunt Halé said, reminding him of his errand and the time set for dinner. Then she went through the permanent guest list for the family get-together, which was as unvaried as the dinner menu, naming each like a radio announcer deliberately calling the names of players already set for a soccer match as if to entice the listeners: "Your mother, your Aunt Suzan, your Uncle Melih, Jelal if he shows up, and of course your father; Coals and Vasıf, and your Aunt Halé." She didn't laugh her croupy laugh to punctuate the teams. And after she said, "I'm making puff *böreks* for you," she hung up.

As Galip gazed vacantly at the phone which began ringing as soon as he hung up, he remembered the old story of Aunt Halé's plans for marriage which had gone sour at the last minute but, for some reason, he couldn't remember the prospective groom's odd name which he had in his mind only moments ago. So that his mind wouldn't get accustomed to slacking off, he told himself: "I am not going to pick up the phone until I remember the name that's at the tip of my tongue." The phone rang seven times before it stopped. When it started again, Galip was thinking of the visit—a year before Rüya's folks moved to Istanbul—that the prospective groom had made to ask for Aunt Halé's hand, his uncle and older brother in tow. The phone fell silent once more, and when next it rang, it was dark and the furniture in the office had become hazy. Galip still couldn't remember the name but he recalled with trepidation the strange shoes the man had worn that day. The man had an Aleppo boil on his face. "Are these people Arabs?" Grandpa had wanted to know. "Halé, you really want to marry this Arab, or what? And just where did he meet you?" By coincidence, that's how! Around seven in the evening, just before Galip left the vacated business building, examining under the streetlights the dossier of a client who wanted to change his name, he came up with the odd name. As he walked to the Nişantaşı *dolmuş* stop he thought that the world was just too extensive to fit into any one memory bank, and as he walked to the apartment building in Nişantaşı, that mankind extracted meaning out of coincidences . . .

The building was on one of the backstreets of Nişantaşı. Aunt Halé lived with Vasıf and Mrs. Esma in one apartment, and Uncle Melih and Aunt Suzan lived in another (formerly with Rüya too). Perhaps others wouldn't call it a backstreet, seeing how it was only a five-minute walk and three streets down from the main street, Aladdin's store, and the police station at the corner. But the relatives who now lived in apartments on this backstreet had watched it get transformed at a distance, without paying much attention, from muddy fields into irrigated vegetable gardens, into cobblestones, and later into pavement; for them the heart of Nişantaşı could never be a street less interesting than the main street on which they had constructed their own apartment building. Lining up the symmetry of their psychic world as well as the geographical one, they had long before established in their minds the Heart-of-the-City Apartments in its central position, even when they already had an inkling that they'd end up selling it flat by flat, leaving the building Aunt Halé said "commanded all Nişantaşı," and resorting to renting shabby apartments elsewhere. Even in the early days when they had moved into this derelict building only in an unhappy and remote corner of their minds, they never failed to bring up the word "backstreet," perhaps to exaggerate the calamity that befell them so as to blame each other, as if to take advantage of an opportunity that must not be missed. Three years before his death, the first day he moved out of the Heart-of-the-City Apartments to his backstreet flat, when Mehmet Sabit Bey (Grandpa) sat in his gimpy-legged armchair which was now placed at a new angle to the window in the new flat, overlooking the street, but at the same old angle (as in the old place) to the heavy stand that carried the radio, he had said, inspired somewhat by the skinny nag that had pulled the horse cart that transported the furniture: "So, we get off the horse to ride the ass. Well then, good luck!" Then he'd turned on the radio on which the dog figurine, sleeping on its crocheted doily, had already been placed.

That was eighteen years ago. But at eight in the evening when all the stores had been zipped up, except the florist's, the nuts 'n dried fruits store, and Aladdin's, a light slushy snow fell through the air dirty with car exhaust, furnace soot, and the smell of coal and sulphur, and Galip had a feeling, when he saw the old lights in the apartments, that the memories connected with this building and the flats went beyond eighteen years. It wasn't the width of the street, or the name of the new building (which none of them had ever used) that was important, nor the location; it was as if they'd lived in flats above and below each other since time immemorial. Climbing the stairs that always smelled the same (according to the analysis in Jelal's column which had brought on such a furor, the smell was a mixture of apartment-building well stench, wet cement, mold, frying fat, and onions), he hurried through the scenes and images that he anticipated with the routine and impatience of a reader riffling through a book that he's read many times:

Seeing how it's eight o'clock, I will see Uncle Melih sitting in Grandpa's old chair rereading the newspapers that he himself brought down, as if he hadn't already read them upstairs, as if "the same news might conceivably be interpreted differently downstairs than it was upstairs," or as if "I might as well take a last look before Vasıf scissors these into bits." I will think that the unfortunate slipper flapping all day long at the tip of my uncle's agitated foot is painfully calling out to me with the unrelenting irritation and impatience of childhood, "I am bored, gotta do something; I am bored, gotta do something." I will hear Mrs. Esma, chased out of the kitchen so that Aunt Halé can fry up the puff pastry to her heart's content without interference from anyone, setting the table with the unfiltered Bafra (which doesn't hold a candle to the old Yeni Harman) dangling from her lip, asking the room in general, as if she didn't already know the answer and the others knew what she didn't, "How many for supper tonight?" I will register the silence from Aunt Suzan and Uncle Melih who sit with the radio between them and Mom and Dad across, just as Grandma and Grandpa used to; and a while later, Aunt Suzan will turn hopefully toward Mrs. Esma and say, "Is Jelal coming tonight, Mrs. Esma?" and Uncle Melih with his customary, "He will never pull his wits together, never"; and Dad, with the pride and · pleasure of being the more responsible and balanced brother and being able to defend his nephew against Uncle Melih, will announce with delight that he'd read one of Jelal's latest newspaper columns. Then, to add to the pleasure of defending his nephew against his older brother the pleasure of showing off in front of me, I will hear Dad venture a few words of praise and appropriate "positive" criticism on Jelal's essay concerning some national problem or some life crisis, which would have immediately incurred Jelal's ridicule were he within earshot. And I'll see Mom nod in agreement (Mom, at least, you stay out of it!) and join Dad (since she considers it her duty to defend Jelal against Uncle Melih's ire by saying, "But he's basically a good sort"). Unable to help myself, I will hear myself ask uselessly, "Have you seen today's column?" knowing full well that they could never in a hundred years get the same pleasure nor the meaning out of Jelal's essays that I so enjoyed. Then I will hear Uncle Melih say, despite holding the newspaper open perhaps to the page with Jelal's column that very minute, "What day is it today?" or, "They're having him write every day now, are they? No, I didn't see it!"; and Dad will say, "I don't approve of him using foul language against the prime minister though," and Mom, "One ought to respect a writer's person even if one doesn't respect his opinions," putting out one of those ambiguous sentences that don't reveal whether it's the prime minister, Dad, or Jelal she's defending. Encouraged by the ambiguity of the moment, Aunt Suzan will bring up the subject of cigarettes and tobacco by saying, "What he thinks of Immortality, Atheism, and Tobacco reminds me of the French." And I will leave the room as the old altercation heats up between Uncle Melih and Mrs. Esma who, still undecided as to how many people to set the table for, spreads the tablecloth like a large sheet on a bed, holding one end and flipping up the other, watching it fall nice and easy through the cigarette smoke coming out of her mouth: "See how your cigarette smoke exacerbates my asthma, Mrs. Esma!" "Then, you quit smoking yourself first, Mr. Melih!" In the kitchen, inside a cloud that smells of dough, melted white cheese, and frying fat, looking like a witch brewing up a magic potion in a cauldron all by herself (her head is covered so her hair won't get greasy), Aunt Halé who's been frying up the puff *böreks* will say "Don't let anyone else see it," and quickly pop in my mouth one of those piping-hot puffs as if to bribe me to get special attention, love, or even a kiss, and she'll ask "Too hot?" as tears of pain roll down my eyes, and I won't even be able to say, "Too hot!" I will leave the scene and enter the room where Grandpa and Grandma spent nights of insomnia wrapped up in the blue quilt on which Grandma gave Rüya and me drawing, math, and reading lessons, and where Vasıf moved with his precious goldfish after their death, and I will see Vasıf and Rüya. They'll be watching the goldfish or looking through Vasıf's collection of newspaper and magazine clippings. I will join them and as always, as if to conceal the fact that Vasıf is deaf and dumb, Rüya and I won't talk for a while and then, as we did in our childhood, using the hand and arm gestures we invented for ourselves, we will enact for Vasıf a scene from the old film we saw on TV recently. Or, neither of us having seen any films to reenact these last few weeks, we will play out in full detail, as if we'd just seen it, a scene from *The Phantom of the Opera* which has always turned Vasıf on. A little later, because Vasıf, who has more empathy than anyone, has turned aside or moved closer to his precious fish, Rüya and I will gaze at each other, and then I will say to you whom I haven't seen since this morning and with whom I haven't talked face-to-face since last night,

"How are you?" and you, as always, will answer: "Oh, all right," and I will pause and think over carefully the intentional and unintentional implications of your response and to hide the emptiness of my train of thought; this time, perhaps, as if I didn't already know that instead of starting to translate the mystery novel you said you'd do some day, you'd spent the day lolling about turning the pages of old mysteries none of which I've ever been able to read, I will ask, "What did you do today?" I will ask you, "Rüya, what did you do today?"

In another of his columns, Jelal had written that the stairwells of backstreet apartment buildings smelled of sleep, garlic, mold, lye, coal, and frying fat, putting forth a somewhat different formula. Before ringing the bell, Galip thought: I'll ask Rüya if she was the one who rang three times this evening.

Aunt Halé opened the door and asked, "What! Where's Rüya then?"

"Hasn't she shown up?" Galip said. "Did you call her?"

"I did, but no one answered," said Aunt Halé. "So I supposed you'd let her know."

"Perhaps she's upstairs, at her father's," Galip said.

"Your uncle and company are downstairs already," Aunt Halé said.

They fell silent for a while.

"She must be at home," Galip ventured. "I'll run home and get her."

"Your phone never answered," Aunt Halé said, but Galip was already headed back down the stairs.

"All right, but be quick about it," Aunt Halé said. "Mrs. Esma is already frying up your puff *böreks*."

As the cold wind that drove the wet snow flipped open his nine-year-old overcoat (the subject of another one of Jelal's columns), Galip hurried along. He had calculated long ago that if he didn't take the main street but walked along backstreets, went by the closed grocery stores, the bespectacled tailor who was still working, the doormen's flats, and the dim neons for Coca-Cola and nylons, it would take twelve minutes to reach his apartment from his aunt and uncle's building. If he returned via the same streets and the same sidewalks (the tailor was putting new thread through his needle, the same material still on the same knee), the round trip took twenty-six minutes total.

When he returned, Galip told Aunt Suzan who opened the door and the others as they sat down to dinner that Rüya was sick with a cold and, having taken too many antibiotics (she swallowed everything she found in the drawers), that she had fallen into a stupefied sleep. Although she had heard the phone ring, she had been too groggy to answer, had no appetite, and sent everyone her love from her sickbed. He knew his words would stir the imagination of those at the table (Poor Rüya in her sickbed), and he had also guessed that he would stir up a verbal phenomenon: recounted and revealed were the names of the antibiotics sold over the counter at the drugstores, the penicillins, the cough syrups and the lozenges, the vasodilators and the painkillers taken for the flu and, as if talking about cream topping for dessert, the name brand vitamins that must be taken along with these, Turkicized by being pronounced with extra vowels stuck in between the consonants, along with directions as to how to take the medications. Another time, this festival of creative pronunciation and amateur medicine might have provided Galip with the same pleasure as reading a good poem. But the image of Rüya in her sickbed was on his mind and, later on, he could no longer discern how pure or how manufactured were the images that he'd fetched up. Sick Rüya's foot sticking out of the quilt or her bobby pins scattered in the bed were presumably real images, but the image of her hair spread out on the pillow, for example, or the boxes of medicine, the water glass, the pitcher, and the books on the nightstand came from somewhere else (the movies, or the badly translated novels she read the way she devoured the pistachios she bought at Aladdin's), images that were learned and imitated. Later, when Galip gave short answers to their "affectionate" questions, at least he made a special effort to distinguish, with the attentiveness of a mystery-novel detective which he wanted to acquire and to emulate, the pure images of Rüya from the secondhand.

Yes (as they all sat down to dinner), Rüya would be asleep now. No, she wasn't hungry, so there was no need for Aunt Suzan to go and make her some soup. And she had said she didn't want that doctor whose breath smelled like garlic and whose bag stank like a tannery. No, she hadn't managed to see the dentist this month either. True, lately Rüya went out hardly at all and spent her time cooped up in the apartment. But no, she hadn't gone out at all today. Did you happen to see her out in the street? Must be that she had gone out briefly but didn't tell Galip; no, she had actually. So, just where did you run into her? She must've gone out to the notions counter at the fabric shop to buy some purple buttons and passed by the mosque. Of course, she had told him; she must've caught a chill out in this terrible cold. She was coughing and smoking, a whole pack; yes, her face was white as a sheet. Oh, no, Galip hadn't realized just how white his own face was, too; nor did he know when he and Rüya would stop leading such unhealthy lives.

Coat. Buttons. Teakettle. Later on, after this family inquisition, Galip hadn't worried too much why these three words had popped into his head.

In one of Jelal's columns, which had been penned with an anger of baroque proportions, he'd written that the subconscious didn't originate with us but came out of the pompous novels of the Western world and their movie heroes whom we never quite learned to imitate (just then, Jelal had seen *Suddenly Last Summer*, in which Elizabeth Taylor would never comprehend the "dark spot" in Montgomery Clift's mind). When Galip discovered that Jelal had built his private life into a library and a museum, he came to understand that, under the influence of what he had previously read in abridged translations of psychology books replete with pornographic details, Jelal had written a great deal that explained everything, even our miserable lives, in terms of this frightening and incomprehensible subconscious he called darkness.

He was about to change the subject, starting with the preamble of "In Jelal's column today . . ." but scared off by habit, he suddenly blurted out the other thing that came to his mind: "Aunt Halé, I forgot to stop at Aladdin's store." They were sprinkling the walnut meats which had been pounded in the mortar left over from the family candy store of long ago on the pumpkin dessert that Mrs. Esma brought in as carefully as if it were an orange baby in its crib. A quarter of a century before, Galip and Rüya had discovered that, struck on the rim with the flat end of a spoon, the mortar would produce a sound like a church bell: Ding-Dong! "Stop it with that thing already, ding-ding, like a Christian sexton." God, how difficult it was to swallow! There weren't enough nutmeats to go around, so Aunt Halé deftly passed up her turn with the purple bowl (I don't care for any), but she did glance at the bottom of the empty bowl after everybody was through. Suddenly, she started cursing out an old commercial rival she considered responsible not only for this particular curtailment but for all the shortage of money: she was going to file a complaint against him at the police station. In reality, they were all spooked by the police station as if it were a dark navy-blue ghost. After Jelal wrote in one of his columns that the dark spot in our unconscious minds was, in fact, the police station, it was a cop from the station who had subpoenaed him to appear at the prosecutor's office to give a deposition.

The phone rang, and Galip's dad answered with a serious air. They're calling from the cop house, Galip thought. Since his dad, as he spoke on the phone, stared at the surroundings (as a consolation, the wallpaper was the same as in the Heart-of-the-City Apartments: green buttons scattered among the leaves of ivy) with the same noncommittal expression with which he stared at those who were seated at the table (Uncle Melih was having paroxysms of coughing, deaf Vasıf seemed to be listening to the phone conversation, and Galip's mother's hair after being dyed and redyed had finally become the same color as beautiful Aunt Suzan's), Galip too, like everybody else, as he heard half of the conversation, tried to make out who it was on the other end.

"No, not here, didn't come," his dad was saying. "Who am I speaking to? Thank you . . . I am the uncle . . . no, unfortunately, isn't among us this evening."

Somebody's looking for Rüya, Galip thought.

"Somebody's looking for Jelal," his dad said after he hung up. He seemed pleased. "An older woman, a fan, a gentlewoman who loved his column in the paper; she wanted to get in touch with him, asked for his address, phone number."

"Which column was it?" Galip asked.

"You know something, Halé," his dad said, "the odd thing was, her voice sounded just like yours."

"Nothing more natural than my voice sounding like an older woman's," said Aunt Halé. Her lung-colored neck suddenly shot up like a goose's. "But my voice is nothing like hers!"

"What isn't it like?"

"That person you thought was a gentlewoman called this morning too," Aunt Halé said. "More likely, rather than a gentlewoman's, her voice was like a witch trying to sound like a gentlewoman. Perhaps even a man trying to sound like a mature woman."

So where had the older gentlewoman found this phone number, Galip's dad wanted to know. Had Halé inquired?

"Nope," said Aunt Halé, "I didn't think it was necessary. Since the day he began washing our dirty laundry in his column as if he were writing about wrestlers or something, I am never surprised by anything about Jelal, so I thought maybe he had given out our phone number in another column lampooning us, just to provide his readers with extra entertainment. Besides, as I think how our dear departed parents worried over him, I've come to understand now that the only thing about Jelal that could still shock me would be to learn why he's hated us all these years—but not his giving out our number to keep his readers entertained."

"He hates because he's a Communist," Uncle Melih said, lighting up victoriously, having overcome his cough. "When it finally hit them on the head that they'd never be able to seduce the labor force or this nation, the Communists tried seducing the military to stage a Janissary-style Bolshevik revolution. So, he let his column become a tool for this dream that stinks of blood and vengeance."

"No," said Aunt Halé, "that's going too far."

"Rüya told me, I know," Uncle Melih said. He laughed but didn't cough. "He took up studying French on his own because he fell for the promise he'd be appointed either the minister of foreign affairs or else the ambassador to Paris in this *à la Turca* Bolshevik-Janissary order. In the beginning, I was even pleased that my son who hadn't managed to learn a foreign tongue, having wasted all his time in his youth with the riffraff, had at last found a reason to learn French. But when he got out of hand, I wouldn't let Rüya see him."

"None of this ever happened, Melih," Aunt Suzan said. "Rüya and Jelal always saw each other, sought each other out, loved each other as if they were full sister and brother, as if they had the same mother."

"Sure it happened, but I was too late," Uncle Melih said. "When he couldn't seduce the Turkish nation or the army, he seduced his sister. That's how Rüya turned into an anarchist. If my son Galip here hadn't pulled her out of that hotbed of guerrilla thugs, that nest of vermin, Rüya wouldn't be at home in her bed now but who knows where."

Galip stared at his nails as he imagined them all imagining Poor Rüya in her sickbed and wondered if Uncle Melih would add anything new to the list of offenses he enumerated every two to three months.

"Rüya could've even ended up in jail, seeing how she's not as cautious as Jelal," Uncle Melih said and, paying no attention to the "God forbid!"'s, he gave in to the excitement of his list as he recounted: "Then, going along with Jelal, Rüya might have gotten mixed up with those thugs. Poor Rüya might have become involved with those gangsters of Beyoğlu, the heroin traffickers, the casino hoodlums, cocaine-snorting White Russians, all the dissolute gangs he penetrated under the guise of getting interviews. We might have had to look for our daughter among Englishmen who come seeking nasty pleasures, homosexuals who're keen on the wrestlers and articles about wrestling, American bimbos who turn up for bath orgies, con artists, local movie stars who couldn't even be whores in Europe let alone act in films, ex-officers who've been kicked out of the army for insubordination or embezzlement, masculinized singers who have cracked their voices on syphilis, slum beauties who pass themselves off as society women. Tell her to take some Istreptomisin," he finished, mangling the name of a wonder drug.

"What?" said Galip.

"Best antibiotic against the flu, taken along with 'Bekozime Fort.' Every six hours. What time is it? Do you suppose she's awake?"

Aunt Suzan said Rüya was probably asleep right now. Galip thought the same thing that everybody else was thinking: Rüya asleep in her bed.

"No way!" said Mrs. Esma. She was gathering up with care the sorry tablecloth which, due to a bad habit passed on by Grandpa despite Grandma's disapproval, they used like a napkin to wipe their mouths on. "No, I'm not having my Jelal dumped on in this house. My Jelal has become a celebrity."

According to Uncle Melih, his fifty-five-year-old son, because he was of the same opinion concerning his own importance, didn't bother looking up his seventy-five-year-old father. He wouldn't divulge which Istanbul apartment he was staying in to prevent not only his father but everybody in the family from reaching him, including Aunt Halé who was always the first to forgive him; he unplugged his phones on top of keeping the numbers secret. Galip was afraid that a few drops of false tears might appear in Uncle Melih's eyes, not out of sorrow but out of habit. But instead of that, something else he was afraid of came to pass: Uncle Melih reiterated once more, not taking into account the twenty-two-year age difference, that he had always wished for a son like Galip for real, instead of Jelal: sane, mature, quiet as Galip.

Twenty-two years ago (that is, when Jelal was his age), when Galip was embarrassingly tall and his hands and arms perpetrated even more embarrassing clumsinesses, when he first heard these words and imagined they could come true, he thought it might be possible to sit down to dinner with Aunt Suzan, Uncle Melih, and Rüya every night, escaping those colorless and tasteless dinners that were eaten with Mom and Dad where everybody looked at a vanishing point beyond the walls that surrounded the dinner table at straight angles (Mom: There's cold vegetables left over from lunch, want some? Galip: Naah, don't want any. Mom: You? Dad: Me what?). Besides, other things occurred to him which made his head spin: when he went upstairs on Sundays to play with Rüya ("Secret Passage," "Didn't See"), his beautiful Aunt Suzan whom he spied in her blue nightgown, although on rare occasions, would become his mother (much better); Uncle Melih whose African and legal stories he adored, his father (much better); and Rüya, since they were the same age, his twin sister (it was there that his mind stopped with indecision as he scrutinized frightening conclusions).

After the table was cleared, Galip said TV people from the BBC had been looking for Jelal but hadn't managed to find him. But this comment didn't reignite the gossip he expected concerning all of Jelal's addresses and the phone numbers he kept secret from everyone and the diverse gabble that went on about the many flats all over Istanbul and how they could be located. Somebody said it was snowing. So, rising from the table, before they sank into their accustomed easy chairs, they looked out in between the dark chill of the drapes they parted with the backs of their hands, on to the backstreet where a light snow had settled. Silent, clean new snow. (A replica of the scene Jelal fetched up more for parody than for sharing with his readers the nostalgia of "old Ramadan nights"!) Galip followed Vasıf who retired to his own room.

Vasıf sat on the big bed, Galip across from him. Vasıf dangled his hands on his shoulders and then ran them over his white hair: Rüya? Galip struck his fist into his chest and did a coughing fit: She's sick with a cough. Then he put his reclining head down on a pillow he formed by folding his arms together: She's lying down. Vasıf brought out a large cardboard box from under his bed: a selection of the newspaper and magazine clippings he'd collected for the last fifty years, perhaps the best ones. Galip sat down next to him. As if Rüya were sitting on the other side, as if they were laughing together at the ones she pointed out, they examined the photos they pulled out of the box at random: the soapy grin of the famous soccer player who, twenty years ago, had lathered up for a shaving cream commercial and who had died of a brain hemorrhage after countering a corner shot with his head; the corpse of General Kassem, the leader of Iraq, resting in his bloody uniform after a military coup; a re-creation of the famous Şişli Square Murder ("The jealous colonel, discovering after his retirement that he'd been cuckolded for twenty years, guns down the lecherous journalist along with his young wife in the car he'd been tracking for days," Rüya would say in her radio-theater voice); and as Prime Minister Menderes saves the life of the camel to be sacrificed to him, behind him the reporter Jelal and the camel look elsewhere. Galip was about to get up to go home when his attention was drawn by two of Jelal's columns he just happened to pull out of Vasıf's box automatically: "Aladdin's Store" and "The Executioner and the Weeping Face." Preparing reading material for a night that was sure to be spent sleepless! He didn't have to mime too much for Vasıf to let him borrow the columns. The folks, too, were understanding when he didn't drink the coffee Mrs. Esma brought: obviously the expression of "my wife is sick at home" had penetrated his face deeply. He was standing on the threshold with the door open. Even Uncle Melih said, "Sure, he should go home"; Aunt Halé was bent over her cat Coals who'd returned from the snowy street; more voices inside kept calling out: "Tell her, get well; tell her to get well; take Rüya our love; take our love to Rüya!"

On the way back, Galip ran into the bespectacled tailor who was pulling the shutters down on his storefront. They hailed each other in the light of the streetlight on which little icicles hung, and they continued to walk together. "I'm late," the tailor said, perhaps to break the profound silence of the snow. "The wife is home, waiting." "Cold," Galip responded. Listening to the snow crunch under their feet, they walked together until they got to Galip's apartment building at the corner, and upstairs in the corner window the dim bedside light in the bedroom came into view. At times snow fell, and at times, darkness.

The lights in the living room were off as they had been when Galip left, and the lights in the hallway were still on. As soon as he entered, Galip put the teakettle on the burner, took off his overcoat and jacket, hung them up, and went into the bedroom where he changed his wet socks in the dim light. He sat down at the dining table and read once more the goodbye letter Rüya had written and left for him. Written with the green ballpoint pen, the letter was shorter than he remembered: Nineteen words.

Chapter Four

ALADDIN'S STORE

If I have any fault it is digression. —BYRON PASHA

I am a "picturesque" writer. I've looked it up but I still don't quite have the meaning; I just happen to like the word's effect. I always dreamed I'd be writing about different things: knights on chargers, two armies on a dark plain preparing to attack on a foggy morning three centuries ago, unfortunates who on winter nights tell one another love stories in taverns, the never-ending adventures of lovers who vanish into obscure cities tracking down a mystery. But God saddled me with this column where I must tell other kinds of stories, and with you, my readers. We've learned to bear with each other.

If the garden of my memory hadn't begun to dry up, perhaps I wouldn't bellyache about my lot; but as soon as I take pen in hand what I see before my eyes are your expectant faces, my readers, and the traces of my memories take a powder in the desolate garden. To be confronted with the trace instead of the memory itself is like looking through tears at the indentations on the armchair left there by your lover who has abandoned you and will never return.

So I decided to give it straight to Aladdin. Tipped off that I intended to write about him in the paper but wanted to interview him first, he opened his black eyes wide and said, "But wouldn't it bring me a lot of grief?"

I assured him it wouldn't. I told him about the importance his store had for us in Nişantaşı. I told him how the thousand—nay, the ten thousand —kinds of articles he sold there remained alive in our memories color by color, smell by smell. I told him how children sick at home waited impatiently in bed for their mothers to return from Aladdin's store with presents: a toy (lead soldier), or a book (*Red Kid*), or a spaghetti-western photonovel (the seventeenth issue, in which Kinova, who'd been scalped, comes back to life and goes after the Redskins). I told him how thousands of students in the neighborhood schools couldn't wait for the last bell, that bell which had already gone off in their heads, to get to his store after school for chocolate-covered *gaufrette* bars in which came photos of soccer players (Metin of Galatasaray), or wrestlers (Hamit Kaplan), or else movie stars (Jerry Lewis). I told him about the girls who stopped by for little bottles of nail-polish remover to take the pale polish off their fingernails before showing up for classes at the Night Crafts School—the same girls who'd later remember their first star-crossed loves, although stuck now with children and grandchildren in the insipid kitchens of insipid marriages, and dream of Aladdin's store like a distant fairy tale.

We'd already arrived at my place and sat down across from each other. I told Aladdin the stories of the green ballpoint pen I bought at his store years ago and the badly translated detective novel. The heroine of the second story, whom I loved dearly and for whom I'd bought the novel, had been sentenced from then on to do nothing with her life but read detective novels. I told him how the twosome—one a patriotic army officer and the other a journalist—who were planning a conspiracy (the coup that would change the flow not only of our history but of the history of the East) had met at Aladdin's store just prior to the first historic assembly. I also told him that, during the evening hour when this momentous meeting took place, Aladdin, unaware of what was up, stood behind the counter which was piled with books and boxes that towered up to the ceiling, wetted his fingers with his spittle, and counted the newspapers and magazines to be returned in the morning.

On the subject of the skin magazines which he displayed in his store window and strung all the way around the large chestnut tree across from his doorway, I confided that in the dreams of the lonely men who passed by absentmindedly on his sidewalk, the local and foreign playmates who'd bared all for the camera would make whoopee that night like the insatiable slave girls and the sultans' wives in the *Thousand and One Nights* tales. And, since we were on the subject of the *Thousand and One Nights*, I informed him that the tale which bore his name was never told in any of the *Nights* but that when the book was first published in the West a hundred and fifty years ago, it appeared among the pages due to a sleight of hand perpetrated by one Antoine Galland. And I explained that the story was never actually told to Galland by Scheherazade but by a Christian scholar from Aleppo called Youhenna Diab, and that the story was probably Turkish in origin, and that, more likely than not, it took place in Istanbul as indicated by the details about coffee. But, I went on, if truth be known, it was impossible to know what was what as to the origins of any story any more than the origins of any life. I explained this was true because I forgot everything, everything. In truth, I was old, miserable, cranky, alone, and I wanted to die. What drowned one in a flood of sorrow was the noise of the traffic around Nişantaşı Square and the sound of the music on the radio. I told him how, after a life of telling stories, I wanted to hear from Aladdin before I died about everything that I'd forgotten, and be told each and every story about the bottles of cologne in the store, the revenue stamps, the illustrations on match boxes, nylon stockings, postcards, the photographs of movie stars, the annals of sexology, the hairpins, and the books on ritual prayer.

Like all real persons who find themselves snatched into fictions, Aladdin had a superreal presence that challenged the world's boundaries and a simple logic that stretched the rules. He conceded that he was pleased the press showed an interest in his store. For the last thirty years, he'd been keeping shop fourteen hours a day at that corner store which was busy as a beehive; and on Sundays, while everybody listened to the soccer game on the radio, he took a nap at home between two-thirty and four-thirty in the afternoon. His real name was something else but his customers didn't know about it. As for newspapers, he only read the popular *Hürriyet*. He pointed out that no political meeting could ever take place in his store, seeing how the Teşvikiye police station was right across from it; besides, he was not interested in politics at all. It wasn't true that he counted the magazines spitting on his fingers; nor was his store a place out of legends and fairy tales. He was sick of people's goofs. Some poor geezers too, mistaking the plastic toy watches in the window for the real article, would go into a buying frenzy hoping to scoop up merchandise on the cheap. Then, there were those who played the Paper Horse Race or the National Lottery, and when they didn't win, they got angry and started a ruckus, thinking Aladdin fixed these games when, in fact, they'd picked the tickets with their very own hands. Take the woman, for example, whose nylons sprung a run, or the mother of the kid who ate domestic chocolates and broke out all over, or the reader who didn't care for the political views of the newspaper he bought, they all were down on Aladdin who didn't make the stuff, after all, but only sold it. Aladdin was not responsible for the coffee-colored shoe polish that came in the package instead of coffee. Aladdin was not responsible for the domestic battery which, after only one song from Emel Sayın's sultry voice, shook itself empty and gummed up the transistor radio. Aladdin was not responsible for the compass which, instead of always pointing to the North as it should, pointed to the Teşvikiye police station. Aladdin was not responsible for the packet of Bafra cigarettes that contained the love-and-marriage proposal put in there by a romantic factory girl; but even so, the painter's assistant had rushed with bells on to kiss Aladdin's hand and ask him for the girl's name and address, as well as asking him to be the best man.

His store was in what was considered "the best" location in Istanbul, but his customers always, but always, knocked him for a loop. He was amazed that the coat 'n tie set still hadn't caught on to waiting for their turn; sometimes he couldn't help chewing out some people who ought to know better. He had given up selling bus tickets, for example, because of the handful who always rushed in just as the bus was turning the corner, and yelling like Mongolian soldiers on a looting spree, "Ticket, give me a ticket and make it quick!" they made a mess of the store. He'd known old marrieds who got into spats picking lottery tickets, painted ladies who sniffed thirty different brands before choosing a single bar of soap, retired army officers who came in to buy a whistle and ended up blowing on every whistle in the box, one by one. But he'd become used to it. He no longer cared. No longer was he offended by the housewife who grumbled because he didn't stock a back issue of a photonovel from ten years ago, by the fat gent who licked a stamp to check out the flavor, and by the butcher's wife who returned the crepe-paper carnation the next day, good and angry because the artificial flower didn't have any scent.

He'd built up the store tooth and nail. For years he had bound the *Texas* and *Tom Mix* comics himself, with his own hands; he was the one who opened shop and swept it while the city slept; he himself had fastened the newspapers and the magazines on the door and on the chestnut tree; he'd put the trendiest goods in the store window; and, to satisfy his customers' demands, he'd traversed the whole of Istanbul for years, inch by inch, store by store, to procure the oddest of merchandise (like the toy ballerinas who pirouetted as the magnetized mirror was brought close; the tricolored shoe-laces; the plaster-of-Paris statuettes of Atatürk which had blue lightbulbs behind the pupils; the pencil sharpeners in the shape of Dutch windmills;

the signs that said FOR RENT or IN THE NAME OF ALLAH THE COMPASSIONATE, THE MERCIFUL; the pine-flavored bubblegum which came with pictures of birds numbered from one to a hundred; the pink backgammon dice which could only be found at the Covered Bazaar; the transfer pictures of Tarzan and Admiral Barbarossa; the gadgets which were shoehorns on one end and bottle openers on the other; and the soccer hoods in the colors of the teams—he himself had worn a blue one the last ten years). He hadn't yet said "nay" even to the most unreasonable demands (Do you carry rose-scented blue ink? Do you have any of those rings that sing?), reasoning that if something were being asked for, then it must have a prototype. He'd make a note in his book, saying "We'll have it in here by tomorrow," and he'd search the city, store by store, like a traveler questing after a mystery, until he landed his quarry. There'd been times he'd made easy money peddling photonovels which sold like mad, or else cowboy comics, or photos of domestic movie stars whose faces said blah; and then there'd been cold, bitchy, nothing-doing days when coffee and cigarettes ended up on the black market and people had to line up in cues. When you looked out of your store window, you wouldn't think people who flowed down the sidewalk were "this way and that way," but . . . but people were "something else."

People who each seemed to march to a different drum suddenly all wanted musical cigarette boxes as if they were going out of style, or they all went ape over Japanese fountain pens no larger than your little finger; then they'd lose interest the next month, and they all wanted pistol-shaped cigarette lighters so bad that Aladdin had a time and a half keeping the lighters in stock. Then there'd be a fad for plastic cigarette holders, and, for the next six months, they'd all be watching the tar build up on the plastic with the obsession of a mad scientist. Then, abandoning that, all of them, the leftist and the conservative, the God-fearing and the godless, they all purchased at Aladdin's the rosaries that came in all colors and all shapes, and they went to town fingering the beads. Before the bead storm was over and Aladdin could return the leftover rosaries, a dream fad would surface, and they'd line up at the door to get the little booklet interpreting dreams. Some American film would hit and all the punks had to have dark glasses; an item in the papers, and all the women had to have lip gloss; or the men had to have beanies for their heads as if they were imams. All in all, fads spread unchartered like the Black Death. Otherwise, why else had thousands, tens of thousands of people been inspired, all at the same moment, to place the same wooden sailboat on their radios, their radiators, in the rear window of their cars, in their rooms, on their desks, and on their workbenches? How else would you explain the phenomenon of moms and dads, kids and old folks, all goaded with some inexplicable desire to acquire and tack up on their walls and doors the poster of the waif with European features and a huge tear dripping out of his eye? This nation, these people . . . they're really . . . really . . . "Strange," I said, completing his sentence. It was my task now, not Aladdin's, to find words like "incomprehensible," or even "terrifying." For a while we fell silent.

Later, I figured out that Aladdin and his customers had a bond through which to communicate the words he himself couldn't nail down, say, for the little celluloid geese that nodded, or for the old-fashioned chocolates that were shaped like bottles and contained sour-cherry liquor as well as a sour cherry, or else the place in Istanbul you could get the cheapest wood strips for your kite. He favored equally both the little girl who came in with her grandma for one of those chiming hoops and the pimply youth who attempted, retiring to a dark corner of the store, to make rapid love to the nude in the French magazine he snatched when no one was looking. He also loved the bank teller with spectacles on her nose who bought in the evening the novel revealing the lives of the Rich and the Famous in Hollywood, and having digested it overnight, wanted to return it in the morning, saying, "It turns out I already had it in my collection"; and he loved the old guy who put in a special request to have the poster of the girl reading the Koran wrapped in plain newsprint. Even so, his was a conditional love. He could sympathize somewhat with the mother-daughter team who spread out the pattern sheets in fashion magazines all over the store in an effort to cut their material right then and there, and even with the boys who got their toy tanks into battle only to get them broken in fistfights even before they got out of the store. On the other hand, he got a feeling that signs were being sent him from a world that he neither knew nor understood when people asked him for pencil flashlights or for key chains with plastic skulls. What mystery prompted the man who came into the store on a snowy winter day and insisted on buying a "Summer Scape" instead of the "Winter Scape" being used for student home projects? Just as he was about to close shop one night, two shady individuals had come in and fondled the dolls with the movable arms (which came in all sizes and with their own ready-made wardrobes), holding them carefully, tenderly, and skillfully like doctors holding live babies; then watching the pink creatures open and close their eyes as if enchanted, they'd had Aladdin wrap up a doll for them along with a bottle of *rakı* before they disappeared into the dark night, giving Aladdin the willies. After many such incidents, Aladdin had dreams of the dolls he sold in boxes and plastic bags, hallucinating that after the store was closed at night, the dolls started to open and close their eyes very slowly while their hair grew and grew. Perhaps he was about to ask me what it all meant, but suddenly he let himself fall into the same abject and brooding silence that comes over our countrymen when they feel they've talked too much, occupied the world too much with their own troubles. Certain that it wouldn't be disturbed too soon now, we kept the silence together.

Some time later, as Aladdin left wearing an apologetic look, he said it was all up to me now, and he was sure I'd do my best. Someday I might just do my best and write something good about those dolls and our dreams.

Chapter Five

PERFECTLY CHILDISH

People separate for a reason. They tell you their reason. They give you a chance to reply. They do not run away like that. No, it is perfectly childish.
—MARCEL PROUST

Rüya had written the nineteen-word farewell letter with the green ballpoint pen that Galip wanted kept right next to the phone. The pen was nowhere to be found; considering he couldn't locate it in his subsequent searches throughout the apartment, Galip surmised that Rüya had written the letter the minute before she went out the door and, thinking the pen might come in handy, popped it into her purse. The fat fountain pen she used lovingly once in a blue moon to fuss over a letter (which she would never finish; if she did, she would hardly ever stick it into an envelope, and if she did, she would never mail it) rested in its usual place: the drawer in the bedroom.

Desperate to find the notebook from which she'd torn the piece of paper, Galip wasted chunks of time. He checked the pages against the letter, riffling through the notebooks in the drawers of the old bureau where, heeding Rüya and Jelal's advice, he'd set up a museum dedicated to his personal history: the grade-school math workbook where the price of eggs was calculated at six pennies per dozen; the compulsory prayer notebook kept for religion class with swastikas and caricatures of the cross-eyed religion teacher drawn on the last few pages; and the Turkish Lit. notebook which had sketches of skirts in the margins along with the names of international celebrities, handsome local sports figures, and pop stars ("There may be a question on *Beauty and Love* on the exam").

Later—after going through the same drawers that were so disappointing, getting to the bottoms of boxes that sadly revealed the same reminiscences, and searching for the last time Rüya's pockets, where the self-same scents seemed to conspire against Galip, persuading him that nothing had changed—when he glanced at the old bureau again, sometime after the call to prayer at dawn, he finally chanced upon the school notebook out of which Rüya had torn the sheet. A page had been ripped hastily and recklessly from the middle of one he'd already looked through but without paying careful attention to the pictures and the notes ("The administration's plunder of our national forests was what provoked the army into the coup of May 27th"; "The hydra's cross section resembles the blue vase in Grandma's sideboard"). It was yet another detail that yielded no conclusion other than Rüya's reckless haste, other than the details he'd accumulated all night long, the small discoveries, the reminiscences that piled atop one another like falling dominoes.

A reminiscence: Years ago in middle school, when Galip and Rüya sat at the same desk, the hideous history teacher they suffered patiently and good-naturedly would all of a sudden pop a quiz, "Take out papers and pens!" But in the stillness that fell over the fearful classroom unprepared for a test, she couldn't tolerate hearing the sound of pages getting torn out of notebooks. "Don't rip the pages out of your notebooks!" her shrill voice would screech. "I want loose sheets! Those who rip up their notebooks and destroy this nation's property aren't Turks, but degenerates! I'll hand them zeros!" And she would too!

A small discovery: In the still of the night, shamelessly disturbed only by the refrigerator which switched on and off at gratuitous intervals, in the bottom of Rüya's closet that he'd already gone through umpteen times, stuck between the dark green pumps she hadn't taken along, Galip came across a detective novel in translation. There were hundreds of them in the apartment and he was about to toss it when, flipping through the pages of the black book with the imprint of a small but treacherous owl with huge eyes, and having learned in one night to go through everything in the bottoms of closets and the corners of drawers, his hand found, as if on its own, the photo clipped out of a glossy magazine: a good-looking naked man. Galip instinctively compared the guy's size with his own, looked at the man-tool in the photo, which was flaccid, and thought: She must've cut it out of some magazine she got at Aladdin's.

Reminiscence: Rüya was sure Galip would never touch her books; she knew he couldn't stand detective novels, which was all she had. Galip couldn't bring himself to spend any time in the artificial world of the whodunit where the English were super-English and the fat superfat, where the subjects and the objects including the criminal and the victim didn't behave like themselves but like devices, or rather were forced by the writer to act like them. (Kills time! Rüya used to say as she scarfed up the novel, along with the nuts'n'tachios also bought at Aladdin's.) Galip had once told Rüya that the only detective novel worth reading would be one in which the writer himself didn't know the identity of the murderer. Only then would the objects and the characters not turn into herrings and red herrings devised by the omniscient writer. By virtue of representing their correspondences in reality, they would exist as themselves in the book, instead of as figments of the novelist's imagination. Rüya, who was a better reader of novels than Galip, had inquired how in the world the surfeit of details in such a novel as he proposed could be kept under control. The details in the detective novel were put there, apparently, to foreshadow the outcome.

Details: Before she left, Rüya had sprayed the hell out of the bathroom, the kitchen, and the hallway with the can of bug bomb on which a huge black beetle and three smaller cockroaches served to terrify the consumer. (It still stank in there.) She'd turned on the so-called *chauffe-bain* without thinking (needless, since Thursday was central hot-water day in the building), she'd skimmed through *Milliyet* (it was wrinkled) and worked through some of the crossword puzzle using the pencil she took along: mausoleum, gap, luna, force, improvisation, pious, mystery, listen. She'd had breakfast (tea, feta, bread) and hadn't done the dishes. She'd smoked two cigarettes in the bedroom, four in the living room. She'd taken some of her winter clothes, and some cosmetics which she claimed were bad for her skin, her slippers, the batch of novels she'd been reading, her lucky key chain with no keys which ordinarily dangled from the handle of her drawer, the pearl necklace that was her only jewelry, and her mirror-backed hairbrush. She'd worn the winter coat which was the color of her hair. She must've put the stuff into the old medium-size suitcase she borrowed from her dad (the one Uncle Melih brought back from the Barbary Coast) in case it might come in handy for the trip they never took. She'd closed most of the cupboards (by kicking them in), she'd slid in the drawers, put her paraphernalia back in their places. And she'd written the goodbye letter at one blow, without any hesitation. There were no torn-up rough drafts in the trash nor in the ash cans.

Perhaps it wasn't even a goodbye letter. Rüya had said nothing about returning, but she hadn't said anything about not returning either. It was as if she were leaving the apartment, not Galip. She'd even put in a five-word proposal to draft him as an accomplice, "Handle Mom and the others," a role he'd accepted right away. Not only was he pleased that she hadn't put the blame for her leaving clearly on Galip, he was pleased to be Rüya's accomplice, when all was said and done, to be her partner in crime. In return for this partnership, Rüya had made Galip a four-word promise: "Will keep in touch." But she'd failed to keep in touch all night long.

Instead, the radiator pipes kept in touch all night long with various moans, sighs, and burbles. Snow fell at intervals. The *boza* man hawked his fermented beverage once but didn't return. Rüya's green signature and Galip stared at each other for hours. The objects and the shadows in the rooms assumed a new character; the place seemed to have become another place. Galip thought of saying, "A spider! So that's what the fixture hanging in here looked like all these years!" He wanted to fall asleep, perchance to catch a good dream; but he couldn't sleep. All night, he launched new forays into the apartment at orderly intervals, disregarding his former searches. (He had looked into the box in the wardrobe, hadn't he; he had, he probably had; probably hadn't; no, he had not; and now he had to go through everything all over again.) He was holding either the memory-laden buckle of Rüya's belt or else the empty case of her long-lost sunglasses when, conceding how aimless his efforts were, he put whatever he had in his hand meticulously back into its original place like a diligent researcher taking inventory at a museum. (Those storybook detectives, they were so damned unconvincing, with the writer whispering clues in the detective's ear—what an optimist, to think a smart reader could be taken in!) The phantom legs of a somnambulist kept taking him to the kitchen where he went through the fridge without taking anything out; then he found himself back in the living room sitting in his favorite chair only to initiate the same old search ritual all over again.

On the night he was abandoned, as he sat alone now in the chair in which for all three years of their marriage he'd watched Rüya across from him reading impatiently and nervously her detective novels, Galip kept fetching up the same image of her dangling her legs, twisting her hair, turning the pages with pleasure and passion, sighing deeply from time to time. What was on his mind was not the feelings of worthlessness, defeat, and loneliness (My face is not symmetrical, my hands are clumsy, I am too wishy-washy, my voice is too weak!) which had surfaced when, in high school, he witnessed Rüya at pastry and pudding shops where cockroaches strolled nonchalantly on the tables, hanging out with pimply guys who sprouted hair above their upper lips and began smoking before Galip did. No, not that. Nor was it the image when, three years after high school, he'd gone up to their flat one Saturday afternoon ("I'm here to see if you have any blue labels") and seen Rüya glance at her watch and dangle her legs impatiently as Aunt Suzan sat at her dilapidated dressing table putting on makeup. It wasn't even the image of Rüya looking pale and tired as he'd never seen her before, when he learned she had consummated a marriage which was not merely political to a young politico considered valiant and devoted by those around him, who already signed his own name to the first political analyses published in *The Dawn of Labor*. What was really before Galip's eyes all night was the picture of a slice of life he'd missed, an opportunity, a bit of fun: snow falling into the light streaming out of Aladdin's store that glimmered faintly on the white sidewalk.

It was a Friday evening when they were in the third grade; that is, a year and a half after Rüya's folks moved into the attic apartment. As darkness fell, and the winter eve's roar of automobiles and streetcars reverberated on Nişantaşı Square, they'd just started to play a new game they'd invented: "I've Vanished," a game combining the rules of "Secret Passage" and "Didn't See." One of the two "vanished" into a corner in their grandparents', uncles', or fathers' apartments, and the other searched until the vanished one was found. A fairly simple game, and since it was against the rules to turn on the lights, and there was no time limit, it hearkened to the imagination and the patience of the seeker. When it was his turn to "vanish," Galip had hid himself on top of the wardrobe in Grandma's bedroom (stepping first on the arm of the chair then, carefully, on the back) and convinced that Rüya would never find him up there, he'd fantasized her moves in the dark. He'd put himself in Rüya's shoes who was yearning for him so that he might better empathize with Rüya's emotions, excruciated by his absence! Rüya must be near tears; Rüya must be bored to death; Rüya must be begging tearfully that he come out, come out, wherever he was! Then, having waited as long as the eternity of childhood, he suddenly slipped off the top of the wardrobe impatiently, not yet aware that the game was already over because of impatience, and once his eyes got used to the dim lights, it was now Galip himself who began searching for Rüya through the apartment building. His searches through the flats completed, an odd and ghostly feeling came over him, an intimation of failure, and he'd resorted to questioning Grandma. "Good grief, you're dusty all over!" said Grandma, who sat across from him. "Where have you been? They've all been looking for you!" Then she added, "Jelal showed up. He and Rüya went to Aladdin's store." Galip had run to the window at once, to that cold, dark, ink-blue window. It was snowing outside, a slow and pathetic snow that summoned you out; a light streamed out of Aladdin's store, through the toys, the picture books, balls, yo-yos, the colored bottles. A light that was the color of Rüya's complexion glimmered faintly on the snowy sidewalk.

All through that long night, each time Galip recalled this twenty-four-year-old image, he felt the same impatience rise up in him with all the unpleasantness of a pot of milk that suddenly boils over. Where was that slice of life he'd missed out on? Now he heard the endless and derisive tick-tock of the grandfather clock that had awaited Grandma and Grandpa's time eternal in the hallway, the same clock that when they were first married, he had removed from Aunt Halé's apartment, eager to keep alive the myths and memories of their shared childhood, and placed with zeal and perseverance against the wall of his own nest of happiness. All through the three years of their married life, it had always been Rüya who seemed disgruntled to be missing the fun and games of some other unapprehended life, not Galip.

Galip went to work every morning and returned home in the evening on the bus or the *dolmuş*, grappling with unidentified elbows and legs in the impersonal crowd that wore such a dark face on its return. All through the day he'd keep finding reasons, flimsy enough for Rüya to raise an eyebrow, to call her from the office. Once he returned to the warmth of his home, he'd approximate, without missing the mark by much, what Rüya had been up to that day by taking an inventory of the ashtrays, the number of the butts and the brands. In a moment of happiness (an exception) or a moment of suspicion, aping the husbands in films that came from the West, as he'd contemplated doing last night, if he came out and asked his wife what she'd done that day, they'd both feel the discomfort of entering an indefinite and slippery realm that was never clearly explained in the movies, whether those from the East or those from the West. It was after he got married that Galip stumbled on that secret, mysterious, and slippery zone in the life of the anonymous personage referred to in the statistics and among the bureaucrats as "a housewife" (the woman with detergents and children bore no relation to Rüya in Galip's mind).

Galip was well aware that the garden in this clandestine world that swarmed with uncanny plants and terrifying flowers was closed to him totally, just like the uncharted depths of Rüya's memory. That forbidden zone was the common subject and the goal of all detergent commercials, of photonovels, of the latest information translated from foreign publications, of most radio programs, and of the colorful supplements that came in the Sunday papers; but it was still beyond everybody's ken and more mysterious and enigmatic than anybody knew. Sometimes when he wondered uninspiredly why and how the paper scissors, for example, had been placed next to the copper bowl that sat on the radiator in the hallway, or when out on a Sunday excursion they ran into some woman he hadn't seen in years but with whom he knew Rüya had kept in constant touch, Galip was momentarily startled and forestalled by the clue he'd come across, the sign that emerged from a realm forbidden to him, as if he were brought face-to-face with the secrets of a widespread sect that had been pushed underground but which no longer needed to be hidden. The frightening thing was not only the contagiousness of the mysteries, like the mysteries of an outlawed cult, spreading among those generic persons called "housewives," but the pretense that no such enigma ever existed, nor any esoteric rites, no shared misdemeanors, no rapture or history, as if their behavior didn't rise out of a sense of secrecy but out of an inner desire. Like the confidences kept by harem eunuchs, locked and with the key thrown away, the mystery was both attractive and repulsive: since its existence was known, perhaps it wasn't dreadful like a nightmare, but since it had never been described and named although handed down through the centuries, it was a pathetic mystery because it could never be a source of pride, assurance, or victory. Sometimes Galip thought this realm was some kind of curse, like a curse that hounds the members of a family for hundreds of years; yet, having witnessed many a woman quit her job all of a sudden and return to the accursed region voluntarily under the pretext of marriage, motherhood, or some other murky reason, he had come to understand it was some kind of gravitational pull of the cult. So much so that, observing certain women who'd gone through hell to be rid of the curse and become somebody, he thought he detected symptoms of the desire to return to the secret rites, the enchanting moments they'd left behind, and back to the dark, silken zone he'd never understand.

Sometimes when Rüya laughed at one of his stupid jokes or puns so hard that it surprised him, or when she cooperated with his joy in running his clumsy hands through the dark forest of her mink-colored hair, that is, free of all the rituals learned from picture magazines, in a moment of true closeness between husband and wife free of all the past and the future, suddenly Galip would feel a desire to ask his wife a question concerning that mysterious realm, to ask her what she'd done at home that day, at a particular hour, aside from the laundry, the dishes, the detective novels, and going out (the doctor had said they'd be unable to have children, and Rüya hadn't shown much interest in working); but the chasm that might open between them following that question was so frightening and the knowledge targeted so alien to the vocabulary of the common language between them that he could not question Rüya but held her in his arms while his face went blank for a moment, completely vacant. "You've vacated your face again!" she'd say. Blithely fetching up the words that her mom said when he was a child, she'd repeat: "Your face is white as a sheet!"

After the call to morning prayer, Galip dozed off sitting up in his chair in the living room. In his dream where the Japanese goldfish in the aquarium swayed drowsily in a liquid that was as green as the ink in a ballpoint pen, Rüya, Galip, and Vasıf spoke about a mistake that had been made and, later, it was understood that Vasıf was not the one who was deaf and dumb, it was Galip. Still, they didn't get too upset: after all, things would soon be all right.

Upon waking, Galip sat down at the table and, as he imagined Rüya had done about nineteen or twenty hours ago, he looked for a clean sheet of paper on the table. And when he didn't come across any paper—just as Rüya hadn't—he began writing on the back of Rüya's letter, making a list of all the people and the places that had gone through his mind overnight. It was an unnerving list that grew longer as he wrote and forced him to write as it grew, giving Galip a sensation that he was imitating a protagonist in some detective novel: Rüya's old flames, her "zany" girlfriends, the chums she occasionally mentioned, her sometime "political" allies, and the friends they had in common who shouldn't be confided in, Galip decided, not until he actually found Rüya. As he jotted down their names made up of particular vowels and consonants, the strokes that went up and down, as their faces and figures cumulatively gained meaning and double entendres, they waved gleefully at Galip, the inexperienced detective, winking treacherously and transmitting false leads. Soon after the garbagemen went by banging the larger cans on the gate of the truck, Galip stuck the list, to stop himself from lengthening it, in the inside pocket of the coat he'd wear that day.

Galip turned off all the lights in the apartment, which at daybreak was illuminated only with the blue light of snow. In an effort to foil the suspicions of the nosy doorman, he put out the trash can, but only after he had checked through the contents once more. He made tea, slipped a fresh blade in his razor and shaved, put on clean but unpressed underwear and shirt, and straightened out the rooms he'd ransacked all night. He drank his tea and read in the *Milliyet*, which the doorman had slid under the door as he got dressed, Jelal's column in which he mentioned the subject of an "eye" he'd. encountered walking around in the slums, years ago, at midnight. Galip remembered having read the article, which had already been published some time back, but still he felt the terror of the same "eye" trained on him. That's when the phone rang.

It must be Rüya! Galip thought. By the time he picked up the receiver, he even had the movie theater picked where they'd go together that evening: the Palace Theater. But he didn't hesitate at all coming up with a story to throw off Aunt Suzan, the disappointing voice on the line: Yes, yes, Rüya's fever had gone down; not only had she slept well, she'd even had a dream; sure, she'd like to speak to her mom; just one moment. "Rüya!" Galip shouted down the hallway, "Rüya, your mom's on the phone!" He imagined Rüya getting out of bed, yawning and stretching languorously as she looked around for her slippers; then he put a different reel in his mind's projector: solicitous husband Galip goes down the hallway to call his wife to the phone, only to find her in bed sleeping like a baby. He even faked "effects" walking up and down the hallway to flesh out the second film and produce a believable ambience for Aunt Suzan. He returned to the phone. "She's gone back to sleep, Aunt Suzan. Her eyes were crusted with fever goop. Seems she washed her face and got back in bed and dozed off again." "Tell her to drink plenty of orange juice," said Aunt Suzan, painstakingly telling him where in Nişantaşı the most reasonable blood oranges could be purchased. "We might go to the Palace Theater tonight," Galip said confidently. "Just so she doesn't catch another chill," Aunt Suzan said and, perhaps worried that she might be interfering too much, she changed the subject completely: "Did you know that your voice sounds just like Jelal's on the phone? Or do you have a cold too? Make sure you don't catch Rüya's bug." Then they hung up at the same moment, gently, not so much out of fear of awakening Rüya but as if not to hurt the receivers, moved by the same feelings of respect, tenderness, and silence.

Soon after hanging up and starting in again on Jelal's old article, somewhere between the persona he'd assumed moments ago, the eyeballing of the aforementioned "eye," and his own foggy thoughts, Galip suddenly decided: "Of course, Rüya has returned to her ex-husband!" He was amazed at himself for not seeing the obvious all night, obscured as it was by his runaway imagination. It was with the same decisiveness that he proceeded to call Jelal, to inform him on the conclusion of the mental torment he'd gone through: "I'm leaving now to go and find them. When I find Rüya with her first husband—which shouldn't take too long—I'm afraid I may not be able to convince her to return home. Only you'd know how to cajole her to come back home ("to me," he meant to say but couldn't get it out), so what should I say to get her to come back?" "First, get ahold of yourself,"

Jelal would say sincerely. "Just when did Rüya leave? Steady now. Let's think this thing through together. Come over, come to the newsroom."

But Jelal was neither at his place nor at the newsroom, not yet. As he went out the door, Galip envisioned leaving the phone off the hook, but he didn't. Just in case Aunt Suzan said, "I called and called, but it was always busy," he'd have been able to say, "Rüya failed to replace the receiver properly. You know how absentminded she is, how she forgets things."

Chapter Six

MASTER BEDII'S CHILDREN

. . . sighs rising and trembling through the timeless air.
——DANTE, *The Inferno*, Canto IV

Ever since we recklessly invited the problems of the populace into our column, no matter what the origin, class, or creed, we have been inundated with reader mail, and some of the letters are doozies. Some readers, who've caught on to the fact that their material too can be articulated at last, don't even bother to write it all down but dash to our press offices personally and tell us their stories until they're blue in the face. Still others, aware of our skepticism concerning the fishy escapades and the gruesome details they have offered up, whisk us away from our desk, in an effort to justify themselves and their stories, and lead us to the murky and mystifying obscurities in our culture which have never been investigated or written about. This is how we got wind of the morbid history of Turkish mannequin making which, it turns out, was forced underground.

For centuries, our culture wasn't even aware of the art of mannequin making aside from some "folkloric" phenomena which smell of dung and villages, such as the scarecrow. The first artisan to take it up, the patron saint of mannequin making, was Master Bedii who created the necessary mannequins for the Naval Museum—our first—founded under Sultan Abdülhamit's edict and the patronage of the Honorable Osman Jelalettin, one of the crown princes at the time. Master Bedii is also responsible for the esoteric history of his craft. According to eyewitness accounts, the guests at the museum's opening were astounded to see our two-fisted corsairs and our strapping valiants who routed Italian and Spanish galleons on the Mediterranean some three hundred years ago erect in all their glory, bristling with handlebar mustaches, and placed in between the royal launches and the men-of-war. Master Bedii used wood, plaster, wax, sheepskin, camelskin, and doeskin, as well as human hair and beard for his materials to create his original prodigies. When the contemporary narrow-minded Sheikh of Islam came face-to-face with these miraculous creatures which had been executed with great artistic skill, he threw a fit: since imitating Allah's creatures perfectly was to engage in a kind of competition with Him, the mannequins were removed from the museum and banisters were placed in between the ships-of-war.

Prohibition, which occurs very frequently in our history of never-ending Westernization, did not snuff out Master Bedii's spontaneously ignited fire of craftsmanship. Not only was he busy making new mannequins in his house, he also attempted to come to an understanding with the authorities to place his masterpieces, which he called his "children," into a museum once more, or at least in some other place where they could be exhibited. When he failed to get the support he needed, he soured on the authorities and the administration but not on his art. He continued to produce mannequins in the basement of his house, which he'd turned into a workshop. Later on, he moved away from old Istanbul into the Christian quarter in Galata, primarily as a precaution against his neighbors' allegations of "witchcraft, perversion, and heresy." Moreover, he could no longer fit all of his "children," whose numbers steadily increased, into a modest Moslem domicile.

In this curious house in Kuledibi (where I was taken), Master Bedii continued his fastidious work with passion and faith, and he also taught his son the craft he'd mastered on his own. After twenty years of steady work, he noticed that those famous haberdashers in Beyoğlu began to place mannequins in their store windows when, during the excitement of the initial wave of Westernization in the early years of our Republic, gentlemen discarded their fezzes in favor of panama hats and ladies peeled off their veils and slipped on high-heeled shoes. When Master Bedii first saw those imported mannequins, he thought that the moment of victory he'd anticipated for years had arrived, and he bolted out of his underground workshop into the street. But it was in the flashy streets of commerce and entertainment in Beyoğlu where he met up with a new disappointment which would, until the day he died, exile him to a life of darkness lived underground.

The owners of the grand department stores who'd seen examples of the work Master Bedii presented, and the purveyors of ready-made suits, skirts, outfits, stockings, topcoats, hats, as well as the window dressers who came to his cellar workshop, all rejected him one by one. Apparently, the mannequins he made didn't look like the models from the West who taught us style; instead, they resembled our own people. "The customer," one of the storeowners said, "doesn't want the topcoat shown on the back of a mustachioed, bowlegged, dark and skinny citizen who's seen every day by the tens of thousands in the streets; he wants to slip into a jacket worn by a new and beautiful person from a distant and unfamiliar land, so that putting on the jacket he can believe he, too, has changed and turned into someone else." A hardboiled window dresser, after being dazzled by Master Bedii's masterpieces, explained that in the interests of his own livelihood, he unfortunately could not place these "authentic Turks, these real citizens" in his windows: Turks nowadays didn't want to be "Turks" anymore but something else. That's how come they'd instigated a code of proper attire, shaved their beards, reformed their tongues and their alphabet. A more laconic storeowner pointed out that his customers did not buy an outfit but, in truth, bought a dream. What they really wanted to purchase was the dream of being like the "others" who wore the same outfit.

Master Bedii didn't even consider making mannequins that would be consistent with such notions. He realized he could never compete with those curiously postured mannequins imported from Europe with their constantly modified toothpaste smiles. So he returned to his own dark workshop where he'd abandoned his own true dreams. In the next fifteen years, until his death, he made over one hundred and fifty new mannequins, each a masterpiece of art, transforming his uncanny domestic dreams into manifestations that were like flesh and bone. His son, who'd come all the way to our newsroom to take us to his father's underground workshop, showed us these mannequins one by one, explaining that our "essence," that which makes us "us," was reposited in these peculiar dusty masterpieces.

We stood in the basement of the cold and dark house, where we had come after a descent down a muddy slope below the huge Galata Tower and after walking on a filthy sidewalk with crooked stairs. We were surrounded by mannequins struggling to wiggle and fidget, as if they were trying to do something in order to live. In the half-light of the cellar, hidden in the shadows, hundreds of faces with expressive eyes stared at us and at each other. Some were seated, some were speaking, some were busy eating, some laughing, some in prayer, and some seemed to defy the life outside with their "existence" which, at that moment, seemed unbearable. It was obvious: these mannequins possessed an élan that could not be perceived in the crowds on the Galata Bridge, let alone in the store windows in Beyoğlu or the Mahmut Paşa bazaar. Life flowed like light through the skin of this wiggling and fidgeting, breathless crowd of mannequins. I was mesmerized. I remember approaching one of the mannequins next to me with awe and yearning. I remember touching this being (avuncular, sunk deep into his own troubles), wanting to engage this thing, to help myself to his vital force and acquire the secret of his reality, of his world. But the unyielding skin was as cold and horrifying as the room itself.

"My father used to say," the son of the mannequin maker explained with pride, "that, above all, we must pay attention to the gestures that make us who we are." After long and exhausting hours of work, he and his father would emerge out of the darkness of Kuledibi into the world, where they'd take a table with a view at the pimps' café in Taksim, order their tea, and observe the "gestures" of the crowd in the square. In those years his father believed that a nation's lifestyle, history, technology, culture, art, and literature could change, but there was no chance that the gestures could be altered. As the son went on explaining, he delineated the details in the stance of a cab driver lighting his cigarette; he described how and why the arms of a Beyoğlu thug stood away from his body as he walked sideways down the street like a crab; and he pointed out the chin of a roasted-garbanzo vendor's apprentice, laughing like the rest of us with his mouth wide open. He revealed the horror in a woman's downcast gaze, who walked alone on the street with a net shopping bag in her hand, and he explained why our people always look down while walking in the city and look up at the sky when in the country. He kept on pointing out again and again the gestures of the mannequins, their postures, and the essence that was "us" in those stances, as they waited for the hour of eternity when they'd be animated at last. What's more, you just knew these wondrous creatures could very well wear and model beautiful clothes too.

But looking at these mannequins, these sad creatures, you still sensed something that compelled you back outside to a life that was well-lighted. How do I say it? It was a kind of terror—gruesome, grievous, and dark! When the son blurted out, "Eventually, my father stopped observing even the most ordinary of movements," I had the feeling that I'd already guessed this awful truth. The father and son began to notice that those movements

I tried to describe as "gestures," be they nose wiping or belly laughing, walking or casting unfriendly looks, shaking hands or uncorking a bottle, all those ordinary movements had changed and lost their authenticity. At first, observing the crowds from the pimps' café, they couldn't figure out who the man in the street modeled himself after, given that he saw nobody other than himself and those who looked so much like him. The gestures which he and his father called "mankind's greatest treasure," the small body movements people performed in their everyday lives, changed slowly and congruously, vanished as if under the orders of an invisible "chief," only to be replaced by a slew of movements modeled after some indiscernible original. Some time later, as the father and son worked on a line of mannequin children, it all became clear to them: "Those damn movies!" cried the son.

The man in the street began to lose his authenticity because of those damn movies that came in canisters from the West and played by the hour in the cinemas. Abandoning their own, our people began to adopt other people's gestures with an unaccountable speed. I won't go into the son's justifications of his father's rage, which he portrayed in great detail, concerning these new, pretentious, and incomprehensible movements. He sketched in, line by line, all those fine manners and the violent behaviors that have annihilated our own crude innocence: bursting into laughter or opening a window or banging a door shut; holding a teacup or putting on a jacket; all those acquired and inappropriate gestures—the nodding, the polite coughing, the shows of anger, the winking, the shadowboxing, raising the eyebrows and rolling the eyes—all learned from the movies. His father didn't even want to see these impure, crossbred movements anymore. Afraid of the influence of these false movements which threatened his "children's" innocence, he decided not to leave his workshop. He shut himself into the cellar of his house, proclaiming that he'd already discovered for some time "the meaning that has to unfold and the essence of the mystery."

As I viewed the masterworks Master Bedii had created in the last fifteen years of his life, I perceived, with the terror of a "wolf child" who discovers his true identity after many years, what this vague essence might be: among this crowd of mannequins who eyed me, who moved toward me, among the uncles, aunts, friends, relatives, acquaintances, among the grocers and the laborers, my likeness also existed. Even I was present in that moth-eaten, abject darkness. Almost covered by a layer of leaden dust, the mannequins of my compatriots (among whom were Beyoğlu gangsters as well as seamstresses, Cevdet Bey whose wealth was legendary, Salahattin Bey the encyclopedist, the firefighters and the singular dwarves, old beggars and pregnant women) reminded me of the gods who had suffered the loss of their innocence as well as the loss of their awesome shadows exaggerated in the dim light; of penitents who consume themselves for not being someone else; of the unfortunates who kill one another because they cannot fall into bed and make love. They too, like me, like us, had perhaps discovered the mystery one day in a past as far away as a remnant of paradise, but they'd forgotten the secret meaning of their vague existence which they'd tumbled into by chance. We suffered from memory loss, we were doubled over, but still we insisted on being ourselves. The gestures which made us ourselves, the way we wiped our noses, scratched our heads, stepped upstairs, our looks of sadness and defeat, were in fact punishment for our insistence on being ourselves. When his son characterized Master Bedii by saying, "My father never lost hope that some day mankind would achieve the felicity of not having to imitate others," I'd been thinking that this crowd of mannequins was also dying to get out of this bleak and dusty dungeon as soon as possible and, like myself, emerge on the face of the earth, to observe other people under the sun, to imitate them, and live happily ever after like ourselves by trying to become someone else.

That desire, as I learned later, wasn't all that unrealistic! One day a shopkeeper, whose hobby was to attract attention through curiosities, bought some of the "merchandise" at the workshop, perhaps because he knew he could get them on the cheap. But the gestures and the stances of the mannequins that he bought and displayed so much resembled the customers and the crowd that flowed by his store window, they were so ordinary, so real, and so much "of us," that nobody paid them any attention. So the skinflint shopkeeper sawed them into pieces, and when the totality that gave meaning to their gestures vanished, the arms, the legs, the feet were utilized for years in the tiny window of the tiny shop where umbrellas, gloves, boots, and shoes were displayed for the benefit of the crowds in Beyoğlu.

Chapter Seven

THE LETTERS IN
MOUNT KAF

"Must a name mean something?"
— LEWIS CARROLL, *Through the Looking Glass*

Stepping out into the anomalous bright white that coated the routine gray of Nişantaşı, Galip realized it had snowed through his sleepless night harder than he'd imagined. The crowd on the sidewalk didn't seem quite aware of the sharp, semitransparent icicles that pointed down from the eaves of the buildings. In Nişantaşı Square, Galip entered the City Bank—which Rüya called the Sooty Bank, referring to the dust, smoke, car exhaust, and the dirty blue fumes that gushed out of the neighborhood's chimneys—and found out that Rüya hadn't withdrawn any appreciable amount from their joint account within the last few days, that the heat in the bank building was off, and that everybody was pleased with the small National Lottery prize which had befallen one of the bank tellers with the atrociously made-up faces. He walked past the florist's fogged window, past the arcades where the tea boys ventured with trays of morning tea, past the Şişli Progressive High where he and Rüya went to school, under the wraith-like chestnut tree hung with ice, and into Aladdin's store. Aladdin had pulled over his head the blue hood that Jelal mentioned in his article nine years ago. He was busy blowing his nose.

"What's wrong, Aladdin? You sick or something?"

"Caught myself a cold."

Enunciating the titles precisely, Galip asked for one copy of each of the leftist political periodicals for which Rüya's ex-husband used to write articles and some of which were okay by Galip. Aladdin, wearing a look first of childish fear and then of suspicion that could never be construed as hostile, said that only university students read such magazines. "What would you want with them?"

"Do the crosswords," Galip said.

Aladdin laughed pointedly to make it clear that he got the joke. "But brother, these things don't run any crosswords!" he said ruefully, like a **true** crossword addict. "These two are new on the stands, you want them too?"

"Sure," Galip said. He whispered like an old man picking up some dirty magazines: "Wrap them up, will you?"

On the Eminönü bus, he noticed the package getting curiously heavier; then, with the same odd feeling, he got the impression that an eye was watching him. But it wasn't an eye that belonged to the throng on the bus; the passengers swayed as if on a small steamboat on the high seas and stared out distractedly at the snowy streets and the crowds milling outside. That's when he realized Aladdin had wrapped the political magazines in an old copy of *Milliyet*. On the corner of one of the folds, Jelal stared out at him from his photograph in its usual place at the head of his column. The unaccountable thing was that the photograph of Jelal, which was the same every morning, now gave Galip a completely different look. Jelal appeared to say, "I'm on to you and I've got an eye on you!" Galip placed his finger on the "eye" that read his soul, but he still felt its presence under his finger the whole time he was on the bus.

He phoned Jelal as soon as he got to the office but couldn't get him. Carefully he put away the old newspaper and started reading the leftist magazines he'd unwrapped. At first, the magazines brought back the feelings of excitement, tension, and expectation that Galip had long forgotten; they reminded him of the intimations of the day of liberation, victory, and judgment which he had given up on a long time ago but didn't know just when. But after long bouts of making calls to Rüya's old friends, whose numbers he'd scribbled on the back of her letter, the memories of his left-wing days seemed as alluring and incredible as the films he'd seen in his childhood at open-air cinemas set up back behind the walls of mosques and outdoor cafés. When he watched those black-and-white Yeşilçam Films, critical of their weak plots, Galip used to think that either he didn't get the whole picture, or else he was being drawn into a world that was unintentionally transformed into a fairy tale, replete with rich but heartless fathers, the penniless Goody-Two-Shoes, the cooks, the butlers, the beggars, and the cars with the fins (the DeSoto, Rüya would remember, had the same license plates as in a previous movie), and just as he scoffed at the audience weeping in the chairs all around him, yes, yes, at that very moment—careful now!—as a result of some hocus-pocus he couldn't make out, he'd suddenly find himself in tears, sharing the sorrows of pale and pathetic altruists on the screen and the torments of resolute but selfless heroes. So as to be better informed about the black-and-white fairy-tale world of the small leftist factions where he'd once found Rüya with her ex-husband, he phoned an old friend who kept all the back issues of all the political journals.

"You're still collecting periodicals, aren't you?" Galip said with conviction. "I have a client who's in real trouble. Do you think I could use your archives for a while to work up his defense?"

"Sure enough," said Saim with his usual goodwill, pleased to be sought after for his "archives." He'd be looking for Galip around eight-thirty tonight.

Galip worked in the office until it got dark. He called Jelal a couple more times but couldn't get him. After each conversation, the secretary informed him that Jelal Bey either hadn't come in "yet" or else had "just" gone out. Galip had the uneasy feeling that he was still being watched by Jelal's "eye" in the newspaper he'd stuck in one of the shelves left over from Uncle Melih's days. Indeed, he felt the tangible presence of Jelal as he listened to the story of an altercation that ensued among the heirs to a small store in the Covered Bazaar, told by an excessively obese mother-son team who kept interrupting each other, and as he tried to explain to a traffic cop, who wore shades and wanted to sue the government for giving him short shrift on his retirement benefits, that according to the laws prevailing in the land the two years he had spent in the loony bin could not be counted as employment.

He phoned Rüya's friends one by one. For each call, he came up with fresh and diverse pretexts. He asked her high-school chum Macide for the phone number of Gül, whose name, meaning "rose," had once entranced him; he needed to get in touch with her in the interests of a case. He was told by the gracious maid of the gracious household that Gül with the pretty name, whom Macide didn't like, had given birth the day before yesterday to her third and fourth children simultaneously at the Gülbahçe (Rose Garden!) hospital, and that if he rushed he still had time to view the darling twins, who'd been named Hüsün and Aşk (Beauty and Love), through the plate glass nursery window. Figen promised she'd return *What Is to Be Done?*

(Chernyshevsky's), as well as the Raymond Chandler, and wished Rüya a speedy recovery. As for Behiye, no, Galip was mistaken, she had no uncle who was an agent at the Narcotics Bureau; and no, Galip was sure of it, there was not a hint in her voice that she knew anything of Rüya's whereabouts. What amazed Semih was how Galip had gotten wind of the underground textile mill: yes, they had indeed put together a crew of engineers and technicians to start a project to actualize the first Turkish-made zipper; but no, since he was not apprised of the trafficking in bobbins reported in the papers recently, he was unable to provide any legal information. He could only send Rüya his most heartfelt regards (which Galip could well believe).

He altered his voice when he made his calls, or he assumed other identities—a school principal, a theater manager, a building superintendent—but none of it helped him to track Rüya down. Süleyman, who sold medical encyclopedias door to door which he imported from England, where they had been published forty years ago, explained in all sincerity to the middle-school principal Galip impersonated who had him called to the phone that never mind having a daughter named Rüya in middle school, he didn't even have any children. Likewise, Ilyas, who freighted coal from the Black Sea coast on his father's barge, protested that he couldn't possibly have left his dream log behind at the Rüya Theater since he had not been to the movies in months nor did he own such a notebook; and the lift importer Asım explained that his company could not be held responsible for the hitch at the Rüya Building elevator because he'd never heard of a building or a street called Rüya; when they said the word *rüya* neither man displayed any hint of anxiety or guilt, they both spoke with all the innocence of sincerity. Tarık, who manufactured rat poison at his father's chemical plant by day and who wrote poetry relating to the alchemy of death at night, accepted with pleasure some law students' invitation to speak on the theme of "dreams and the enigmas of dreams" as seen in his poems, and he promised to meet his new friends in front of the old pimps' café at Taksim. As for Kemal and Bülent, they were both on excursions into Anatolia. One had gone after the memoirs of a seamstress from Izmir who some fifty years ago, after dancing the waltz with Atatürk surrounded by much applause and lots of journalists, had immediately sat down at her pedal-model Singer and dashed off a pair of European-style trousers. And the other was traversing the whole of Eastern Anatolia on muleback, village by village, coffeehouse by coffeehouse, to unload magical backgammon dice that had been carved out of the thousand-year-old thighbone of the avuncular personage known to the Christians as Santa Claus.

On top of having to relinquish the rest of the names on his list to wrong numbers and bleeps on the phone lines, which were at their worst on the days it snowed or rained, nowhere in the pages of the political journals he read all day—looking through the names of those who'd changed factions, or confessed, or who underwent torture and were killed, or were given jail sentences, or were killed in a scuffle and given funerals, those whose letters the editors answered or returned or published, or the names and assumed names of those who drew political cartoons, wrote poetry, or worked in the editorial cadres—did he come across Rüya's ex-husband's name or pen name.

As evening descended, he stayed stuck in his chair, sad and motionless. Outside the window a curious crow gave him sideways glances; he could hear the din of the Friday evening crowd in the street. Galip slowly settled into a blissful and magnetic sleep. When he woke up much later the room was completely dark, but he still felt the crow's eye watching him just like Jelal's "eye" in the newspaper. Still sitting in the dark, he slid the drawers in slowly, felt for his overcoat and put it on, and left the office. All the hallway lights had been turned off in the building. The apprentice in the tea room was busy cleaning the urinals.

He felt really cold as he crossed the snow-covered Galata Bridge: a stiff wind came down the Bosphorus. He stopped off at a pudding shop in Karaköy which had marble tabletops. He turned away from the mirrors that reflected each other and had some vermicelli chicken soup and potted eggs. On the only wall in the pudding shop that wasn't hung with mirrors, there was the view of a mountain inspired by postcards and Pan American Airways calendars. The brilliant white peak of the mountain, seen through the pines and behind the mirror-like lake, looked more like Mount Kaf, where Galip and Rüya had so often taken magic trips in their childhood, than like any of the Postcard Alps which had inspired it.

On the short trip up to Beyoğlu on the funicular, Galip was drawn into an altercation with an old man he didn't know: was it because the cable had snapped that day that the cars had been derailed and bolted into Karaköy Square, breaking through walls and the glass frame like unbridled horses mad with joy? Or was it because the engineer was drunk? Turns out the drunk engineer was the anonymous geezer's fellow townsman from Trabzon. In Cihangir, not far from the crowded streets of Taksim and Beyoğlu, nobody was out in the streets. Saim's wife, who came to the door, was pleased but in a hurry to get back; she and Saim had apparently been watching the same TV program cabbies and doormen would watch together in a basement coffeehouse.

The program, "Things We Left Behind," was a diatribe lamenting the passing of the old mosques, fountains, and caravanserais built by the Ottomans in the Balkans into the hands of Yugoslavians, Albanians, and Greeks. Saim and his wife seemed oblivious to Galip, who watched the images of forlorn mosques on the tube—like some neighbor boy who'd come in to see the soccer game—from the fake rococo armchair the springs of which had sprung long ago. Saim looked like that wrestler with Olympic medals who'd gone to his eternal rest but whose pictures still graced the walls of greengrocery stores. His wife resembled a cute, fat mouse. There was a dust-colored table in the room and a dust-colored lamp; a grandfather who looked more like the wife than like Saim (could her name be Remziye? Galip wondered wearily) was hung up on the wall inside a gilt frame; there they all were: the calendar from an insurance company, the ashtray from a bank, the cordial set, the silver candy dish, the buffet with the coffee cups. And there were the two walls of dust, paper, and periodicals, Saim's "library archive": the reason for Galip's presence there in the first place.

Saim had created this library, referred to as "the archive of our revolution" by the sarcastic university crowd even ten years ago, out of his own indecision, which he once owned up to in an uncharacteristic confessional moment. It was an indecision born not from the choice "between the two classes" but from that between political factions.

Saim used to show up at all the political meetings, the "forums," running from university to university and canteen to canteen, listening to everyone and his brother, in pursuit of "all opinions, all convictions," but hesitant to ask too many questions; he'd get hold of all kinds of leftist circulars (Pardon me, but do you happen to have the report handed out by the "eliminators" at the School of Technology yesterday?), including all the white papers, the propaganda brochures, the handbills, and he'd read like mad. When he no longer had the time to read everything, but still couldn't settle on a "political line," he must have started accumulating what he couldn't read. Later on, when reading and coming to a resolution ceased to be big concerns for him, his goal was to build a dam in order to prevent this "river of documents," which had gathered affluence, from flowing along uselessly (the metaphor originated with Saim who was a construction engineer), and it was to this end that Saim had generously dedicated the rest of his life.

With the TV program over, the set turned off, and polite conversation got through, the husband and wife cast quizzical glances at Galip in the ensuing silence, requiring that he tell his story immediately: His defendant was a student who'd been accused of a political crime he hadn't committed. No, it wasn't like there was no dead party. It followed a bungled bank robbery planned by three bungling kids, and as they tried to make it to the getaway car which was a stolen taxi, one of them had accidentally bumped into a little old lady, bumping her off. Seems the poor dear lady fell and hit her head on the sidewalk and died on the spot ("Wouldn't you know it!" said Saim's wife). The only one they caught on the scene, carrying a gun, was a quiet boy who came from a "good family." Naturally, he tried to withhold the names of comrades whom he admired too much and, what's more amazing, he was successful in keeping his mouth shut despite the torture he underwent; but the bad news, according to Galip's subsequent investigations, was that he ended up quietly assuming the responsibility for the little old lady's death. The real perpetrator, a student of archaeology named Mehmet Yılmaz, was gunned down three weeks later by unidentified persons as he wrote ciphered slogans on a factory wall in a new squatters' district behind Umraniye. Under the circumstances, it could be expected that the kid from the good family would divulge the name of the real perpetrator, but not only did the police not believe that the dead Mehmet Yılmaz was the real Mehmet Yılmaz but the leaders of the faction who were behind the bank robbery, taking an unexpected stance, claimed that Mehmet Yılmaz was still in their ranks and, what's more, that he continued to write articles for their publication with all his former resolve.

Now that he'd taken on the case, more for the sake of the father, who was a wealthy, well-meaning man, than for the boy in the big house, Galip wanted: 1) to make sure that the "Mehmet Yılmaz" was not the real Mehmet Yılmaz by going through his articles; 2) to discover who in fact was writing the articles under the guise of the dead Mehmet Yılmaz by checking out articles written under other assumed names; 3) as Saim and his wife must have already surmised, seeing how this odd happenstance had been arranged by the cadre in which Rüya's ex-husband once figured, he wanted to glance through the activities of this political splinter group over the last six months; and 4) he was determined to make a serious inquiry into ghostwriters who assumed the identity of dead writers, and into the mystery of missing persons in general.

They embarked immediately upon the research, which now excited Saim. In the first couple of hours, while they drank tea and gobbled up slices of cake served by the wife whose name Galip finally recalled (Rukiyé), they looked through the publications only for the names and the assumed names of the contributors. Then they augmented the list with the pen names of those who made confessions, those who were dead, and those who worked for the periodicals. Soon their heads were reeling with the enigma of a semisecret world which was impermanent, built on death notices, threats, confessions, bombs, errors of typesetting, poems, and slogans.

They came across assumed names that were no secret, names derived from these assumed names, names that were portions of the derivative names. They deciphered acrostics, letter codes that were less than perfect, and semi-transparent anagrams which might have been intentional or entirely accidental. Rukiyé sat at one end of the table where Saim and Galip were sitting. The atmosphere in the room had assumed the same impatient but somewhat customary sadness of people listening to the radio on New Year's Eve while playing bingo or the Paper Horse Race, rather than the effort to clear a young man falsely accused of murder, or to track down a woman who was missing. Between the open curtains, one could see the snow flurries outside.

With the same satisfaction as that of a patient teacher who waits to witness the successful maturation of a bright new student he's discovered, they delighted in tracking down the assumed names' adventures, their zigzags through the magazines, their ups and their downs. At times when they saw the photograph of one among them who had been arrested, put to torture, given a sentence, or had disappeared, they fell silent with a sorrow that curtailed their excitement; then, stumbling across some new wordplay, a new coincidence, or something erratic, they returned once more to the life of letters.

According to Saim, never mind the imaginary nature of the names and the heroes that they came across in the publications, even the demonstrations, the meetings, the secret councils, the congresses of underground parties, and the bank robberies organized by these names had never taken place. As an extreme example of what he was saying, he pulled out the account of a popular uprising some twenty years ago in the town of Little Çeruh, situated between Erzincan and Kemah in Eastern Anatolia: during the insurrection, for which one of the publications had provided a definite date, a provisional government had been established, a pink stamp bearing a dove had been issued, the provincial governor had been brained by a falling vase, a daily paper composed entirely of poems had been published, opticians and pharmacies had handed out free eyeglasses to cross-eyed persons, firewood was obtained for the stove at the elementary school, and, just as the bridge to connect the town to civilization was about to be built, Atatürkist forces of government arrived, taking the matter in hand, and, before the cows had a chance to finish munching up the stinky prayer rugs that covered the dirt floor in the mosque, they'd strung up the rebels on the oak tree in the middle of the town square. In reality—as Saim pointed out the enigma in the logograms and the maps—on top of there being no town called Çeruh, Little or Otherwise, the names of those who took part in the insurrection that arose like the legendary bird were all false. The false names got buried under poetry with rhymes or word repetitions, but there was one instance when they came upon a clue concerning Mehmet Yılmaz (the reference was to a murder committed in Umraniye during the same period that Galip had spoken about). They pored over the accounts and the reports, which read like domestic films that keep breaking and getting spliced, but they could never find the end to the story in the subsequent issues of the journal.

At one point Galip rose from the table and called home, telling Rüya tenderly that he was going to work late with Saim and not to wait up but to go to sleep. The phone was at the far end of the room. Saim and his wife sent Rüya their regards: Rüya responded in kind, naturally.

While they were deep into the game of discovering the assumed names, deciphering them, and making logographs out of them, Saim's wife went to bed, leaving the two men alone in the room, every inch of which was covered under piles of papers, periodicals, newspapers, and reports. It was way past midnight; Istanbul was under the bewitching silence of snow. While Galip indulged himself in the typesetting and spelling errors in the fascinating collection ("Too incomplete, too inadequate!" Saim said with his usual modesty) which was made up largely of sheets that had been faintly duplicated by the same mimeograph machines and dispersed in university canteens that smell of cigarette smoke, during strikes held in tents on rainy days and in remote train stations, Saim brought out from another room a tract which he called "very rare" and showed it to him with the pride of a collector: *Anti Ibn Zerhani or The Sufi Traveler Who Has His Feet on the Ground.*

Carefully, Galip began to turn the pages of the bound book, which was nonetheless in typescript. "A fellow who lives in the province of Kayseri, in a town that doesn't show up on a medium-size map of Turkey," Saim explained. "He received training in religion and Sufi mysticism in his childhood from his dad who was the master of a small tekke. Years later, as he read the thirteenth-century Arab mystic philosopher Ibn Zerhani's book called *The Inner Meaning of the Lost Mystery*, he wrote in the margins, emulating Lenin reading Hegel, a running 'materialist' commentary. He then made a fair copy of these notes, which he expanded with long and unnecessary parenthetical substantiations. As if his notes were the work of someone else whose notions were totally incomprehensible and esoteric, he next wrote a long explication, a kind of treatise. Then he put these together as if both were the work of other people, typed it all up including a 'publisher's foreword,' which he also wrote himself. In the first thirty pages, he added the tale of his own religious and subsequent revolutionary life history. What was interesting in these tales was the account of how the author discovered, as he strolled in the town cemetery one afternoon, the strong connection between Sufi mysticism, which the West terms 'pantheism,' and the philosophical 'thingism' as propounded by the author in reaction to his father, a Sufi master. When he saw in the tall cypress trees the same crow he'd seen years ago in this very cemetery where the sheep graze and where even the ghosts are asleep—you know that the Turkish crow has a life span of two hundred years, don't you?—he understood that the winged, shameless flying beast called 'higher thought' retained always, always, the same head and feet and especially the same body and wings. He drew the picture of the same crow, inscribed on the bound cover, himself. This book proves that any Turk who desires immortality has to be his own Boswell to his own Johnson, both his own Goethe and his own Eckermann. Six copies were typed in all. I bet there isn't one in the archives of the National Bureau of Investigation."

It was as if the ghost of a third person bonded the two men in the room to the author of the book with the crow on the cover, to the imaginative power of the sad, insignificant, isolated life that was spent going back and forth between a house in a provincial town and the small hardware store he inherited from his father. Galip felt like saying: "There is only one story told in all that's been written, in all those letters, all the words, all the hopes of salvation and the recollections of torture and disgrace, penned with the joy and sorrow of all those hopes and the recollections, a single story." It was as if Saim had captured the story somewhere in his collection of white papers, periodicals, and newsprint which he'd pulled together with the patience of a fisherman who's thrown his net into the ocean for years. And he knew he got it too. But besides being unable to seize the naked story hidden in all the material that he'd stacked up and put into order, he'd lost the word that would unlock it.

When they came across Mehmet Yılmaz's name in a periodical published four years ago, Galip began saying that it was just a coincidence and that he ought to go home, but Saim stopped him declaring that nothing was coincidental in his periodicals—he spoke of them as "my periodicals" now. Making a superhuman effort for the next two hours, leaping from one periodical into another, rolling his eyes like projectors, Galip discovered Mehmet Yılmaz had been converted to Ahmet Yılmaz; in a periodical which had a well on the cover and which roiled with chickens and peasants, Ahmet Yılmaz had now turned into a Mete Çakmaz; it was not too difficult for Saim to put together that Metin Çakmaz and Ferit Çakmaz were also the same individual; in the meantime, the pen name had given up on theoretical articles and gone for writing lyrics for songs that are sung accompanied by stringed instruments and cigarette smoke at memorials held in wedding halls. But he hadn't stayed with that too long, either; for a while, he'd turned into a pen name which was convinced that everybody except itself was part of the police, then into an ambitious and highstrung math-oriented economist who deciphered the perversities of British academicians. But he wasn't someone who could long tolerate dark and dire clichés. Saim found his hero in an issue of another periodical collection for which he'd tiptoed into the bedroom, published some three years ago, as if he'd planted him there himself: the guy's name was now Ali Celan, who expounded on the details of how life would be lived in a classless society in a beautiful future: cobbled streets would remain cobbled and not covered under asphalt; detective novels which were a waste of time would be banned as well as mystifying newspaper columns; the habit of having barbers come home to give haircuts would be broken. And when Galip read that the education of children, in order to prevent them from getting brainwashed by their parents' stupid prejudices, would be delegated to their grandparents who lived upstairs, he had no doubt left as to the identity of the pen name, and he came to the painful realization that Rüya had shared her childhood recollections with her ex-husband. Surprisingly enough, it was announced in the next issue that the same pen name belonged to a professor of mathematics who was a member of the Academy of Albanian Studies. There, below the professor's life story, not hidden under some assumed moniker, stood Rüya's ex-husband's real name, silent and motionless like a bewildered bug caught under the kitchen light turned on suddenly.

"Nothing can be as astounding as life," Saim said exultantly, "except writing."

He tiptoed into the bedroom once more and came out with two cardboard Sana margarine cases piled up with periodicals. "These are the periodicals of a splinter group that has some connection to Albania. I'm going to relate to you a strange mystery I've managed to solve only because I've devoted to it so many years of my life. I have a feeling it's related to the object you're looking for."

He brewed a fresh pot of tea, took some periodicals out of the boxes and some books off the shelves that he deemed necessary for the telling of his story, and placed them on the table.

"It was six years ago," he began, "a Saturday afternoon. I was looking through the magazines put out by fellow travelers of the Albanian Labor Party and its leader Enver Hoxha (and there were three publications back then which were all sworn enemies of each other); as I was leafing through the last issue of one called *The Labor of the People* to see if there was anything of interest, my eye caught a photograph and an article: it was about a ceremony in honor of new recruits inducted into the faction. What caught my attention was not the disclosure that the recruits were inducted into a Marxist organization with songs and poems in a country where all Communist activity is illegal, no; I knew that, in spite of the danger, all the small leftist splinter groups published similar articles in each issue in order to stay alive, to make it known that their numbers were growing. What did catch my attention was the caption that mentioned pointedly the 'twelve' columns in the black-and-white photo which showed a crowd smoking passionately as if it were performing a sacred duty, the posters of Enver Hoxha and Mao, and the reciters of poetry. Even more strange, the assumed names of the new recruits mentioned in the interview were always chosen from the names of the Alawite order, names like Hasan, Hüseyin, Ali and, as I was to discover later, the names of the Bektaşi sheiks, spiritual leaders. Had I not known that Bektaşi Sufi orders had been big in Albania at one time, perhaps I would never have suspected anything about this incredible mystery, but I went at the events and the articles hammer and tongs. For four whole years I read books constantly on the Bektaşi order, the Janissary army, Hurufism, and Albanian Communism, and I unraveled a hundred-and-fifty-year-old conspiracy."

"You know all this anyway," Saim said but went on to recite the Bektaşi history of seven hundred years, beginning with Hacı Bektaş Veli. He gave an account of how the order had Alawite, Sufi, and shamanistic origins, how it was related to the periods of inception and rise of the Ottoman Empire and the tradition of revolution and rebellion in the Janissary army, the center of which was rooted in the Bektaşi order. If you considered, after all, that each Janissary soldier was a Bektaşi, then you saw instantly its mystery stamped on the history of Istanbul. The first time the Bektaşis got the boot out of Istanbul, it was due to the Janissaries: while the barracks got blitzed in 1826 under the orders of Mahmut the Second, seeing how the rebellious army was unwilling to accept his program of Westernization, the tekkes which maintained the spiritual health of the Janissaries were shut down and the Bektaşi dervishes kicked out of town.

Twenty years after going underground, the Bektaşis returned to Istanbul, but this time under the guise of the Nakşbendi order. Until Atatürk banned all the activities of the orders seventy years later, the Bektaşis presented themselves to the world as Nakşis, but they lived among themselves as Bektaşis, burying their secrets even deeper.

Galip studied an engraving from an English travel book that represented a Bektaşi ritual which probably reflected the fantasy in the mind of the artist-traveler rather than reality. He counted the *twelve* columns in the engraving one by one.

"The third time the Bektaşis manifested themselves," Saim said, "it was fifty years after the Republic, not under the Nakşbendi order this time but wearing a Marxist-Leninist guise . . ." Following a silence, he gave an excited recital, producing by way of illustration articles, photos, engravings he'd cut out of journals, books, brochures. All that was performed, written, and experienced in the Bektaşi order corresponded exactly to all that went on in the political factions: the rituals of initiation; the periods of severe trials and self-denial before the initiation; the pain endured by the youthful aspirants during these periods; the veneration for the fallen, the sainted, and the dead among the order's or the faction's past members, and the rites of paying homage to them; the sacred meaning assigned to the word "road"; the repetition of words and expressions for the sake of the spirit of oneness and community; the litanies; the fact that adepts who travel the same road recognize each other by their beards, mustaches, even the expressions in their eyes; the meter and the rhyme scheme in the poems recited and the songs played during their ceremonies; etc., etc. "Ostensibly, unless all this is only coincidence," said Saim, "unless God is playing a cruel epistolic joke on me, then I'd have to be blind not to see that the logogriphs and the anagrams the Bektaşis took over from the Hurufis are, without any doubt, being reiterated in the leftist publications." In the silence which was unbroken except for the whistles of the night watchmen in distant quarters, Saim slowly began to recite for Galip the word games he'd figured out, lining them up with their secondary meanings, as if he were repeating his prayers.

Much later, somewhere between sleep and wakefulness, in the wee hours when he went back and forth between dreams of Rüya and memories of happier times, Galip became aware of Saim saying: "the most striking aspect and the essence of the subject . . ." and began to pay attention. The kids who joined political factions, Saim was saying, had no idea they'd turned Bektaşi. Since the whole thing was cooked up between the party middle management and the Bektaşi masters in Albania, those in the rank and file were completely unaware; all those well-intentioned altruistic kids who joined up at the cost of abandoning their daily habits and altering their entire lives from tip to toe had no clue that their photos taken at the ceremonies and rituals, the marches and meals, were all evaluated by some dervishes in Albania as an extension of their own order. "At first, in my innocence, I thought it was a terrible conspiracy, an incredible secret, that these kids were being hoodwinked despicably," Saim went on. "So much so that, in the first flush of excitement, for the first time in fifteen years I thought of putting it all on paper, down to the last detail, and publishing it, but I decided against it immediately." In the snowy silence, listening for a while to the moan of a dark tanker sailing through the Bosphorus, the sound reverberating lightly on the casements of the entire city, he added: "I have finally understood that nothing can be changed by proving that the life we lead is someone else's dream."

Then Saim told the story of the Zeriban tribe who settled on an inaccessible mountain in Eastern Anatolia and for the next two hundred years prepared for the journey that would take them to Mount Kaf. The idea of going on the journey to the mythic Mount Kaf, a journey on which they'd never set forth, had come from a dream book published three hundred and twenty years ago. What would be changed by informing the members of the tribe that their spiritual leaders, who handed down the truth from generation to generation as if it were a secret, had already made a deal with the Ottomans stipulating that the trip to Mount Kaf would never be made? It would be like trying to explain to the soldiers who crowd into small-town movie houses on Sunday afternoons that the scheming priest on the screen who tries to get the brave Turkish warrior to drink poisoned wine is only a humble actor who, in real life, is devoted to Islam. Where would it get you? You'd end up depriving these people of their sole pleasure, the pleasure of getting mad.

Toward morning, as Galip drowsed on the sofa, Saim was busy soliloquizing that, in all probability, the elderly Bektaşi masters in Albania who got together with the party leadership in the dreamlike empty ballroom of a white colonial hotel left over from the turn of the century, looking through tearful eyes at the photos of the Turkish youths, had no inkling that it wasn't the mysteries of the order that were being recited at the ceremonies, but exuberant Marxist-Leninist analyses. For the alchemists, not knowing that they'd never be able to transmute matter into gold was not their misfortune but their reason for being. No matter how much the modern illusionist revealed the tricks of his trade, the fervent audience was still gratified in persuading itself, for a moment, that this was not a deception but a brush with sorcery. A whole lot of young people, too, fell in love under the influence of some talk they'd heard at some period of their lives, or in a story, or a book they'd shared; they married their flames in a fever and, never comprehending the fallacy that lay behind their romance, merrily spent the rest of their lives. As Saim's wife cleared the table of periodicals in order to set the table for breakfast, Saim, while he glanced at the daily paper that had been slipped under the door, was still carrying on about how nothing could be changed by the knowledge that everything that's written, everything in the authoritative texts, alludes not to life but, simply by virtue of having been written, alludes to some dream.

Chapter Eight

THE THREE MUSKETEERS

I asked him about his enemies: He recounted, recounted, and recounted.
—Conversations with Yahya Kemal

His funeral turned out exactly as he feared, as he'd predicted it thirty-two years ago: one inmate and one orderly from the small nursing home for the indigent, one retired journalist who'd been his protégé when he was at the height of his career as a columnist, two confused relatives who had no knowledge of the writer's life and work, one bizarre-looking Greek dowager wearing a hat with a gauzy veil and a brooch that resembled a sultan's aigrette, the reverend imam, myself, and the body in the coffin. We were nine in all. The coffin was lowered into the ground during yesterday's snowstorm, so the imam hurried through the prayers, and the rest of us were in a rush to scatter earth into the grave. Then, before I knew it, we were all on our way. At the Kısıklı stop, there was no one waiting for the streetcar besides me. Once I crossed over to this side, I went up to Beyoğlu where Edward G. Robinson's *Scarlet Street* was playing at the Alhambra. I went in and gave myself the thrill of seeing it. I've always loved Edward G. Robinson. Here he plays a failed bureaucrat and an amateur painter, who acquires ritzy duds and identity and pretends to be a billionaire, hoping to impress his love object. But it turns out that his sweetheart, Joan Bennett, has cheated on him all along. He gets two-timed, grief-stricken, destroyed, and we get depressed watching him suffer.

When the dearly departed and I first met (to begin the paragraph, as I did the first, with words he often used himself), he was a veteran columnist of seventy and I thirty. On my way to see a friend in Bakırköy, I was about to step into the commuter train at the Sirkeci Station, and who should I see! There he was, seated at a table in one of the platform eateries, drinking *rakı* with two other legendary columnists of my childhood and youth. What surprised me was not running into the three septuagenarians who inhabited the Mount Kaf of my literary imagination among the mortal multitudes and the rumpus in the Sirkeci train station, but seeing them seated together at all, at the same table drinking like the three musketeers at Dumas *père's* tavern, when all through their literary lives these three pen wielders had laid into each other with bitter insults. During their literary careers of a half century when they wore out two sultans, one caliph, and three presidents, these three belligerent penmen had accused each other (at times rightfully) of many things: of atheism, Young Turkism, francophilism, nationalism, Masonism, Kemalism, republicanism, of treason, of royalism, Westernism, mysticism, plagiarism, Nazism, Judaism, Arabism, Armenianism, of homosexuality, of being turncoats, of religious canonism, of Communism, Americanism, and, in keeping with the fashionable topic of the times, existentialism. (At the time, one of them had claimed that "the existentialist of all time" had been Ibn Arabi who'd not only been imitated seven centuries later but also been robbed blind by the Western World.) I studied the three penmen carefully for a while; then heeding an inner compulsion, I walked over to their table, introduced myself, and paid all three compliments that I made sure were equally distributed.

Now, I want my readers to understand: I was excited, passionate, young, creative, bright, successful, but I vacillated unresolved between narcissism and self-confidence, shifted back and forth between good intentions and opportunism. Despite my youthful excitement as a dewy-eyed columnist, had I not been so sure that I was better read than all three of them, that I received more letters from the readers, that I was a better writer, of course, and that they were painfully aware of at least the first two of these facts, I wouldn't have had the guts to approach the three great masters of my trade.

That's why I joyfully interpreted their turning up their noses at me as a sign of victory. Had I not been a young and successful columnist but an ordinary reader gushing with admiration, naturally they'd have treated me much better. First, they wouldn't ask me to sit down, so I waited. Then, when they did let me sit, they sent me to the kitchen as if I were the waiter; so I waited on them. They wanted to check out a certain weekly, so I ran to the newspaper kiosk and got it for them. I peeled his orange for one, retrieved the other's napkin before he could stoop for it, and I responded, cringing as they wanted me to, no sir, unfortunately I didn't have much French but in the evenings, with the aid of a dictionary, I worked on deciphering *Les Fleurs du mal.* My ignorance had rendered my victory over them even less tolerable, but my excessive self-effacement seemed to lighten my transgression.

Years later, when I myself pulled the same act on younger journalists, I'd come to understand that, although they appeared to be completely uninterested in me and only addressed each other, the three masters were actually making sure I was getting properly influenced. Silent and respectful, I listened to them spout off. Concerning the German atomic scientist who'd hit the headlines the last few days, what were the actual forces behind his conversion to Islam? When the Honorable Ahmet Mithat, the father of Turkish columnists, cornered Elastic Sait, who'd bested him in the battle of words, in a dark alley one night and gave him a thorough beating, had he stipulated that Sait renounce the polemics in which they were engaged? Was Bergson a mystic, or a materialist? Where was the proof that hidden mysteriously within the world there was a "second creation"? Who were the poets getting themselves chewed out in the last verses of the twenty-sixth sura of the Koran for professing beliefs and deeds they neither believed in nor performed? In the same vein, was André Gide a real homosexual, or like the Arabian poet Abu Nuwas, did he date girls but pretend to like boys, aware that the predilection would bring him notoriety? In the first paragraph of *Kéreban le têtu* where Jules Verne describes Tophane Square and the Fountain of Mahmut the First, did he screw up because he'd extrapolated the scene from a particular engraving by Melling, or because he'd lifted the whole thing out of Lamartine's *Voyage en Orient*? Had Rumi included the account of the woman who dies fornicating with a donkey in the fifth volume of his *Mathnawi* for the story or for the lesson?

Seeing how their eyes shot glances at me and their white eyebrows posed questions as they debated the last subject cautiously and courteously, I too tossed in my two cents' worth: The story was included there for the story, as are all stories, but an effort had been made to cover it under the gauzy veil of a lesson. "Son," said the one whose funeral I attended yesterday, "do you pen your columns to instruct, or to entertain?" In an effort to prove that I had already had definite ideas on any given subject, I went for the first thing that popped into my head: "To entertain." They didn't go for it. "You're young and new at your métier," they said; "allow us to give you some free advice." I shot to my feet all stirred up. "Sirs!" I said, "I want to take down all your advice!" and, sprinting up to the cash register, I got the host to give me a sheaf of paper. I wish to share with you, my readers, the advice I received.

I know that among my readers some are impatient to hear the long-forgotten names of the three masters; they probably expect that I will whisper, at least, the names in their ears, but seeing how I've avoided giving away the three penmen up to this point, I am not about to do it now. Not so much to make sure the threesome sleep peacefully in their graves, but to weed out the readers who don't deserve this bit of information from those who do. For this end, I will refer to each deceased writer by one of the three pseudonyms that three Ottoman sultans signed under their poems. Those who can figure out which pseudonym belongs to which sultan, provided they also reason through the parallels between the names of the poet-sultans and the names of my masters, can perhaps decipher the puzzle that isn't all that consequential. But the real enigma is hidden in the game of vanity-chess the three masters played, building the mystery on the moves they called advice. Given that I'm still not clear about the beauty of the mystery, like some unfortunate incompetents who interpret the grand masters' moves through the aid of newspaper columns on chess I too have inserted my abject interpretations and pitiful thoughts parenthetically within the pieces of advice from my masters.

A: *Adli*. On that winter day, he wore a cream-colored suit made of English wool (in our country all costly material gets dubbed "English") and a dark tie. Tall, well-groomed, combed white mustache. Carries a cane. Looks like an English gentleman who doesn't have money, though it is not for me to say whether, if one doesn't have money, one can still be an English gentleman.

B: *Bahti*. His tie is loose and awry like his face. He has on an old jacket, stained and unpressed. Looped through one buttonhole of his vest, the chain of the pocket watch he wears in his vest pocket is visible. Broad in the beam and slovenly. The ubiquitous cigarette in his hand which he passionately calls "my only friend" and which, betraying his unrequited love, will kill him of a heart attack.

C: *Cemali*. Short, cantankerous. Even though he tries to be neat and clean, he still can't change the look of his retired teacher's clothes. The faded jacket of mail carriers, the pants, the thick rubber-soled shoes from the state's Sümerbank shops. Thick lenses, terribly myopic, "violently" ugly.

Here are the masters' nuggets of advice and my unworthy interpolations:

1. C: Writing merely for entertainment leaves the columnist without a compass in the wild blue yonder.

2. B: The columnist being neither Aesop nor Rumi, the lesson emerges out of the story; the story won't emerge out of the lesson.

3. C: Don't aim for the intelligence of the reader, aim for your own.

4. A: Your compass is the lesson. (An obvious reference to C's 1.)

5. C: Without digging into the mystery of our graveyards and history, you can talk about neither "us" nor the East.

6. B: On the subject of East 'n West, the key is hidden in a saying by Arif the Beard: "You poor slobs who look Westward as your ship sails East!" (Arif the Beard was one of the heroes in B's columns, modeled after an actual person.)

7. A, B, C: Get hold of proverbs, sayings, anecdotes for yourself, and jokes, lines of poetry, adages, poetry anthologies.

8. C: You won't be scratching around for the maxim with which to crown your piece; instead, you will be looking for an appropriate topic to wear the crowning maxim you've already chosen.

9. A: Don't even sit down before you've got your first sentence.

10. C: You've got to have some kind of sincere belief.

11. A: Even if you don't have some kind of a sincere belief, make sure the reader believes that your beliefs are sincere.

12. B: The reader is a child who wants to go to the carnival.

13. C: The reader never forgives the writer who blasphemes against Muhammad; besides, God will strike him with paralysis. (Sensing that 11 is persiflage directed against him, he's insinuating that the slight paralysis in the corner of A's mouth is a result of the piece A's written on Muhammad's conjugal and business affairs.)

14. A: Dote on dwarves; the reader does. (He's responding to C's 13 by making an innuendo about C's lack of stature.)

15. B: The mysterious home for dwarves in Üsküdar, for example, is a fine topic.

16. C: Wrestling is also a fine topic but only when it's done, or written about, for the sport. (Figuring 15 is an insult aimed at himself, he's referring to B's interest in wrestling and his serials on wrestling which have given rise to talk that he's a pederast.)

17. A: The reader has the IQ of a twelve-year-old, he's married, has four children, and can't make ends meet.

18. C: The reader bites the hand that feeds him, like the cat.

19. *B:* The cat, being an intelligent animal, does not bite the hand that feeds him; he only knows not to trust writers who fancy dogs.

20. *A:* Don't make observations on cats and dogs, concern yourself with the problems of your homeland.

21. *B:* Make sure you know the addresses of consulates. (Innuendo about the rumor that, during the Second World War, C was in the pay of the German Consulate, and A of the British.)

22. *B:* Get embroiled in polemics, but only if you know how to hurt a guy.

23. *A:* Get embroiled in polemics, but only if you can get your boss to back you up.

24. *C:* Get embroiled in polemics, but only if you have a greatcoat to take along. (Allusion to B's famous line explaining why he avoided the War of Independence and remained in occupied Istanbul: "I can't take Ankara winters.")

25. *B:* Answer reader mail; if nobody's writing, then go ahead and answer the letters you've faked yourself.

26. *C:* Our teacher and master is Scheherazade; remember, you merely tack ten- or fifteen-page stories in between events that constitute "life."

27. *B:* Read a little, but read with love; you'll appear better read than those who read like a tomcat eating a grindstone.

28. *C:* Be pushy, get to know important people so that you'll have some reminiscences to write about when they kick the bucket.

29. *A:* Don't begin an obituary piece with "dearly departed" only to end up insulting the dead.

30. *A, B, C:* Do everything in your power to avoid the following sentences: *a)* The dearly departed was alive only yesterday. *b)* Our profession is fraught with ingratitude: what we write today is forgotten tomorrow. *c)* Did you happen to hear such and such a program on the radio last night? *d)* How time flies! *e)* Had the dearly departed been alive today, what would he have said about this crying shame? *f)* They don't do that in Europe. *g)* Bread cost only this many *kuruş* this many years ago. *h)* Then the event also reminded me of such and such.

31. *C:* "Then" is a word that belongs only to those who don't know the writer's art.

32. *B:* Whatever smacks of art in a column does not belong in the column; whatever it is that's in the column, it is not art.

33. *C:* Don't adulate the intelligence of anyone who rapes poetry to satisfy his lust for art. (Tweaking B's poetic aspirations.)

34. A: Write easy; you'll get read easily.

35. C: Write hard; you'll get read easily.

36. B: If you write hard, you'll get ulcers.

37. A: If you get ulcers, you'll become an artist. (Seeing how one of them spoke affably to another for the first time, they all chortled at this point; they laughed together.)

38. B: Get old quick.

39. C: Yes, get old as fast as you can. How else will you be able to write a good autumnal piece?

40. A: The three big themes are, of course, death, love, and music.

41. C: But you've got to decide on the subject of love: what it is.

42. B: Search for love.

(I might remind my readers that long silences, stillnesses, and sulks intervene.)

43. C: Conceal love; you are, after all, a writer!

44. B: Love is a quest.

45. C: Conceal yourself, so that they assume you have something to hide.

46. A: Make them guess you have a secret, and the women will love you.

47. C: Every woman is a mirror. (Here, breaking out another bottle, they offered me some *rakı*, too.)

48. B: Remember us well. (Of course, I will, sir! I said and I have, as my more attentive readers will attest, written many of my pieces minding them and their stories.)

49. A: Get out on the street, study faces; there's a topic for you.

50. C: Let them imagine you know an historical enigma; too bad, though, you can't write in that vein. (Here, C told another story, the story where the lover says "I am Thou" to his beloved—which I will transpose into another piece at a later date—and I felt the presence of the mystery that brought to the same table three writers who'd insulted each other for half a century.)

51. A: And don't you ever forget that the whole world hates Turks.

52. B: As a nation we love our generals, our childhood, and our mothers; do likewise.

53. A: Do not use epigraphs; they will only kill the mystery in the piece!

54. B: If it's to die, then go ahead, kill the mystery; kill the false prophet too who pushes mystery!

55. C: If you must use epigraphs, don't extract any out of books that come from the West where neither the writers nor the heroes resemble us, and definitely not any out of books you haven't read; after all, that's the very eschatology of the Dadjdjal.

56. A: Remember, you are both Satan and the Angel, both the Dadjdjal

and Him too—readers have a way of growing weary of someone who's all good or all bad.

57. B: But should the reader figure out that he's been had, that he's been fooled by the Dadjdjal in His guise, that what ostensibly seemed to be his savior was the Dadjdjal all along, he just might strike you dead in a dark alley, take my word for it!

58. A: That's right, that's why you must keep the mystery concealed. Don't you ever sell out the secrets of the trade!

59. C: The mystery is love, and don't you forget it. The key word is love.

60. B: No, no, the key word is written on our faces. Look and listen.

61. A: It's love, it's love, it's love, love!

62. B: Don't be fainthearted about plagiarism either; the secret of our two-bit efforts in reading and writing is, after all, hidden in the mirror of mysticism, as are the rest of our secrets. Do you know Rumi's story, "The Contest of the Two Painters"? He too lifted the story from somewhere else, but he himself . . . (I know the story, sir, I said.)

63. C: When you too grow old and ask the question whether a man can be himself, you'll also be asking yourself if you comprehend the mystery at all, and don't you forget it! (I haven't forgotten.)

64. B: And don't forget worn-out buses, books written in haste, those who endure, and those who don't comprehend as well as those who do!

A song was being played somewhere in the station, perhaps in that very restaurant, the lyrics descanting on love, pain, and the emptiness of life; that's when they became oblivious of me; remembering that they were all elderly Scheherazades sporting mustachios, they began telling each other stories in friendship, in brotherhood, and sorrow. Here are some of them:

The tragicomic story about the unfortunate columnist whose lifelong passion had been expounding on Muhammad's journey into the Seven Heavens, who went into a depression upon finding out that Dante had taken the same trip; the story about a crazy and perverted sultan and his sister who behaved like vegetable-garden scarecrows in their childhood; the story about the writer whose dream life dried up when his wife ran off; the story about the reader who began imagining that he was both Proust and Albertine; the story about the columnist who disguised himself as Sultan Mehmet the Conqueror; et cetera, et cetera, et cetera.

Chapter Nine

SOMEBODY'S FOLLOWING ME

At *times snow fell, and at times, darkness.* —ŞEYH GALIP

Galip was to recall all day, as if it were the sole detail left over from a vile nightmare, the gutted armchair he saw as he descended the step-down side-walks along the ancient streets in Cihangir on his way down to Karaköy after he left his archivist friend Saim's house in the morning. The armchair had been abandoned in front of the closed shutters of one of those shops for wallpaper, or vinyl upholstery, or carpentry, or plaster-of-Paris ceilings, back behind the steep streets in Tophane where Jelal once stalked the trail of busy opium traffickers. The varnish had completely flaked off the arms and the legs, the seatcover had been gashed like wounded skin, and, underneath, the rusty springs had spilled out hopelessly like the greenish intestines of a cavalry horse whose belly had been slashed.

The square in Karaköy was forsaken although it was past eight o'clock. Galip was beginning to associate the deserted street where he saw the armchair and now this forsaken square with a cataclysm for which everybody else had already read the signs. It was as if some impending disaster was the reason why ships scheduled to sail had been roped to one another, why people had made themselves scarce at the docks, and why the street peddlers, the instant photographers, and the beggars with disfigured faces who worked the Galata Bridge had all decided to take a vacation on the last day of their lives. Leaning over the railing, Galip contemplated the murky water and remembered it was on this end of the bridge that swarms of children would once dive for the coins Christian tourists tossed into the Golden Horn, then wondered why, when Jelal had imagined the day the Bosphorus dries up, he had made no mention of these thick coins which, years later, would end up signifying things other than themselves.

Once in his office upstairs in the building, he settled down to read Jelal's column for the day. He noticed it wasn't a new piece but one that had already been printed some time back. This could be taken as a sign that Jelal hadn't offered any new columns to his editors in quite a while, as well as the hidden signal for something totally different. The central question in the piece, "Do you have difficulty being yourself," and Jelal's barber protagonist who posed it, did not perhaps refer to the surface meanings in what Jelal had written but pointed to other meanings in the world outside it.

Galip remembered Jelal lecturing him on this subject some time ago: "Most people," Jelal had said, "don't perceive the essential characteristics of a substance, given that these characteristics are right under their noses, but they recognize and acknowledge the secondary qualities which attract attention by virtue of being on the surface. That's why I don't openly reveal what I intend to expose, but I drop it in as if it were merely an aside. Naturally, the spot where I stash the meaning is not too obscure a corner—my gambit is a hide-and-seek that's no more than child's play—but they will believe it right off the bat, like children, if they find it there themselves: that's how come I do it. Besides, what's worse, the newspaper gets tossed aside before the intended meaning and its contingent allusions, which require a little patience and intelligence to discover, can be perceived in the main body of the piece."

Heeding an inner urge, Galip tossed the newspaper aside and took off for the *Milliyet* offices to see Jelal. He knew that Jelal was more likely to make it down to the paper on the weekend when the place was less crowded, so he figured he'd find Jelal alone in his room. He walked up the steep hill, planning to tell Jelal that Rüya was slightly under the weather. Then he'd tell him the story of a client who'd been left helpless because his wife left him. How would Jelal respond to such a story? A well-loved wife, going against all that is best in our traditions and culture, suddenly abandons a fine fellow who's upstanding, industrious, well-balanced, well-tempered, and well off. What did such a thing imply? The indication of what secret and hidden significance? The mark of what apocalypse? Jelal would listen carefully to the particulars Galip narrated and then he'd put it together; the more Jelal explained, the more the world would make sense, transforming the "hidden" realities right under our noses into the rich fare of an astonishing story that we already knew but didn't know that we knew, thereby making life more bearable. Galip noticed the glistening branches of the wet trees in the Iranian Consulate garden, and he thought that, rather than live in his own world, he'd prefer living in a world described lovingly by Jelal.

He didn't find Jelal in his room. His desk was neat, the ashtray empty, and there was no teacup. Galip sat in the purple chair he always sat in and began to wait. He was convinced that he'd soon hear Jelal laugh in one of the other rooms.

By the time he lost the conviction, he'd managed to remember a lot: his first visit to the newspaper, unbeknownst to the family, under the pretext of getting an invitation to a radio quiz show, when he'd brought along a classmate who'd later fall in love with Rüya ("He would've taken us on a tour of the printing press too," Galip had said with embarrassment on the way back, "but he didn't have the time." "Did you take a look at the photos of all those women on his desk?" said his schoolmate), and the first time he and Rüya had come up and Jelal had taken them through the printing rooms ("Do you want to grow up to be a journalist too, little lady?" the old printer had asked Rüya and, on the way back, Rüya had put the same question to Galip), and how he used to think this was a room out of the *Thousand and One Nights*, full of marvelous stories, lives, and dreams constructed on paper that he couldn't imagine himself.

He began going through Jelal's desk in a hurry to find new papers and new stories, and perchance to forget, to forget; he came across unopened reader mail, half-bitten pencils, newspaper clippings in various sizes (a story about the murder committed by a jealous husband marked in green ballpoint pen), mug shots cut out of foreign publications, portraits, Jelal's handwritten notes on scraps of paper (Do not forget: the story of the crown prince), empty ink bottles, matches, a repulsive necktie, crude popular books on shamanism, Hurufism, and improving your memory, a bottle of sleeping pills, vasodilating medications, buttons, a watch that had stopped, scissors, photos that had come in reader mail that had been opened (one showed Jelal with a bald army officer and in another, a couple of oil wrestlers and a pleasant Kangal sheep dog looked good-naturedly into the camera at some country café), colored pencils, combs, cigarette holders, and ballpoints in many colors . . .

He found two folders tucked in the blotter on the desk, one marked "In Print" and the other "Backlog." The folder for the columns "In Print" contained the typescripts of the pieces printed over the last six days as well as the Sunday column which was yet to be published. The Sunday piece, which had to be in the paper tomorrow morning, must have already been set, illustrated, and put back into the folder.

He found only three pieces in the folder marked "Backlog." All three had already been published many years ago. A fourth piece to be published on Monday may be somewhere downstairs on a typesetter's table, so the spares would suffice only for three or four more days after Sunday. Could this mean that Jelal had gone on a trip or taken a vacation without informing anyone? But Jelal never stirred outside of Istanbul.

Galip entered the large editorial room and his feet took him to a table where two elderly persons were confabulating. One, known by his pen name of Neşati, was an angry old-timer who'd embarked years ago on an intense war of words with Jelal. Nowadays the paper gave him a less prominent column than Jelal's, one read by fewer people, where he wrote memoirs driven by a furious sense of righteousness.

"Jelal hasn't been around these last few days," he said, frowning with the bulldog face that appeared in the photo above his column. "What relation are you to him anyway?"

When the second journalist inquired why he was looking for Jelal, Galip was about to track down the fellow's identity in the messy files of his memory bank. This guy, who always wore dark glasses and didn't take any wooden nickels, was the Sherlock Holmes of the magazine section. He knew in just which posh madam's house which elegant movie star—they all put on the airs of aristocratic Ottoman ladies—had once turned tricks at what date on what backstreet in Beyoğlu. He knew, for example, that the prodigious singer brought to Istanbul under the guise of an Argentine countess who had been discovered rope dancing in a French provincial town was, in reality, a poor Moslem woman from Algiers.

"So, you're a relative," said the magazine writer; "I'd understood that Jelal had nobody close to him other than his dear departed mom."

"Phooey!" said the old polemicist. "If it hadn't been for those relatives of his, would Jelal be where he is today? He had a brother-in-law, for example, who gave him a leg up. The same fellow who taught him to write, a sincerely religious man whom Jelal eventually betrayed. The brother-in-law belonged to a Nakşi sect that carried on their secret rites in an abandoned soap factory in Kumkapı. He'd partake in the rites, during which a slew of chains, olive presses, candles, and soap molds were also used, then he'd sit down by the

week and report to the National Bureau of Investigation inside information
on the activities of the sect. The fellow kept trying to prove that the disciples
of the religious order he snitched on for the military were not, in reality,
engaged in anything harmful to the government. He'd share his intelligence
reports with Jelal, hoping the literature buff might read and learn, get a taste
for good prose. In those years when Jelal bent his views according to a wind
that blew from the left, he availed himself pitilessly of the style of those
reports, which was woven with similes and metaphors lifted straight from
Attar, Abu Khorosani, Ibn Arabi, and the translations of Bottfolio. Sure,
some people see in his similes new bridges that span to our past culture—
although they all hinge on the same stereotyped origin; they cannot know
that the inventor of these pastiches is someone else entirely. The ingenious
brother-in-law with many talents whose existence Jelal would rather forget
was also a true jack-of-all-trades: he manufactured mirrored scissors which
made barbers' lives easier, developed a circumcision device that does away
with the grave mistakes that ruin the future of many a boy, and invented
gallows which were painless on account of being fitted with a chain instead
of a greased noose and the sliding platform instead of a chair. In the years
when Jelal felt he needed the affection of his dear older sister and the brother-
in-law, he used to introduce the inventions exuberantly in his so-called
'Believe It or Not' column."

"Pardon me, but you've got it all wrong," countered the magazine writer.
"During the years he ran the 'Believe It or Not' column, Jelal was completely
on his own. Let me put to you a scene I didn't get secondhand but saw with
my own two eyes."

It was a scene right out of a schlock Yeşilçam movie depicting the poor
and lonesome years of a deserving kid who'll eventually make good. On a
New Year's Eve, in their shabby house in the poor district, the cub reporter
Jelal tells his mother that the well-off branch of the family has invited him
to a New Year's Eve entertainment at their place in Nişantaşı. There he'll
spend a noisy and fun evening with his uncles' and aunts' cheerful daughters
and boisterous sons and end up at goodness knows which hot spot around
town. The mother, who happens to be a seamstress, relishes imagining her
son's pleasure and has a surprise in store for him: just for tonight, she has
quietly fixed his father's old jacket to fit him. Jelal puts on the jacket, which
fits him perfectly (the scene jerks the tears right out of the mother's eyes:
"You look exactly like your dad"), and the happy mother is relieved to hear
that a fellow journalist has also been invited to the entertainment. When
the journalist, who's the witness of our story, and Jelal go down the cold

and dark stairs of the wooden house and out into the muddy street, he learns that neither Jelal's relations nor anybody else has invited poor Jelal to any New Year's Eve entertainment. What's more, Jelal is on duty at the newspaper so that he might earn the money to pay for the surgery his mother needs because she's going blind from sewing in candlelight.

Following the silence after the story was over, Galip pointed out that some of the details didn't jibe with Jelal's life, but they didn't much pay attention to his explanations. Sure, they could be mistaken as to the degree of the relationships and how far back the dates went; if Jelal's father was still alive (Are you absolutely sure of that, sir?), they might have substituted the father for the grandfather, or the older sister for the aunt, but they were not about to make too big a deal of their inaccuracies. They had Galip sit down at the table, offered him a cigarette, asked him a question but didn't listen to his reply (How did you say you're related to him again?), then they started pulling reminiscences out of the bag like pieces they'd placed on an imaginary chessboard.

Jelal was so inundated with familial affection that even in those hopeless days when all subjects aside from the municipal problems had been prohibited, he could knock off a piece neither his readers nor the censors could make out, relating to his childhood memories of a great mansion where a different linden tree could be seen out of each window.

No, no, Jelal's interpersonal skills outside of journalism were so limited that whenever he had to attend a big affair, he made sure he took along a friend whose every gesture and word, whose clothes and table manners he could safely imitate.

Not so at all! An aspiring young journalist, whose beat is the crossword puzzles and advice in the women's section, who within three years lands the best-read column not only in his own country but also in the entire Balkans and the Middle East, and commences to slander folks left and right without any compunction. How else could the scenario be explained besides the tender love and care, albeit undeserved, of powerful friends and relations who pulled strings for him?

Take the "birthday party," one of the cornerstones of the Western civilization, a human custom one of our forward-looking statesmen hoped to establish within our culture as well. So he invited journalists, along with a Levantine biddy who tinkled the piano, to a well-meaning "birthday party" he organized for his eight-year-old son, replete with eight lit candles on a butter-cream strawberry cake. Jelal lampooned the party in his column, running it into the ground mercilessly and pigheadedly, not for ideological, political, or even aesthetic reasons as it was surmised, but because he was stricken by the apprehension that in all his life he had never received any fatherly love, or any other kind of love, at all.

The fact that he couldn't be located anywhere now, the revelation that he'd given out wrong or false telephone numbers and addresses, stemmed from the odd and unfathomable hatred he felt for these near relations, whose love he was unable to reciprocate, and for these distant relatives—nay, even for all mankind. (All Galip had done was to ask where he could find Jelal.)

Oh, well, the reason why he was hiding out in a remote corner of the city, having exiled himself from all humankind, had to depend on something else, naturally: he'd understood at last that he'd never recover from the disease of being a loner, that incurable feeling of loneliness that surrounded him like an unlucky halo since the day he was born. Like an invalid who'd surrendered to his disease, he'd finally let go, resigning himself in a room somewhere out of the way into the arms of an abject loneliness he couldn't escape.

Galip brought up the fact that a TV crew "from Europe" was looking for Jelal, who was holed up somewhere in this out-of-the-way room.

"In any case," interrupted the polemicist writer Neşati, "Jelal is about to get the boot. He hasn't sent in anything new for ten days now. Everybody's all too aware that the stuff he's trying to palm off as backlog is nothing but twenty-year-old pieces retyped to make them look like new copy."

The magazine writer disagreed, as Galip had hoped and expected he might: the columns were being read with even greater interest, the phones were ringing off the hook, and Jelal's share of mail was no less than twenty letters a day.

"Yes!" said the polemicist. "The letters he gets are nothing but propositions from whores, pimps, terrorists, hedonists, dope dealers, and veteran gangsters whom he glorified."

"You read his mail on the sly then?" the magazine writer said.

"So do you!" said the polemicist.

Both sat up in their chairs like a pair of chess players, pleased with their opening moves. The polemicist brought a small box out of the deep pocket of his coat. He displayed the box to Galip with the fastidiousness of a magician about to make an object disappear. "The only thing I now have in common with the man you call your relative is this stomach medicine. It blocks stomach acid instantly. Care to have one?"

Galip couldn't figure out where this game started and where it ended, but he wanted in; so he took one of the white pills and swallowed it.

"How do you like our game so far?" said the old columnist, smiling.

"I'm still trying to figure out the rules," Galip said mistrustfully.

"Do you read my column?"

"I do."

"When you pick up the paper, do you read mine first, or Jelal's?"

"Jelal happens to be my cousin."

"Is that the only reason you read him first?" said the old writer. "Do family ties constitute a stronger bond than good writing?"

"Jelal writes well too!" Galip said.

"Anybody can do what he does, don't you get it?" said the old columnist. "What's more, most are too long to be proper columns. Fake stories. Artsy embellishment. Frivolous bunk. He has a couple of tricks that are his stock-in-trade, that's all. Reminiscences and descants sweeter than honey are the order of the day. Every now and then, a paradox must be seized. Games of irony the courtly poets called 'erudite ignorance' must be resorted to. What isn't likely must be told as if it is, and what's gone down as if it has not. And if all this doesn't work out, then the vacuousness of the piece must be hidden under highfalutin sentences that his fans take for good writing. Everybody has a life, memories, and a past which are no less than his. Anybody can play his game. Even you. Tell me a story!"

"What kind of a story?"

"Whatever comes to you: a story."

"A man's beautiful wife, whom he loves very much," said Galip, "deserts him. So he sets out to look for her. He comes across her tracks everywhere in the city but not her . . ."

"Go on."

"That's all."

"No, no! There has to be more to it!" said the old columnist. "What does he read into his wife's traces in the city, this man? Is the wife a real beauty? Who did she leave him for?"

"This man reads his own past in the traces he finds all over the city. His own tracks together with his beautiful wife's. He doesn't know, nor does he want to know, for whom she's given him the slip. He tends to think that the man, or the place, his wife made tracks for must exist somewhere in his own past."

"Good subject," said the old columnist. "Like Poe said: a beautiful woman who dies or is lost! But the storyteller has to be more decisive. The reader doesn't trust a writer who cannot make up his mind. Let's see, we might finish the story using one of Jelal's tricks. Reminiscences: the city swarms with the man's happier memories. Style: the clues in the reminiscences are buried in a highfalutin language that points to a void. Erudite Ignorance:

the man pretends he can't figure out the identity of the other man. The Paradox: therefore, the man the wife ran off with is the man himself. How's that? See, you can do it. Anybody can."

"But Jelal's the one who does it."

"That's right! But from now on, you can do it too!" said the old writer, signaling that the subject was closed.

"If you want to track him down, study his columns," said the magazine writer. "He's got to be in there somewhere. His columns are full of messages sent hither and yon, small private messages. Do you get my meaning?"

By way of an answer, Galip said that when he was a child Jelal had shown him how to make sentences using the first and last words in his paragraphs. He had revealed the logogriphs he constructed to get around the censor and the press prosecutor, word chains he formed on the first and last syllables of sentences, the sentences based on all the capital letters, and the word games that made "our aunt" angry.

The magazine writer asked: "Was your aunt an old maid?"

"She never married," Galip said.

Did Jelal and his father have a falling out over a flat?

Galip said it was "a very old" altercation.

Was it true that there was a lawyer uncle who confused his court records, writs, and bylaws with restaurant menus and ferryboat schedules?

Galip said he imagined this too was a story like all the others.

"Get a clue, young man!" the old writer said unpleasantly. "Jelal didn't let him in on all that stuff! I bet our friend here, who's keen on detective work and Hurufism, unearthed the meanings himself out of the letters Jelal concealed in his columns, excavating bit by bit, as if digging out a well with a sewing needle."

The magazine writer said it was possible that the word games had a meaning, that perhaps they signaled messages from the unknown, and that perhaps it was his deep association with the unknowable that elevated Jelal above other writers who shall go nameless. Besides, he wanted to remind him that there was truth in the saying that "journalists who get too big for their breeches get buried either by donation or by the city."

"Maybe, God forbid, he's even dead!" said the old journalist. "How do you like our game?"

"And the matter of him losing his memory," said the magazine writer, "is it true, or fiction?"

"Both," Galip said. "Fact and fiction."

"And his hideouts all over the city?"

"They too."

"Perhaps he's breathing his last in one of his hideouts all alone," said the columnist. "You know, he loves this kind of conjecture game himself."

"If he were dying, he'd have summoned someone he feels close to," the magazine writer said.

"There is no such person," said the old columnist. "He feels close to no one."

"I bet this young man doesn't see it that way," the magazine writer said. "You haven't even told us your name."

Galip told them.

"In that case, tell me, Galip," said the magazine writer. "In this place he's holed up—who knows under what compulsion—there must be somebody to whom Jelal feels close enough to pass on, at least, his literary secrets and his last testament, mustn't there? He isn't that much of a loner, after all."

Galip thought it over. "He isn't that much of a loner," he said apprehensively.

"Who would he summon then?" said the magazine writer. "You?"

"His sister," Galip blurted out. "He has a half-sister who's twenty years younger than him, that's who he would have called." Then he fell into thought. He recalled the armchair with the rusty springs poking out of its belly. He went on thinking.

"Perhaps you've begun to catch on to the logic of our game," the old columnist said. "You're perhaps beginning to relish arriving at logical conclusions. That's why I have to tell you this without any reservation: All Hurufis invariably come to a bad end. Fazlallah of Astarabad, who's the founder of Hurufism, was put to death like a dog, and his corpse was dragged through markets and streets by a rope tied to his feet. Did you know that six hundred years ago, he too broke into his trade by interpreting dreams—just like Jelal? He didn't ply his trade at some newspaper though, but in a cave just outside of town . . ."

"What can we know about a person," the magazine writer said, "through this kind of comparison? How far can one penetrate into the secrets of someone's life? It's been more than thirty years that I've been trying to penetrate the secrets of the pitiful film artists we call 'stars' in imitation of the Americans. And this is what I've found out: Those who say that each human being has a double are wrong. Nobody is like anybody else. Every poor girl is poor in her own way. Each one of our stars is singular like the ones in the sky, all alone, a pitiful starlet that has no look-alike."

"Aside from the original model in Hollywood," said the old columnist. "Did I ever mention to you the list of originals that Jelal emulates? Aside

from Dante, Dostoevsky, and Rumi, he's cribbed liberally from our great
divan poet Şeyh Galip's *Beauty and Love*.

"Each life is unique!" the magazine writer said. "Each story is a story
because it has no double. Every writer is singularly himself, a two-bit writer
in his own way."

"Phooey!" said the old writer. "Let's take the bit he presumably likes so
well, the one called 'The Day the Bosphorus Dries Up.' Aren't all the signs
of the apocalypse lifted straight out of books that are thousands of years old
describing the days of destruction before the arrival of the Messiah? Out of
the Koran, the suras on the Day of Judgment? And out of Ibn Khaldun and
Abu Khorosani? He then tacks on a vulgar story about some hoodlum. It
has no artistic merit. Of course, all that hokum in the piece is not what
heats up the excited reception a certain narrow spectrum accords it, or the
hundreds of phone calls that hysterical women make on that day. There
happen to be secret messages in the letters that are deciphered, not by you
and me, but only by disciples who have the codebook in their possession.
Scattered all over the country, these disciples, half of whom are prostitutes
and the other half pederasts, who consider these messages sacred orders, call
the paper day and night so that we don't kick their sheikh Jelal Bey right out
of the door for writing a bunch of nonsense. Besides, there are always one
or two persons waiting for him in front of the door. How do we know, Mr.
Galip, that you aren't one of them?"

"But it turns out we like Galip," the magazine writer said. "We detected
something of our own youth in him. We took him to our hearts enough to
give away all these confidences. That's how we know what's what. Her
ladyship Samiye Samim, a brilliant star a while back, once told me during
her last days at a nursing home: 'The disease called jealousy . . .' What?
Are you leaving, young man?"

"Galip, my son, now that you're leaving, answer me this one question,"
the old columnist said. "Why in hell does British TV want to interview Jelal
and not me?"

"Because he's the better writer," Galip said. He'd risen from the table and
was about to step into the silent corridor that led to the stairs. He heard the
old writer shout after him with a powerful voice that had lost nothing of its
gusto.

"Did you really think what you swallowed was a stomach pill?"

Galip looked around him carefully when he got out on the street. On the
opposite sidewalk, on the corner where the seminary school students had
once burned the paper that contained the column of Jelal's they considered
blasphemous, an orange vendor and a bald-headed man stood around aim-

lessly. There didn't seem to be anyone waiting around for Jelal. He went across and bought an orange. Peeling the orange and eating it, he was gripped by a feeling that somebody was following him. At Cağaloğlu Square he turned to go to his office, still not having figured out why he was spooked at that very moment. He walked down the street slowly, looking into bookstore windows, but he didn't get anywhere analyzing why the feeling seemed so real. It felt as if there was the vague presence of an "eye" just behind his neck, that's all.

Slowing down as he passed by one of the bookstores, his eyes met another pair of eyes in the window which, the moment they met, excited him as if he'd realized how fond he'd been of an intimate all along. This was the window of the publishing house that printed most of the detective novels that Rüya read as if she were gulping them down. The treacherous little owl he often noticed on the novels now patiently watched Galip and the Saturday crowds that went by the store window. Galip went in the store and had them wrap up three old volumes he didn't think Rüya had read and another one called *Women, Love, and Whiskey* which was being advertised as the publication of the week. A largish poster tacked on one of the upper shelves said: "No other series in Turkey has ever reached Number 126: Our Number is the guarantee of the quality of our Detective Novels." The store sold other books besides the "Literary Romances" and the "Owl Series of Humorous Novels" also published by the same house, so he inquired if they had a book on Hurufism. A stocky old man, who sat in the chair he'd placed in the doorway from where he managed to watch simultaneously the pale young man at the register and the crowd that went by on the muddy sidewalk, gave him the answer he expected.

"We don't carry it. Ask for it at Stingy Ismail's store." Then he added: "Some time ago I got hold of the rough drafts of detective novels translated from the French by the Crown Prince the Honorable Osman Jelalettin who happened to be a Hurufi himself. Do you know how he got killed?"

Outside the store, Galip looked up and down both sidewalks but didn't see anything that might attract his attention: a woman and her kid whose coat was too big studying the window of the sandwich shop, two schoolgirls who wore identical green socks, and an old man in a brown coat waiting to cross the street. But as soon as he began walking toward his office, he felt the same watchful "eye" on his neck.

Galip, who'd never been followed nor been gripped by a feeling of being followed, was limited to the films he'd seen, or scenes in Rüya's detective novels, for his expertise on the subject. Although he'd read only a few detective novels, he often ranted and raved about the genre: it should be possible to construct a novel in which the first and last chapters were identical; somebody should write a story that had no "ending" because the real ending had been concealed somewhere in the text; there ought to be a novel imagined where all the characters were blind, etc., etc. Constructing these premises Rüya turned up her nose at, Galip dreamed that perhaps someday he could become some other person.

He imagined that the legless beggar ensconced in the alcove next to the entrance to the office building was blind in both eyes; that's when he decided that the nightmare he was becoming increasingly involved in must be due to a lack of sleep as much as Rüya's absence. Upon entering his office, instead of sitting at his desk, he opened the window and looked down. He watched all movement on the sidewalk for a short period. When he sat at his desk, his hand went, seemingly on its own, not to the telephone but to a folder that contained paper. He took out a fresh sheet. He began to write without doing too much thinking.

"Places where Rüya might be: Her ex-husband's house. My uncle's house. Banu's house. A 'safe' house. A semi-safe house. A house where poetry is discussed. A house where anything is discussed. Some other house in Nişantaşı. Any old house. A house." Realizing he wasn't thinking well while he wrote, he put the pencil down. Then he picked up the pencil again and struck out all the possibilities aside from "Her ex-husband's house," and he wrote this: "Places where Rüya and Jelal might be: One of Jelal's hideouts. Rüya and Jelal in a hotel room. Rüya and Jelal going to a movie theater. Rüya and Jelal? Rüya and Jelal?"

Writing on paper gave him an impression that he resembled the heroes of all those detective novels he'd projected; consequently, he felt as if he was approaching the entrance of a door that was suggestive of Rüya, a new world, and the new person he wanted to become. The world glimpsed through the door was a world where the sensation of being followed was serenely accepted. If a person believed that he was being followed, then he must at least believe he was someone capable of sitting down at his desk and making a list of all the clues necessary to find another person who had vanished. Galip knew he was nothing like a hero in a detective novel, but presuming that he resembled that person, or being "like him," somewhat lightened the oppression of the objects and the stories that beset him. Some time later when the young waiter, whose hair was parted in the middle with an astonishing symmetry, served the meal he'd ordered brought in from the restaurant, Galip's world so closely approximated the world of the detective novels that, now that he had filled sheets of paper with clues, the dish of pilav topped with gyros and the carrot salad which sat on the dirty tray no longer seemed the same old stuff he always ate but had become unusual fare that he was seeing for the first time.

The phone rang in the middle of his meal. He picked it up like someone who was expecting the call: wrong number. After he finished eating and got rid of the tray, he called his own apartment in Nişantaşı. He let the phone ring a long time, imagining Rüya, who'd returned home tired, getting out of bed, but he wasn't surprised when no one answered, either. He dialed Aunt Halé's number.

Hoping to forestall new questions from his aunt, Galip ran through explanations in one breath: Their phone was out of order and that's why they couldn't get in touch; Rüya had recovered that same night, she was right as rain, nothing the matter with her at all, there she was in her purple coat, pleased with herself, sitting in the '56 Chevvy taxicab, waiting for Galip; they were about to take off on a trip to Izmir, to see an old friend who was seriously ill; the boat would sail shortly, Galip was calling from a grocery store on the way; he thanked the grocer who let him use the phone when the store was really jumping; goodbye, Aunt, goodbye! But Aunt Halé still managed to ask: Did they make sure the door was locked, had Rüya taken along her green sweater?

When Saim called, Galip had been wondering if a person could change significantly by staring at the map of a city where he'd never set foot. Saim said he had continued researching in his archives after Galip left in the morning and had come across some clues that might be useful: this Mehmet Yılmaz who was responsible for the old lady's death, yes, he was possibly still alive, didn't go under the names of either Ahmet Kaçar or Haldun Kara as they had previously supposed, but went around town like a ghost calling himself Muammer Ergener which didn't smack of a pseudonym at all. When he came across this name in a publication that espoused totally "opposing views," Saim was not surprised; what surprised him was that another person, who went under the name of Salih Gölbaşı, had used the same prose style and made the same spelling errors in two pieces sharply criticizing a couple of Jelal's columns. After reasoning through that the first and the last name both rhymed with Rüya's ex-husband's first and last names, besides being made up of the same consonants, he saw the person's name now listed in a small educational publication called *The Hour of Labor* as the editor-in-chief; so Saim had secured for Galip the address of the editorial offices, which were on the western outskirts of the city: Refet Bey Street, No. 13, Sunny Heights, Sinan Paşa, Bakırköy.

Following the phone conversation, Galip located the map of the Sinan Paşa District in the City Directory. He was amazed: the Sunny Heights development covered the whole area of the barren hill where Rüya had moved into a squatter's shack with her ex-husband, twelve years ago when they were first married, so that the husband could conduct his "studies" on laborers. Galip examined the map and figured out that the hill that he had once visited had been subdivided into streets each named after a hero of the War of Independence. In one corner, there was a square indicated by the green of a small park, the minaret of a mosque, and the tiny oblong of a statue of Atatürk. This was a realm that Galip wouldn't have dreamed of in a thousand years.

He called up the paper and was informed that Jelal hadn't arrived yet, then he phoned İskender. He told İskender that he'd located Jelal, that he'd told him British TV wanted to interview him, that Jelal didn't seem opposed to the idea, but that he was too busy at this particular time. And while he ran through his story, he could hear a little girl crying on the other end, not too far away from the telephone. İskender told him that the British would be in Istanbul for six more days at least. They'd been hearing good things about Jelal, so he was sure they'd wait; if Galip wished, he could look them up at the Pera Palas Hotel himself.

He put the lunch tray in front of the door and left the building; as he walked down the hill toward the sea, he noticed that the sky was a paler color than he'd ever seen it before. It seemed about to snow down ashes, and yet the Saturday crowd would probably act as if that were par for the course. Perhaps that was why people walked along the muddy streets looking at their feet; they were hoping to get used to the idea. He sensed that the detective novels under his arm calmed him down. Perhaps it was thanks to their having been written in distant, magical countries and translated into "our tongue" by unhappy housewives who regretted not continuing the training they began in one of the foreign-language high schools that now everybody could go about his business as usual, so that the peddlers in faded suits who refill lighters at the entrances to business buildings, the hunchbacked men who look like old colorless rags, and the silent passengers at the *dolmuş* stops could all keep on breathing their usual breaths.

He got on the bus in Eminönü and off at Harbiye, not far from the apartment, where he saw the crowd in front of the Palace Theater. The crowd was waiting for the 2:45 Saturday afternoon movie. Twenty years ago, amidst an identical trenchcoated and pimpled crowd of students, Galip too would come to this matinee with Rüya and her other schoolmates; he'd descend the stairs, which were covered with sawdust then as they were now, examine the tinted stills of the coming attractions lit by tiny bulbs, and, quietly patient, he'd watch to see just who Rüya was talking to. The previous showing seemed never to end, the doors never to open, and the moment he and Rüya would sit side-by-side when the lights went out never seemed to come. Today, when he found there were still tickets available for the 2:45 show, Galip was gripped by a sense of freedom. Inside the theater, the air left over from the previous audience was hot and close. Galip knew he'd fall asleep as soon as the lights went off and the ads came on.

The moment he awoke, he sat up in his seat. On the screen was a beautiful woman, a real beauty, who was as troubled as she was beautiful. Then came a scene of a wide and tranquil river, a farmhouse, an American farm set in dense greenery. Then, the troubled beautiful girl began talking to a middle-aged man Galip had never seen before in any movie. He could see the deep trouble that beset their lives in their faces and in their gestures, which were as slow and placid as their speech. It was beyond mere understanding: he *knew*. Life was full of trouble, pain, deep misery which made our faces alike, pain that just as we got used to it surpassed itself with new pain that was much worse. Even when miseries arrived suddenly, we knew that they had always been on the way; we'd readied ourselves, but still, when trouble beset us like a nightmare, we found ourselves seized by a kind of loneliness, a hopeless and addictive loneliness, and imagined that sharing it with others would make us happy. For a moment Galip felt that his trouble and the trouble of the woman on the screen were the same—maybe it wasn't trouble they had in common but a world, an orderly world where you never expected too much, which never turned away from you, which summoned you to be humble. Galip felt so close to the woman that it was as if he were watching himself as he watched her fetch water out of a well, take a trip in an old Ford pickup, talk to the child in her lap as she was getting him ready for bed. What made him want to embrace her was not the woman's beauty, her artlessness, or her forthright attitude, it was the belief that he lived in her world: were he able to embrace her, the slender woman with light brown hair could have shared his belief. Galip felt as if he were watching the movie all by himself, as if what he saw could be seen by no one else. Soon, though, when a fight broke out in the sultry town divided by a wide asphalt road, and a male who was the "strong and dominant type" took matters in hand, Galip knew that he was about to lose the partnership he shared with the woman. He read the subtitles word by word; he could feel the fidgeting humanity in the theater. He rose and walked home under the snow that fell slowly from a sky that was nearly dark.

Much later, as he napped under the blue-checkered quilt somewhere between sleep and wakefulness, he realized he'd left behind at the movie theater the detective novels which he'd bought for Rüya.

Chapter Ten

THE EYE

During that cycle of productivity in his life, his daily literary yield never numbered less than five pages. —ABDURRAHMAN ŞEREF

The incident I'm about to relate happened to me on a winter's night. I was going through a melancholic period of my life: I'd already survived the first years as a journalist, which are the most difficult, but the things I had to endure in order to establish myself a little had already burned out my initial enthusiasm for the profession. On cold winter nights when I told myself "I made it after all!" I also knew that I'd been emptied out inside. That winter, I'd been stricken with the insomnia which was to follow me around the rest of my life; so some nights during the work week the night clerk and I would keep late hours at the paper, and I'd finish some articles which I couldn't write during the workday hustle and bustle. The "Believe It or Not" column, a fad European newspapers and magazines had also entertained at that time, was made to order for my nocturnal labors. I'd turn the pages of one of those European papers that had already been clipped into bits and pieces, examine the pictures in the "Believe It or Not" section, and, inspired by the picture (I've always deemed learning a foreign language not only unnecessary but downright detrimental to my imagination), I'd expatiate on my impressions with a kind of artistic fervor.

On that winter's night, having briefly glanced at the picture of a monster (one eye was above, the other below) in a French publication (an old copy of *L'Illustration*), I quickly worked up a piece on the subject of the Cyclops: having outlined the reincarnations of this doughty creature who scares young girls in the Dede Korkut legends, who is transformed into the perfidious Cyclops in Homer, who is the Dadjdjal himself in Bukhari's *History of the Prophets*, who penetrates the harems of viziers in the *Thousand and One Nights*, who puts in a brief appearance wearing purple in the *Paradiso* just before Dante finds his sweetheart Beatrice (who seems so familiar to me), who waylays caravans in Rumi, and who assumes the shape of a Negress in William Beckford's novel *Vathek*, which I really love, I speculated on what in the world that single eye like a dark well in the middle of the forehead resembled, why it startled us, why we had to fear and avoid it. And, carried away with my excitement, I added to my short "monograph" a couple of little stories that flowed out of my pen: one about the Cyclops Number One who was reputed to live in one of the slum districts around the Golden Horn and made his way goodness knows where through the muddy, oily, turbid water at night to meet up with Cyclops Number Two, either one and the same as the first, or else an aristocratic Cyclops (they called him "Lord") who, upon removing his fur headgear at midnight at some posh Pera whorehouse, knocked many a working girl unconscious with fear.

I scribbled a note for the illustrator ("No mustache, please!") who really fancied this sort of theme, and I left a little past midnight; I had no desire to go back to my cold and lonely flat, so I decided to take a walk through the streets of old Istanbul. As usual, I wasn't pleased with myself, but I was pleased with my column and stories. If I fantasized the success of my piece while taking a long walk, I thought I might perhaps postpone the sensation of grief that clung to me like an incurable disease.

I walked through the backstreets, which got increasingly narrow and darker, crisscrossing each other in haphazard diagonals. Listening to my own footsteps, I walked between the dark houses that leaned into each other, their enclosed balconies bent out of shape and their windows pitch black. I walked through those forgotten streets where even the dog packs, sleepy night watchmen, dopeheads, and ghosts didn't dare set foot.

When I was seized by a feeling that an eye was watching me from somewhere, I wasn't alarmed at first. It would be a false sensation that stemmed from the piece I'd just written, I surmised, because there was no eye watching me either from the window of the crooked enclosed balcony, where I felt it was, or out of the darkness of the vacant lot. The presence that I sensed was nothing more than a vague illusion; I didn't want to attach any importance to it. But in the stillness where nothing could be heard besides the whistles of the night watchmen and the ululations of dog packs fighting in distant quarters, the awareness that I was being watched slowly increased until it reached such an intensity that I could no longer be rid of the oppressive sensation by ignoring it.

An all-seeing, omnipresent eye now watched me without concealing itself. No, it had no relationship to the heroes of the stories I had made up that evening; unlike them, this one was not frightening, or hideous, or ridiculous, nor was it alien or inimical. It was even, yes, an acquaintance; the eye knew me and I knew it. We had known about each other for a long time, but acknowledging each other openly had required the particular sensation that had just overcome me in the middle of the night, the particular street I walked on, and the intensity of the scene in that street.

I won't mention the name of this street in the hills behind the Golden Horn since it won't mean much to readers who don't know that part of Istanbul really well. All you have to imagine is a pallid cobblestone street, characterized by dark wooden houses (most of which I see still standing thirty years after the metaphysical incident that befell me) and the shadows of enclosed balconies, where the illumination from a single lamppost is obscured by crooked branches. The sidewalks were dirty and narrow. The wall of a small mosque stretched into a seemingly endless darkness. Where the street—or the perspective—came to a dark point, this ridiculous eye (what else can I call it?) awaited me. I imagine it has already become clear: the "eye" was waiting to help me gain access to the "metaphysical experiment" (which was more like a dream, I thought later) rather than to do me harm —say, to frighten, to strangle, to knife or kill.

Not a sound. Instantly, I knew that the whole experiment was related to what journalism had taken away from me, something to do with the emptiness that I felt inside. One has the most convincing nightmares when one is really tired. But this was not a nightmare; it was a sharper, clearer—even a mathematical—sensation. "I know I'm completely empty inside." That was what I'd thought, and then, leaning up against the mosque wall: "It knows I'm completely empty inside." It knew what I was thinking, knew all that I had done so far, but even these things were not important; the "eye" signaled something else, something that was all too obvious. I had created it, and it had created me! I thought maybe this idea would just dart through my mind, like one of those stupid words that sometimes appear at the tip of your pen and vanish, but it remained there. And the idea opened the door through which, like that English girl who followed a rabbit down his hole under the hedge, I entered a new world.

In the very beginning, I was the one who created the "eye" so that, obviously, it would see me and observe me. I didn't want to be outside its gaze. I'd created myself under the gaze and the consciousness of this eye: I was pleased with its surveillance. My existence depended on my knowledge that I was being constantly observed—as if I'd cease to exist if the eye didn't see me. The obvious truth was that, having forgotten that I was the one who created it, I felt grateful to the eye that made my existence possible. I wanted to comply with its commands! Only then would I be included in a more pleasant "existence"! But it was difficult to accomplish this, although the difficulty was not painful (life was like that), it was something familiar we'd come to accept as natural. The contemplative world I fell into while leaning up against the mosque wall was not a nightmare but a kind of happiness fabricated out of reminiscences and familiar images, like the imaginary paintings "produced" by nonexistent painters I invented which I had once described in the column called "Believe It or Not."

Leaning up against the wall of the mosque and observing my own perception, I saw that I was in the center of this garden of happiness.

I knew instantly that what I saw in the center of my perception, or imagination, or illusion—whatever you want to call it—was not a being that resembled me; it was me, myself. That's how I could understand that the gaze of the "eye" that I'd sensed moments before was my own gaze. I had become that "eye" and was now observing myself. Besides not being a weird or foreign sensation, it was not at all frightening. As soon as I observed myself from outside myself, I recognized and understood that I had a long-standing habit of keeping an eye on myself. That's how I had managed to pull myself together over the years, checking myself out from the outside. "Okay, everything is in its place," I would say. Or, scanning myself, "Ugh, I don't make it today," I would say. "I don't look enough like what I want to look like." Or I said: "I look something like it, but I must try harder." And after many years, observing myself, "All right! I look like what I want to look like at last!" I could say joyfully: "Yes, I've made it, I've become *him*."

Who was this "him" anyway? First, I understood why "he," whom I wanted to be so much like, appeared to me at this point of my journey to Wonderland: because, during my long walk through the night, I hadn't been trying to imitate "him" or anybody else. Don't get me wrong. I don't believe for a moment that people can live without impersonation, without desiring to be someone else, but that night I was so tired, so empty, and the desire in me had hit such a low that *he* (who must be obeyed) and I had become "equals" at last. You can attest to our "relative" equality, seeing how I was neither afraid of him nor reluctant to get involved in the world of fantasy into which he had summoned me. I still lived under his eyes, but on that beautiful winter night I was also free. Even though it was a sensation that I'd earned through fatigue and defeat, instead of through willpower and victory, still this feeling of freedom and equality had paved the way for an informal familiarity between him and me. (This cordiality must be self-evident in my style.) For the first time in years, he divulged his secrets to me, and I understood him. Sure enough, I was talking to myself, but what is this kind of conversation but whispering like chums with a second person, or even a third person, we've buried deep inside?

My more attentive readers have long figured out the references I've used interchangeably, but let me reiterate them anyway: "He" was, of course, the "eye." The eye was the person I wanted to be. I had first created not the "eye" but "him," the person I wanted to become. And the "he" who I wanted to be had let loose that powerful, stultifying gaze on me across the distance between us. The "eye" that put limits on my freedom, the insouciant gaze that had me under total surveillance and passed judgment on me, stood hanging over my head like an accursed sun that wouldn't let me off. Don't assume that I am complaining. I was pleased with the brilliant scene that the "eye" presented to me.

Watching myself in this geometrical and fastidiously precise landscape (which was the pleasure of the thing, after all), I'd instantly perceived that I'd created "him" myself, but I had only a vague idea how I'd gone about it. There were some clues which revealed to me that I'd abstracted him out of my own life materials and experiences. He (whom I wanted to become) had been affected by the heroes of the comics I'd read in my childhood, the heavy-duty *littérateurs* whose photos I studied in foreign publications, or these posturing persons' libraries, their desks, the sanctified haunts where they cogitated their "deep and meaningful" thoughts and in front of which they posed for the photographers. Sure I'd wanted to be like them too! But how much, though? In this metaphysical geography, I came across some disheartening clues as well, vis-à-vis my having created "him" out of the details of my own past: a wealthy and industrious neighbor whose virtues my mother extolled; the shadow of a Westernized pasha who'd pledged himself to the rescue of his homeland; the image of the hero in a book which had been read five times through from beginning to end; a teacher who punished us by giving us the silent treatment; a classmate who was so classy that, besides being able to afford to put on clean socks every day, he addressed his parents in the second person plural; the intelligent, resourceful, and witty

protagonists in foreign films shown at Beyoğlu and Şehzadebaşı theaters—
the way they handle their drink glasses, the way they are so humorous, so
appropriately decisive, and so totally at ease with women, even with beautiful
ones; famous writers, philosophers, scientists, discoverers, and inventors,
whose life histories I read in the forewords to their books; a few military men;
and the insomniac hero who saves the city from a catastrophic flood . . .
All these persons put in appearances one by one, hailing me here and there
like familiar districts on the map as I stood, way past midnight, leaning up
against the wall of the mosque. Like a person who's startled upon finding
on a map the district and the street where he's lived most of his life, I felt
the same childish excitement at first. Then, I too sampled the same unsavory
aftertaste as that person who's looked at the map for the first time, who's
bound to be disappointed when he realizes that the buildings, the streets,
the parks, the houses, all the places loaded with memories the recollections
of which will haunt him for a lifetime, are shown perfunctorily on the great
big map as tiny lines and dots which, compared to other lines and signs,
look insignificant and meaningless.

I had reproduced him out of my memories and memorialized persons.
This monstrosity, which was the collage of the crowd that I recollected one
by one, existed as the soul of the "eye" that he'd turned loose on me, which
had now become my own gaze. Within it, I now apprehended myself and
my whole life. I lived my life, pleased to be under the scrutiny of this gaze,
pulling myself together under its auspices, imitating "him," trying to reach
him through impersonation, assured that someday I would actually become
him, or at least something like him. I lived not hopefully, but hoping for
the hope of becoming someone else: him. Don't let my readers assume that
this "metaphysical experiment" constitutes some sort of awakening, an exemplary tale in the genre of "opening your eyes to reality." In the Wonderland
where I found myself, leaning up against the wall of the mosque, everything
sparkled in the light of a scintillating geometry, purified of crime and sin,
pleasure and punishment. I'd once dreamed of the full moon, hung up in
the same midnight-blue sky above this very street and this very perspective,
slowly transforming itself into the bright dial of a clock. The landscape I
experienced now had the clarity, the transparence, the symmetry of that
dream. I felt like going on observing at my leisure, recounting what seemed
self-evident by pointing out the amusing variations one by one.

It's not that I didn't go at it, either: As if divining the configurations of
stones standing on a dark-blue marble slab on which a game of draughts is
played, I told myself, "The 'me' who stands leaning against the wall of the
mosque desires to be him." "The man wants to become at one with him

whom he envies." "On the other hand, 'he' pretends not to be aware that he's been concocted by 'me' who impersonates him." "That's why the 'eye' is so self-assured." "*He* seems not to know that the 'eye' has been created to make it possible for the man who leans up against the mosque wall to reach him, but the man who leans up against the wall is well aware of this vague apprehension." "If the man makes a move to reach him and manages to become him, then the 'eye' would be left at an impasse or else in a lacuna." "Besides, what's more . . ." Etc., etc.

Those were the things on my mind as I observed myself from the outside. Then the "I" which I observed began walking home to his own bed along the wall of the mosque and, when the wall came to an end, along the wooden houses with the enclosed balconies that duplicated each other, along past vacant lots, public fountains, past zipped-up stores and the graveyards.

I was constantly astonished as I observed myself, the way we are startled when, walking along a crowded street and glancing at the impressions of people going by, we suddenly catch ourselves in a plate glass window or in a huge mirror behind a row of mannequins. But, simultaneously, I knew it was not astonishing that this "I" that I observed as if in a dream was nobody besides myself. What astonished me was the unbelievably gentle, sweet, and loving affinity I felt for this person. I knew how fragile and pitiful he really was, how helpless and sad. I was the only one who knew this person was not what he seemed; I wanted to protect this touchy kid, this creature, as if I were his father, or even a god, and take him under my wing. But he kept walking on for a long time (What was he thinking of? Why so sad, so tired and defeated?), and he finally arrived on the main street. Occasionally, he looked into the unlit windows of pudding shops and grocery stores. He'd thrust his hands into his pockets. Then, his chin fell on his chest. He walked on from Şehzadebaşı to Unkapanı without paying any attention to the occasional vehicle or the vacant taxi that zoomed by. Perhaps he didn't have any money on him either.

Walking on the Unkapanı bridge, he momentarily glanced at the Golden Horn. In the dark, a barely visible crew was pulling on a rope tied to the long and slim stack of a tugboat which was set to sail under the bridge. Walking up Şişhane hill, he exchanged a few words with a drunk who was coming down the street; he paid no attention to the well-lit windows on İstiklâl Avenue, except one, a silversmith's display which he studied thoroughly. What was on his mind? Watching him with nervous apprehension and affection, I was anxious for him.

At Taksim, he bought some cigarettes and matches at a stand. He opened the pack with the lingering gestures characteristic of the sorry Turk in the street, and he lit a cigarette: Oh, the sad wisp of smoke that curled out of his mouth! I was a know-it-all, I recognized everything and had a great deal of experience, but I was fearfully anxious as if I were face-to-face with a human being's existence for the first time. I wanted to say, "Watch it, kid!" Every time he crossed a street, I was thankful that he hadn't met up with something dreadful, seeing how I kept reading the signs of some calamity lurking in the street, the dark façades of the apartment buildings, and in the unlit windows.

Thank goodness, he managed to get home safely, at a Nişantaşı apartment building (Heart-of-the-City Apartments). Once up in his attic flat, you'd think he'd take his troubles to bed, the same troubles I wanted to understand and alleviate. But no, he sat down in a chair, began smoking and going through the daily papers for a while. Then he paced up and down among the old furniture, the dilapidated table, the faded drapes, all the papers and books. Suddenly he sat down at the table, squirmed on the squeaky chair and, grabbing a pen, he leaned over a clean sheet of paper to write something.

I stood immediately next to him; I felt as if I were on top of his messy table. I observed him close up: He wrote with a childlike concentration, with the unruffled pleasure of watching a favorite film, but introspectively. I watched him, proud as a father observing his son pen his first letter. He pursed his lips together when he reached the end of his sentences, his eye bobbled along the paper with the same speed as the words. When he filled up the entire page, I read what he'd been writing, and I shuddered with a deep ache.

He hadn't managed to quote from his own soul, with which I was dying to acquaint myself, but had only scripted the sentences you've been reading. It wasn't his world, but mine, not his words, but the very words across which you're speeding now (slow down, please!), which belonged to me. I wanted to stand up to him and demand that he write his own words, but I could do nothing but watch him as in a dream. The words and sentences followed each other, each one causing me further pain.

At the beginning of a new paragraph he paused for a bit. He looked at me—as if he saw me, as if our eyes met! Remember the scenes in old books and magazines where the writer and his muse have an agreeable chat? Playful illustrators depict in the margin the sweet muse, who is no larger than a pen, and the absentminded writer smiling at each other. Well, that's the smile we gave each other. Now that we'd given each other smiles of empathy, I assumed, optimistically, that everything would be illumined. He would become aware of what's what, write the stories out of his own world for which I had so much curiosity, and I'd read his opinions on being himself with great pleasure.

Nice try! But nothing. Zilch. He shot another beatific smile at me, as if all that needed clarification were clear as a bell; he paused, emotionally worked up as if he'd solved a problem in a game of checkers, and wrote the final words that plunged my world into an impenetrable darkness.

Chapter Eleven

WE LOST OUR MEMORIES
AT THE MOVIES

The movies not only ruin a child's eyesight; they ruin his mind. —ULUNAY

As soon as Galip woke up, he knew it had snowed again. Perhaps he'd known it in his sleep; he'd sensed silence envelop city noises in the dream he remembered upon waking but lost instantly when he looked out the window. It had been dark for quite some time. Galip bathed in the water the gas heater never quite warmed and then got dressed. He took paper and pen to the table, sat down, and worked on the clues for a while. He shaved, put on the herringbone jacket Rüya liked, which was identical to the one Jelal wore, and over it he put on his thick and coarse winter coat.

It had stopped snowing. A couple of inches of the stuff covered the parked cars and the sidewalks. Saturday-evening shoppers with packages in their hands walked home gingerly, as if stepping on the spongy surface of an alien planet they were just getting used to walking on.

At Nişantaşı Square, he felt pleased that the main thoroughfare was clear. He pulled a copy of the next morning's *Milliyet* out of the stack of girlie and scandal magazines on the stand, which was set up in the entryway of a grocery store, as it usually was at night. He walked over to the restaurant across the street, sat in a corner that couldn't be seen by the pedestrians, and ordered tomato soup and grilled *köftes*. While he waited for the food, he placed the paper on the table and read Jelal's Sunday column carefully.

The piece was one of those that had first appeared many years ago; reading it now for the second time, Galip had memories of some of Jelal's individual sentences, which related to memory. While he drank his coffee, he marked the text. Upon leaving the restaurant, he hailed a taxi to take him to Sinan Paşa in the suburb of Bakırköy.

On the protracted taxi ride, Galip felt as if he were not in Istanbul but in some other city, seeing the sights. Where Gümüşsuyu Ramp slopes into Dolmabahçe, three municipal buses had plowed into each other and a crowd had gathered around them. There was absolutely nobody at the bus and *dolmuş* stops. Snow had descended on the city like some kind of oppression, the street lights had grown dimmer, the nighttime activity which makes a city into a city had stopped, and it had regressed to a blank medieval night where the doors are closed and the sidewalks deserted. The snow on the domes of the mosques, on the warehouses, and on the squatter's shacks was not white but blue. He saw whores with purple lips and blue faces hanging about in Aksaray, youngsters sliding down along the city walls on wooden ladders used as sleds, the revolving blue lights of the squad cars parked by the terminal where the buses took off carrying passengers who looked out fearfully. The elderly taxi driver told a dubious story relating to an implausible winter long ago when the Golden Horn froze over. Working in the taxi's top light, Galip marked Jelal's column all over with numbers, signs, and letters, but he still didn't get anywhere. When the driver protested that he could drive no further, Galip got off at Sinan Paşa and walked.

Sunny Heights was closer to the main street than he'd remembered. The road, which ran along two-story concrete-block houses (upgraded from squatter's shacks) with their curtains drawn shut, and along store windows which showed no light, went up a slight slope and suddenly came to a halt at a small square where the bust of Atatürk stood (it wasn't a statue after all) that was represented by the oblong sign he'd seen in the City Directory that morning. Counting on his memory, he took a street off the fair-sized mosque, which had political slogans written all over its walls.

He didn't even want to imagine Rüya in one of these houses where the stovepipes poked out of the middle of the windows, where some of the balconies sloped slightly downwards; but ten years ago he'd quietly approached the open windows, seen for himself what he didn't even want to imagine, and beat a hasty retreat. On that hot August evening, Rüya sat in a sleeveless cotton print dress, working at the table piled with papers, and twirled a curl in her hair round and round; her husband, who sat with his back turned to the window, was stirring his tea; and the moth which was soon to get zapped went in less and less orderly circles around and around the bare bulb that hung overhead. On the table between the husband and wife there was a plate of figs and a mosquito spray. Galip recalled perfectly the tinkle of the spoon in the teacup and the chirr of the cicadas in the bushes nearby, but he could fetch up no associations with the corner where he saw the sign on the post half buried in the snow: Refet Bey Street.

He walked down and back the full length of the street, where kids were throwing snowballs at one end and at the other a lamp illuminated a movie poster showing a nondescript woman whose eyes had been blocked out, blinded. All the houses had two stories and none had any numbers on the doors, so he went by them the first time being nonchalantly forgetful. The second time, though, he reluctantly remembered the window, the door handle he was loath to touch ten years ago, and the dull, unplastered walls. Another floor had been added. A garden wall had been built. And concrete had replaced the mud yard. The first floor was in pitch darkness. The bluish light of a TV screen filtered through the closed curtains on the second floor, which had a separate entrance, and a sulphur-yellow fume of lignite coal smoked out of the stovepipe which stuck out of the wall into the street like the barrel of a gun, announcing the good news that an unexpected guest who knocked on the door would find here something hot to eat, a warm hearth, and warmhearted people watching TV like dummies.

Galip went up the snow-covered steps cautiously, accompanied by the foreboding barks of the dog in the next yard. "I won't take too much time talking to Rüya!" Galip said to himself, but he wasn't sure whether he was speaking to himself or to the ex-husband in his imagination. He'd request that she explain the reasons she hadn't divulged in the goodbye letter, then he'd ask her to come as soon as possible and get all her stuff, her books, cigarettes, the odd pairs of stockings, the empty pill bottles, her bobby pins, the cases for all her prescription glasses, the half-eaten chocolates, her barrettes, the wooden ducklings that were her childhood toys; and be gone. "Anything that reminds me of you gives me more pain than I can bear." Since he couldn't say all this in front of the guy, he'd best convince Rüya to go somewhere to sit down and talk "like adults." Once they went to this place and the subject of "adults" came up, it was possible to convince Rüya of other things as well; but how was he to find such a spot in this place where there was nowhere to go aside from all-male coffeehouses?

When Galip heard a child's voice first (Mom, the door!) and then a woman's voice which was in no way anything like his wife's, his sweetheart for twenty years and his friend for more than that, he knew how stupid he'd been to come here to find Rüya. For a moment he thought he'd beat it, but the door was already open. Galip recognized the ex-husband immediately, but the ex didn't recognize Galip. He was of an average age and of average height; he was just like what Galip had imagined and was also someone Galip would never imagine again.

While the ex-husband got his eyes accustomed to the darkness of the dangerous world outside, and Galip waited to grant the man enough time to recognize him, the inquisitive heads of first the wife, next a child, next another child, appeared one by one: "Who is it, Dad?" Dad, already stuck for an answer, was bewildered for the moment. And Galip, having decided this was his chance to escape without having to go inside, gave his account all in one breath.

He was sorry he was disturbing them in the middle of the night, but he was in a real tight spot; he was here at their home, where he'd come again for a friendly visit some other time (with Rüya even), to get information on an extremely pressing problem concerning a person, or a name. He was defending a university student accused of a murder he hadn't committed. No, it wasn't as if there weren't a dead party, but the real murderer who went around the city like a ghost was at one time . . .

As soon as he got all his story out, Galip was whisked inside; once he removed his shoes, he was presented with a pair of slippers too small for his feet, a cup of coffee was pressed into his hand, and he was told the tea was being brewed. Galip mentioned again the name of the person in question (making up a completely different name to avoid any coincidence), then Rüya's ex-husband took over. Galip had a feeling the stories would anesthetize him, and the more the man went on narrating, the more difficult it would be to get out the door. Later, he'd remember how he thought that resting there a minute, he could find out something about Rüya, or a few clues at least, but it was more like a terminal patient deluding himself as he went under before surgery. Two hours later, when at last he got to the door he thought would never open again, what he learned listening to the ex-husband, whose stories had cascaded like waters overflowing a dam unimpeded, were these facts:

We thought we knew a lot of things, but we knew nothing.

We knew, for example, that most of the Jews in Eastern Europe and America were descendants of the Jewish Khazar Kingdom which existed between the Volga and the Caucasus a thousand years ago. We also knew that the Khazars were really a Turkish tribe who'd accepted Judaism. But what we didn't know was that the Turks were as much Jews as the Jews were Turks. How very interesting it was! To observe these two sibling peoples undulate through migrations for the last twenty centuries, as if dancing together to the rhythm of a secret music, without ever uniting but always tangential, condemned to each other like a pair of hopeless twins.

Once the map was brought in, Galip awoke from the anesthetic of the stories, got up, moved his muscles which had slackened in the heat, and looked in amazement at the arrows marked in green ballpoint on the storybook planet spread on the table.

The host was now considering that historical symmetry as an unassailable fact; we had to prepare ourselves for an eventual misery that would last as long as our present happiness, etc., etc.

Initially, a new state would be set up on the Straits of Bosphorus and the Dardanelles. This time, they would not bring in new settlers to populate this new country, as was the case a thousand years ago; they would transform the old inhabitants into a "new people" that could serve their purposes. It wasn't even necessary to read Ibn Khaldun to surmise they'd have to detach our memories and turn us into wretches existing out of time, without a past, without a history. It was a known fact that students were given lavender liquids to drink in order to destroy our national consciousness ("Take note of the name of the color," said Mom, who was listening to her husband attentively) at the gloomy missionary schools settled on the hills of the Bosphorus and the backstreets in Beyoğlu. Later, this reckless method, due to the chemical considerations, was deemed too dangerous by the "humanitarian component" of the Western Bloc, and "a kinder, gentler," but more durable solution had been applied through their "movie-music" method.

There was no doubt that the movie method utilizing the iconographic faces of beautiful women, the symmetric and powerful music of church organs, the visual repetitions that were reminiscent of hymns, and the eye-catching, brilliant depictions of booze, guns, planes, and clothes had proved to be more radical and conclusive than the methodology tried out by missionaries in Africa and Latin America. (Galip wondered who else had heard these long sentences obviously constructed beforehand: neighbors in the district? co-workers? anonymous passengers on the *dolmuş*? the mother-in-law?) Soon after movie theaters in Şehzadebaşı and Beyoğlu first went into operation, hundreds of people had virtually gone blind. The cries of those who rebelled, having perceived the horrifying thing being perpetrated on them, had been silenced by the police and the head doctors. Nowadays, they could only alleviate the same inner reactions seen in some kids whose eyes had been blinded by these new images by doling out free glasses through National Health. Yet incidents happened now that couldn't be so easily smoothed over. When he saw a sixteen-year-old boy put futile bullets through a movie poster a couple of districts away, he'd immediately understood why. And somebody else, who'd been caught at the foyer of a movie theater carrying a couple of cans of gasoline, had demanded his eyes back from the bouncers who were roughing him up. Yes, he wanted his eyes back, eyes which had once seen the old images. And the newspapers had reported on the shepherd boy from Malatya who'd been induced to develop such an addiction to the movies within one week that he lost his memory, everything he knew including his way back home. Had Mr. Galip seen it by any chance? There were not enough days in the week to go through all the stories about people who couldn't resume their former lives and had become bums because they coveted the streets, the clothes, the women they saw on the silver screen. People who identified with the characters on the screen were so numerous that not only were they not considered "sick" or "felonious," but our new masters made them partners in their enterprises. We'd all been blinded! All of us! All of us!

The host, Rüya's ex-husband, now wanted to know: Was any administrator in the government aware of the parallel between the rise of the movie theaters and the fall of Istanbul? He wanted to know: Was it mere chance that whorehouses and the movie theaters operated on the same streets? He further wanted to know: Why were movie theaters so dark, so thoroughly and cruelly black?

Ten years ago, here in this house, he and Ms. Rüya had tried living under pseudonyms and false identities, all for the sake of a cause they believed in deep in their hearts. (Galip kept glancing at his fingernails.) They translated into our "tongue" manifestos in the language of a country where they'd never been, trying to make the texts sound like that language; they wrote political predictions in this new language which they'd gleaned from persons they'd never seen, and they typed and duplicated these to inform people they would never meet. In fact, they only wanted, naturally, to be someone else. How happy it made them to find out that someone they met took their pseudonyms for real. Sometimes one of them would forget the weariness of the hours spent working at the battery factory, or writing all those articles, or stuffing all the manifestos into envelopes, and would stare and stare at the new identification cards they got their mitts on. In their youthful enthusiasm and optimism, they got such a kick out of saying, "I have changed! I am a totally different person!" that they jumped at the chance to egg each other on to say these words. Thanks to their new identities they read meanings in a world they hadn't been able to see before: the world was a brand-new encyclopedia which could be read from the beginning to the end; the more you read it the more the encyclopedia changed, and so did you; so much so that once they finished reading it, they went back to read again the encyclopedia-world beginning with volume one, and they went into a trance, inebriated with the umpteen new identities they found within the pages. (As the host got lost within the pages of the encyclopedia metaphor in the rest of his lecture, Galip noted the volumes of the *Treasury of Knowledge* one of the newspapers gave away as a supplement, fascicle by fascicle, which was being kept on one of the shelves of the buffet.) Now years later, however, he had understood that this vicious circle was a kind of diversion contrived by "them": it was deluded optimism to think that we could return to the happiness of our original identity after we turned into someone else, then another, and yet another. They had understood, somewhere in the middle of the road, that the husband and wife had lost their way among the signs, letters, manifestos, photos, faces, guns to which they could no longer assign meanings. At that time this house had stood all by itself on this barren hill. One evening Rüya had stuffed a couple of things into her small bag and gone back to her family, back to her old home and life where she thought it was safe.

The host (whose goggling eyes reminded Galip at times of Bugs Bunny) got up to walk up and down whenever the force of his own words overwhelmed him, making Galip's sleepy head spin, as he explained why he'd decided that we had to return to the beginning of things, way back to the origins, in order to nullify "their" games. Mr. Galip could see it for himself: this house was exactly like a dwelling for a "petit bourgeois" or a "middle-class person," or a "traditional citizen." There were old easy chairs slipcovered with printed cotton, drapes made out of a synthetic material, enamel dinner plates with butterflies on the rims, an ugly "buffet" where they kept the candy dish that only came out for guests during holidays and the cordial set that was never used, the faded rugs beaten to a pulp. He was aware that his wife was not an educated, stunning woman like Rüya: she was more like his own mom, plain, simple, harmless (here the wife gave Galip, then her husband a smile the meaning of which Galip couldn't decipher), and she was his cousin, his uncle's daughter. Their children, too, were just like them. Had he been alive and never changed, this was the life his own father would've set up. He'd chosen this life intentionally; lived it consciously, insisted on his own

"true" identity, thereby thwarting a thousand-year-old conspiracy by refusing
to be someone other than himself.

All the objects in this room Mr. Galip might suppose were here by chance
had been in fact arranged in accordance with the same purpose. The wall
clock had been specially selected because a house like this needed the ticking
of this sort of wall clock. Since the TV was always on at this time in houses
like this, it was left on as if it were a streetlight, and the hand-crocheted
doily was laid on the television because sets that belonged to this kind of
family had to have this sort of doily. Everything was the end result of a
carefully thought out plan: the disorder on the table, the old newspapers
tossed aside once the coupons were clipped, the drop of jam on the side of
the gift box of chocolates which had been put to use as a sewing box, and
even things he hadn't devised himself directly, like the teacup handle broken
off by the children which had resembled an ear, the laundry being dried
next to the frightful coal-burning stove. Sometimes he stopped to observe,
as if watching a movie, the things he talked about with his wife and children,
the way they all sat in their chairs at the table, and he was delighted with
the awareness that their conversations and movements were exactly like those
of the kind of family they were. If happiness was to live consciously the life
one desired, then he was happy. What's more, he was even happier that
through this implementation of happiness, he'd frustrated the thousand-year-
old conspiracy.

In an effort to turn the last remarks into the closing statement, Galip got
up saying it was snowing again and stumbled toward the door, feeling he
might pass out despite all the tea and coffee. The host stuck himself between
Galip and his coat, and he continued:

He felt sorry that Mr. Galip had to go back to Istanbul where all this
disintegration had started. Istanbul was the touchstone: let alone live there,
even setting one foot in Istanbul was to surrender, to admit defeat. That
frightful city now roiled with the images that we once only saw in the movies.
Hopeless crowds, dilapidated cars, bridges that slowly sank into the water,
piles of tin cans, highways made out of potholes, incomprehensible large
letters, illegible posters, meaningless torn panels, graffiti with the paint half
washed away, pictures of bottles and cigarettes, minarets devoid of calls to
prayer, mounds of rubble, dust, mud, etc., etc. Nothing could be expected
from such wreckage. If a revitalization could take place—the host was convinced of the existence of others like himself who also resisted with all their
being—he was certain it could only begin here, in these communities be-
littled as "the concrete shantytowns" only because these were the places
where our most precious essence was still being preserved. He was proud to

be the founder, the torchbearer of such a community and he invited Galip to join, even now as he spoke. He could spend the night, they could even debate a little.

Galip had put on his coat, said goodbye to the mom who was quiet and to the children in a stupor, opened the door and stepped out. The host surveyed the snow carefully for a while, then he enunciated the word "white" in a manner that also appealed to Galip. The host had come to know a sheikh who wore only white and, after meeting him, had a dream that was all white. In a pure white dream, he sat with Muhammad in the backseat of a pure white Cadillac. In the front seat were the driver, whose face he couldn't see, and Muhammad's grandchildren, Hasan and Hüseyin, dressed in white. As the white Cadillac went through Beyoğlu, full of posters, ads, movies, and whorehouses, the grandchildren turned around to make disgusted faces for their grandfather's approval.

Galip tried going down the snow-covered stairs, but his host continued: It wasn't as if he put too much stock in dreams. He'd learned to read some of the holy signs, that's all. He wished both Mr. Galip and Rüya could make use of what he'd learned, others certainly helped themselves to it.

It amused him to hear the prime minister now repeat verbatim his own political solutions, his "global analyses" that he'd published under a pseudonym some three years ago when he was in the thick of an active political life. You may be sure "these men" had in their service a wide net of intelligence agencies which scoured the smallest of publications in the land, sending the information "up" when necessary. Not too long ago, his eye had caught an article by Jelal Salik who seemed to have also got hold of the same material through the same channels, but his was a hopeless case: the man searched in vain for the wrong solution to a dead cause in a column where he sold himself.

It was interesting that the ideas of a true believer were being utilized by the prime minister and a famous columnist, ideas they got hold of somehow, when others assumed he was completely depleted and didn't even bother ringing his doorbell. For a while, he'd considered informing the press about the audacious plagiarism perpetrated by these two esteemed personages, proving how they lifted some expressions and even some sentences word for word out of an article in a splinter-group journal which nobody ever read; but the conditions weren't ripe yet for such an ambush. He knew as he knew his own name that it was necessary to wait patiently, that someday these people too would be on his doorstep. Mr. Galip's visit, under the pretext of a pseudonym that wasn't convincing at all, all the way to a distant suburb on a snowy night, had to be a sign. He wanted Mr. Galip to know how well he read these signs and to ask him quietly (when Galip finally made it down to the snowy street) these last questions:

Might Mr. Galip possibly give his revisionist history a chance? In case he had trouble finding his way back to the main street by himself, might the host accompany him there? In the same vein, when might Galip visit again? Very well, then, might he send Rüya his best regards?

Chapter Twelve

THE KISS

The habit of perusing periodical works may be properly added to Averroës'
catalogue of Anti-Mnemonics, or weakeners of the memory.

—COLERIDGE, *Biographia Literaria*

He asked me to give you his regards two weeks ago, to be exact. "I sure will,"
I said, but by the time I got in the car I'd already managed to forget, not
the regards but the man who sent them. I haven't lost any sleep over it,
though. In my opinion, any smart husband ought to push those men who
send his wife their regards out of his memory. After all, you never know,
do you? Especially if your wife happens to be a housewife, that unfortunate
person whose circle consists of relatives and shopkeepers, and who has no
way of knowing any man besides her tedious husband her entire life. Should
someone send her his regards, she might be inclined to think about this
gentle individual; she has the time. When you come right down to it, men
of this sort are truly urbane. But since when did we acquire such customs
anyway? In the good old days, a gentleman might at most send his regards
to an impersonal, nebulous harem. Oldtime streetcars were better too.

Even those readers who know that I am not married, have never been
married, and on account of my profession will never be married, probably

suspect by now that this column, beginning with the opening sentence, is a puzzle that I have devised for them. Just who is this woman whom I address so intimately? Hocus-pocus! Your aging columnist is about to harp on the slow loss of his memory, inviting you to smell the last fading roses in the garden, if you get my meaning. But stand back, so that we can easily pull off our garden-variety sleight of hand without giving away the trick.

Approximately thirty years ago, during my early days as a cub reporter on the Beyoğlu beat, I'd go from door to door in search of a scoop. I'd look for fresh love stories that culminated in death or suicide at the casinos where Beyoğlu gangsters and drug kingpins hang out. I'd go from hotel to hotel, looking through guest registers that hotel clerks let me see—a privilege for which I plunked down two-and-a-half lira notes every month—to sniff out foreign celebrities, or an interesting person from the West whom I could palm off as a foreign celebrity visiting our city. Back in those days, not only did the world not overflow with celebrities, none of them ever showed up in Istanbul. When people that I presented in my paper as celebrities in their own countries but who were not saw their photos in print, they were thrown into a confusion that always ended in disaffection. One among them for whom I had predicted fame and glory eventually achieved real celebrity, becoming a truly famous French—and existentialist—fashion designer twenty years after the appearance of the news that "so-and-so, the famous couturier, visited our city yesterday." But not a word of thanks to me. That's what you get for gratitude from the West.

Regarding those days when I was busy with unqualified celebrities and domestic gangsters (called the mafia these days): I once came across an elderly pharmacist who showed promise as a news story. This man was stricken with insomnia and forgetfulness, which are afflictions that I now suffer from myself. The most horrible aspect of suffering from both of these at the same time is the mistaken notion that it is possible to compensate for one (insomnia) with the other (forgetfulness) when what actually goes on is quite the opposite. During the sleepless nights when neither night nor time would pass, frozen in a world without identity, personality, color, or smell, his memories escaped him so badly (just like mine) that the old man thought he was all alone on the "other side of the moon" referred to so often in magazine articles translated from foreign publications.

The old man had invented a drug in his laboratory (as I have invented prose for the same purpose) in the hope of curing his affliction. At a press conference where a pothead reporter from an evening paper and I were the only two in attendance (the pharmacist made the third), the old man made a great show of pouring out his pink liquid and quaffing it repeatedly for the sake of presenting his drug to the public, thereby achieving at last the sleep he had yearned for all these many years. But since the old pharmacist, who was reunited with not only his sleep but his dreams of paradise, would never wake up again, the public never heard the news it's so hungry for: that a Turk had also managed at last to invent something.

On the day of his funeral, a dark day a couple of days later, if memory serves me right, I kept wondering what it was that he had wanted to remember. I still wonder about it. As we grow older, what is it that our memory throws off like a petulant pack animal who refuses to carry the extra baggage? Is it the most unpleasant? The heaviest? Or the weight that falls off most easily?

Forgetting: I have forgotten how sunlight streamed on our bodies through gauze curtains in small rooms located in the most beautiful spots all over Istanbul. I have forgotten which movie theater entrance was worked by the scalper whose love for the pale Greek girl at the ticket window drove him mad. I have long forgotten the names of the dear readers, and the mystery I divulged to them in personal letters, who dreamed the same dreams as I did during the time I wrote the column interpreting dreams for their newspaper.

Then, years later, researching into time past, your columnist searches for a branch to hold on to in the middle of the night, and he remembers a horrific day he spent in the streets of Istanbul: My entire body, and my entire being, had been wracked by a desire to kiss someone on the lips.

Holed up in an old movie theater one Saturday afternoon, I had viewed an unprolonged kissing scene in an American detective flick (*Scarlet Street*), perhaps older than the theater itself. It was a run-of-the-mill kissing scene, no different than in other black-and-white films, where our censors had already lopped off anything longer than four seconds. I don't quite know how it happened but I was seized by such a desire to kiss a woman the same way, yes, pressing my lips on hers with all my might, that I thought I'd choke on my own misery. I was twenty-four years old, and I had yet to kiss someone on the lips. It wasn't as if I hadn't slept with brothel whores, but not only were those women not prone to kissing, I wouldn't have wanted to put my lips on theirs either.

Even before the film was over, I was out on the street, apprehensive and agitated as if some woman who wanted to kiss me were waiting for me somewhere in the city. I remember walking at a run to the subway, then hurrying back to Beyoğlu, trying hopelessly the whole time, as if looking for something in the dark, to fetch up the memory of a face, a smile, a woman's image. I couldn't come up with an acquaintance or a relative I could kiss on the lips; I had no hope of ever finding myself a sweetheart; I knew of no one who could be my . . . lover! The city that teemed with people seemed totally empty.

Come what may, I still found myself on a bus soon after arriving at Taksim Square. Some distant relatives on my mother's side had taken an interest in us during the years when my father had left us; I had played jacks a few times with their daughter who was a couple of years younger than I. When I rang their doorbell at Fındıkzade an hour later, I suddenly recalled that the girl I dreamed of kissing had been married some time ago. I was invited in by the elderly parents, who have long since passed away. They seemed to be surprised and bewildered as to why I had shown up after all these years. We chitchatted about this and that (they showed no interest in me as a journalist, a profession they considered little better than gossip-mongering), took tea and ate sesame bagels while we listened to the soccer game on the radio. They expected wholeheartedly for me to stay for supper too, but suddenly, mumbling something, I excused myself and bolted out onto the street.

I was still burning up with the desire to kiss when I felt the cold air outdoors on my skin. My skin cold as ice but my flesh and blood on fire, I was suffering from a deep and unbearable discomfort.

Taking the ferryboat at Eminönü, I crossed over to Kadıköy. A schoolmate used to tell tales about a girl in his neighborhood who was a known kisser (that is, known to give kisses before she got married). As I walked to his place at Fenerbahçe I was thinking that my friend must know other girls like her, even if she herself were not available. I went round and round the wood-frame mansions and the cypress gardens where my friend used to live, but I just couldn't find his place. I kept looking into lighted windows as I walked by the old wood structures that have long been torn down, imagining that the girl who was a kisser before she got married lived in one of them. Looking up to a window, I'd say to myself, "There she is, the girl who will kiss me on the lips." There was no great distance between us, just a garden wall, a door, some wooden stairs.

Yet I could not reach her and kiss her. At that moment, how near yet how distant was that kiss! As scary as it was attractive! That mysterious, weird, unbelievable kiss that everyone knew about, yet was as strange and magical as a dream!

Aboard the ferry back to the European side, I remember wondering what would happen if I kissed some woman by force. Or what if I pretended my lips for a moment touched hers accidentally? But on top of not being in any condition to think things through carefully, I did not see a suitable face anywhere around me. There had been periods in my life when I was seized, painfully and hopelessly, by a feeling of the city's emptiness, even as I breathed the same air as the city's crowds, but never had I felt it as powerfully as I did that day.

Pounding the damp sidewalks for quite some time, I kept thinking that I would surely get what I wanted someday when, having achieved fame and glory, I returned to this totally empty city. At the moment, however, your columnist had no other respite than returning to the house where he lived with his mother, to read Balzac's account of poor Rastignac in Turkish translation. Back in those days, I used to read books like a real Young Turk, that is, not for my personal pleasure but out of a sense of duty to prepare myself for the future. But the future could not save the day!

After secluding myself in my room for a while, I reemerged impatiently. I remember looking into the bathroom mirror as I visualized the actors in the movie, thinking a person could at least kiss himself in the mirror. At any rate, I could not get the image of actors' lips (Joan Bennett's and Dan Duryea's) out of my mind. Even so, I would not be kissing myself but the glass. So I left. My mother was sitting at the table among patterns and pieces of silk chiffon obtained from God knew what wealthy relation of a distant relative, trying to get an evening dress made in time for some wedding.

Reviewing my plans for the future, I began explaining things to her, most probably stories and daydreams that involved my successes and desires. But my mother wasn't listening to me heart and soul. I realized that what was important to her was not what I said, no matter what it was; what was important was the fact that I was sitting at home on Saturday night, chatting with her. I was furious. For some reason her hair was well groomed that evening, and her lips were lightly dabbed with lipstick. I stared at my mother's lips, at her mouth that was often said to resemble mine; I was dumbstruck.

"There's a strange look in your eyes," she said apprehensively. "What is it?"

My mother and I fell silent for a time. Then I began walking toward her but stopped dead in my tracks. My legs were trembling. Without getting any closer, I began to shout with all my might. I cannot remember clearly now what it was that I was saying, but before we knew it, we were having one of our terrible fights. We had suddenly lost all fear of being overheard by the neighbors. It was one of those moments of anger when one loses all inhibition and lets it rip. In situations like this, either a teacup gets broken or else the stove barely misses being knocked over.

Eventually, I was able to tear myself away and storm out the door. My mother sat weeping among the pieces of silk chiffon, spools of thread, and imported dressmaker's pins (the first Turkish-made pins were manufactured in 1976 under the trademark of Horseman). I beat the sidewalks all over the city until midnight. I went in the courtyard of the Mosque of Süleyman the Magnificent, crossed the Atatürk Bridge, went up to Beyoğlu. It was as if I were not myself; I felt as if the specter of rage and vengeance were pursuing me; the person I was supposed to be seemed to be on my trail.

Next, I found myself sitting at a pudding shop just to be around other people. But I did not look at anyone for fear of catching the eye of someone who was also trying to fill up the eternity of a Saturday night. People like me recognize each other immediately, only to feel contempt for one another. Not too long after, a man and his wife stopped by my table, and the husband began to talk to me. What was this white-haired ghost doing among my memories?

Turns out, he was the old schoolmate whose house I was unable to find in Fenerbahçe. Not only was he married, he worked for the State Railways, had become prematurely gray, and remembered the good old days only too well. You know how an old friend will astonish you by falling all over you, pretending that he shares with you a great many memories and secrets, just to make his own past sound interesting for the benefit of a wife or companion who's standing next to him. Well, I wasn't taken in. But I wouldn't play the role that made his trumped-up reminiscences more interesting, either. There was no way that I was admitting to being still stuck in the same old sad and miserable life that he himself had long left behind.

Spooning up my unsweetened pudding as I gave them the scoop, I confessed that I myself had been married for quite some time, that you were waiting for me at home, that I had parked my Chevvy at Taksim and had walked here to pick up the chicken-breast pudding you had a sudden craving for, that we lived in Nişantaşı, and that I could drop them off somewhere on my way. He thanked me, but no, seeing how he still lived in Fenerbahçe. He questioned me tentatively to satisfy his own curiosity at first, but then, when he found out that you came from "a good family," he wanted to impress the wife with his familiarity with good families. Not letting the chance go to waste, I insisted that he must remember you. He did, gladly, and he sent you his regards. As I left the shop, the container with the chicken-breast pudding in my hand, first I kissed him and then, aping the breezy Western manner in the movies, I kissed his wife. What a bunch of oddball readers you are! What an oddball country!

Chapter Thirteen

LOOK WHO'S HERE!

We should have met long ago. —TÜRKAN ŞORAY, superstar of Turkish film

On the main drag, where Galip found himself after he left Rüya's ex-husband's place, he couldn't find any transportation. From time to time, city buses roared by, inexorably determined not to slow down, let alone make a stop. He decided to walk all the way to the train station at Bakırköy. Slogging his way through the snow to the train station that looked like one of those dinky refrigerated cases at a corner grocery store, Galip had fantasies of running into Rüya, of things returning to normal, and of almost disregarding Rüya's reasons for leaving, once these were understood to be clear and simple; but not even in the fantasies of resuming their life together could he find any way of telling Rüya about his interview with her ex-husband.

On the train, which left half an hour later, an old man told Galip the story of something that happened to him some forty years ago on a winter's night that had been equally cold. The old man's brigade had put in a difficult winter at a village in Thrace during the years of dearth when the big war was expected to spread into our country. One morning, having received a coded order, they had mounted their horses, left the village, and ridden a whole day to reach the outskirts of Istanbul. But they hadn't entered the city. Instead, they had waited for nightfall in the hills above the Golden Horn. Once activity in the city ceased, they had descended into the dark streets and, in the ghostly light of the masked streetlights, they had guided their horses quietly over the frozen cobblestones and handed them over to the slaughterhouse in Sütlüce. The noise of the train made it hard for Galip to make out the words and the syllables describing the scenes of carnage as the horses fell one by one, the bewildered animals with their guts spilled on the bloody stones, their internal organs hanging out like the springs of the gutted armchair, the rage of the butchers, the sad look in the faces of the animals waiting for their turn which resembled the expression in the cavalrymen's faces as they sneaked out of town like criminals.

There was no transportation in front of Sirkeci Station, either. Galip considered for a moment walking up to the office building and spending the night in his office, but then he sensed that the taxi doing a U-turn would pick him up. Yet when the taxi stopped further down the sidewalk, a man carrying a briefcase, who seemed to have stepped out of some black-and-white film, yanked the door open and got in. The driver, after picking up his fare, also stopped for Galip, saying that he could drop him off at Galata Palace along with the "gentleman."

When Galip got out of the taxi at Galata Palace, he regretted not having spoken with the man who looked like a character out of a black-and-white film. He contemplated the ferryboats docked at Karaköy Bridge, which were not in service yet fully lighted, imagining the conversation he could have struck up with the man. "Sir," he could have said, "once upon a time many years ago, on a snowy night like this . . ." If only he had begun the story, he could have finished it with the same ease with which he began, and the man might have listened to Galip with the interest he anticipated.

A little down the road from the Atlas Theater, Galip was looking into the window of a women's shoestore (Rüya wore a size seven shoe), when a small, skinny man approached him. He was carrying one of those imitation leather cases carried door to door by bill collectors from the municipal gas company. "Do you fancy the stars?" he said. He wore his jacket buttoned up to his neck like an overcoat. Galip surmised he had met up with a colleague of the man who set up his telescope at Taksim Square on cloudless nights, offering the curious a look at the stars for a hundred liras a shot, but the man pulled an album out of his case. He turned the pages of the album himself, giving Galip a look at his incredible photographs showing some of our famous movie stars, printed on good quality stock.

And yet, the photographs were not of the famous movie stars but of their look-alikes, wearing costumes and jewelry modeled after the stars', who imitated their poses and gestures, such as the way they smoked their cigarettes or puckered up for a kiss. Pasted on each movie star's page was the star's name in bold print cut out of newspaper headlines and a color picture of her clipped from a magazine, and arranged all around it were many "attractive" poses of the impersonator striving to look like the original.

Aware of Galip's lack of interest, the thin man with the case pulled him into a narrow, deserted street behind the New Angel Theater and proffered the album to him so that he could flip through it with his own hands. In the light of an odd little shop window where gloves, umbrellas, purses, and stockings were displayed on severed mannequin's hands, arms, and legs dangling from the ceiling on strings, Galip carefully studied "Türkan Şoray" dancing in a gypsy outfit that swirled out into infinity or wearily lighting a cigarette, "Müjde Ar" peeling a banana, staring wantonly into the camera or laughing recklessly, and "Hülya Koçyiğit" wearing glasses to mend the bra she'd taken off, leaning into the sink to do the dishes, then weeping, troubled and disconsolate. The owner of the album, who had been studying Galip with the same attentiveness, suddenly ripped the album out of Galip's hand with the resolve of a high-school teacher who has caught his student reading a forbidden book and stuffed it back into his case.

"Want me to take you to them?"

"Where do they hang out?"

"You look like a gentleman. Follow me."

As they wended their way through back alleys, Galip was pestered to make a choice and obliged to divulge that he liked Türkan Şoray the best.

"In person," said the man with the briefcase as if giving away a secret. "She'll be tickled pink. She'll get a real kick out of you."

They went in the first floor of an old stone house next to the Beyoğlu police station that had the inscription COMPANIONS over the door. It smelled of dust and fabrics. In the semilit room, although there were no sewing machines or materials anywhere around, Galip nonetheless had an impulse to name the place The Companions' Haberdashers. The brilliantly lit second room they entered through a tall white door reminded Galip that he ought to give the pimp his cut.

"Türkan!" said the man as he put the money in his pocket. "Türkan, look, İzzet is here asking for you."

The two women playing cards tittered as they turned to look at Galip. In the room that called to mind an old, dilapidated stage set, there was that sleep-inducing lack of air that is endemic to those rooms where the stove isn't well-ventilated, the smell of perfume is heavy, and the racket of domestic-pop music tiresome. Reclining on the sofa was a woman riffling through a humor magazine, who had assumed Rüya's typical pose as she read detective novels (one leg on the back of the sofa), although she looked neither like a movie star nor like Rüya. One could tell "Müjde Ar" was Müjde Ar because her T-shirt said so. An older man who looked like a waiter had fallen asleep in front of a TV show on which a panel was discussing the significance of the conquest of Constantinopole in world history.

Galip thought the woman with the permed hair who was wearing blue jeans looked vaguely like an American movie star whose name escaped him, but he wasn't sure whether the resemblance was intentionally cultivated. Another man who entered through the other door approached "Müjde Ar," and with the seriousness of a drunk, swallowing the first two syllables, he concentrated on reading her name on her T-shirt like those people who believe what's going on only when they read about it in the headlines.

Galip guessed the woman wearing a leopard print dress must be "Türkan Şoray": not only was she approaching him, her walk had a modicum of grace. Perhaps she was the one who most looked like the original; she had pulled long blond hair over her right shoulder.

"May I smoke?" she said, smiling pleasantly. She placed an unfiltered cigarette between her lips. "Will you light it for me?"

As soon as Galip lit her cigarette with his lighter, an incredibly dense cloud of smoke formed around the woman's head. When her head and her long-lashed eyes emerged out of the cloud like a saint's head materializing in the mist, a strange silence seemed to overcome the loud music (as in romantic movies), making Galip think, for the first time in his life, that he could go to bed with a woman other than Rüya. Upstairs, in a room that was carefully appointed, the woman stubbed her cigarette in an ashtray that had the insignia of the Ak Bank, and she took another one out of her pack.

"May I smoke?" she said with the same voice and manner as before. She placed the cigarette in the corner of her mouth, smiling pleasantly but holding her head high. "Will you light it for me?"

Noticing that she leaned her head exactly in the same way as before toward an imaginary lighter, thereby exposing her cleavage, Galip figured that her lines and the gesture of lighting her cigarette must have come out of a Türkan Şoray movie, and that he himself was supposed to play the actor İzzet Günay who was the male lead in the same flick. When he lit her cigarette, the same incredibly dense cloud formed around the woman's head, and the long-lashed black eyes once more emerged slowly out of the mist. How was she able to blow out so much smoke? He would've thought an effect like this could only be simulated in a studio.

"Why so quiet?" said the woman, smiling.

"I'm not quiet," Galip said.

"You're some piece of work, aren't you?" the woman said, pretending to be simultaneously curious and angry. "Or are you too innocent for words?" She repeated the same lines once more. Her long earrings dangled on her bare shoulders.

The lobby photos stuck into her round vanity mirror reminded Galip that Türkan Şoray had worn the leopard print dress, which was cut way down to her buttocks in the back, when she played the nightclub doxy in the movie called *My Disorderly Babe* in which she shared the lead with İzzet Günay some twenty years ago; then he heard the woman say other lines that also came out of the Türkan Şoray movie: (*Hanging her head like a wistful, spoiled child, her hands suddenly flying out from where they were clasped under her chin*) "But I can't go to sleep now! When I drink, I want to have fun!"; (*With the air of a kindly aunt worrying over a neighbor's child*) "Stay with me, İzzet, stay until the bridge opens!"; (*With sudden exuberance*) "It was kismet that it happened with you, and today!"; (*In a ladylike manner*) "I am pleased to meet you, I am pleased to meet you, I am pleased to meet you . . ."

Galip took the chair next to the door, and the woman sat before the round vanity mirror that looked a lot like the original in the movie, brushing her long bleached blond hair. Stuck in the mirror, there was also a photo of this particular scene. The woman's back was even more beautiful than the original. For an instant, she looked at Galip's image in the mirror.

"We should have met long ago . . ."

"We did meet long ago," Galip said, observing the woman's face in the mirror. "We didn't sit at the same desk at school, but on a warm spring day when the window was opened after a long class discussion, I watched your face reflected like this in the pane which the blackness of the chalkboard right behind it had turned into a mirror."

"Hmmm . . . We should have met long ago."

"We met long ago," said Galip. "When we first met, your legs looked so thin and so delicate that I was afraid they would break. Your skin was rough when you were a kid, but as you got older, after we graduated from middle school, your complexion became rosy and incredibly fine. If they took us to the beach on hot summer days when we went crazy from playing indoors, coming back with ice-cream cones we bought at Tarabya, we would scratch letters with our long nails into the salt on each other's arms. I loved the fuzz on your skinny arms. I loved the peachy color of your suntanned legs. I loved the way your hair spilled over your face when you reached for something on the shelf above my head."

"We should have met long ago."

"I used to love the strap marks left on your shoulders by the bathing suit you borrowed from your mother, the way you absentmindedly tugged at your hair when you were nervous, the way you caught between your middle finger and thumb a speck of tobacco left by your filterless cigarette on the tip of your tongue, the way your mouth fell open watching a movie, the way you unwittingly scarfed up the roasted garbanzos and nuts in the dish under your hand while you read a book, the way you kept losing your keys, the way you screwed up your eyes to see because you refused to accept you were nearsighted. When you narrowed your eyes on a distant point and absconded for parts unknown, I understood that you were thinking of something else, and I loved you apprehensively. Oh my God! I loved with fear and trepidation what I couldn't know of your mind as much as I loved what I did know."

Galip shut up when he saw a vague anxiety in Türkan Şoray's face in the mirror. The woman lay down on the bed next to the vanity.

"Come to me now," she said. "Nothing is worth it, nothing, you understand?" But Galip just sat there, unsure. "Or don't you love your Türkan Şoray?" she added jealously, though Galip couldn't decide for sure if it was real or make-believe.

"I do."

"You loved the way I batted my eyelashes too, didn't you?"

"I did."

"You used to love the sensuous way I went down the stairs in *Maşallah Beach*, the way I lit my cigarette in *My Disorderly Babe*, and the way I smoked through a cigarette holder in *Hell of a Girl*. Didn't you?"

"I did."

"Then, come to me, my darling."

"Let's talk some more."

"What?"

Galip was pensive.

"What's your name? What do you do for a living?"

"I am a lawyer."

"I used to have a lawyer," the woman said. "He took all my money but he could not get this car that was registered to me out of my husband's mitts. It's my car, understand? Mine. Now some whore has got hold of it. A '56

Chevrolet, fire-engine red. What's a lawyer good for, I ask you, if he can't get my car back? Can you get my husband to give me back my car?"

"I can," said Galip.

"You can?" the woman said hopefully. "You can. You do it, and I will marry you. You'll save me from the life I am leading, that is, the life of living in the movies. I am sick and tired of being a movie star. This retarded nation thinks a movie star is just a whore, not an artist. I am not a movie star, I am an artist. You understand?"

"Sure."

"Will you marry me?" the woman said exuberantly. "If we were married, we could drive around in my car. Will you marry me? But you'd have to fall in love with me."

"I will marry you."

"No, no, you ask me . . . Ask me if I will marry you."

"Türkan, will you marry me?"

"Not like that! Ask sincerely, with feeling, like in the movies! But first get on your feet. No one ever pops the question sitting down."

Galip got on his feet as if he were going to sing the national anthem. "Türkan, will you, will you, marry me?"

"But I am not a virgin," said the woman. "I had an accident."

"What, riding a horse? Or sliding down the banister?"

"No, doing the ironing. You laugh, but only yesterday I heard that the Sultan wants your head. You married?"

"I am."

"I always get stuck with the married guys anyway," said the woman, her manner lifted out of *My Disorderly Babe*. "But it's not important. What is important is the State Railways. Which team do you think will win the cup this year? How do you think things will end up? When do you think the military will put a stop to all this anarchy? You know, you'd look better if you got your hair cut."

"Don't make personal remarks," said Galip. "It's not polite."

"What did I say now?" the woman said opening her eyes wide and blinking like Türkan Şoray to feign surprise. "I only asked if you married me, would you win back my car? No, no. I said if you get my car back, will you marry me. Here's the license number: 34 JG 19 May 1919. Same day Atatürk hit the road in Samsun to liberate Anatolia. My darling '56 Chevvy."

"Tell me about it!" Galip said.

"Yes, but they'll soon be knocking on the door. Your *visite* is just about up."

"The Turkish expression is 'paying your respects.' "

"Excuse me?"

"Money is no object," Galip said.

"For me, neither," said the woman. "The '56 Chevvy was red as my nails, the same color exactly. I got a broken nail, don't I? Maybe my Chevvy too hit something. Before that creep who's supposed to be my husband presented my car to that whore, I used to drive it here every day. But these days I only get to see him in the street, I mean, the car. Sometimes I see it being driven around Taksim by some driver or other, and sometimes at the Karaköy ferry station with yet another cabby sitting in it, waiting for a fare. The broad is obsessed with the car; she has it painted a different color every other day. Sometimes, lo and behold, it's been painted chestnut brown, next day it's the color of coffee with cream, dripping with chrome and fitted with lights. The day after, it's wreathed with flowers, with a doll sitting on the dashboard, and it's become a pink bridal limousine! And then a week later, there it is painted black, six cops with black mustaches sitting in it, and wouldn't you know it, now it's a squad car! You can't mistake it, seeing how it even says POLICE on it and everything. But, of course, the license plates are changed every time, so that I won't catch on."

"Of course."

"Of course," the woman said. "Both the cops and the drivers are that broad's tricks, but that cuckold of a husband of mine doesn't have a clue. He left me just like that one day. Has anyone left you just like that? What's the date today?"

"The twelfth."

"How time passes! Look how you make me talk a blue streak! Do you want something special by any chance? Go ahead, tell me, I've taken to you. You are a well-bred man, so how bad could it be? You have a lot of money on you? Are you really rich? Or just a greengrocer like İzzet? No, you're a lawyer. Go ahead and tell me a riddle, Mr. Lawyer. All right, I will tell you one. What's the difference between the Sultan and the Bosphorus Bridge?"

"Beats me."

"Between Atatürk and Muhammad?"

"I give up."

"You give up too easy!" the woman said. She rose from the vanity where she'd been watching herself and, giggling, she whispered the answers into Galip's ear. Then she twined her arms around Galip's neck. "Let's get married," she murmured. "Let's go to Mount Kaf. Let's belong to one another. Let's become some other persons. Marry me, marry me, marry me."

They kissed in the spirit of the game. Was there anything about this woman that was reminiscent of Rüya? There was not, but Galip was still pleased with himself. When they fell into bed, the woman did something that reminded him of Rüya, but she didn't do it exactly like Rüya. Every time Rüya put her tongue in his mouth, Galip would be upset thinking that his wife had for a moment turned into someone else. But when the pretend Türkan Şoray stuck her tongue, which was larger and heavier than Rüya's, into Galip's mouth somewhat victoriously, but tenderly and playfully, he felt that it was not the woman in his arms who was different but it was he that had completely become someone else; and he was terribly aroused. Goaded by the woman's sense of play, they rolled rough-and-tumble from one end of the bed to the other, first one on top and then the other, as in the totally unrealistic kissing scenes in domestic films. "You're making me dizzy!" said the woman, making as though she was really dizzy in imitation of a ghostly figure that was not present. When Galip realized that they could see themselves in the mirror on this end of the bed, he figured out why this tender rolling scene had been deemed necessary. The woman watched with pleasure the image of taking off her own clothes and then Galip's in the mirror. As if watching a third person together, perhaps somewhat more congenially than the judges evaluating the contestants going through the compulsory movements in a gymnastic competition, they watched in the mirror the woman's tricks, one after the other, to their hearts' content. At a moment when Galip couldn't see the mirror while they were bouncing on the quiet springs of the bed, the woman said, "We have both become other people." She asked, "Who am I, who am I, who am I?" but Galip didn't manage to give her the answer she wanted to hear: he'd let himself go completely. He heard the woman say, "Two times two makes four," murmuring "Listen, listen, listen!" and then barely audibly speaking about a sultan and his unfortunate crown prince as if she were telling a fairy tale, or a dream, using the special past tense for telling stories.

"If I am you, then you are me," the woman said later as they put their clothes back on. "So what? What if you have become me, and I you?" She gave him a foxy smile. "How did you like your Türkan Şoray?"

"I liked her."

"Then save me from the life, save me, take me away from here, marry me, let's go somewhere else, let's elope, get married, and begin a new life."

From what film did this segment come, or from what game? Galip was not certain. Perhaps this was what the woman wanted. She told Galip that she did not believe he was married, seeing how she knew a lot about married men. If they really did get married, and if Galip managed getting the '56 Chevvy liberated, the two of them would go on an outing on the Bosphorus; they'd get wafer *helva* at Emirgân, view the sea at Tarabya, and eat somewhere in Büyük Dere.

"I don't care for Büyük Dere," Galip said.

"In that case, you're waiting for Him in vain," said the woman. "He will never come."

"I am in no hurry."

"But I am," the woman said stubbornly. "I am afraid of not recognizing Him when He comes. I am afraid I'll be the last one to get to see Him. I am afraid of being the very last person."

"Who is He?"

The woman smiled mysteriously. "Don't you ever see any movies? Don't you know the rules of the game? Do you suppose people who blab such things are allowed to remain alive in this country? I want to live."

Someone began to knock on the door before she finished telling the story of a friend of hers who vanished mysteriously and was, in all likelihood, murdered and her body dumped in the Bosphorus. The woman fell silent. As he walked out the door, the woman whispered after him:

"We are all waiting for Him, all of us; we are all waiting for Him."

Chapter Fourteen

WE ARE ALL WAITING
FOR HIM

I am crazy about mysterious things. —DOSTOEVSKY

We are all waiting for Him. We have been waiting for Him all these centuries. Some of us, weary of the crowds on the Galata Bridge, wait for Him as we dolorously watch the lead-colored waters of the Golden Horn; some of us wait as we throw a couple more sticks in a stove that just won't heat a two-room flat at Surdibi; some of us wait as we climb a seemingly endless staircase up a certain Greek building on a back street in Cihangir; some of us wait in a podunk town in Anatolia as we do the crossword puzzle in an Istanbul paper to pass the time until we meet our friends at a tavern; some of us wait as we fantasize about boarding the airplanes mentioned and shown in the same newspaper, or about entering a well-lit room, or embracing beautiful bodies. We await Him as we sorrowfully walk on muddy sidewalks, in our hands paper bags that have been made out of newspapers read over at least a hundred times, or plastic bags that inundate the apples inside with a synthetic smell, or string market-bags that leave purplish marks on our fingers and palms. We are all waiting for Him at the movie theaters where we watch tough guys break bottles and windows on a Saturday night and the delightful adventures of world-class dolls; returning from whorehouses where we sleep with whores who only manage to make us feel even more lonely, or from taverns where our friends poke merciless fun at our small obsessions, or from the neighbors' where we can't get any pleasure out of listening to the radio theater because their noisy children cannot manage to go to bed, we wait for Him in the street. Some of us say that He will first appear in the darkest corners of the slums where urchins knock out the streetlights with their slingshots, while others say it will be in front of stores where sinful tradesmen sell tickets for the National Sweepstakes and Sports Lotto, and skin magazines, toys, tobacco, condoms, and stuff like that. Everyone says that no matter where He is first seen, be it at *köfte* shops where children are kept kneading hamburger twelve hours a day, or at the movie theaters where a thousand eyes burning with the same desire become a single eye, or on the green hills where angelically innocent shepherds fall under the spell of the graveyard cypresses, the fortunate person who first sees Him will recognize Him instantly, and it will be understood that the waiting, which has been as long as eternity and as short as an eye blink, is at an end, and that the hour of salvation is at hand.

The Koran is quite explicit on the subject only for those who can make out the "meaning" of the Arabic alphabet (as in the 97th verse of the sura called *Al-Isra*, or The Israelites, or the 23rd verse of *Al-Zumar*, or The Companies, where it is explained that the Koran is revealed *mutashabih* and *mathani*: "consistent in its various parts" and "repeated," etc., etc.). According to Mutahhar Ibn Tahir from Jerusalem, who wrote three hundred years after the revelation of the Koran, in his book *Origins and History*, the only evidence on this subject is what he says concerning Muhammad's "name, appearance, or else the guidance of someone whose work is consistent with mine," or else, the depositions of the other witnesses who supplied the information for this particular hadith and others like it. And we also know that it is briefly noted in Ibn Batuta's *Journeys* that the Shiites await His manifestation ceremonially in the underground passages below the shrine of *Hakim-al Wakt* (Sage of the Time) at Samarra. According to what Firuz Shah dictated to his scribe thirty years after that, there were thousands of unfortunates in the dusty yellow streets in Delhi who awaited Him and the mystery of the letters that He would reveal. We also know that yet another point is stressed once again during the same time period, in Ibn Khaldun's *Introduction* where he considers each hadith concerning His appearance, which he selected by sifting through extreme Shiite sources: that He would slay Dadjdjal, or Satan, or, in keeping with the Christian concept and language, the Antichrist, who would appear together with Him on the Day of Judgment and Salvation.

The surprising thing was that none among those who awaited and dreamed of the Messiah found it possible to imagine His face: not my worthy reader Mehmet Yılmaz who has written to me concerning the vision he experienced in his house at a remote town in the Anatolian hinterland, not even Ibn Arabi who dreamed up the same vision seven hundred years before him and wrote about it in his *Phoenix*, not the philosopher al-Kindi who had a dream that He, along with all those He had saved, would conquer Constantinople from the Christians, and not the salesgirl who daydreamed about Him as she sat surrounded by bobbins, buttons, and nylon stockings in a dry-goods store on a backstreet of the Beyoğlu district in Istanbul where al-Kindi's dream had eventually come true.

On the other hand, we are able to imagine Dadjdjal all too well: according to al-Bukhari's *Prophets*, Dadjdjal is single-eyed and red-haired, according to *Pilgrimage* his identity is written on his face; Dadjdjal, who is supposed to be thick-necked according to Tayalisi, has red eyes and a heavy frame according to *Tawhid* by Reverend Nizamettin Bey who did his daydreaming in Istanbul. In the humor rag called *Karagöz*, which was read extensively in the hinterland during the years I was a cub reporter, there was a cartoon-strip romance concerning the derring-do of a Turkish warrior, in which Dadjdjal was represented as deformed and crooked-mouthed. Dadjdjal, who came up with incredible ruses in his battles against our warriors, who were known to make love to the beauties of Constantinople, which was as yet unconquered, had a broad forehead, a large nose, but no mustache (in keeping with the suggestions I sometimes gave the illustrators). In opposition to Dadjdjal, who stirs our powers of imagination so vividly, our only writer who was able to personify our long-awaited Messiah in all His glory was Dr. Ferit Kemal who wrote his *Le Grand Pacha* in French, and the fact that it could only be published in Paris in 1870 is considered, by some, a loss for our national literature.

Placing this unique work which portrays Him in all his aspects outside of our literature, just because it has been penned in French, is as wrong as it is pitiful to claim that "The Grand Inquisitor" in the Russian author Dostoevsky's *Brothers Karamazov* has been lifted out of this slim treatise, as some have done, although with some embarrassment, in East-oriented publications such as *The Ritual Fountain* or *The Grand East*. On the subject of the litany concerning what the West has stolen from the East, or the East from the West, I am always reminded of a notion I had: If this realm of dreams that we call the world is a house into which we enter disoriented as a somnambulist, then the various literatures are like clocks hung up on the walls of the rooms in this house to which we wish to orient ourselves. Now:

1. It's stupid to say that one of the clocks ticking away in one of the rooms in the house of dreams is right while another one is wrong.

2. It's also stupid to say that one of the clocks in the rooms is five hours ahead of another since, by virtue of the same logic, it can be said that the same clock is seven hours behind.

3. It's even more stupid to conclude that one clock is imitating another if one clock says nine thirty-five and then, after some period of time has elapsed, another one now says nine thirty-five.

Ibn Arabi, who wrote more than two hundred mystical books, was in Morocco, a year before he attended Averroës' funeral in Cordova, where he had written a book inspired by the story (dream) of how Muhammad had been taken to Jerusalem and ascended to the sky on a ladder (*mirach* in Arabic) where he took a good look at both Heaven and Hell as it is related in the Israelites sura mentioned above (note to the typesetter: if we are on top of the column now, then substitute "below" for "above"). Now, after taking into account what Ibn Arabi says about perambulating the seven heavens with his guide, what he saw there, and what he and the prophets confabulated about, and also taking into account that he wrote this book when he was thirty-three years of age (in 1198), coming to the conclusion that the dream girl called Nizam in his book is "true" while Beatrice is "false," or that Ibn Arabi is "right" while Dante is "wrong," or that "The Book of the Israelites" and *Makan al-Asra* are "correct" while *The Divine Comedy* is "incorrect," is an example of the first kind of stupidity that I mentioned.

Since the Andalusian philosopher Ibn Tufeyl penned in the eleventh century a book about a child abandoned on a desert island where he lived for years and came to appreciate nature, the sustenance he nursed from a doe, the ocean, death, the heavens above, and "the divine truths," claiming that *Hayy Ibn Yakzan (The Self-Taught Philosopher)* is six hundred years "ahead" of Robinson Crusoe, or, since the second book gives much more information about tools and things, claiming that Ibn Tufeyl is six hundred years "behind" Daniel Defoe is an example of the second kind of stupidity.

The Reverend Veliyyudin Bey, who was one of the Sheikhs of Islam during the reign of Mustapha the Third, suddenly inspired by the disrespectful and inopportune remark made by a loose-tongued friend (who was visiting on a Friday evening and, upon seeing a magnificent escritoire in the Sheikh's study, said, "Reverend Teacher, seems like your cupboard is as messy as your mind"), began writing a lengthy poem in couplets, in March of 1761, in order to prove that everything was in its place both in his mind and in his walnut escritoire, making much of the similarities between the two. Since he propounded in his work the view that our minds also had twelve compartments—just like the splendid Armenian-make escritoire which had two cabinets, four shelves, and twelve drawers—where we stored time, places, numbers, papers, all the odds and ends we call today "cause-and-effect," "existence," and "necessity," and since he beat by twenty years Kant's categorization of Pure Reason into twelve compartments, deducing that the German appropriated the idea from the Turk is an example of stupidity of the third kind.

When Dr. Ferit Kemal was at work portraying the long-awaited Messiah in all His glory, he wouldn't have been surprised to learn that his compatriots would approach his book a hundred years later displaying such stupidities: his whole life was already surrounded by a nimbus of neglect and disinterest which had exiled him to the silence of a dream. Today, I can only imagine his face, which was never photographed, as the face of a somnambulist: he was an addict. He turned many of his patients into addicts like himself, as we are told in Abdurrahman Şeref's derogatory study called *The New Ottomans and Liberty*. He went to Paris in 1866, heeding some vague sense of rebellion—that's right, a year before Dostoevsky's second trip to Europe!—and had a couple of articles in the newspapers called *Liberty* and *Reporter*, both of which were published in Europe, but he remained in Paris after the Young Turks reconciled their differences with the Palace and returned one by one to Istanbul. There's no other trace of him. Since he refers to Baudelaire's *Les Paradis artificiels* in his foreword, perhaps he also knew about De Quincey, who is a favorite of mine; perhaps he was experimenting with opium, but in the pages where he talks about Him there are few hints of any such experiments; quite to the contrary, there are signs of a powerful logic that we are in desperate need of today. I am writing this column in order to promulgate this logic and to introduce the irresistible ideas put forth in *Le Grand Pacha* to the patriotic officers serving in our armed forces.

But in order to get the logic, one must first get the book's ambience. Imagine a book bound in blue, printed on paper made of straw, and published by Poulet-Malassis in the year of 1861, in Paris. It has only ninety-six pages. Imagine the illustrations by a French artist (De Tennielle) which, rather than showing old Istanbul, look like today's Istanbul with its stone buildings, sidewalks, and parquet-stone paved streets; imagine the pictures of today's concrete rat holes, and of shadows, furniture, and surroundings that suggest suspended and electrified instruments of torture rather than the stone cells and primitive torture devices that were the order of the day back then.

The book begins with the description of one of the backstreets in Istanbul. There is no sound besides the night watchmen's nightsticks beating on the sidewalks and the ululations of dog packs fighting each other in distant neighborhoods. No light seeps through the latticework windows of the wood-frame houses. The wisp of smoke that comes out of a stovepipe diffuses into the gossamer fog that has descended on the domes and rooftops. In this profound silence, one can hear the sound of footsteps on the deserted side-walks. Everyone interprets this strange, novel, unexpected sound of footsteps as joyful tidings, even those who have put on several layers of sweaters in preparation for diving into their chilly beds, also those who are already dreaming deep under a pile of quilts.

The next day, far from the gloom of the night before, is festive. Everyone has recognized Him, realized that He is Him, and knows that the hour of eternity loaded with sorrows that all thought would never end is finally over. He is present among the festive merry-go-rounds, the old enemies who have made up, children eating apple candy and taffy on a stick, men and women joking together, people dancing and playing. He is more like an older brother among his siblings than the supreme Messiah walking among the unfortu-nates that He will lead to better days and to victory upon victory. But there is the shadow of a doubt in His face, a misgiving, a premonition. Then, as He walks in the streets lost in thought, the Grand Pasha's men arrest him and stick him into one of those stone-vaulted dungeons. At midnight, the Grand Pasha himself arrives with a candle in his hand to visit Him in his cell and converse with him throughout the night.

Who was this Grand Pasha? I too, like the author, want the reader to come to a conclusion without any interference, so I cannot even translate his proper name into Turkish outright. Seeing that he is a pasha, we might think of him as a great statesman, or a great soldier, or else simply as someone who has achieved high rank. From the logical nature of his discourse, we might assume that he is a philosopher or a lofty personage who has achieved a certain kind of wisdom that we sense in certain people who place the interests of the nation and the country above themselves, which is a recurrent phenomenon among us Turks. All night long, the Grand Pasha holds forth, and He listens. Here is the Grand Pasha's logic and the words which strike Him speechless:

1. Like everyone else, I too knew at once that you are Him (the Grand Pasha begins to speak). Knowing this didn't depend on my consulting oracles concerning you, or signs in the heavens and in the Koran, or the secrets in letters and numbers—as has been the custom for hundreds and thousands of years. I knew you were Him the moment I saw the joy and the thrill of

victory in the faces of the multitude. Now they expect you to obliterate their pains and sorrows, restore their lost hopes, and lead them on to victory. But can you do it? Hundreds of years ago, Muhammad was able to provide happiness for the unfortunate because his sword opened the way for them to rush from victory to victory. Today, on the other hand, no matter what strength our faith has, the enemies of Islam possess more powerful weapons. No chance of a military victory! Can this fact be better illustrated than in the case of some false Messiahs who have claimed to be Him and managed to make things very difficult for the English and the French in India and Africa for a brief period, only to be completely crushed and annihilated themselves, thereby leading the people to greater catastrophe? (These pages abound with military and economic comparisons that demonstrate why a massive victory over the West has to be dismissed as a mere fantasy, not only for Islam, but for the East as a whole. The Grand Pasha compares the levels of wealth in the West to the poverty of the East with the honesty of a realistic statesman. And He, because He is He and not a fake, quietly and sadly confirms the depressing prospects as they are delineated.)

2. And yet (the Grand Pasha continues in the wee hours of the morning), it does not mean that no hope of victory can be provided for the unfortunate. We cannot fight only against "external" enemies. What about foes that are internal? Might it not be that the authors of all our poverty and suffering are the sinners, the usurers, the vampires, and the sadists amongst us who palm themselves off as ordinary citizens? You do see, don't you, that you can give the hope of victory and happiness to your unfortunate brethren only by waging war against the enemy inside? Then you must have also realized that yours is not a war that can be fought through the agency of gallant warriors, the champions of Islam; it must be fought under the auspices of informers, torturers, executioners, and the police. The hopeless have to be presented with the criminal responsible for their misery so that they can believe that his defeat will render heaven on earth possible. That is all we have been able to do for the last three hundred years. In order to give them hope, we reveal to our brothers the criminals among them. And they believe us, for they are as hungry for hope as they are for bread. Before these criminals are sentenced, the smartest and the straightest among them, those who understand why they are being condemned, admit to more crimes, exaggerating even the smallest, so that hope can be stirred all the more in their unfortunate brothers' hearts. We even pardon some who join us in hunting down the criminal element. Like the Koran, hope supports not so much our spiritual lives as our material existence: we expect to receive hope and freedom from the same source that provides us with our daily bread.

3. I know that you have the resolve to accomplish all the difficult tasks that are put before you, the sense of justice to pluck the criminals out of the crowd without batting an eyelash, and the strength to put them through torture, even though unwillingly, and rise above it all: after all, you are Him. But for how long can you expect hope to distract the multitudes? They are bound to catch on all too soon that things are not getting any better. When they see that their slice of bread is getting no larger, the hope they have been offered will begin to diminish. Once more they will lose their trust in the Book and their faith in both worlds; they will surrender themselves to the depression, immorality, and spiritual poverty of the life they led yesterday. Worst of all, they will begin to suspect you, even to hate you. The informers will begin to feel guilty about the criminals they've willingly handed over to your executioners and your diligent torturers; the police and the guards will become so sick of the vapidity of the torture they have perpetrated that neither the latest methods nor the hope you have offered will keep them distracted; they will end up by becoming convinced that the unfortunates who were hung from the gallows like bunches of grapes have been sacrificed in vain. You must have already realized that on Judgment Day they will believe neither you nor the stories you tell them; and when there remains no single story that they can all believe in collectively, then they will begin believing their own private fictions; everyone will have his own story which he will want to tell. Millions of wretches, wearing their tales like haloes of woe around their heads, will stumble dolorously like somnambulists on dirty city streets and on muddy squares that never seem to get tidied up. Then, in their eyes, you will be the Dadjdjal, and the Dadjdjal, you! Now they will want to put their faith in Dadjdjal's tales, and not in yours anymore. Returning in glory, Dadjdjal will either be me, or else someone like me. And he will tell them that you have been fooling them for all these years, that it was not hope that you infected them with but lies, that you had been Dadjdjal all along and not Him. Perhaps there will be no need for all this. At midnight some night, in a dark alley, either Dadjdjal himself or some unfortunate who has come to the conclusion that you had deceived him for too long will empty his gun into your mortal body which was once supposed to be bulletproof. That is how, because you offered them hope and deceived them all these years, they will find your body some night on a dirty sidewalk, in one of those muddy streets that you had come to know and cherish.

Chapter Fifteen

LOVE TALES ON
A SNOWY NIGHT

. . . idle men and the like, who seek stories and fairy tales . . . —RUMI

The next time he saw the man with whom he'd shared the cab, the one who looked like a character from a black-and-white film, Galip had just left Türkan Şoray's look-alike's room. He was standing in front of the Beyoğlu police station, unable to decide which way to go, when a squad car with its flashing blue light suddenly came around the corner and pulled to a stop at the curb. He at once recognized the man who came out of the rear door, which was flung open in a hurry; the man's face had exchanged the look of black-and-white films for the vivid dark blue colors that befit the night and crime. An officer preceded him out of the car, a second officer followed. One of them carried the man's briefcase. In the brilliant light that flooded the façade of the police station, safeguarding it against unexpected attacks, a dark red bloodstain appeared at the corner of the man's mouth, but he did not wipe it off. He walked with resignation, his head down like someone who'd owned up to his crime, but he also seemed to be terribly pleased with himself. When he caught sight of Galip standing in front of the station steps, he gave him a satisfied look for a moment that was odd and scary.

"Good evening, sir!"

"Good evening," Galip said diffidently.

"Who's he?" said one of the cops, pointing at Galip.

Galip couldn't hear the rest of the conversation as they pushed and shoved the man into the station house.

When he got to the main drag, it was a little after midnight; there still were people on the snowy sidewalks. "On one of the streets parallel to the British Consulate," Galip thought to himself, "there's supposed to be an all-night place frequented not only by the nouveau riche who arrive from Anatolia to throw their money around, but by the intellectuals as well!" It was Rüya who gleaned this kind of information from artsy magazines which mention such places using language that's supposed to be sarcastic.

In front of the old building that once housed the Tokatlıyan Hotel, Galip ran into İskender. His breath betrayed the fact that he'd had plenty of *rakı:* he'd picked up the BBC television crew at the Pera Palas Hotel, given them the thousand-and-one-nights tour of Istanbul (dogs on garbage patrol, dope and rug dealers, potbellied belly dancers, nightclub hooligans, etc.), then he'd taken them to a club on one of the back streets. There, an odd-looking man with a briefcase had started a squabble over an incomprehensible word, not with his party but with some others; the cops had arrived and nabbed the man, one of the patrons had climbed out of a window to escape; then people around the place had come to sit at their table, and so, it had shaped up to be a fun evening which Galip could join in if he wished. Galip walked up and down Beyoğlu with İskender who was out looking for unfiltered cigarettes, then accompanied him into the club, which had a sign, NIGHT-CLUB, on the door.

Galip was met with noise, merriment, and indifference. One of the British journalists, a good-looking woman, was telling a story. The classical Turkish music ensemble had stopped playing, the magician had begun his number by taking boxes out of boxes out of boxes. His assistant had bow legs and, just below her navel, the scar of a C-section. Galip mused that the woman didn't seem capable of giving birth to any child other than the sleepy rabbit she held in her hands. After performing the Vanishing Radio Trick cribbed from Zati Sungur, the legendary Turkish illusionist, the magician once more began taking boxes out of more boxes, losing the audience.

As the beautiful Englishwoman who sat at the other end of the table told her story, İskender translated it into Turkish. Galip listened to the story, optimistically assuming that he could figure out the gist of it from the woman's expressive face, although he'd missed the beginning. The rest of the story revealed that a woman (Galip thought it must be the same woman who was telling the story) had tried to convince a man, who had known and loved her since she was nine, to believe in a self-evident truth, a distinct sign on a Byzantine coin found by a diver, but that the man could not see anything besides his love for the woman, that his eyes were blind to the magic that they both beheld, and that all he could do was write poems inspired by the ardor of his love. "So, on account of a Byzantine coin a diver found on the ocean floor," İskender said, rendering the woman's story into Turkish, "the two cousins were married at last. But whereas the woman's life was changed completely through her belief in the magical face she saw on the coin, the man didn't get any of it." For this reason, the woman was supposed to have spent the rest of her days alone, shut up in a tower. (Galip imagined the woman had left the guy in the lurch.) When it was understood that the tale had come to an end, the "humane" silence respectful of "human sentiments" affected by the listeners who sat at the long table struck Galip as stupid. Perhaps he couldn't expect everyone to be as pleased as he was because a beautiful woman had dumped some dumb guy, but although he'd heard only half of it, the bathetic ending of the story (with all of them entering the idiotic and pretentious silence that follows such highfalutin language) was patently ridiculous. The whole scene was ridiculous, aside from the woman's beauty. Galip thought he might downgrade the storyteller's charms to merely attractive but not beautiful.

Galip caught İskender's drift that the tall man who started yet another story was a writer whose name he'd previously heard bandied about. The bespectacled writer warned his audience that since his account concerned another writer, the identity of the protagonist must not be confused with his own. Observing the odd way the writer smiled as he spoke, his countenance somewhat embarrassed and somewhat currying favor with the company, Galip could not nail down the writer's motivation.

According to the narrative, this guy wrote stories and novels (which he showed no one, or, if he did, he would not publish) cooped up in his house for many a year. He had surrendered himself so obsessively to his profession (which could not even be called a profession back then), it had become a kind of habit. It wasn't because he was a misanthrope, or because he was critical of others' lives that he was not seen in company, but because he could not drag himself away from his desk where he wrote behind closed doors. Having spent so much of his life at his desk, the writer's "social skills" were so atrophied that when he stepped out once in a blue moon, he was totally bewildered by social intercourse and retreated to a corner where he waited for the hour he could return to his desk. After spending more than fourteen hours working, he would get into bed toward dawn as the calls to early prayer were repeated on the minarets and echoed against the hills, and he would dream of his sweetheart whom he saw only once a year, and then only accidentally. Yet he did not dream of this woman with the passion or the sexual desire that other people talk about, but with yearning for an imaginary companion, the only antidote for his loneliness.

Some years later, as it turned out, this writer, who admitted to knowing about love only through books and not being all that crazy about sex either, ended up marrying an extraordinarily beautiful woman. Much like the publication of his work, which also happened around then, his marriage did not manage to change his life. He still spent fourteen hours a day at his desk, slowly constructing sentences for his stories just as patiently as he had before, and imagining details for new work as he stared at the blank sheets of paper on his desk. The only change in his life happened to be the correspondence he felt between the dreams his silent and beautiful wife was dreaming when he came to bed just before dawn and the daydreams he habitually constructed as he listened to the call to morning prayer. Now, when he lay down to daydream next to his wife, the writer had a sense that there was a connection between his and his wife's dreams, not unlike the harmony unconsciously established in their breathing that was reminiscent of notes going up and down in a modest piece of music. The writer was pleased with his new life, and it wasn't difficult for him to fall asleep next to someone after so many years of solitude; he liked listening to his beautiful wife's breathing as he fetched up his own dreams, liked believing that their dreams were indeed tangled together.

When his wife left him on a winter's day without giving a substantial excuse, the writer was in for some bad times. He just could not come up with any dreams as in the old days when he lay in bed listening to the summons to early prayer. The tales which he had so easily constructed and which had culminated in peaceful sleep before and during his marriage could no longer achieve the level of "credibility" or "brilliance" that he desired. Aside from not being content with the novel he was writing, there seemed to be an inadequacy and indecisiveness that would not surrender its secret in his dreams and left the writer stranded, at a dead end. When his wife first left him, his daydreams were in such an abysmal state that he could not fall asleep even after the summons to early prayer, nor until long after the first birds sang in the trees, the seagulls left the rooftops where they collectively spent the night, the garbage truck went by and then the first municipal bus. What's worse, the deficiency in his dreams and sleep also dogged him in the pages he attempted to write. The writer was aware that he could not put any snap into the simplest of sentences, not even if he wrote it over twenty times.

The writer struggled to beat the depression that invaded his whole world; he put himself under strict discipline, forcing himself to remember all his erstwhile dreams in turn so that he might, perchance, rediscover their harmony. After many weeks, having finally succeeded in falling asleep peacefully while he listened to the call to prayer, he woke up, went to his desk like a somnambulist, and realized that his depression was over when he began writing sentences with the attendant beauty and vividness that he had so desired; he was also aware of the small trick he had unconsciously invented in order to achieve this end.

The person whose wife had left him, that is, the writer who could no longer invent tales to his heart's content, began imagining his old self, the self that did not share his bed with anyone, whose dreams were not entangled in any beautiful woman's dreams. He conjured up the persona he had abandoned with such force and intensity that he became the persona he envisioned and was thereby able to fall into a peaceful sleep dreaming that person's dreams. Since he was soon able to adjust to this double life, he no longer had to force himself to dream or to write. Having assumed the identity of his former self, he became someone else when he wrote, filling the ashtray with the same butts, having coffee in the same coffeecup, sleeping peacefully at the same time, in the same bed, as his own ghost.

When one day his wife returned to him ("home," as the woman put it), again without giving any substantial excuse, the writer was once more in for some bad times, which didn't sit well with him. The same uncertainty that had cropped up in his dreams when he had initially been forsaken pervaded his entire existence once more. After having the devil of a time falling asleep, he would be awakened by nightmares, restlessly going back and forth between his old self and the new, wavering between the two, aimless as a drunk who cannot find his way back home. After one sleepless morning, he got up with his pillow in his hand and went to his workroom that smelled of dust and papers, and there curled up on the small sofa beside his desk and papers and fell fast asleep. From that time on, the writer no longer lay next to his silent and mysterious wife, entangled in her dreams, but slept there, next to his desk and his papers. As soon as he got up, somewhere between sleep and wakefulness, he sat at his desk and was at ease writing stories that seemed to be the continuation of his dreams; but now he had another problem that scared him stiff.

Before his wife had left him, he'd written a novel on the subject of a pair of look-alikes who had exchanged lives, a book that was considered by his readers to be "historical." When the writer played the role of his old self so that he could sleep and write, he became the author of the aforementioned novel and, since he could experience neither his own future nor that of his ghost, he found himself writing again the same old story about the "look-alikes" with all the same enthusiasm as before! After a while, this world, in which everything imitated everything else—where all the stories and the people were simultaneously themselves and their own imitations, and where all stories alluded to other stories—began to look so real to the writer that, thinking no one would swallow stories that had been written with such "obvious" realism, he decided to seek out an irreal world which might provide him with pleasure in writing of it and his readers with pleasure in falling for it. To this end, while his beautiful, mysterious wife quietly slept in the bed, the writer haunted dark streets in the city at midnight, districts where street-lights had been smashed, underground passages inherited from Byzantium, taverns, nightclubs, and opium dens where pathetic people hang out. What he had seen up to now had taught him that life in "our city" was as real as it was in an imagined world: this fact alone confirmed that the universe was indeed a book. He was so stuck on reading this book of life, gadding about here and there, walking the streets for hours where the city offered him each day new pages in which to read faces, signs, and stories, that he was now afraid that he'd return neither to his beautiful wife fast asleep in her bed, nor to the story that he'd left half told.

Since the writer's story dealt with loneliness rather than love, and told about storytelling rather than telling a story, it left the audience cold. Galip thought they must be particularly curious as to why the writer's wife had left him, seeing how everyone knows something about getting dumped inexplicably.

The next storyteller, who Galip thought must be one of the house B-girls, repeated several times that hers was a true story and wanted to be assured that "our tourist friends" got the point; she wanted her story to serve as an example not only for Turkey but for the entire world. It all began at this very club, not too long ago. Two cousins met each other here after many years and rekindled their childhood passion. Since the woman was a party girl and the guy a fancy man ("in other words," the woman said for the benefit of the tourists, "a pimp") there was no question of "honor" that might lead a guy in situations like this to take advantage of the girl, to "waste" her. Back then, there was peace and quiet in the nightclub, as in the country; young people weren't gunning for one another in the streets, but kissing and hugging and sending each other packages of real candy during the holidays rather than bombs. The girl and the boy were happy. The girl's father had suddenly died, so the young couple were able to live under the same roof, although they slept in separate beds, chafing for the day they would marry.

On their wedding day, while the girl and her fellow Beyoğlu party girls were busy getting all dolled up, putting on makeup and perfumes, the guy got his nuptial-day shave and strolled out on the main drag where he was captivated by a woman who was gorgeous beyond belief. The woman, who instantly robbed him of his reason, took him to her room in the Pera Palas Hotel where, after they made copious love, the luckless woman divulged that she was the bastard daughter of the Shah of Iran, sired on the Queen of England. She had come to Turkey to instigate the first phase of her master plan of revenge against her parents who'd abandoned the fruit of their one-night stand. What she wanted from the young man was for him to get hold of a map, half of which was being held by the National Bureau of Security and the other half by the Secret Police.

Inflamed by passion, the young man begged for her permission to leave and hurried off to the hall where the wedding was to take place; the guests had already drifted away but the girl was still weeping in the corner. He consoled her first and then confessed that he'd been recruited in the interests of a "national cause." They put off their nuptials, and they sent out word to all the party girls, belly dancers, madams, and Sulukule gypsies that each and every cop who'd fallen prey to the dens of iniquity throughout Istanbul was to be pumped for information. When they finally got hold of the two halves of the map and put it together, the girl also put it together that her cousin had pulled a fast one on her, as well as on all the industrious working girls in Istanbul: he was really in love with the daughter of the Queen of England and the Shah of Iran. She hid the map in the left cup of her bra and holed up in a room where she exiled herself in her sorrow, at a brothel in Kuledibi frequented only by the cheapest whores and the worst perverts.

The shrewish princess ordered the boy cousin to go through Istanbul with a fine-tooth comb and get that map. As he conducted the search, he finally understood that he loved, not the instigator of the hunt, but the hunted one, not just any woman but the beloved, not the princess but his childhood love. He finally tracked her down to the brothel in Kuledibi, and when he observed through a peephole in a mirror his childhood love do an "innocent girl" number on a rich guy with a bow tie, he broke in and saved the girl. A huge mole appeared on his eye, the same eye he'd fitted to the peephole and thereby broken his heart (from watching his half-naked sweetheart joyfully playing the flute), and it would not go away. The identical mark of love also appeared under the girl's left breast. When they got the police to raid the virago's room at the Pera Palas to apprehend her, in her dresser drawers they found butt-naked photos of thousands of innocent young men who'd been enticed by the man-eating princess into having their pictures taken in various positions for her "political" blackmail collection. There were also mug shots of terrorists, manifestos stamped with the hammer and sickle, various political books and pamphlets, the will of the last sultan, who was a "queer," and the master plan to carve up Turkey, which had been marked by the Byzantine Cross. The Secret Police knew all too well that it was this broad who was responsible for importing into the country the plague of terrorism, as if it were the French plague of syphilis, but since her collection contained innumerable photos of the members of the police force, wearing only their birthday suits and their "nightsticks," her involvement was covered up, for fear that some journalists might get hold of the photos. The only news seen fit to print was the notice concerning the cousins' nuptials, along with their wedding picture. The B-girl pulled out of her purse the notice she'd personally clipped from the newspaper, in which she herself could be seen wearing her snazzy coat with the fox collar and the same pearl earrings she wore this very minute, and she wanted it passed around the table.

Seeing that her story was received with some skepticism and, at times, with outright ridicule, the woman became cross and, saying her account was true, she called out to someone: the photographer who'd taken the innumerable dirty pictures showing the princess with her victims happened to be on the premises. The gray-haired photographer approached the table, and when the woman told him that in return for a good love story "our guests" would be happy to have their pictures taken, and compensate him liberally, the elderly photographer began to tell a story.

Some thirty-odd years ago, a manservant had stopped by his tiny studio to summon him to a house in the posh quarter of Şişli on the streetcar route. Since he had made his mark as a nightclub photographer, as he went up to the house he wondered why he'd been chosen for the job when, in his opinion, another colleague of his was more appropriate for upper-class shindigs. There, a young and good-looking widow invited our photographer in and proposed a deal: in return for a sizable bit of cash, she wanted him to drop off in the morning copies of the hundreds of photos he snapped at the Beyoğlu clubs every night.

The photographer, suspecting that there was some love entanglement behind this deal that he'd accepted somewhat out of curiosity, decided to keep an eye on the brown-haired woman, who had slightly crossed eyes, as best he could. After a couple of years, he realized the woman was not looking for the picture of a particular man she'd known or whose picture she'd seen before; neither the faces nor the ages of the men she chose from the hundreds she sifted through and wanted to see blown up or shown from other vantage points, were ever the same. In time the woman, having become familiar by virtue of their joint venture and more trusting by virtue of their shared secret, began to confide in the photographer.

"It's useless to bring me the photos of these vacant faces, these blank looks, these expressionless visages," she said. "I cannot make them out; I cannot see any letters anywhere in their faces!" The vague meanings she could hardly *read* (she used this word insistently) in other exposures of the same face always left her disappointed, leading her to say: "If this is all we can get at the nightclubs frequented by the melancholic and the depressed, my God, how blank, how vacant their faces must be when they are at their places of business, behind store counters, sitting at office desks!"

Yet it wasn't as if they had not run into a couple of specimens that gave them both some hope. Once, the woman read a meaning that she dwelled on for some time in the terribly wrinkled face of an old man who, as they discovered later, was a jeweler, but the meaning was very ancient and quite stagnant. The wrinkles on his forehead and the abundance of letters under his eyes were nothing more than the final refrain of an obscure meaning that shed no light on the present but kept on repeating itself. Three years later they came across a face alive with muscular letters that did signify, they discovered, the meanings of the day. Excited by the stormy face, they had enlarged the photograph and soon learned that the subject was an accountant. On a dark morning, the woman showed the photographer a huge picture of the man that had appeared in all the papers with headlines like HE BILKED BANK OF TWENTY MILLIONS. Now that his fling with crime and transgression was over, the accountant's relaxed face stared peacefully at the reader, as vacant as the henna-dyed face of a sacrificial sheep.

The listeners had already decided, of course, whispering among themselves and signaling with their eyes and eyebrows, that the real love story was the one between the woman and the photographer, but at the end the hero turned out to be someone entirely different: one cool summer morning, the moment the woman clapped eyes on that incredible, brilliant face among all the meaningless faces in a photo of a crowded table at a nightclub, she realized that the search she had conducted for the past ten years had not been in vain. A very plain, simple, and clear meaning could be read in all the subsequent photos of that young and fabulous face, easily taken at the nightclub that very same night and enlarged: it was LOVE. The woman could read the four letters of the new Latin alphabet so effortlessly in the open and clear face of the thirty-three-year-old man, who as they found out later repaired watches in a small shop in Karagümrük, that she snapped at the photographer when he said he couldn't make out any of the letters that he must be blind. She spent the following days trembling like a prospective bride being shown to matchmakers, already suffering like a lover who knows in the beginning that she's slated for defeat, and splitting hairs as she imagined the possibility of happiness when she sensed the smallest flicker of hope. Within a week, the woman's salon was plastered all over with hundreds of photos of the watch repairman, who had been tricked under various pretexts into having his picture taken many times.

When the watch repairman with the incredible face stopped showing up at the club the night after the photographer managed to get closeups which showed him in more detail, the woman went berserk. She sent the photographer after the repairman in Karagümrük, but the man could not be found at his shop nor at his house pointed out by the neighbors. When he went back a week later, the shop was up for sale "as a going concern" and the house had been vacated. The woman was no longer interested in the photos the photographer brought from then on "for love"; she refused even to glance at intriguing faces other than the watch repairman's. One of those windy mornings when autumn arrives early, he showed up at the woman's door armed with a "piece" that he thought might pique her interest, only to be greeted by the nosy doorman who was pleased to tell him that the lady had moved to an undisclosed address. The photographer was sad that the story had come to an end—he had to confess to his listeners that he was indeed in love with the woman—but he told himself at the time that now he could perhaps embark on his own story, one he would construct by remembering the past.

But the real end of the story came many years later when he was absent-mindedly reading a picture caption: "She Doused His Face with Nitric Acid!" Neither the name, the face, nor the age of the jealous woman armed with nitric acid was consistent with the lady who lived in Şişli, and the husband whose face got splashed with nitric acid was not a watch repairman but a public prosecutor in the Central Anatolian town where the news had originated. Nevertheless, although none of the details jibed with the characteristics of either his dream woman or the handsome watch repairman, the moment he saw the words "nitric acid" our photographer had intuited that this couple was none other than "them," and he figured out that they'd been together all these years, that he'd been part of their game plan to elope, and that they'd used the ploy to eliminate many an unhappy fellow like himself who came between them. He realized how right he was when he bought another scandal sheet that day and saw the watch repairman's face which, having completely melted away, had been altogether relieved of any letters and meaning.

The photographer, who could see that the story he had told while looking expressly at the foreign journalists was received with approval and interest, offered up a final detail, as if imparting a military secret that would crown his victory: the same scandal sheet had printed the same melted face (once again, many years later), claiming that it was the picture of the last victim of a Middle East war that had gone on much too long, with the following caption: "As they say, all is for love, after all."

The company at the table was pleased to pose for the photographer. Among them were a couple of journalists and an adman Galip knew slightly, along with a bald-headed man who looked familiar and several foreigners who sat gingerly at one end. The sort of fortuitous friendship and curiosity that forms among people who share an inn for a night or a small accident had also developed at the table. Since most of the patrons had left, the club had become quiet, and the stage lights had been turned off some time ago.

Galip had a feeling the club might have been the actual location of *My Disorderly Babe* in which Türkan Şoray had played a call girl; so he put the question to the elderly waiter whom he'd summoned to the table. The waiter, perhaps because everyone had turned toward him, or else spurred on by the stories he'd been overhearing, told a brief story himself.

No, his story didn't concern the movie that was mentioned but another, older movie that had been filmed at this very club in which he'd watched himself fourteen times during the week it played at the Rüya Theater. Since both the producer and the beautiful woman who played the lead had requested that he take part in a couple of the scenes, the waiter had been happy to oblige. When he saw the movie several months later, he recognized his face and his hands as his own, but his back, shoulders, and neck in another scene belonged to someone else; each time he watched the film, the waiter, though spooked by this, also tingled with an odd pleasure. What's more, he could not get used to hearing someone else's voice come out of his own mouth, a voice that he was to hear again in many other films. His friends and relations who saw the film were not as interested as he was in the hair-raising, mind-boggling, dreamlike substitutions, nor were they aware of any trick photography. Even more important, they never knew that a small trick could fool one into believing that one was someone else, or that someone else was oneself.

The waiter had waited in vain for years, hoping they'd show the film in which he appeared briefly when they played double features at the Beyoğlu theaters during the summer months. Had he been able to see the film once more, he believed he could have embarked on a new life, not because he would again meet himself as a young man but because of the other "obvious" reason that his friends didn't comprehend but would be comprehensible to the distinguished company present.

The subject of "the obvious reason" was discussed extensively behind the waiter's back. For most, the reason was, of course, love; the waiter was in love with himself, or with the world he saw in himself, or else with the "art of the cinema." The B-girl put the kibosh on the subject by saying the waiter, like all ex-wrestlers, was nothing but a fag, seeing how he had been caught stark naked abusing himself looking in the mirror, as well as putting the pinch on the bus boys in the kitchen.

The bald-headed man who looked familiar to Galip opposed the B-girl's "unfounded allegation" against our wrestlers who practice the sport of our ancestors and began recounting his own observations concerning the exemplary family lives of these exceptional people he had once followed closely during his stay in Thrace. In the meantime, İskender clued Galip in as to who the old guy was: he had run into this bald man in the lobby of the Pera Palas Hotel at the height of the commotion when İskender was tearing out his hair trying to make an itinerary for the British journalists and hoping to locate Jelal—yes, it was possible that he'd called Galip that same evening. The old guy had joined in the quest saying that he knew Jelal, and that he also needed to find him for a personal reason. In the days that followed, he'd cropped up here and there, not only in search of Jelal but also to help him and the British journalists with small details thanks to his large circle of influence (he was a retired army officer). The guy got a real kick out of putting his limited English into use. Obviously, he was the sort of retiree who wanted to do something useful for the country with his time; he liked making friends and knew Istanbul quite well. After he got through talking about the Thracian wrestlers, the old guy began to narrate his own story.

Actually, it was more of a conundrum than a story: an old shepherd comes home at midday in pursuit of his flock which, on account of an eclipse of the sun, make for home on their own; so, after securing the sheep in the pen, he goes in the house only to find his beloved wife in bed with her lover. After a moment of hesitation, he gets hold of a knife and kills them both. He gives himself up, and he defends himself in front of the judge, putting forth a logic that sounds simple when he says that he didn't kill his wife and her lover but some unknown woman and her paramour whom he'd caught in his own bed. Since it was impossible for the "woman" whom he knew, trusted, and with whom he cohabitated lovingly for many years, to do this to "him," both the woman in the bed and he "himself" were two other people. The shepherd had no trouble believing this astounding substitution, seeing how the supernatural omen of the eclipse had bolstered his conviction. Naturally, the shepherd was ready to take the rap for the other self he remembered assuming momentarily, but he wanted the man and the woman he killed in his own bed to be considered a pair of thieves who'd broken into his house and shamelessly took advantage of his bed. After he did his time, no matter how long, he intended to set out on the road in search of his wife whom he hadn't seen since the day of the eclipse; once he found her, and perhaps with her help, he would begin to look for his own lost self.

So, what was the punishment the judge meted out to the shepherd?

Galip listened to the solutions the company offered the retired colonel, thinking he had read or heard this old chestnut somewhere before but he just couldn't remember where. As he examined one of the pictures the photographer had developed and handed out to the company, he thought for a moment that he would be able to remember just how it was that he knew the bald man and his story; he felt as if he'd then be able to inform the man of his real identity and that, just at that moment, the mystery of another illegible face would also be solved as it was in the photographer's story about faces. When his turn came, while Galip concluded that it was necessary for the judge to forgive the shepherd, he was also considering that he might have solved the hidden meaning in the retired colonel's face: it was as if the retired soldier had been one person when he began to tell his story, and when he finished it, he was another. What had happened to him as he told the story? What had changed him when he was through telling it?

Taking his turn to tell a story, Galip began an account which he said he had heard from a columnist, concerning the obsession of an elderly newsman who was single. This fellow had spent his entire life working for the Babıali dailies, doing translations for magazines, and writing film and theater criticism. Since he was interested in women's wear and jewelry rather than the women themselves, he had never married. He lived in a small two-room apartment on a backstreet in Beyoğlu, keeping company only with his tabby, who seemed even older and lonelier than himself. The only rub in his uneventful life was toward the end when he began reading Marcel Proust's seemingly endless book in search of time past.

The elderly journalist loved the book so much that for a long time he didn't want to talk about anything else, but not only was he unable to find someone willing to invest himself as he had in the struggle to read all those beloved volumes in French, he didn't even chance upon someone with whom to share his zeal. As a result, he became introverted and began retelling himself all the stories and the scenes in those volumes that he had read so many times that he'd lost count. All day long, whenever he met with adversity, or had to put up with rudeness and ruthlessness from unfeeling, unrefined, and greedy people whose sort also tended to be "uncultured" as well, he said to himself, "I am not here; I am at home now, in my bedroom, and I am thinking of my Albertine sleeping, or waking, in the next room, or else I am listening with pleasure and joy to Albertine's soft and gentle footsteps padding around the apartment!" Whenever he was walking, out on the street, and feeling miserable, he imagined, like the narrator in Proust's novel, that a beautiful young woman was waiting at home, that Albertine, even a casual meeting with whom he would have once considered a great happiness, was waiting for him, and he fantasized about Albertine's movements while she waited. When the elderly journalist returned to his two rooms where the stove never put out enough heat, he would remember with sorrow other pages in which Albertine left Proust, internalizing the feeling of sadness that pervaded the forsaken rooms, and he would keep on recollecting things, as if he were both Proust and also his mistress Albertine: how it was just here that he and Albertine talked, laughing together; how she would visit him only after ringing the bell; his own endless fits of jealousy; the dreams of the trip to Venice that they'd take together—until tears of joy and sorrow flowed out of his eyes.

On Sunday mornings, spent in the company of his tabby cat, when he was irritated with the coarse stories published by the paper, or remembered the words of ridicule spoken by curious neighbors, insensitive distant relatives, and sharp-tongued rude children, he'd pretend he had found a ring in a compartment in his old chest, imagining it was the ring Albertine had left behind which his maid Françoise had found in a drawer in the rosewood desk; and then, turning to the imaginary maid, "No, Françoise," he'd say loud enough for only the tabby to hear, "Albertine did not forget it; returning the ring would be futile, since Albertine will soon be coming back."

What a pathetic and miserable country we live in, the old journalist reflected, where no one has come upon Albertine or knows Proust. The day someone who can understand Proust and Albertine appears will be the day, yes, when those poor mustachioed fellows in the street can perhaps begin to live better lives; perhaps then, instead of knifing each other at the first hint of jealousy, they too, like Proust, will reflect on reveries in which they bring to life the images of their lovers. All those writers and translators, who were given work at the newspapers since they were supposed to be literate, were as mean and obtuse as they were because they did not read Proust, did not know Albertine, and had no idea that the old journalist had read Proust, nor comprehended that he was personally both Proust and Albertine.

The astonishing aspect of the story was not the fact that the old journalist considered himself the hero of a novel or its author; after all, any Turk who passionately loves a masterpiece from the West which remains unread by his compatriots begins after a while to believe in all sincerity that not only does he love reading the book, but that he has written it himself. Eventually, this person will end up despising the people around him, not only because they have not read the book but because they have not written a book of the same caliber as his. That's why the surprising thing was not the fact that the old journalist had considered himself Proust or Albertine for a long time, but that he had one day divulged the secret he'd kept to himself all these years to a young columnist.

It was perhaps because the old journalist had a very special feeling for the young columnist that he could confide in him; the young fellow possessed a beauty that was reminiscent of Proust and Albertine: he had the bud of a mustache on his upper lip, a strong and classical build, nice hips, long lashes, and, like Proust and Albertine, he was dark and somewhat short in stature; his silky soft skin had the shimmer of a Pakistani's complexion. But the similarities ended there. The young and beautiful columnist, whose taste for European literature didn't go beyond Paul de Kock and Pitigrilli, laughed uproariously when he first heard the tale of the old journalist's secret love; then he announced that he would use this interesting account in one of his columns.

Realizing his mistake, the old journalist begged his young and beautiful colleague to forget everything, but the other turned a deaf ear and kept right on laughing. Once the old journalist returned home, he knew at once that his whole world had been demolished: in his deserted rooms he could imagine neither Proust's jealousies, nor the time he spent with Albertine, nor even where Albertine had gone. That magical love that he alone lived and breathed in all of Istanbul, that sublime love that was his only source of pride and which no one could ever besmirch, was soon to be coarsely related to hundreds of obtuse readers in a way that would be like raping Albertine whom he'd worshipped all these years. The old journalist just wanted to die, thinking that Albertine's name—the beautiful name that belonged to dear Albertine whom he loved so much, for whom he could die of jealousy, whose leaving destroyed him, and the sight of whom he could never, ever forget since the time that he first saw her riding a bicycle in Balbec—would be printed on pieces of newspaper which dumb readers, who never read of anything besides the ex-prime minister's larcenies and the mistakes in the latest radio programs, would then spread under garbage pails or under fish to be cleaned.

It was this notion that gave him the courage and determination to phone the columnist with the silken complexion and the bud of a mustache, and explaining that "only but only" he could comprehend such a special but uncurable love, this human condition, his abject and boundless jealousy, he begged him never to touch on the subject of Proust or Albertine in any of his columns. "Besides," he added with fortitude, "you haven't even read Marcel Proust's masterpiece!" "Whose what masterpiece?" asked the young man, who had already forgotten about the subject and the old journalist's obsession. So the old man retold his story, and the insouciant young columnist once again shrieked with laughter, saying gleefully that yes, yes, it was the very story that he should write. He might have even been under the impression that the old guy actually wanted the subject ventilated.

And he went ahead and wrote it. In the column that was something like a short story, the old journalist was characterized much as in the account you have heard: a pitiful, lonely old man from Istanbul who falls in love with a weird novel from the West, imagining that he is both the heroine and the author of the book. The old journalist in the story has a tabby cat just like the real old journalist's. The old journalist in the story is also shaken to see himself being ridiculed in a newspaper column. In the story within the story that was being told, the old journalist also wants to die upon seeing Albertine's and Proust's names in the paper. Lonely newsmen, Albertines, and Prousts in the story within the story within the story kept reappearing in infinite regression out of one bottomless well after another in the old writer's nightmares during the last, unhappy nights of his life. When he woke from his nightmares at midnight, the old writer could no longer have the happiness of a love no one knew about. When his door was broken down three days after the publication of the cruel column, it was discovered that the old journalist had quietly died in his sleep, asphyxiated by the smoke that leaked from the stove that had refused to put out any heat. The tabby had not been fed in three days, but she still hadn't mustered up the courage to chew on her master.

Despite its sadness, Galip's story had cheered his audience by virtue of drawing them together. Several people, some of whom were foreign journalists, got up to dance with the party girls to the music that came from an invisible radio, laughing and enjoying themselves until it was time to close the place.

Chapter Sixteen

I MUST BE MYSELF

If you wanted to be cheerful, or melancholic, or wistful, or thoughtful, or courteous, you simply had to act those things with every gesture.
—PATRICIA HIGHSMITH, *The Talented Mr. Ripley*

Some time back I remembered a metaphysical experiment that befell me twenty-six years ago on a winter's night and which I related briefly in these columns. It must be ten or twelve years ago, I can't be sure (these days when my memory is really shot, the "secret archives" I keep on hand unfortunately aren't available for reference), but when I wrote on the subject, it brought on piles of letters. Among the letters from my readers, irate that I hadn't written the sort of column they'd come to expect from me (why hadn't I discussed national concerns, why hadn't I described the sadness of Istanbul streets in the rain), there was one from a reader who had "intuited" that I was of the same opinion as himself on a "very important matter." He divulged that he'd soon pay me a visit and put to me questions concerning some "special" and "deep" subjects on which, he believed, we were in agreement.

Just as I was about to write off this reader—who was a barber (this was odd in itself)—he turned up for real one afternoon. I had no time for him. Besides, I thought the barber might go on and on about his troubles and give me grief for not giving enough space to his endless woes in my column. Just to get rid of him, I told him to come back another time. He reminded me that he'd written that he'd be coming; on top of that, he had no time for "another time"; he had only two questions, ones that I could answer at once, on my feet. Pleased that the barber approached the subject so directly, I told him to ask away.

"Do you have difficulty being yourself?"

Expecting something strange, a joke we could share later—that an entertainment was about to break loose—a small crowd had gathered around my desk: younger journalists I'd taken under my wing, the loud and fat soccer correspondent who kept everyone in stitches. So, in answer to the question put to me, I came up with one of my "witticisms," which had come to be expected of me in situations like this. The barber, after listening to the putdown as if it were the very response he thought I would make, asked his second question.

"Is there a way a man can be only himself?"

This time he made his query as if he were inquiring on behalf of someone else and not to satisfy his own curiosity. Obviously he'd prepared the question ahead of time and committed it to memory. The effect of my initial joke was still in the air; and other people, hearing the merriment, had joined us. Under the circumstances, what could be more natural than nailing a second joke on the head instead of holding forth on the ontological question of man's being himself? On top of that, a second joke would aggrandize the first, making it even more impressive, turning it into an elegant story that could be repeated in my absence. After the second joke was cracked, which I cannot remember now, the barber said, "I just knew it!" and he left.

Since our people appreciate double entendres only if the second meaning is insulting or derogatory, I paid no attention to the barber's thin skin. I can even say that I looked down on him as I would on the enthusiastic reader who, upon recognizing your columnist in the public urinal, inquires, as he buttons up his fly, about the meaning of life or if yours truly has faith in God.

But as time went by . . . Misconstruing the half-finished sentence, the readers who think I regretted my insolence (that I thought the barber's question was moot, or that I even had nightmares about him one night and woke up with guilt feelings), those readers haven't yet come to know me. I didn't even think of the barber, except once. And the one time I did think of him, my chain of thought didn't start with the barber. What came to my mind was the continuum of an idea I'd first had years ago. In fact, at the beginning, it could hardly be called an idea. It was more like a refrain stuck in my mind since childhood which had suddenly surfaced in my ears—no, more like out of the depths of my soul: "I must be myself. I must be myself. I must be myself."

At the end of a day spent in crowds and among relatives and co-workers, before going to bed at midnight, I sat in the old armchair in the other room, my feet propped on a stool, as I smoked and stared at the ceiling. The incessant chatter of the people I listened to all day, their noise, their demands, had all come together into a single tone that reverberated like a nasty and tiresome headache, or even like a sinister toothache. The old refrain that I can't call an "idea" began at first in response to this reverberation like—how to say it—a countertone. To shield me from the relentless noise of the crowds, it offered up a reminder of the way to my inner voice, my own peace, my own happiness, and even my very own smell: "You must be yourself. You must be yourself. You must be yourself."

It was then at midnight that I realized how pleased I was to live far away from all the crowds and the muck of that revolting disorder which "they" (the imam sermonizing on Friday, teachers, my aunt, my father, politicians, all of them) consider "Life," desiring that I immerse myself, that we all immerse ourselves in it. I was so pleased to roam in the garden of my own dreams, and not in their plain and tasteless tales, that I even regarded my poor legs, stretched from the armchair to the stool, with affection, and I examined with tolerance my ugly hand that brought back and forth to my mouth the cigarette whose smoke I blew at the ceiling. For the first time in so many years I was able to be myself! For the first time in so many years I was able to love myself because I could be myself. Stronger than the refrain of the village idiot who repeats the same word as he goes by each stone along the wall of the mosque, more concentrated than the effort of an old passenger who counts the telegraph poles out of the window of a moving train, this feeling turned into a kind of force enveloping with its fury and impatience not only me but also the pitiful old room in which I sat—enveloping all "reality." It was with this force that I repeated these words, not as a refrain but with a felicitous anger.

I must be myself, I repeated, without paying any attention to them, their voices, smells, desires, their love, their hate. If I can't be myself, then I become who they want me to be, and I cannot bear the person they want me to be; and rather than be that intolerable person they want me to be, I thought, it would be better that I be nothing at all, or not be.

In my youth, when I visited my uncle's and my aunt's, I became the person who was thought of as someone who "works as a journalist, which is too bad, but he works hard at it, and if he keeps on working like this,

chances are he will succeed someday." And when, after working for years
to escape being that person, I entered as a grown man the apartment building
in which my father too lived now with his new wife, I became the person
who "worked hard and after many years was somewhat successful." And
what's worse, unable to see myself any other way, I let this person I didn't
like cling to my flesh like an ugly skin, and before long I caught myself
speaking not my own words but the words of this person; when I returned
home at night, just to torture myself I reminded myself of how I'd spoken
the words of this person I didn't care for, repeating trite sentences like "I
touched on this subject in my long article this week," "I considered this
problem in my latest Sunday article," "This coming Tuesday, I will delve
into that too, in my long article," until I thought I'd drown in my own
unhappiness—when, at last, I could be somewhat myself.

My entire life was full of these sorts of horrible memories. In the armchair
where I sat stretching my legs, I recalled the times, one by one, that I was
not myself, just to revel in my present state of selfhood.

I recalled how, just because my "comrades-in-arms" had decided on
the first day of my military service just what kind of a person I was, I'd
spent my entire army days as "someone who didn't give up joking around
even in the worst of times." Because I had once imagined that in the eyes
of the idle crowd who stood smoking during the five-minute intermission at
the trashy movies I then frequented—not to kill time but just to sit alone
in the dark—I must appear as "a valuable young man destined to do worth-
while work," I would behave, I remembered, as if I were "an absentminded
young man deep in meaningful, even sacred, contemplation." In those days
when we planned a military coup and were deeply involved in dreaming of
a future when we'd be at the helm of the state, I remember behaving like a
patriotic person who loved his people so greatly that he couldn't sleep nights,
lest the coup be delayed, thereby prolonging the suffering of the people. I
recalled how at the whorehouses I surreptitiously frequented, I pretended to
be a lovelorn soul who'd recently gone through a terrible and impossible
love affair because the whores gave such guys a better time. I'd walk by
police stations (in case I hadn't already had the presence of mind to change
sidewalks) trying to appear like an ordinary good citizen. I'd pretend to have
great fun playing bingo at my grandmother's, where I went just because I
didn't have the courage to spend New Year's Eve alone. I recalled how,
when talking to attractive women, instead of being myself I pretended to be
someone who thought of nothing but (assuming this was what they wanted)
matrimony and responsibility, or that I was someone who had no time for

anything but the struggle to save our country, or that I was a sensitive person sick and tired of the general lack of empathy and understanding in our land, or, to put it in banal terms, that I was a closet poet. And at the end (yes, at the very end), I recalled how at my barber's, where I went every two months, I was not myself but the impersonator of my self who was the subtotal of all these personages I impersonated.

Actually, I went to the barber's to loosen up (another barber, of course, than the one at the beginning). But as the barber and I looked in the mirror together, we saw there, along with the hair that was to be cut, this head that carries the hair, the shoulders, the trunk; and I sensed at once that the person whom we watched in the mirror sitting in the chair was not "I" but somebody else. This head that the barber held in his hands as he asked, "How much off the front?", the neck that carried the head, the shoulders, and the trunk weren't mine, but belonged to Jelal Bey, Columnist. I had indeed no connection to this man! Such an obvious fact that I thought the barber would notice it, but he didn't seem to catch on. What's more, as if to rub it in that I was not me but "the Columnist," he asked me the sort of questions columnists get asked, like: "If war broke out, could we whip the Greeks?" "Is it true that the prime minister's wife is a slut?" "Are greengrocers responsible for the high prices?" And some mysterious power the origin of which I cannot discern would not let me answer these questions myself. But the columnist I watched in the mirror with utter amazement would answer for me, murmuring with his usual pedantic air something like: "Peace is a good thing." "Prices won't go down, you know, just because some people are strung up."

I hated this columnist who thought he knew everything, who knew it when he didn't know it, and who'd pedantically taught himself to accept his shortcomings and excesses. I even hated the barber who, with each of his questions, turned me that much more into Jelal the Columnist . . . And it was then, as I was recollecting my bad times, that I remembered the other barber, the one who came into the newsroom to ask his strange questions.

At that point, late at night, as I sat in my own armchair that made me myself, my legs stretched out on the stool, listening to the new fury in the old refrain that reminded me of my bad moments, "Yes sir, barber," I said to myself, "they won't allow a man to be himself; they won't let him; they won't ever." But these words, which I spoke with the same rhythm and anger as the old refrain, managed only to settle me deeper into the tranquility I so wanted. That's when I discerned an order that I've spoken of before in these columns and that my most faithful readers will detect—a meaning and even a "mysterious symmetry," if I may say so, in the complete story of the visit to the newsroom of that barber, the memory of whom was refreshed through the mediation of another barber. It was a sign indicative of my future: After a long day's night, a man's being left alone to sit in his own armchair and be himself is like a traveler's coming home after a long and adventurous journey.

Chapter Seventeen

DO YOU REMEMBER ME?

Whenever I cast a restorative gaze on the past, I seem to perceive a throng perambulating in the dark. —AHMET RASIM

The storytellers did not disperse when they came out of the nightclub but stood around under the flakes of snow that fell sporadically, staring at each other in anticipation of some new entertainment which was not as yet determined, riveted to the scene like people who have witnessed a fire, or a shooting, just in case it breaks out again. "But it's not the sort of place that's open to everyone, İskender Bey," said the bald guy, who'd already donned a huge fedora. "They cannot possibly accommodate a crowd this large. I'd like to take only the Brits. They might as well get an eyeful of yet another aspect of our country." Then he turned to Galip. "Of course, you too may come along . . ." They took off toward Tepebaşı, joined by two more who could not be gotten rid of like the others, a woman who was an antiques dealer and a middle-aged architect with a mustache stiff as a brush.

They were going past the American Consulate when the man with the fedora asked, "Were you ever in Jelal Bey's apartments in Nişantaşı and in Şişli?" "What for?" said Galip, scrutinizing the man's face which he did not find expressive. "It's just that İskender Bey said you are Jelal Salik's nephew. Don't you ever look him up? Wouldn't it be dandy if he were the one to acquaint the Brits with the situation in our country? Look, at last the world shows some interest in us!" "For sure," said Galip. "Do you happen to have his addresses?" the fedora hat said. "No," Galip said, "he gives his addresses out to no one." "Is it true that he uses those apartments for trysts with women?" "No," Galip said. "Forgive me," said the man; "it's just gossip. Tongues will wag! You can't shut people up. Especially about someone who is a legend in his own time like Jelal Bey. I know him well." "That so?" "Yes, it is. Once he had me come up to one of his places in Nişantaşı." "Where was it?" Galip asked. "The place is long gone," the man said, "a two-story stone house where he complained one afternoon about being lonely. He told me to look him up whenever I felt like it." "But he wants to be left alone," Galip said. "Perhaps you don't know him very well," said the man. "A voice inside me tells me he needs my help. You sure you don't know his address at all?" "Not at all," Galip said, "but it's not for nothing that people identify with him." "An extraordinary personality!" the fedora hat said, summarizing the situation. That's how they embarked on a discussion of Jelal's latest pieces.

When they heard a night watchman's whistle, which was more appropriate to a slum than one of the well-lit streets that led to the subway, they all turned and looked at the snowy sidewalks in the narrow street lit by purple neon, and when they turned into one of the streets that went up to the Galata Tower, Galip had the sensation that the upper stories of the buildings on either side of the street drew together slowly like the curtains at a movie theater. The red lights on top of the Tower were lit to indicate that it was going to snow tomorrow. It was two in the morning. Somewhere close by, the metal roll-down shutter of a store made a great deal of noise as it was lowered.

Skirting the Tower, they entered an alley Galip had never seen before and walked along a dark sidewalk where a sheet of ice had formed. The man with the fedora knocked on the dilapidated door of a small two-story house. A bit later, a light went on above, a window opened, and a blue-tinged head poked out. "It's me, open the door," said the man with the fedora. "We have some visitors from England." He turned around to cast an embarrassed smile at the Brits.

A pale, unshaven, thirtyish fellow opened the door, which said MARS MANNEQUIN ATELIER. His face was sleepy. He wore black slacks and a blue-striped pajama top. After shaking hands with all the visitors, the man, who wore a mysterious expression as if they were all brothers in a secret cause, took them into a brightly lit room that smelled of paint and was full of boxes, molds, tins, and various mannequin parts. Handing out some pamphlets he produced, he began a speech that was delivered in a monotone.

"Our establishment is the oldest mannequin-making enterprise in all the Middle East and the Balkans. The stage we have arrived at after one hundred years of history is an indicator of the Turkish achievement concerning modernization and industrialization. Today not only are arms, legs, hips produced in our country one hundred percent . . ."

"Mr. Cebbar," said the bald man with exasperation, "our friends have not come to take a look around here but to see, under your guidance, the levels below, the underground, the unfortunates, our history, and the things that make us 'us.' "

When the guide turned a knob angrily, the hundreds of arms, legs, heads, bodies in the fair-sized room were plunged into darkness, and a bare lightbulb went on in a small landing that opened to a stairway. The group started to walk down the iron staircase when a dank smell that rose from below made Galip stop. Mr. Cebbar came up to Galip with an ease that seemed surprising.

"Have no fear, you will find here what you are looking for!" he said in a know-it-all manner. "I was sent by Him. He has no desire at all for you to stray on the wrong paths and get lost."

Was he speaking these ambiguous words for the benefit of the others as well? In the first room they descended into, the guide introduced the mannequins they saw there: "My father's early work." In the next room they viewed in the light of a bare bulb some mannequins representing Ottoman seamen, corsairs, scribes, as well as a bunch of peasants sitting cross-legged around a meal on a tablecloth spread out on the floor, and the guide murmured something or other. It was in yet another room, where they saw the mannequins of a washerwoman, a beheaded atheist, and an executioner carrying the tools of his trade, that Galip first understood the guide's utterances.

"One hundred years ago, when my grandfather created his first works of art, he had no other concept in his head aside from this simple thought that anybody should be able to get through his head: the mannequins displayed in the store windows ought to represent our own people. That's what my grandfather thought. But he was forestalled by the unfortunate victims of a historical and international plot cooked up two hundred years ago."

They saw hundreds of mannequins as they went down more stairs, passing through more rooms which opened on to more steps that led down to where a single electric cable carrying naked lightbulbs wound around overhead like a clothesline.

They saw the mannequin of Field Marshal Fevzi Çakmak who during his thirty years as the chief of staff, fearing that the citizens might collaborate with the enemy, had conceived of blowing up all the bridges in the country, of pulling down all the minarets in order to rob the Russians of landmarks, and of evacuating Istanbul and proclaiming it a ghost town, thereby turning the city into a labyrinth where an occupying enemy would be lost. They saw the mannequins of peasants from the Konya region who, having intermarried for so long, look exactly alike—mothers, fathers, daughters, grandfathers, uncles, and all. They saw itinerant junk dealers who go door to door collecting the old stuff that makes us, without our being conscious of it, who we are. They saw film actors who could not be themselves playing movie heroes who could not be themselves, because they could neither be themselves nor anyone else, and they saw the Turkish superstars and actors who simply play themselves. They saw the poor bewildered souls who dedicate their entire lives to translations and adaptations in order to bring home Western arts and sciences, and they saw the dreamers who die and whose grave sites are obliterated before any of their dreams come true, who have worked their entire lives with magnifying glass in hand in order to turn the jumble of streets in Istanbul into the linden-lined streets of Berlin, or the boulevards of Paris radiating outward like a star, or the bridged avenues of St. Petersburg, imagining modern sidewalks where our generals too, like their European counterparts, could take their dogs out on leashes for an evening crap. They saw members of the secret service who are forced into early retirement because where torture is concerned they want to be true to local and traditional procedures rather than the new international methods, and peddlers who, their wares on a yoke across their shoulders, sell their fermented cereal, bonito, and yogurt in the neighborhoods. They saw a group entitled "Scenes from the Coffeehouse," which the guide described as "a line launched by my grandfather and developed by my father, and which I took over." Among them were the unemployed whose heads were sunk into their shoulders, and the lucky ones who could happily manage to forget themselves, together with the century in which they lived, during a game of backgammon or checkers, and compatriots who stared at the vanishing point on the horizon as if trying to remember the reason for their existence which had somehow got lost while they drank their tea and smoked their cheap cigarettes, or those who had withdrawn into themselves, or having failed to withdraw, abused the cards, the dice, or each other.

"The magnitude of the international powers that be finally hit my grandfather on his deathbed," their guide explained. "Historical forces which are against letting our nation be itself, in an effort to deprive us of our daily gestures which are our most precious treasure, had my grandfather thrown out of the stores in Beyoğlu and the display windows on İstiklâl Avenue. When my father understood that my dying grandfather had left him the underground, yes, the underground, as a prospect, he hadn't yet recognized the fact that Istanbul has always been an underground city throughout its history. He came to realize it by living through it and by coming across passageways as he excavated the mud for more chambers in which to place his mannequins."

Going down the stairs that connected to these passageways, through the landings and chambers that were more like caverns, they beheld the mannequins of wretches by the hundreds. In the light of the bare bulbs, the mannequins sometimes reminded Galip of our long-suffering countrymen who, covered under the dust and mud of ages, wait at some forgotten bus stop for a bus that will never arrive, and who sometimes gave him the illusion that all the unfortunates in the streets of Istanbul must be each other's brothers. He saw bingo men with their draw sacks. He saw snotty, stressed-out university students. He saw apprentice nut roasters, bird fanciers, and treasure seekers. He saw those who have read Dante in order to prove that all Western art and thought has been appropriated from the East, and those who have drawn maps in order to prove that the objects called minarets are in fact signal posts erected by extraterrestrials, and he saw the mannequins of theological-school students who, having been struck by a high-tension cable, were jolted into a collective blue funk which enabled them to recite daily events that had happened some two hundred years back. In the muddy chambers, he saw mannequins who had been teamed into groups of mountebanks, impersonators, sinners, and imposters. He saw couples who were unhappily married, ghosts who were restless, and war dead who had bolted their sepulchres. He saw mysterious persons who had letters written on their faces and foreheads, sages who had divulged the mystery in these letters, and even famous personages of our day who were the successors to those sages.

In one corner, among the contemporary Turkish artists and scribblers, even a mannequin of Jelal was present, wearing the raincoat he used to wear twenty years ago. As they went by this mannequin, the guide mentioned that this was a writer for whom his father had such great expectations that he'd revealed to him the mystery of letters, which the writer had used for his own sleazy ends, having sold out for cheap success. The piece that Jelal had written twenty years ago on the subject of the guide's father and grandfather had been framed and hung around the mannequin's neck like an edict of execution. Galip's lungs felt full of the irritating smell of mold and dampness that oozed off the walls in the muddy chambers, which had been excavated, as is the case for many a shopkeeper, without a permit from the city. All the while, the guide was giving an account of how his father, betrayed time and again, had put all his hopes on the mystery of letters which he had learned of in his trips to Anatolia, and how the underground passages, which made Istanbul what it was, had gradually disclosed to him, while he was busy modeling his mannequins, the mystery that he represented in the faces of the mannequins of the unfortunate. Galip remained stuck for quite a while in front of Jelal's corpulent mannequin, which had a huge torso, a gentle expression, and tiny hands. "You are the reason why I could never be myself," he felt like saying. "You are the reason I believed in all these fictions which managed to turn me into you." He studied Jelal's mannequin for a long time, like a son examining attentively a good photo of his father many years after it was taken. He remembered that the material for the trousers had been bought at discount from a distant relative's store in Sirkeci, that Jelal really liked the raincoat which he thought made him look like the sleuths in English detective novels, that the seams in corners of his pockets were ripped away because he so often stuck his hands in his pockets forcefully, that these past few years there had no longer been any razor cuts visible under his lower lip and on his Adam's apple, and that Jelal still used the fountain pen he kept in the pocket of his jacket. Galip loved him and yet feared him; he wanted to be in Jelal's shoes and yet he wanted to get away from him; he was looking for him and yet he wanted to put him out of his mind. He got hold of Jelal's jacket by the lapels as if to demand that he be told the meaning of his life, which he couldn't decipher by himself—the secret that Jelal knew but kept from him, the mystery of the parallel universe, and the escape clause in the game that had begun as a joke but turned into a nightmare. In the distance, he heard the guide's voice, which had an undertone of excitement as well as of habit and routine.

"Using his knowledge of letters, my father imparted to the faces of his mannequins meanings that cannot be seen any longer either in our streets or in our houses, working at such a pace that we ran out of room in the underground chambers that we had dug and had to dig further. That was when we began to come across passageways which connected us to the history of the underground, and this fact cannot be explained away as mere coincidence. My father saw clearly that from then on our history could only take place underground, that the life below gave a clear warning of the final collapse above, that each of the passages that eventually connected to our house, these pathways that teemed with skeletons, provided us with a historical opportunity that could give life and meaning to the faces of true compatriots which only we could now create."

When Galip let go of the lapels of Jelal's mannequin, it slowly rocked on its feet from side to side like a lead soldier. Galip backed off and lit a cigarette, thinking that he would not be able to forget, ever, this weird, horrific, ridiculous image of his mentor. He didn't feel at all like descending along with the others down to the brink of the underground city which would, one day, teem with mannequins as it did with skeletons.

When they had descended, the guide showed his guests the maw of the underground passage that ended on this side of the Golden Horn, one which the Byzantines, fearing that Attila might attack, had tunneled under the Horn one thousand, five hundred and thirty-six years ago; and he went on indignantly to tell the story of the skeletons he said they'd be able to see if they entered from this end carrying a light—and their tables and chairs as well, obscured under spider's webs, where the skeletons had guarded the treasures hidden away from Latin invaders seven hundred and seventy-five years ago. While he listened, Galip kept thinking that he'd already read about all this long ago in one of Jelal's pieces concerning the puzzle which these images and stories signified. As the guide was explaining how his father, having read the powerful signs of an absolute collapse, had decided to go underground, he mentioned that each incarnation of Istanbul (a.k.a. Byzantium, Vizant, Nova Roma, Anthusa, Tsargrad, Miklagrad, Constantinopole, Cospoli, Istin-Polin) had its historical origin in the inevitable and necessary passageways and tunnels below in which the previous civilization had sought refuge, which in turn had created the incredible double-level construct below the city—but, as the guide explained with considerable heat, the civilization below had always managed to wreak vengeance on the one above for having pushed it under. Galip remembered one of Jelal's pieces in which he had mentioned that apartment buildings were the extension of this underground civilization. The guide, his voice now tinged with anger, went on to tell how, in order to join the colossal collapse foretold by the underground, to become a part of that irresistible doomsday, his father had wanted to see his mannequins populate all these passages, these underground corridors chock-full of treasures and infested with rats, skeletons, spiders— how the dream of celebrating this colossal collapse had brought new meaning to his father's life, and how the guide himself had followed in his father's footsteps, creating letters and their meaning in the faces of his masterworks.

As he listened, Galip was ready to believe that this guide bought a copy of *Milliyet* at the crack of dawn just in order to read Jelal's column with the greed, jealousy, hate, and anger that he now displayed. Galip became convinced that the guide had carefully read Jelal's latest column when the fellow remarked that those who had the nerve for it could certainly venture into an incredible passage, hung with gold necklaces and bracelets, where they would see the skeletons of Byzantines, whom the siege of the Abbasites had scared into going underground, and the timeless skeletons of Jews holding each other in fear of the Crusaders. There were the skeletons of Genoans, Amalfians, and Pisans who escaped the city when the Byzantines were decimating the Italian population that had numbered more than six thousand, and the six-hundred-year-old skeletons of those who had fled from the Black Death—which had arrived on board a ship from the Sea of Azov—and sat leaning against each other at tables which had been brought underground during the siege of the Avars, all of them waiting patiently for the Day of Judgment. Listening restlessly to the fellow go on and on, Galip wondered how he had found the same kind of patience that had been granted Jelal. The guide pointed out that passageways extended from Saint Sophia to Saint Irene, and from there to Pantocrator, which then had to be dug out all the way to this end when they ran out of room, all in order to hide from the Ottomans who sacked Byzantium. And then he went on to say that two hundred years later those who beat it down here, trying to avoid Murat the Fourth's ban on coffee, tobacco, and opium, were slowly covered under a silky layer of dust that fell on them like snow while they waited for the mannequins to show them the way to salvation, holding onto their coffee grinders, their coffeepots and their waterpipes, their long tobacco pipes, their tobacco and opium pouches. Galip imagined the same silky layer of dust would one day cover Jelal's skeleton. The guide informed them that, aside from the skeleton of Ahmet the Third's heir apparent, who had been forced after a failed palace conspiracy to go underground in the same passages where Jews had taken refuge when they were kicked out of Byzantium seven hundred years ago, and the skeleton of the Georgian slave girl who escaped the seraglio with her lover, they would be able to see contemporary counterfeiters holding wet banknotes which they check for accuracy of color, or else, because there is no dressing room at the little theater, the Moslem Lady Macbeth who is forced to go one flight below to sit at her dressing-table mirror and dip her hands into a barrel of contraband water-buffalo blood, dying them a red so true to life that its like has never been seen on another stage in the entire world, or else our young chemists distilling prime-grade heroin in glass globes which they are zealous to export to America on rusty Bulgarian ships. Galip had the feeling that he could read all this in Jelal's face as well as in one of his pieces.

Later, when the guide had completed his lecture, he spoke of the event which was his and his father's fondest dream, one that would unfold on a hot summer's day when all Istanbul was taking a sluggish, heavy siesta above, immersed in vapors thick with flies, the stench of garbage, and dust. In the cool, moist, and dark passages below, a great celebration, a great entertainment, a festival that went beyond time, history, and social constraints in its sanctification of life and of death would be organized by the forbearing skeletons and the mannequins alive with the life force of our countrymen. On the way back to the surface, thinking with horror of the pain the visitors had seen in the faces of the hundreds of "citizen" mannequins, Galip felt the weight of all the stories he'd heard and all the faces he'd beheld, and he imagined the skeletons and the mannequins gaily dancing together at the festival, the broken wine cups and bowls, the music and the silence, the horror of copulating couples clacking away in abandon. The weakness he felt in his legs had resulted neither from the steep passages they'd climbed nor from the fatigue of the long day he'd put in. His own body felt the weariness he saw in the faces of his brothers, those figures that he met on slippery steps under the light of bare bulbs and in the damp rooms that he had constantly crossed. Their lowered heads, bent spines, hunched backs, splayed legs, their troubles and their stories, were extensions of his own body. Since he felt that all the faces were his face, and all their misfortunes his misfortune, he wanted to stop looking at the lively mannequins as they approached and avoid their eyes, but he could no more tear his eyes away than he could have torn himself away from his identical twin. He wanted to convince himself, as he had when he read Jelal's pieces as a teenager, that behind the visible world there was a simple secret he could get out from under if he discovered it, a mystery that would liberate a person once its recipe was known. But, just as when he had read Jelal in those earlier days, he found he was so deeply immersed in the world that every time he forced himself to seek for a solution to the mystery he sensed that he was becoming more and more helpless and childish, like someone in a fugue state. He was not aware of the meaning of the world signified by the mannequins; he did not know what he was doing here with all these foreigners; nor did he know anything of the mystery of letters, the meaning of faces, or the secret of his own existence. What's more, the nearer they got to the surface, the farther up they went and the farther away from the secrets below, the stronger became his sense that he was already beginning to forget what he had seen and learned. When he saw in one of the upper rooms a line of "ordinary citizens" that the guide didn't bother commenting on, he felt that he shared with them the same fate and the same vision: Once upon a time they had all lived a bright and meaningful life together, but due to an unknown cause they'd now lost that meaning along with their memory. Anytime they attempted to recover the meaning, they got lost in the spider-filled passages of their minds, they could not find their way back through their minds' dark blind alleys, they could never locate the key to a new life, which had dropped down to the bottom of their lost memory banks, leaving them seized by the same helpless pain felt by those who have lost their homes, their countries, their past, and their history. The pain of exile and of loss was so intense and so unbearable that it was best to give up trying to remember the lost meaning or the mystery, and simply be patient and resign oneself to waiting quietly for the end of time. But as he got closer to the top, Galip sensed that he could never endure the suffocating sensation of waiting like this, and that he could not find peace unless he located what he was looking for. Was it not far better to be a bad imitation of someone else than to be somebody who had lost his past, his memory, and his dreams? At the threshold of the iron staircase, he wanted to have a go at being Jelal, scoffing at the mannequins and the driving idea that created them: it was nothing more than the obsessive repetition of a stupid notion; it was nothing but a caricature, a joke that fell flat; it was a miserable idiocy that signified nothing! And, as if to prove Galip's case, there was the guide, a caricature of himself, babbling on about how his father did not go along with "Islam's prohibition against pictorial representation," how the faculty of thought was nothing more or less than pictorial representation, and how what they'd seen here was also a series of representations. Now the guide was standing in the room they'd been let into when they first arrived, explaining the necessity of doing business with the mannequin market in order to keep this colossal conception alive, and requesting that the visitors kindly drop whatever amount they wished in the green contribution box.

Galip had just dropped a thousand-lira note in the box when his eyes met the eyes of the antiques dealer.

"Do you remember me?" said the woman. Her face had a dreamy look and a playful childlike expression. "Turns out my grandmother's stories were all true." In the half-light, her eyes gleamed like a cat's.

"Beg your pardon?" Galip said with embarrassment.

"You don't remember me," said the woman. "We were in the same class at middle school. Belkis."

"Belkis," Galip said, realizing for a second that he could not picture any other girl in the class aside from Rüya.

"I have a car," the woman said. "I live in Nişantaşı too. I could drop you off."

Once out in the open air, the crowd gradually dispersed. The British took off for the Pera Palas; the man with the fedora hat gave Galip his card, sent Jelal his regards, and disappeared into one of the backstreets in Cihangir.

İskender hopped a taxi, and the architect with the brush mustache walked alongside of Belkis and Galip. At the intersection a little beyond the Atlas Theater, they bought a dish of pilav from a vendor who had set up in the street, and they ate it. They looked at the watches displayed in a frosty showcase as if they were seeing magic toys. Galip studied a torn poster which was the same color as the murky dark blue of the night and in a photographer's window the photo of a prime minister who had been murdered long ago. That was when the architect suggested taking them to the Mosque of Süleyman the Magnificent. There, he would show them something even more remarkable than what they'd seen at the place he called "the Mannequin Hell." The four-hundred-year-old mosque was apparently moving out of place a little at a time! They got into Belkis's car, which she'd parked on a back alley in Talimhane, and set out quietly. As they drove past the dark and dreadful two-story buildings, Galip felt like saying, "Dreadful, dreadful!" It was snowing lightly and the city was asleep.

When they arrived at the mosque after driving for a considerable time, the architect told them the story: He was well acquainted with the underground passages below the mosque, having worked on its restoration and repairs, and he was also familiar with the imam, who'd be willing to open the doors in return for a tip. When the engine stopped, Galip said he would stay in the car and wait for them.

"You'll freeze!" Belkis said.

Galip noted that Belkis spoke to him familiarly and also that despite her rather attractive appearance, under the weight of her coat and with the scarf on her head she looked more like a distant aunt. The marzipan offered by that aunt when they visited on religious holidays used to be so sweet that Galip had first to down a drink of water before he could eat another of the pieces that she forced on him. Why had Rüya always refused to go on these holiday visits?

"I don't want to come," said Galip, sounding determined.

"But why not?" said the woman. "We'll go up the minaret afterwards." She turned to the architect. "Can we?"

There was a moment of silence. A dog barked somewhere, not too far off. Galip heard the roar of the city under the blanket of snow.

"My heart can't take all those stairs," the architect said. "You two go up."

The idea of going up the minaret appealed to Galip, so he got out of the car. They went past the outer courtyard, where the snow-covered trees were lit by naked lightbulbs. In the courtyard, with the great mass of stone suddenly seeming smaller than it actually was, the mosque was transformed into a familiar building which couldn't hide its secrets. The icy layer of snow that covered the marble was dark and pitted like the surface of the moon in its closeup photographs.

The architect began monkeying officiously with the padlock on the metal door that stood where the arcade formed a corner. At the same time, he kept explaining how the mosque, due to its own weight and that of the hill where it stood, had been slipping into the Golden Horn for centuries by some two to four inches a year. In reality, it should have hit the water by this time, but the mosque's progress was being slowed down by "these stone walls" that circumvented the foundations, the secret of which had yet to be discovered; and by "this sewer system" the technical sophistication of which was unsurpassed to this day; by the "water table" that had been balanced so accurately; and by the "system of passageways" that had been calculated four hundred years ago. When the door was unlocked and opened into a dark passageway, Galip noticed the sparkle of a life-affirming curiosity in the woman's eyes. Perhaps Belkis did not possess unusual beauty, but one was curious as to what she would do next. "The West has been unable to solve this secret," the architect said as if intoxicated and reeled into the passageway with Belkis like a drunk. Galip stayed outside.

Galip was listening to the squeaky sounds that came from the passageway when the imam turned up out of the shadows of the columns, which were edged with ice. The imam didn't seem at all upset that he'd been awakened in the wee hours of the morning. After listening to the voices in the passageway, he asked, "Is the woman a tourist?" "No," said Galip, thinking that the imam's beard made him look older than he was. "Are you a teacher?" the imam asked. "I am a teacher." "A professor, like Fikret Bey!" "Right." "Is it true that the mosque is on the loose?" "It's true. That's why we are here." "May God recompense you," the imam said. He looked dubious. "Does the woman have a child with her?" "No," said Galip. "There is a child hiding inside, somewhere deep under," the imam said. "Apparently, the mosque has been slipping for ages," Galip said uncertainly. "I know that," said the imam. "Although entering that way is also forbidden, some tourist woman and her kid went in that way, I saw them. Then she came out alone. The kid was left behind." "You should've told the cops," Galip said. "Not necessary," said the imam. "Both the woman's and the kid's pictures were in the papers: turns out the kid is the grandson of the Ethiopian King. High time that they came and got him." "So, what was on the kid's face?" Galip asked. "See!" the imam said suspiciously. "Even you know about it. One couldn't look the kid in the eye." "What was written on his face?" Galip insisted. "There was a lot written on his face," the imam said, losing his self-confidence. "You know how to read faces?" Galip asked. The imam kept quiet. "Is it sufficient for a person to pursue the meaning in faces in order to find the face that he has lost?" "You'd know that stuff better than me," the imam said apprehensively. "Is the mosque open?" Galip said. "I just opened the portals," the imam said. "They'll soon be coming in for the morning prayer. Go on in."

The mosque was empty inside. The fluorescent lights illuminated the bare walls rather than the purple rugs that stretched out like the surface of an ocean. Having taken off his shoes, Galip felt his feet turn into ice in his socks. He looked up at the dome, the columns, and the imposing mass of stonework above, wishing to be moved but he could get no feeling stirred up other than the wish to be moved: a sense of waiting, a vaguely perceptible curiosity about what might happen . . . He felt the mosque was a colossal and closed object which was as self-sufficient as the stones that went into building it. The place neither summoned one anywhere, nor sent one somewhere else. Just as nothing signified anything, anything could also signify everything. For a moment it was as if he perceived a blue light, then he heard the rapid flutter of something like the wings of a pigeon, but immediately everything went back to the same old silent stagnance that awaited a new meaning. Then he had the thought that things and stones are more "naked" than they were supposed to be: it was as if things called out to him, saying "Give us a meaning!" A little later, when a couple of geezers approached the holy niche whispering to each other and went down on their knees, Galip could no longer hear the call of things.

That was why Galip had no premonition as he went up the minaret. When the architect informed him that Belkis had gone up without waiting, Galip had begun to go up the stairs quickly, but not too long after, feeling the beat of his heart in his temples, he came to a stop. And when a pain started up in his legs and hips, he sat down for a moment. From then on, every time he went past another of the bare bulbs that lit the way up the stairs, he sat down and then started up again. When he heard the woman's footsteps somewhere above him, he speeded up, though he knew he would catch up with her later when he came out on the balcony. Once he was there, he and the woman stood looking down on Istanbul shrouded in darkness for a long time without speaking, watching the city's lights, which were hardly visible, and the snow that fell sporadically.

When Galip became aware that the darkness was slowly being dispelled, the city itself seemed to retain the night for a long time like the dark side of a distant planet. Some time later he thought, as he shivered with the cold, that the light that reflected off the chimney smoke, the walls of the mosque, and the piles of concrete did not originate from somewhere outside of the city but leaked out from somewhere within it. Just as on the surface of a planet that was still being formed, it felt as if the uneven pieces of the city buried under concrete, stone, wood, plexiglass, and domes might slowly part and the flame-colored light of the mysterious underground seep through the darkness. As the larger letters on the billboards for banks and cigarettes gradually became visible in between walls, chimneys, roofs, they heard the imam's metallic call to prayer boom out of the loudspeaker right next to them.

As they were going down the stairs, Belkis inquired after Rüya. She was waiting up for him at home, Galip said; he had bought her three detective novels today; Rüya liked reading at night.

When Belkis asked about Rüya again, it was after they'd got into the woman's nondescript Turkish Fiat, dropped off the brush-mustachioed architect on Cihangir Avenue, which was wide and always uncrowded, and were going up toward Taksim. Galip said Rüya didn't have a job, but read detective novels; she also took her own sweet time, sometimes translating one she had read. As they took the traffic circle around Taksim Square, the woman asked Galip how Rüya did these translations and Galip said "Very slowly." He went to his office in the morning and Rüya got down to work at the table after clearing away the breakfast things, but he couldn't visualize Rüya working at the table since he had never seen her doing it. Galip responded to another question absentmindedly, saying that some mornings he left before Rüya got out of bed. He said they went to dinner once a week at the aunt's whom they had in common, and some evenings to movies at the Palace Theater.

"I know," Belkis said. "I used to see you at the movies. You seemed content with your life, looking at the photos in the lobby, holding your wife's arm tenderly as you led her in the crowd going up to the balcony door. Yet she would be scanning the crowd and the posters for the face which would open the world's doors to her. From where I sat at a distance from you, I intuited that she read the secret meaning in faces."

Galip kept silent.

"During the five-minute intermission, while you, like the contented, good, and faithful husband that you are, wishing to please your wife with a coconut-filled chocolate bar or a frozen treat, signaled to the vendor tapping the bottom of his wooden tray with a coin, and went through your pockets looking for change, I used to sense that your wife was looking for the traces of a magic sign that might take her into another world, even in the advertisements for carpet sweepers or orange-juice extractors which she watched unhappily on the screen in the dim houselights."

Galip still kept quiet.

"Just before midnight, when people came out of the Palace Theater, leaning more into each other's coats than into each other, I used to see the two of you walk home arm in arm, staring at the sidewalk."

"At most," Galip said resentfully, "it must have been one time that you saw us at the movies."

"Not one time, but twelve times at the movies, more than sixty times in the street, three times at restaurants, six times out shopping. When I got home, I imagined that the girl with you was not Rüya but me—just like I did when I was a young girl."

Silence ensued.

"In middle school," the woman went on, driving past the Palace Theater they were just talking about, "at recess, while she laughed at jokes told by the sort of boys who run the combs they take out of their back pockets through their wetted hair and hang their key chains on their belt buckles, I used to imagine it was not Rüya that you watched out of the corner of your eye, without looking up from the book on your desk, but me. On winter mornings, I used to imagine myself as the carefree girl, instead of Rüya, who crossed the street without looking, since you were there with her. Some Saturday afternoons when I saw you walk to the Taksim *dolmuş* stop with an uncle who made you two smile, I used to imagine you and I were being taken to Beyoğlu."

"How long did this game go on?" Galip said, turning on the car radio.

"It wasn't a game," said the woman, and as she took the intersection without slowing down, she added, "I'm not making a turn into your street."

"I remember this music," Galip said, glancing at the street he lived on as if looking at a postcard from a distant town. "Trini Lopez used to sing it."

Neither in the windows nor in the curtains was there a sign that Rüya had returned home. Galip didn't know what else to do with his hands but fiddle with the radio dial. A well-modulated, kindly male voice was giving pointers on rat control in our barns. "Didn't you get married?" asked Galip as the car turned into one of the backstreets in Nişantaşı.

"I am a widow," said Belkis. "My husband died."

"I just don't remember you from school," Galip said, being pointlessly unkind. "I recall another face that looked like you. A shy and very cute Jewish girl, Meri Tavaşi, her dad owned Vogue Hosiery; at New Year's, some boys and even some teachers used to ask her for Vogue calendars that had pictures of girls putting on their stockings, and she'd dutifully bring them to school, embarrassed and abashed."

"Nihat and I were happy during the first years of our marriage," said the woman, telling her story after a brief silence. "He was delicate, quiet, and smoked too much. On Sundays he looked through the papers, listened to the game on the radio, and tried playing the flute that he'd acquired around that time. He drank, but very little, yet his face was very often sadder than the sorriest drunk's. For a while he complained about a headache with embarrassment. Turns out he had been patiently growing a huge tumor in one corner of his brain. You know, there are some quietly stubborn children who won't give up what they've got in their fists no matter how hard you try? Well, he protected the tumor in his brain just like those children. Just like those kids who smile for an instant when they finally give up the bead in their fists he gave me that same pleased smile as he was being wheeled in for brain surgery where he died quietly."

They entered a building, which was a dead ringer for the Heart-of-the-City Apartments, not too far from Aunt Halé's on a corner Galip didn't go by very often but knew as well as the street he himself lived on.

"I knew that he took some sort of revenge on me by dying," the woman continued on the dilapidated elevator. "He had realized that as much as I was an imitation of Rüya, he had to become an imitation of you. Some evenings when I overdid the cognac, I couldn't keep myself from going on and on, telling him about you and Rüya."

They fell silent and entered her place, and after settling down among furnishings that looked much like those at home, Galip said anxiously, "I remember Nihat from our class."

"Would you say that he looked like you?"

Galip forced himself to extract a couple of scenes out of the depths of his memory: Galip and Nihat standing there with notes in their hands from their parents asking to be excused while the gym teacher accuses them of being lardasses; on a warm spring day, Galip and Nihat drink water, sticking their mouths on the faucets in the putrid student latrine. He was fat, clumsy, and none too bright. Galip could not feel any closeness for his look-alike he couldn't quite remember despite all his goodwill.

"Yes," said Galip. "Nihat looked a bit like me."

"He didn't look like you in the slightest," Belkis said. For a moment her eyes had the same dangerous gleam in them as when Galip first noticed her. "I know he didn't look at all like you. But we were in the same class. And I had managed to make him look at me the way you looked at Rüya. During lunch break when Rüya and I smoked with the other boys in the Milk Company pudding shop, I'd see him out on the sidewalk, glancing anxiously in the shop where he knew I was with the cool crowd. And on those sad fall evenings when night comes early, looking at the naked trees in the pale light that came from the apartment buildings, I knew that he would think of me the same way you thought of Rüya when you looked at those trees."

When they sat down to breakfast, there was bright sunlight shining into the room in between the curtains that remained drawn.

"I know how difficult it is to be oneself," Belkis said, bringing up the subject suddenly, as people do when they have been contemplating the same thing for a long time. "But I realized it only after I was thirty. Before that, if you asked me, the problem seemed like a mere desire to be like someone else or a case of simple jealousy. Lying on my back, sleepless, watching the shadows on the ceiling at midnight, I wanted to stand in for someone else so bad that I believed I could slip out of my skin like a hand slipping out of a glove and, through the vehemence of my wish, I could wrap myself into someone else's skin and begin a new life. Sometimes, thinking about this other person, the pain of not being able to live my life as hers was so intense that, as I sat in a movie theater or watched self-absorbed people in a crowded bazaar, tears would pour out of my eyes."

The woman passed her knife absentmindedly over the thin slice of bread hardened from being toasted too much as if she were buttering it, although there was no butter on the knife.

"After all these years, I still cannot figure out why anyone would want to live someone else's life rather than her own," the woman went on. "I cannot even say why I wanted to be Rüya rather than this or that person. All I can say is that for years I thought it was a disease that must be kept a secret. I was ashamed of my disease, of my soul that had contracted the disease, and of my body that had been condemned to carry the disease around. I thought my life was an imitation of what ought to be my 'real life,' and that, like all fake things, it was pitiful and shameful. Back then, I had no other recourse than imitating my 'original' to dispel my unhappiness. For a while, I even fantasized about changing schools, neighborhoods, and my circle of friends, but I knew that going away would not result in anything but thinking about you all the more. On a rainy autumn day, in the afternoon, when I felt like doing nothing, I'd sit in an easy chair for hours, watching the raindrops on the window pane. I'd think of the two of you: Rüya and Galip. I'd consider the clues such as I had, imagining what Rüya and Galip might be up to right about now, so much so that, after a couple of hours of it, I'd begin to believe that the person sitting in the chair in the dark room was not me but Rüya, and I began to derive a terrific delight from these horrible thoughts."

Since the woman was able to smile amiably as if she were relating a pleasant story about a mere acquaintance while she went in and out of the kitchen to bring more toast or tea, Galip listened to what she had to say without feeling uneasy.

"The disease raged on until my husband died. Perhaps it still rages on, but I no longer experience it as a disease. During those days of loneliness and regret following my husband's death, I came to the conclusion that there was no way one could be oneself. Back in those days, prompted by a massive feeling of regret which is another version of the disease, I was burning up with the desire to live through my life with Nihat again, all of it, identically, only this time as myself. In the middle of the one night when I became aware that regret would ruin the rest of my life, this weird thought went through my mind: I was going to spend the second half of my life as someone else who regretted that she couldn't manage being herself, just like I had spent the first half not being myself because I'd wanted to be someone else. The notion seemed so ridiculous to me that the horror and the sorrow that I saw as my past and my future instantly metamorphosed into a destiny I shared with everyone else, which I didn't wish to dwell on too much. I had at last learned a piece of knowledge that could never be forgotten: no one could ever be himself. I knew full well that the old fellow that I saw as someone sunk deep in his own troubles waiting in line at the bus stop was in fact keeping alive the ghost of some 'real' person whose shoes he had wished to step into many years ago. I knew that the hale and hearty mom who took her kid out sunning in the park had sacrificed herself to become the copy of another mother who took her child to the park. I knew that melancholics walking slowly out of movie houses, or unfortunates fidgeting in crowded streets and noisy coffeeshops were all being haunted day and night by the ghosts of their originals that they wanted to emulate."

They sat smoking at the breakfast table. The more the woman went on, and the warmer the room got, the more Galip felt an irresistible feeling of sleepiness wrap itself gradually around his body; it was like the feeling of innocence that can be experienced only in one's dreams. When he asked if he could take a nap on the sofa next to the radiator, Belkis began telling him the story of the Prince, which she thought was "related to all this stuff."

Yes, long ago there lived a prince who had discovered that the most crucial problem in life was to be oneself, or not to be oneself, but as soon as Galip began animating the story's details in his imagination, he initially felt that he was being transformed into someone else, and then into someone who fell asleep.

Chapter Eighteen

THE DARK VOID

The aspect of the venerable mansion has always affected me like a human countenance. —NATHANIEL HAWTHORNE, *The House of the Seven Gables*

I went to see the building one afternoon after many years. I'd walked along that perpetually crowded street so very often, on those same sidewalks where during their midday break necktied but slovenly high-school students toting their school bags shove each other around, and where husbands pass on their way home from work and housewives from their get-togethers, but I'd never gone back after all these years just to look at that building again, the apartment building which had once meant so much to me.

It was an evening in winter. Darkness had fallen early and smoke from the chimneys had descended on the narrow avenue like a foggy night. Lights were on in two floors only: dim, dispirited lights in two business offices where people worked late. Otherwise, the façade of the building was in total darkness. Dark curtains had been closed in dark apartments; the windows were as empty and frightening as the eyes of a blind person. What I saw was a cold, insipid, and unprepossessing sight when compared to its past. One could not even imagine that once an extended family had lived here, on top of each other, in each other's hair, and in a hubbub.

I enjoyed the rack and ruin which had pervaded the building like the punishment for the sins of youth. I knew that I was seized by this feeling only because I could never get my share of sinful bliss, and that seeing the decay gave me a taste of revenge, but at that moment I had something else on my mind: "I wonder what happened to the mystery hidden in the pit which became the air shaft. And what happened to the pit as well as what was inside it?"

I thought of the pit which used to be right next to the building, the bottomless pit that had inspired shivers of fear at night, not only in me but in all the pretty children, girls, and adults who lived on all the floors. It seethed with bats, poisonous snakes, rats, and scorpions like a well in a tale of fantasy. I had a feeling it was the very pit described in Şeyh Galip's *Beauty and Love* and mentioned in Rumi's *Mathnawi*. It so happened that sometimes when a pail was lowered into the pit, its rope was cut, and sometimes they said that there was a black ogre down there who was as big as a house. Don't you kids go anywhere near it! we were told. One time when the doorman was dangled down from a rope that was tied to his belt, he returned from the zero-gravity journey he made into the infinite darkness of time with tears in his eyes and lungs blackened with cigarette tar for all eternity. I was aware of the fact that the desert witch who guarded the pit could also assume the shape of the doorman's moonfaced wife, and that the pit was closely related to a secret that lay deep in the inhabitants' memories. They were afraid of the secret inside themselves as if fearful of a past sin that could not stay buried in the past for all eternity. Eventually they forgot about the pit, its memories and secrets as well as what it contained, like instinctive animals who scratch some dirt to conceal their disgrace. One morning, waking up from a black nightmare that seethed with human faces, I discovered that the pit had been covered over. It was then that I understood with horror, gripped by the same nightmarish feeling, that the pit had been turned inside out, and it now rose out of the site that was once called the pit. They had a new way of referring to this new space that brought mystery and death up to our very windows; they called this dark well the air shaft.

In reality, the new space the inhabitants called the air shaft in disgust and disgruntlement (unlike other Istanbulites who termed this kind of space a light well), was neither an air shaft nor a light well. When the place was first built, there were vacant lots on either side; it was not one of the ugly apartment buildings which later lined the street like a solid dirty wall. When the lot next to it was sold to a builder, the kitchen windows, the windows of the narrow and long inner corridor, and the windows of the little room that was used for different purposes on each floor (storage room, maid's room, nursery, poor relation's room, ironing room, a distant aunt's room), all of which had a view of the mosque and the tram tracks, the girls' lycée, Aladdin's store, and the pit now faced the windows of the tall row-house style apartment building next door, only three yards away. That was how a lightless and oppressive space without a breath of air, which was reminiscent of an infinite well, was formed in between the dirty nondescript concrete walls and the windows that reflected each other and the floors below.

Soon pigeons discovered this space, which within a short time developed its own gloomy, old and heavy smell. They built roosts for their constantly increasing population on concrete ledges, on windowsills that broke off of their own accord, in the elbows of downspouts inaccessible to human hands—which in time became places that no one would want to touch—where they deposited their profusion of droppings. At times insolent seagulls, who are harbingers not only of meteorological catastrophe but also of other nebulous nastinesses, would join them, and so would black crows who lost their bearing at midnight and smashed into the windows in the dark well. One sometimes came across the corpses of these winged creatures, which the mice had picked to shreds on the obscured floor, as one ventured into the doorman's airless low-ceilinged apartment, bending over in order to get through a low iron door that was reminiscent of cell doors (creaked like a dungeon door, too). Other things could be found on the repulsive basement floor that was encrusted with dirt a lot worse than manure: shells of pigeon eggs stolen by mice who went up the spouts to the upper stories, unlucky forks and odd socks that had slipped from flower-print tablecloths and sleepy bedsheets shaken out the windows and fallen into the petroleum-colored void, knives, dust cloths, cigarette butts, shards of glass and lightbulbs and mirrors, rusty bed springs, armless pink dolls that still batted their plastic eyelashes hopelessly yet stubbornly, pages of some compromising magazine and newsprint that had carefully been torn into tiny pieces, busted balls, soiled children's underpants, horrifying photographs that had been ripped to shreds . . .

At times the doorman went from flat to flat showing one of these objects, which he held up by the corner in disgust as if he were taking around a criminal for identification, but the inhabitants in the building would not own up to any suspect articles that returned unexpectedly out of the slime of the nether world: "Not ours," they'd say. "Fell down there, did it?"

It was a place they wanted to escape from like a fear they wanted to consign to oblivion and yet were unable to. They mentioned the place as if talking about some ugly, contagious disease: the void was a cesspool they themselves could, if they were not careful, accidentally fall into like the unfortunate objects swallowed up by it; it was a nest of evil that had been slyly insinuated into their lives. No doubt, the children were sick so often because this place gave them germs, those germs that were constantly discussed in the newspapers, as well as giving them the fear of ghosts and of death, which they began talking about at an early age. The strange odors that came in the windows and at times surrounded the building like free-floating terror also originated from that place; one could very well imagine that the whammies and the jinxes, too, seeped in from the dark gap between the buildings. Like the heavy dark-blue smoke in the gap, the catastrophes that befell the inhabitants (bankruptcy, debt, runaway dads, incest, divorce, infidelity, jealousy, death) were also connected in their minds to the history of this dark void: like the pages of books they didn't want to remember which got jumbled together in their memory banks.

But, thank God, there is always someone who's willing to go through the forbidden pages of such books to find treasures. Children (ah, children!), shivering with fear in the corridor where the light was kept off in order to save on electricity, slipped through the deliberately drawn curtains to press their foreheads curiously on the windows overlooking the dark void. Back in the days when all the cooking was done in Grandpa's flat, the maid would yell into the dark void that dinner was on the table for the benefit of the inhabitants below (and in the next flat), and when the mother and son duo exiled to the attic apartment was not invited, they'd leave their kitchen window open to keep an eye on the subterfuges and the food prepared below. Some nights a deaf mute would stare into the dark void until his grandmother caught him at it. The servant girl daydreamed in her tiny room, staring into that place as she sorrowed along with the downspouts on rainy days, and so did the young man who would return victoriously to the building where a family which subsequently collapsed could not manage to survive.

Let us take a cursory look at the treasures they saw: the images of women and girls on the foggy kitchen windows but whose voices could not be heard; the back of a ghostly shadow slowly bending and rising in prayer; the leg of an elderly woman resting next to an illustrated magazine on a bed where the quilt has not been turned down (if one stays put, one will see a hand flip the pages and languorously scratch the leg); the forehead pressed on the cold windowpane that belongs to the young man who has decided that he will one day return victoriously to the bottomless pit and discover the secret concealed by the inhabitants. (The same young man watching his own reflection would sometimes see, reflected in the window opposite his from the flat below, his enchantingly beautiful stepmother who was in a reverie like himself.) Let us also add that these images are framed by the heads and bodies of pigeons crouched in the darkness, that the frame is dark blue, that slight movements of the curtains, lights that momentarily go on and off, and rooms that are well lighted will make bright orange tracks on the windows and in the sad and guilty memories transformed into these images: We live but for a short time, we see but very little, and we know almost nothing; so, at least, let's do some dreaming. Have yourselves a very good Sunday, my dear readers.

Chapter Nineteen

SIGNS OF THE CITY

Was I the same when I got up this morning? I almost think I can remember feeling a little different. But if I'm not the same, the next question is "Who in the world am I?" —LEWIS CARROLL, *Alice in Wonderland*

When Galip woke up, he saw that Belkis had changed her clothes and was now wearing a petroleum-colored skirt which reminded him that he was in a strange place with a strange woman. She had also completely changed her face and her hair. She'd combed her hair back like Ava Gardner's in *55 Days at Peking*, and she had painted her lips the same Supertechnirama Red as in the film. Looking at her new face, Galip suddenly thought that people had been taking him in for quite some time.

Not long after, Galip had already removed the newspaper in the pocket of his overcoat, which the woman had fastidiously slipped on a hanger and put in the closet, and had spread the paper on the breakfast table, which had been cleared with the same fastidiousness. When he reread Jelal's column, the notes he'd previously made in the margins and the words and syllables he had underlined seemed silly to him. It was so obvious the marked words were not the ones which would reveal the secret in the piece that Galip entertained the passing thought that the secret did not exist: it seemed as if the sentences he was reading signified themselves and, at the same time, something else. So much so that every sentence regarding the hero in Jelal's Sunday column, who could not communicate to mankind an incredible discovery he had made on account of having lost his memory, seemed like it was a sentence that came out of another story concerning some other human condition known and understood by everyone. This was so clear and so true that there was no necessity to rewrite and to rearrange certain letters, syllables, and words he had chosen. In order to decipher the "hidden" meaning in the piece, all that was needed was merely to read the piece in good faith. As his eyes traveled from word to word, Galip believed that he was studying the City's and Life's secrets, as well as seeking the location and the significance of the place where Rüya and Jelal were hiding out; but each time he raised his head from the text and saw Belkis's new face, he lost his good faith. He hoped he could keep his optimism intact and tried for a while to start from scratch rereading the text, but he could not clearly discern the secret meaning that he thought might become apparent to him. He felt the thrill of almost discovering the mystery concerning existence and the world, but whenever he tried thinking through the secret he was looking for by spelling it out, the face of the woman who watched him from her corner appeared in front of his eyes. After a while, having decided that he might be able to get close to the secret through the intellect, not through faith and intuition, he began making fresh notes in the margins and marking entirely different syllables and words. He had lost himself in his task when Belkis approached the table.

"Jelal Salik's column," she said. "I'm aware that he's your uncle. Do you know why his underground mannequin looked so creepy last night?"

"No, I don't," said Galip. "But he's not my uncle, he's my uncle's son."

"Because the mannequin looked so much like him," Belkis said. "Sometimes when I went up to Nişantaşı in hopes of running into you, I'd see him instead wearing the same outfit."

"That's the raincoat he wore years ago," Galip said. "He used to wear it a lot back then."

"He still wears it, going around Nişantaşı like a ghost," said Belkis. "What are those notes you're taking in the margins?"

"They are not about the column," Galip said, folding the newspaper. "They concern a polar explorer who gets lost. Because he is lost, someone else steps in and gets lost in his place. The first missing person, the mystery of whose loss is deepened by the loss of the second person, apparently goes on to live in a godforsaken town under a different name, but it seems he gets himself killed one day."

When Galip got through telling his story, he realized that he'd have to tell it again. As he told it again, he felt great anger against all the people who forced him to tell a story over and over again. He felt like saying: "Why can't everyone be himself so that no one needs to tell any stories!" He'd gotten to his feet while he was retelling the story, and now he slipped the folded newspaper back into the pocket of his old overcoat.

"Are you leaving?" Belkis asked timidly.

"I haven't finished my story yet," Galip said with irritation.

As he finished telling the story, Galip had a feeling that there was a mask on the woman's face. If he pulled away the mask with the Supertechnirama Red lips from the woman's face, the total meaning would be clearly visible on the countenance underneath it, but he couldn't figure out what that meaning might be. It was as if he were playing the game of "Why Are We Here?" he played in his childhood when he was bored out of his skull. Consequently, he was able to tell his story, as he did in his childhood, focusing on something else while playing the game. For a moment he thought the reason why Jelal was so attractive to women was because he could tell a story while he simultaneously thought about other things; but then, Belkis did not look like a woman who was listening to one of Jelal's stories.

"Doesn't Rüya ever wonder where you are?" Belkis said.

"No, she doesn't," said Galip. "I've been known to go home past midnight lots of times. On account of missing politicos, or swindlers who take out loans under false names. I've been gone until morning many a time, having had to deal with mysterious tenants who vanish without paying the rent, or unhappy bigamists who remarry using false identifications."

"But it's past noon," Belkis said. "If I were Rüya waiting for you at home, I'd wish you'd call soon as you could."

"I don't want to call."

"If it were me waiting for you, I'd be worried sick," Belkis went on. "I'd be at the window, listening for the phone to ring. I'd be unhappier still, thinking that you didn't call in spite of the fact that you knew I was worried and unhappy. Come on, give her a ring. Tell her you're here, with me."

When the woman brought the receiver to him as if it were a toy, Galip called home. There was no answer.

"Nobody's home."

"Where could she be?" said the woman playfully.

"Don't know," said Galip.

He opened up the newspaper again and turned back to Jelal's column. He read the text again and again, so many times and for such a long time that the words lost their meaning and turned into mere shapes composed of letters. A while later, Galip thought he could write this piece himself, that he could write like Jelal. Before long he took his coat out of the closet and put it on, folded the paper carefully, and put the column, which he'd ripped out of it, into his pocket.

"You leaving?" said Belkis. "Don't go."

In the taxi he finally managed to flag down, Galip took a final look at the familiar street, afraid that he wouldn't be able to forget Belkis's face insisting that he not go; he wished the woman could have stayed in his mind wearing another face, inhabiting another story. He thought of instructing the driver, "Such and such street and step on it," as in Rüya's detective novels, but merely said he was going to the Galata Bridge.

As he was walking across the bridge, lost in the Sunday crowd, he was seized by a feeling that the solution to the secret he had been blindly searching for all these years, without ever realizing until just now that it was what he sought, was immediately at hand. Somewhere in a dark corner of his mind, as in a dream, he was aware that this feeling was a misapprehension, but the two sensations existed together in Galip's mind without disturbing him in the least. He observed conscripts out on a pass, people out fishing, families with children hurrying to catch the boat. They all inhabited the secret Galip was working on, but they were not aware of it. When, in a moment, Galip solved it, they would all become aware of this fact which had for many years been impressed deeply on their lives—including the father out for a Sunday visit along with his sneakered son and the infant he was carrying, and the mother and daughter who both wore scarves sitting on a bus that went by.

He was on the bridge, walking on the Sea of Marmara side, when he began making for people as if he were going to run into them: the meaning in their faces which had been missing, stale, or used up for many years seemed to light up for a moment. While they tried figuring out who the reckless person was, Galip looked into their eyes and their faces as if reading their secret.

Most wore old jackets and overcoats, worn and faded. Walking along, they considered the whole world as ordinary as the sidewalk they were on, but they did not have a real foothold on this world. They were preoccupied; yet if they were provoked a little, a kind of curiosity that connected them to a profound meaning in their past surfaced from the depths of their memory banks and appeared, for a moment, on the masklike expressions on their faces. "I wish I could bother them!" Galip thought. "I wish I could tell them the story of the Prince." The story he had in mind was now brand-new; he felt he had lived through the story himself and remembered it.

Most people on the bridge were carrying plastic bags. He stared at the bags, which had paper sacks, bits of metal, plastic, or newspapers sticking out of them, as if he were seeing plastic bags for the first time, and he assiduously read what was written on them. He was heartened for a moment, having sensed that the words and the letters on the bags signified the "other" or the "real" reality. But just as the meaning in the faces that went by him faded following the moment of brightness, the words and syllables on the plastic bags, after being momentarily suffused with a new meaning, also vanished in turn. Still, Galip kept on reading for quite some time: ". . . Pudding Shop . . . Ata Village . . . Turkmanufac . . . Dried fruits . . . it is the hour of . . . Palaces . . ."

On a bag that belonged to an old guy who was out fishing, he saw the picture of a stork instead of letters and realized that pictures could be read just as well as letters. He saw a bag with the faces of a pair of happy parents and their son and daughter who regarded the world with hope, on another bag there were a pair of fish, on others were pictures of shoes, maps of Turkey, silhouettes of buildings, cigarette packs, black cats, roosters, horseshoes, minarets, baklava, trees. Obviously they were all signs of a mystery. But what was the mystery? He saw an owl on the bag sitting next to an old woman who sold bird feed for the pigeons in front of the New Mosque. When he realized that this owl was either the same owl as the one in the imprint on the detective novels that Rüya read or its cunningly concealed twin, Galip clearly felt the presence of a "hand" that secretly brought order to things. There it was, another trick perpetrated by the "hand" which must be tipped and exposed; the owl had a secret significance but nobody besides Galip gave two hoots. Even though they were in it up to their ears, buried deep in the secret that had been lost!

So that he could examine the owl more closely, Galip bought a cup of corn from the old bat who looked like a witch, and he scattered the feed for the pigeons. Instantly, a black and ugly mass of pigeons closed in on the feed like an umbrella of wings. The owl on the bag was the very same owl as the one on Rüya's detective novels. Galip was angry with a pair of parents who were proudly and blithely watching their daughter feed the pigeons because they were unaware of this owl, of this obvious truth, of other signs, of any sign whatsoever, of anything at all. They didn't have a clue, not even a hint of suspicion. They were oblivious. He imagined he was the protagonist of the detective novel he imagined Rüya was reading, waiting for him to come home. The puzzle that had to be solved was between himself and that covert hand which itself remained hidden in spite of having arranged everything masterfully, pointing to a significance that was top secret.

When he himself happened to be in the vicinity of the Mosque of Süleyman the Magnificent, it was enough for him to see an apprentice carrying a framed picture of the same mosque made out of tiny beads to conclude that if words, letters, pictures on the plastic bags were signs, so were what they signified. The loud colors in the picture were more real than the mosque itself. Not only were inscriptions, faces, pictures the pieces in the game played by the hidden hand, but so was everything. As soon as he understood this, he realized that the district known as Dungeon Door, where he was walking through a jumble of streets, also had a special significance that nobody was aware of. Patient like someone nearing the end of a crossword puzzle, he felt that everything was about to fall into place.

He sensed that the garden shears he saw in jerry-built stores and on crooked sidewalks in the neighborhood, the screwdrivers ornamented with stars, the NO PARKING signs, the tomato-paste tins, the calendars on the walls of cheap restaurants, the Byzantine aqueduct hung with plexiglass letters, the ponderous padlocks on roll-down store shutters, were all signs of the secret meaning. If he wished, he could read these articles and signs as if reading human faces. That was how, having realized that pliers were the sign for "attentiveness," bottled olives for "patience," and the contented driver in the billboard advertising tires for "approaching the goal," he decided he was approaching his goal with attentiveness and patience. Yet all around him were signs which were much more formidable to fathom: telephone wires, a circumcisor's signboard, traffic signs, detergent boxes, shovels without handles, illegible political slogans, pieces of shattered icicles on the sidewalks, numbers on doors pertaining to the municipal electric services, traffic arrows, pieces of blank paper . . . They might perhaps be clarified shortly, yet everything was completely messed up, wearisome, and noisy. On the other hand, the protagonists in Rüya's detective novels lived in a snug and equanimous world determined by a requisite number of clues that the author had presented them.

Even so, the Mosque of Ahi Çelebi consoled him, serving as the sign of a comprehensible fiction. Many years ago, Jelal had written about a dream in which he saw himself in this little mosque in the company of Muhammad and some of the saints. When he'd gone to consult an oracle in the Kasımpaşa district to get his dream interpreted, he was told he would keep writing until the very end of his life. He would have such a career of writing and imagining that he would remember his life as a long journey even if he never stirred out of his house. Galip had figured out much later that the article was an adaptation of a well-known piece by Evliya Çelebi, the historical travel writer.

He went by the Fruit Market, thinking, "Therefore, the first time I read it, the story presented one meaning, then a completely different meaning after the second reading." He had no doubt that the third and fourth readings of Jelal's column would each time reveal yet other meanings: Jelal's stories, even if they signified something else each time, gave Galip the impression that he was on target, going through a series of doors just like the puzzles in children's magazines. Absentmindedly walking through the jumble of streets in the Market, Galip wished he could instantly be someplace where he could go through all of Jelal's columns once more.

Just outside the Market, he saw a junk dealer. The dealer had spread a large bedsheet on the sidewalk and put out a series of objects that enthralled Galip, who'd come out of the racket and stench of the marketplace without having arrived at any sort of conclusion: a couple of pipe elbows, old records, a pair of black shoes, a lamp base, a broken pair of pliers, a black telephone, two bedsprings, a mother-of-pearl cigarette holder, a wall clock that wasn't running, White Russian banknotes, a brass faucet, a figurine carrying quivers which depicted a Roman goddess (Diana?), a picture frame, an old radio, a couple of doorknobs, a candy dish.

Galip named all of them, deliberately enunciating the words, as he examined each one carefully. He felt that what actually made objects enchanting did not reside in the objects themselves but in the way they were being displayed. The elderly dealer had arranged these articles, which could be seen in any junk dealer's display, four down and four across on the bedsheet, as if it were a great big checkerboard. The objects were equidistant from each other like checkers on a board with the requisite sixty-four squares; they did not touch each other, yet the acuity and the simplicity in their arrangement seemed to be not accidental but deliberate. So much so that Galip immediately thought of vocabulary tests in foreign-language textbooks; on those pages too he'd seen the pictures of sixteen objects, all lined up just like this, which he'd named with nouns in the new language. Galip felt like saying, with similar enthusiasm, "pipe, record, shoe, pliers . . ."

But what scared him was the definite feeling that the objects had other meanings as well. While he stared at the brass faucet, he thought it signified "brass faucet" as in the vocabulary exercise, but he was excited to sense that the faucet could just as well signify something else. The black telephone on the sheet, in addition to representing the concept of the telephone as in the pages of a foreign-language textbook, denoting that familiar instrument which once plugged in connects us to other voices, also connoted another meaning that made Galip shiver with excitement.

How could he enter the arcane world of secondary meanings and discover the mystery? He felt the thrill of being at the threshold of this realm, but he just couldn't take the first step in. In Rüya's detective novels, when the puzzle was solved at the end, while the second realm which had been under wraps was illuminated the first one would now sink into the darkness of oblivion. When around midnight, stuffing her face with the roasted chickpeas from Aladdin's, Rüya announced, "The murderer turns out to be the retired colonel avenging himself for an insult!" Galip surmised that his wife had already forgotten all the details in the book rife with English butlers, cigarette lighters, dinner tables, porcelain cups, guns, and that she would only remember the new secret meaning of the world that these objects and persons signified. But, at the end of the horribly translated book, the reposited objects, with the help of the hardboiled detective, placed Rüya in another world. Such objects, however, could so far offer Galip no more than the hope for a new world. In an effort to solve the enigma, Galip carefully observed the junk dealer who had arranged these mysterious objects on the sheet, as if to read the meaning in the old guy's face.

"How much for the telephone?"

"You a buyer?" said the junk dealer, initiating the bargaining procedure guardedly.

Galip was thrown by the unexpected question concerning his identity. A thought flashed through his mind: "See, I too am considered the signpost for something other than myself!" Still, the world he wanted to enter was not this one but another sphere that Jelal had spent his life creating. He felt that Jelal, by naming things and telling stories, had been building the walls and concealing the keys to this world where he had secreted himself. The dealer's face lit up for a moment with the prospect of making a deal, then it reassumed its former dullness.

"What's this for?" Galip said, pointing out a simple little lamp base.

"Table leg," said the dealer, "but some people stick 'em on the ends of curtain cornices. Could make a doorknob too."

When Galip got to the Atatürk Bridge, he was thinking, "From now on, I will only observe faces." The brief brightness in the faces that went by on the bridge was for a moment aggrandized in his mind like the dilating question marks in photonovels translated from other languages, then, along with the question, the face was also nullified, having left only a slight trace. Even though he came close to making a connection between the view of the city from the bridge and the cumulative meaning the faces created in his mind, it was a misapprehension. Although it was possible to perceive the city's old age, its misfortune, its lost splendor, its sorrow and pathos in the faces of the citizens, it was not the symptom of a specifically contrived secret but of a collective defeat, history, and complicity. In the wake of the tugboats, the cold leaden-blue waters of the Golden Horn took on a frightening brown hue.

By the time he entered a coffeehouse on a backstreet behind the so-called subway, Galip had observed seventy-three new faces. He sat down at a table, pleased with what he had seen. After ordering his tea, he took the page of newsprint out of his coat pocket and began automatically rereading Jelal's column. The words, the sentences, and the letters were no longer fresh, yet, as he read them, Galip felt that some ideas that had not previously occurred to him were being verified: although these ideas did not emerge out of Jelal's article but were Galip's own, in some odd way Jelal's article included them too. When he became aware of the parallels between his own ideas and Jelal's, Galip felt the same sort of inner peace as in his childhood when he was sure at times that he had succeeded in impersonating someone he wanted to emulate.

On the table, there was a piece of paper that had been shaped into a cone. The sunflower-seed hulls scattered next to it indicated that some vendor had sold the seeds in this paper cone to persons who'd sat at this table prior to Galip. Looking at the edges of the paper, Galip realized that it had been torn out of a school notebook. He read the painstaking child's handwriting on the other side: "September 6, 1972. Unit 12. Homework: Our home, our garden. There are four trees in our garden. Two poplars, a large willow and a small willow. My father built a wall around our garden using stones and wire fencing. A house is a shelter that protects people from the cold in the winter and the heat in the summer. Home is a place that safeguards us against harm. Our house has 1 door, 6 windows, 2 chimneys." Underneath the text, drawn with colored pencils, there was an illustration of the house inside a walled garden. The roof tiles had initially been drawn individually, then the whole roof had been impatiently scratched over in red. Galip felt his sense of inner peace increase when he realized that the number of doors, windows, trees, and chimneys verified those in the essay.

It was with this feeling of peace that he turned the unused side of the page over and began to write rapidly. He had no doubt the words he wrote in between the lines in the paper signified certain facts that became real just like the words that the kid had written. It was as if he had lost his words and his tongue for many years and had now retrieved them thanks to this page of homework. He made a list of all the clues, which he wrote in small letters; and when he came to the end of the page, he thought, "It was all so easy!" Then he thought, "Just to make sure that Jelal and I think alike, I have to see many more faces."

After drinking his tea while watching the faces in the coffeehouse, he went back out into the cold. On one of the streets behind Galata Palace Lycée, he saw an elderly woman wearing a kerchief who walked along talking to herself. He read that all lives are similar in the face of a little girl who stooped down to emerge from under the half-closed shutter of a grocery store. On the face of a young girl in a faded dress, who walked staring at her rubber shoes that kept slipping on the ice, it was written that she knew the nature of anxiety.

When Galip went in and sat down in another coffeehouse, he took the page of homework out of his pocket and quickly began reading it as if reading Jelal's column. He was well aware now that he could locate Jelal if he acquired Jelal's memory bank by reading his work over and over. That meant, in order to get the memory, he first had to discover the repository where Jelal's complete works were hidden. It was having read the homework so many times that had made it possible for him to figure out that such a museum had to be a "home": "A place that safeguards us against harm." As he kept reading the homework, he felt deep inside himself the innocence of the kid who could dauntlessly name all objects, so much so that he thought he could easily come up with the location of the place where Rüya and Jelal were waiting for him. But sitting at the table, he was unable to do much more than write in new clues on the other side of the homework every time he went into a tizzy with the realization.

By the time he was out on the street once again, Galip had eliminated some of the clues and given prominence to others: They could not be outside of the city since Jelal could not live anywhere but in Istanbul. They couldn't be on the Anatolian side, across the Bosphorus, seeing how it wasn't "historical" enough to suit him. Rüya and Jelal couldn't have holed up at a mutual friend's since they didn't have such a friend. Rüya couldn't be at one of her friends' either because Jelal would never be caught dead going to such a place. They couldn't stay in those hotel rooms devoid of memories, even though they were brother and sister, because a man and a woman together would look fishy.

In the next coffeehouse, he was sure that he was at least on the right track. He wanted to walk to Taksim through the backstreets in Beyoğlu, toward Nişantaşı, Şişli, and the very heart of his own past. He remembered Jelal expounding in one of his pieces on the names of Istanbul streets. He noticed the photo on the wall of a late-lamented wrestler about whom Jelal had written at length. It was a black-and-white photo, the kind that came as the centerfold of the old *Life* magazines which got framed and graced the walls of many a barber, haberdasher, and greengrocer. Galip was studying the expression in the face of the Olympic medalist, who had his hands planted on his hips and smiled modestly at the camera, when he remembered that the man had died in a traffic accident. That's why the accident that took place seventeen years ago and the modest expression in the wrestler's face were fused together in his mind, as had happened so many times before, and Galip couldn't help but think the traffic accident was some sort of sign.

It went to show that moments of coincidence were necessary which would fuse the facts with the imagination, creating the signs of an entirely different story. "Incidentally," Galip reflected when he had come out of the coffee-house and was walking toward Taksim on one of the backstreets, "looking at the tired old horse in front of that cart next to the curb on Hasnun Galip Street, I need to consult the recollection of the large horse that I'd seen in my alphabet book when Grandma was teaching me to read and write. In turn, the large alphabet horse under which it said HORSE reminds me of Jelal who lived alone during the same years in the attic apartment in the building on Teşvikiye Avenue, and of the apartment itself which Jelal had furnished in accordance with his taste and memories. Then, I am led to think that the apartment could be a sign of the hold Jelal has on my own life."

But years had gone by since Jelal had vacated the flat. Galip came to a halt, thinking he might also be screwing up interpreting the signs. He had no doubt that he'd be lost in the city if he came to think his senses were misleading him. Fictions were what kept him aloft, tales that his senses stumbled on, groping like a blindman to locate and recognize objects. He was still on his feet only because he had managed to construct a story out of the signs and images as he went all over the city. He was sure that the people and the world around him also managed to abide on the strength of stories.

When he went into yet another coffeehouse to sit down, hanging on to his optimism, Galip was able to review "his situation." The words in the list of clues seemed as simple and comprehensible as the words in the homework on the other side of the page. On the black-and-white TV in the far corner of the room, a soccer game was in progress on a snowy field. The marking lines on the field and the muddy soccer ball were black. Aside from those who played cards on the bare tables, everyone watched this black soccer ball.

Walking out of the coffeehouse, Galip thought the mystery he was seeking was as clear as the black-and-white soccer match. All that was necessary was to keep looking at faces and manifestations and going wherever his feet took him. Istanbul was chock-full of coffeehouses; a person could walk the entire city, stopping at some coffeehouse every couple of hundred yards.

He suddenly found himself in the crowd that came out of a movie house near Taksim. The faces of the people who walked out absentmindedly, staring at their feet, their hands in their pockets, or walking arm in arm up the steps into the street, were loaded with such suggestive meaning that Galip thought even his own nightmarish story was not all that significant. In the faces of the moviegoers was the serenity of those who, having immersed themselves in some fiction up to their ears, have managed to forget their own sorrow. They were simultaneously in this miserable street and also in the tale where they wished to be. Their memory banks which had long been bankrupted by dolor and defeat were now replenished by a profound story which had fully and gently soothed their recollections of pain. "They are under the impression that they are someone else!" Galip thought longingly. For a moment he wished he too had seen the same movie as the crowd and could disappear and become someone else. He could see that these people, as they looked into ordinary store windows, were returning to the boring world of familiar and recognizable things. "They go easy on themselves!" Galip thought.

On the other hand, to become someone else, you needed to use all your determination. By the time Galip ended up at Taksim Square, he was resolved to jog his whole willpower to this end. "I am someone else!" he told himself. It was a pleasant feeling, altering not only the frozen sidewalks under his feet, and the square surrounded by billboards for Coca-Cola and canned food, but also his own person from head to toe. Repeating the sentence with resolution, one could make oneself believe the whole world had been transformed, but going that far wasn't all that necessary. "I am someone else," Galip said to himself. He listened with pleasure to the music suffused with the memories and the sorrows of a person he didn't wish to name, rising inside him like a new life. Taksim Square, one of the basic landmarks of his life, with buses circling around it like overgrown turkeys, slow trolleys like absentminded lobsters, and obscure areas resolved to remain in the dark, was gradually transformed within the music and turned into the gussied-up "modern" square in an impoverished, hopeless country where Galip had set foot for the first time. The snow-covered Statue of the Republic, the grand Ionic Stairway that led nowhere, and the "Opera" House which Galip had been pleased to watch going up in a blaze ten years ago had also become transformed into the actual pieces that belonged to the imaginary country they were meant to signify. Among the agitated crowds at the bus stops, or the people who elbowed their way into transports, Galip could not see any mysterious faces, not even a plastic bag which could be a sign for a parallel universe under wraps.

So, without feeling any need to go into coffeehouses, he made his way from Harbiye straight to Nişantaşı. Much later, when he believed that he had found the place he was looking for, he would remain uncertain as to the identity he had assumed along the way. "I had not yet totally convinced myself by then of having become Jelal," he would reason later on, surrounded by the old pieces, old notebooks, and newspaper clippings that illuminated Jelal's past in its entirety. "I hadn't yet totally left myself behind then." He had regarded what he saw like a tourist who, on account of his plane having been delayed, was spending half a day at some city he had never imagined himself visiting: The statue of Atatürk signified that there had been a prominent military hero in this country's past; the crowds jammed into the muddy but brightly lit movie theater entrances signaled that the populace, bored on a Sunday afternoon, distracted themselves watching dreams imported from other countries; the salesmen in sandwich and pastry shops looking out the store windows into the street holding their knives meant that their sad dreams and memories were fading out; and the dark, bare trees in the middle of the avenue were the sign of a national sorrow that became darker as it descended in the afternoon. "My God, what is there to do in this city, on this avenue, at this hour?" Galip had murmured only to remember that he had picked up this invocation from one of Jelal's old pieces which he'd clipped and saved.

It had become dark by the time he got to Nişantaşı. The smell of engine exhaust intensified by traffic jams on winter evenings and the smoke from the chimneys of the apartment buildings pervaded the narrow sidewalks. Galip calmly inhaled the pungent smell which he thought was strangely particular to this quarter. On Nişantaşı Corner, the desire to be someone else arose so strongly in him that he imagined he could apprehend the façades of apartment buildings, storefronts, bank billboards, and neon signs as completely different and novel things. The feeling of lightness and adventure that transformed the quarter where he'd lived for so many years into someplace else altogether penetrated deep inside Galip as if it would never leave him again.

Instead of crossing the street to his own place, he turned left on Teşvikiye Avenue. Galip was so pleased with the feeling that permeated his whole body, and the possibilities offered by the personality he'd assumed were so attractive, that he filled his eyes with new sights like a patient released from the hospital where he'd been sick for years within four walls. "So, the display window of the pudding shop looked all along like the well-lit showcase of a jewelry store," he felt like saying. "So, the street was quite narrow and the sidewalks all crooked!"

In his childhood, too, it so happened that he used to watch objectively his second self who left his own body and soul behind. "Now he's going by the Ottoman Bank," Galip thought, as if he were tracking down the alternative identity he used to assume in his childhood; "Now he's going by the Heart-of-the-City Apartments, without even giving it a glance, where he lived for years with his mom, dad, and grandparents. Now he stops to look in the window of the pharmacy where the son of the woman who gave shots sits at the cash register. Now he goes by the police station without any trepidation, and now he fondly regards the mannequins placed among the Singer sewing machines as if they were old friends. Now he walks like a goal-oriented, determined person toward the mystery, toward the heart of a plot that has been schemed painstakingly for so many years."

He crossed to the other side of the street and doubled back, only to cross the street once more and walk under the precious few linden trees, billboards, and balconies all the way to the mosque. By going a little farther up or down the street each time, he enlarged his "field of research," and each time he carefully observed and recorded in his memory the details he hadn't been able to perceive before on account of his hapless former personality: In Aladdin's display window, among the piles of old newspapers, toy guns, and nylon stockings, there happened to be a switchblade; the traffic arrow indicating the obligatory direction into Teşvikiye Avenue pointed instead to the Heart-of-the-City Apartments; despite the cold weather, the crusts of bread that had been left for pigeons and cats on the low walls around the mosque had become moldy; some of the words in the political slogans scrawled along the portals of the girls' lycée had double meanings; out of his photo on the wall in a classroom where the lights had been left on, Atatürk was looking at the Heart-of-the-City Apartments through dusty windowpanes; the hand of someone with strange sensibilities had pinned safety pins on the rosebuds in the florist's window. The snazzy mannequins in the window of a new leather apparel shop were also staring at the Heart-of-the-City Apartments, at the top floor where once Jelal had lived and later Rüya with her parents.

Galip joined the mannequins in staring at the top floor for quite some time. It seemed reasonable to Galip that Jelal and Rüya could be up there, on the top floor that the mannequins' gazes pointed to, feeling as he did like a fake hero modeled after those in the translated detective novels, which he heard about from Rüya, who had also been conceived in foreign lands, as were the mannequins themselves. He practically fled the premises and walked toward the mosque.

But he had to use all his power to do it. It was as if his legs refused to take him away from the Heart-of-the-City Apartments but wanted to go in the building immediately, run up the stairs to the top floor, and show him something upon arriving at that dark and scary place. Galip did not wish to dwell on the particulars of this image. While he walked away from the place using all his strength, he had a feeling that the sidewalks, the shops, the letters on the billboards, and the traffic signs went back to indicating their former significations. As soon as it hit him that the two of them were up there, he had an instant premonition of disaster and was frightened out of his skull. When he arrived at Aladdin's corner, he couldn't figure out if his fear intensified because he was near the police station or because he realized the traffic arrow no longer pointed at the Heart-of-the-City Apartments. He was so tired and confused, he needed to sit down somewhere so he could do a little thinking.

He went into the long-standing diner on the corner by the Teşvikiye–Eminönü *dolmuş* stop and asked for tea and a *börek*. Seeing how Jelal was so stuck on his own personal history and his eroding memory, what could be more natural than his renting or buying the flat where he had spent his youth and childhood? That way he'd be returning victoriously to the place he was kicked out of, while those who gave him the boot were broke and rotting in a dusty apartment on one of the unfashionable streets. Galip thought it was totally in character for Jelal to keep his victory from the family, aside from Rüya, and to cover his tracks in spite of living on the main avenue.

For the next few minutes, he turned his attention to a family that showed up at the counter: mom, dad, daughter, and son making do with supper at the diner after taking in their Sunday afternoon movie. The parents were the same age as Galip. From time to time the father buried himself in the newspaper which he'd produced out of his coat pocket; the mother used her eyebrows to supervise the fights that erupted between the kids, her hand traveling continuously between her small handbag and the table to produce things for the other three with the speed and dexterity of a magician pulling strange objects out of a hat: a hankie for the boy's runny nose, a red pill for the father's palm, a bobby pin for the girl's hair, a cigarette lighter for the father, who was reading Jelal's column, the same hankie for the boy's nose, etc.

By the time Galip was done with his *börek* and tea, he had remembered that the father had been a classmate of his in middle school and high school. As he was going out the door, he heeded an inner urge to divulge this fact to the father, and as he became aware of a frightful burn scar on the man's throat and right cheek, he recalled that the mother had been the loudmouth whiz kid who was also in the same class when he and Rüya attended Şişli

Progressive High. The two children saw their chance to get even with each other while the adults went through the obligatory reminiscing and asking after each other, and Rüya, who completed the symmetry with the other, similar marriage, was also remembered with affection. Galip told them they didn't have any children; Rüya waited for him at home reading detective novels; they were going to the Palace Theater in the evening, where he had gone to get tickets ahead of time, and on the way he had run into another one of their classmates, Belkis: Belkis, you know. Brown hair, medium height.

The tedious couple left no room for doubt, making their tedious point: "But there was no one in our class called Belkis!" Apparently they were in the habit of looking through their yearbook now and then, recalling everyone in turn with special anecdotes and reminiscences; that's why they were so damn sure.

Out of the diner into the cold, Galip rapidly made for Nişantaşı Square. He had made up his mind that Rüya and Jelal would go to see the 7:15 Sunday evening show at the Palace, so he ran all the way to the theater; but they were not to be seen anywhere on the sidewalk or at the entrance. While he waited for them, he saw the photo of the woman in the film he'd seen yesterday, and he felt the desire to be with that woman in her world rise inside him once more.

They did not appear, and he wandered around for a time looking into display windows and reading the faces of the people who went by on the sidewalks; when he arrived in front of the Heart-of-the-City Apartments again, it was quite late. By eight o'clock every evening, the bluish light from the TV sets would be flickering in the windows of all the buildings with the exception of the Heart-of-the-City Apartments. Galip was carefully studying the blank windows in the building when he noticed a dark-blue piece of cloth tied on the iron grill of the balcony on the top floor. When the whole family lived here thirty years ago, the same kind of dark-blue cloth tied to the same iron grill used to be a signal for the water-man, who purveyed water in enameled containers loaded on his horse cart. From the position of the blue cloth he could figure out which flats were out of drinking water and brought the water up accordingly.

Galip decided that the cloth must be a signal too, and this presented to his mind different notions of how to read it. It might be a signal to tell him that Jelal and Rüya were there, or it might be a sign of Jelal's nostalgic research into some details out of his past. At eight-thirty, he left his spot on the sidewalk and returned home.

The light cast by the lamps in the living room where he and Rüya sat together once, and not so very long ago, smoking and reading their books and papers, was unbearably full of memories and unbearably sad, like the pictures of a lost paradise that end up on the travel pages of the newspapers. Nowhere was there a sign that Rüya had come home or had stopped by: the familiar scents and shadows wanly greeted the tired husband returning to his nest. Abandoning these silent objects to the sad light of the lamps, Galip went into the dark hallway and then the dark bedroom. He took off his coat, groped for the bed, and fell into it on his back. The light from the living room and the streetlamps that seeped in through the hallway left shadows like thin-faced devils on the ceiling. He could not sleep.

Not long after getting out of bed, Galip knew exactly what he was going to do. He checked the TV programs in the paper, studied the films and the times they were being shown at the neighboring theaters, in spite of the fact that the show times never varied; he took a last glance at Jelal's column; he went to the fridge and lifted out a few olives and a piece of feta cheese from the first signs of spoilage in their containers, found some crusts of bread, and ate. He stuffed random pages of newspaper into a largish envelope that he found in Rüya's closet, and writing Jelal's name on it took it along. By ten-fifteen, he was out of the house and across the street from the Heart-of-the-City Apartments again, this time on a spot further down the sidewalk.

Presently the stairway lights went on and Ismail, who'd been the building's doorman for the longest time, took out the garbage cans and began, his cigarette dangling from his mouth, to empty them into the large barrel next to the chestnut tree. Galip crossed over.

"Ismail, hello there. I'm here to leave this envelope for Jelal."

"It's you, Galip!" the man said with the joy and anxiety of a high-school principal who recognizes an old student many years later. "But Jelal is not here."

"I just happen to know he is here, but I'm not about to let anyone else in on it," Galip said, entering the building resolutely. "Don't you tell anyone, either. He gave me instructions, saying, leave the envelope with Ismail downstairs."

Galip went down the stairs that had the same old stench of natural gas and fried fat and entered the doorman's flat. Ismail's wife, Kamer, was sitting in the same old armchair and watching a TV set that stood on the same stand that had once carried the radio.

"Kamer, look who's here," Galip said.

"Well, I'll be . . ." said the woman, getting up to kiss him. "You all don't remember us anymore."

"How could we forget you?"

"You go past the building, but none of you ever thinks of stopping by!"

"I brought this for Jelal!" said Galip, pointing at the envelope.

"Was it Ismail who told you?"

"No, Jelal told me himself," said Galip. "I definitely know he's here, but don't tell anyone else."

"We're keeping our mouths shut, aren't we," said the woman. "He gave us strict orders."

"I know," Galip said. "Are they upstairs now?"

"We don't know anything at all. He comes and goes in the middle of the night when we're sleeping. We only hear him. We take out his trash and deliver his paper. Sometimes the papers pile up, there under the door for days."

"I'm not going upstairs," Galip said. He scanned the flat as if picking out a place to leave the envelope: the dinner table covered with the same old blue-checkered oilcloth, the same faded curtains that shut out the view of legs going by and muddy automobile tires; the sewing basket, the iron, the candy dish, gas cooking plate, sooty radiators . . . On the nail pounded into the edge of the shelf above the radiator, Galip saw the key, hanging in its usual place.

"Let me make you some tea," she said. "Take a seat on the edge of the bed." She kept an eye on the tube. "What's Rüya up to? Why are you two still without a kid?"

On the screen, which the woman couldn't help but watch now, there appeared a young woman who was slightly reminiscent of Rüya. Her indeterminately colored hair was ruffled, her complexion was light, her gaze had the calmness of the childlike look Rüya affected. She was blithely applying her lipstick.

"Pretty woman," Galip said quietly.

"Rüya is even prettier," said Kamer, also quietly.

They watched respectfully, with an apprehensive kind of admiration. Galip skillfully snatched the key off the nail and put it in his pocket, slipping it next to the page of homework full of clues. The woman was none the wiser.

Through the small curtained window that faced on the street, Galip caught a glimpse of Ismail coming back into the building with the empty trash cans. When the power kicked in on the elevator, the picture on the tube got fuzzy for a moment, which gave Galip the chance to say goodbye. He went up the stairs and noisily made for the door. He opened the door and did not go out, but banged the door shut. Without making a sound, he walked back to the staircase, then tiptoed two flights up, unable to control his jitters. He sat down on the steps between the second and third floors, waiting for Ismail, who was returning the trash cans to the upper floors, to go down on the elevator. The lights in the stairwell went out suddenly. "The time-switch!" Galip murmured; in his childhood he had associated the name with magical journeys on a time machine. The lights went back on. While the doorman took the elevator down, Galip began slowly going up the stairs. On the door to the flat where he had once lived with his mom and dad, a lawyer had put up his brass nameplate. At the entrance to his grandparents' flat, he saw a gynecologist's shingle and an empty trash can. He climbed to the top floor.

On Jelal's door there was neither a sign nor a name. Galip rang the doorbell routinely like an assiduous bill collector from municipal gas. He was ringing the bell a second time when the lights in the stairway went out again. There was no light at all showing under the door. His hand searched for the key in the bottomless well of his pocket while he rang the bell for the third and fourth times, and his finger was still pushing the bell when he found the key. "They are hiding in one of the rooms in there," he reasoned. "They are sitting across from each other in two armchairs and waiting quietly!" At first he couldn't fit the key in the lock; he was about to pronounce it the wrong key when the key clicked into place with an odd felicitousness that was surprising—like an addled memory that in a moment of lucidity becomes aware of both its own dotage and the haphazard order in the world. Galip became aware first of the darkness into which the door opened, and then of a phone beginning to ring in the dark flat.

Part Two

Chapter Twenty

THE PHANTOM ABODE

He felt as dreary as an empty house . . .
                                        —GUSTAVE FLAUBERT, *Madame Bovary*

The phone had begun to ring three to four seconds after he opened the door, but Galip still felt apprehensive. What if there was a mechanical connection between the phone and the door, just like those alarm bells that ring ruthlessly in gangster films? The third time he heard the ring, he thought he might run smack into Jelal anxiously hurrying to get the phone in the dark apartment; on the fourth ring, he surmised that there was no one at home, on the fifth that there must be, reasoning that only someone who knew that the place was inhabited would keep ringing so insistently. On the sixth ring, Galip was groping around to locate the light switches, trying to remember the topography of this phantom-like flat in which he had last set foot fifteen years ago, and he was startled when he crashed into something. In the pitch dark, he made for the phone, running into other things and knocking them over. When he at last held the elusive receiver to his ear, his body had found a chair on its own and sat down.

"Hello?"

"So you finally got home!" said a voice he didn't know at all.

"Yes."

"Jelal Bey, I've been looking for you for days. Sorry to be disturbing you at this hour. But I've got to see you as soon as possible."

"I can't place your voice."

"We met years ago at a Republic Day ball. I'd introduced myself to you, Jelal Bey, but I don't suppose you'd remember it at this date. Later on, I wrote you a couple of letters under pseudonyms that I cannot now recall. One of them put forth a thesis that might bring to light the mystery behind Sultan Abdülhamit's death. The other one concerned the university student conspiracy commonly known as the trunk murder. I was the one who intimated to you that there was a secret agent involved, and you, putting your sharp intelligence to work, looked into the matter and, having found out, brought it to light in your columns."

"Yes."

"Now I have another dossier at hand."

"Leave it at the editorial offices."

"But I know you haven't been there for quite some time. Besides, I don't know that I trust anyone at the paper where this urgent matter is concerned."

"All right, in that case, leave it with the doorman."

"I don't have your address. The phone company won't supply your address if all I have is the number. This phone must be under another name. There is no number for Jelal Salik anywhere in the book. There is, however, a listing for Jelalettin Rumi—which must be a pseudonym."

"Didn't whoever gave you my number also give out my address?"

"No, he didn't."

"Who was it?"

"A friend we have in common. I'd rather tell you all about it when I see you. I've tried every conceivable ruse. I called your relatives. I talked to your dear aunt. I made trips to some places in Istanbul that I knew from reading your columns that you love—like the streets in Kurtuluş, Cihangir, the Palace Theater—hoping to run into you. Meanwhile, I found out that a team from British TV staying at the Pera Palas Hotel was also looking for you. Did you know that?"

"What's this dossier about?"

"I'd rather not get into it on the phone. Let me have your address and I'll be right there. Somewhere in Nişantaşı, isn't it?"

"Yes," Galip said nonchalantly. "But these matters no longer interest me."

"Come again?"

"Had you been reading my columns carefully, you'd have known that I'm no longer into this type of thing."

"No, no, this is subject matter you'd be interested in. You may even want to share it with the British TV people. Go ahead and give me your address."

"I'm sorry," Galip said with such cheerfulness that it even astonished him, "but I no longer talk to literature buffs."

He hung up calmly. When his hand went out instinctively in the dark, he found the switch on the desk lamp next to him and turned it on. The room was lit up with a dull orange light, leading Galip to name the bewilderment and panic that seized him as "the mirage," which is how he would later remember it.

The room was the exact replica of Jelal's digs twenty-five or thirty years ago. The furniture, curtains, lamps, their placement, the colors, shadows, and smells were exactly the same. Some of the new articles were simulations of the old ones, bent on tricking Galip into believing that he had not lived through the quarter of a century that had gone by. But when he looked more closely, Galip almost felt convinced that things were not playing tricks on him, and that his life since his childhood had melted away by magic and was gone. The furniture that suddenly emerged out of the dangerous darkness was not new. The spell that made things seem new was the way these objects, which he would've thought had grown old, fallen apart, and perhaps even ceased to exist like his own memories, had suddenly reappeared after so many years wearing the same guise as when he'd last seen them and yet had all but forgotten. It was as if the old tables, the faded curtains, the dirty ashtrays, and the tuckered-out armchairs had not succumbed to the fate and the fictions dictated by Galip's life and memories but, after a certain date (the day Uncle Melih and his family had arrived from Izmir and moved into the flat), had rebelled against the fate conceived for them and found other means of realizing their own private worlds. Once more, Galip figured out apprehensively that everything had been arranged so that it was identical to the way it had been when Jelal and his mother had lived here forty years ago and then when, as a cub reporter more than thirty years ago, he began to live here alone.

Everything remained the same in the orange light where Galip had left them behind, hoping not to remember them: the same old walnut table with the feet that resembled lion claws, the way it stood the same distance from the windows hung with the same pistachio-colored curtains, the same human-shaped stain made by hair grease and hair-dressing gunk on the headrest of the armchair which was still upholstered by the same material from Sümerbank Textiles (the same ferocious greyhounds chasing the same hapless gazelles with the same blood thirst as thirty years ago in a forest of purple leaves), the patience of the English setter which seemed to have stepped out of an English flick sitting in the copper dish in the dusty curio cabinet to watch the same old world, the same way the nonworking watches, the cups, and the nail scissors stood on the radiator. "There are certain things that we fail to remember, but there are other things that we don't even remember having failed to remember," Jelal had written in one of his recent columns. "They ought to be retrieved!" Galip recalled how, after Rüya's family moved in and Jelal was moved out of the flat, the stuff in here had gradually changed locations, got worn or been replaced, or vanished into a never-never land without leaving any traces in people's memories. When the phone rang again he was certain, as he reached for the all-too-familiar receiver from where he sat in the "old" easy chair, still wearing his coat, that he could imitate Jelal's voice without even being aware that he was doing it.

The same voice was on the phone. Heeding Galip's request, this time he introduced himself by name instead of through his reminiscences: Mahir Ikinci. The name had no association to faces or persons in Galip's mind.

"They are organizing a military coup. A small junta in the Army. It's a religiously oriented group, a brand-new sect. They believe in the Messiah. They think the time has come. What's more, they've been inspired by your stories."

"I've had no dealings with such nonsense."

"Yes, you have, Jelal Bey; yes, you have. You don't remember it now, or don't want to, having lost your memory, as you say, or else because you refuse to remember. Take a good look at your old pieces, read them well, and you will remember."

"I won't remember."

"You will too. From what I know about you, I'd say you are not someone who can sit unfazed on his behind when he gets a tip about a military coup."

"No, I'm not. I'm not myself, even."

"I'll be right over. I'll get you to remember your past, your lost memories. At the end, you will agree with me and go at it hammer and tongs."

"I would like to, but I won't be seeing you."

"But I will see you."

"If you can get hold of my address. I don't go out anymore."

"Look here: the Istanbul phone book has three hundred thousand subscribers. Since I have an idea of what the first digit is, I can scan rapidly five thousand numbers every hour. This means that within five days I'll have your address as well as that pseudonym I'm so curious about."

"All in vain," Galip said, trying to sound confident. "This happens to be an unlisted number."

"You really have a thing for pseudonyms. I've been reading you for years. You're a sucker for pseudonyms, pettifoggery, imposture. I bet you'd just as soon have fun making up a pseudonym as fill out an application to keep your number out of the phone book. I've already checked out some of the likely pseudonyms I bet you'd go for."

"And what might they be?"

The guy ran off at the mouth making a list. After Galip hung up and unplugged the phone, he realized all these names he had listened to one by one were likely to be deleted from his memory without leaving a trace or any associations. He made a list of the names on a piece of paper he took out of his coat pocket. It was so odd and confounding for Galip to come up against the existence of another reader who was hooked on Jelal's columns and remembered them even better than himself that his body seemed to have lost its reality. He sensed, although it was repellent, that he could be bonded to this diligent reader through a feeling of brotherhood. If only he could sit down with him and discuss Jelal's old pieces, the chair where he sat in this surreal room would've achieved a more profound significance.

It was before Rüya and Uncle Melih and Aunt Suzan showed up, when he was six years old, that he began to slip out of Grandma's to sneak up to Jelal's bachelor pad—which his parents didn't much condone—to listen to the Sunday afternoon soccer game on the radio together with him (Vasıf nodding as if he could hear). Galip used to sit in this very chair watching Jelal write the next installment of the series on wrestlers which a persnickety colleague of his had left unfinished, admiring the speed with which Jelal typed as he smoked a cigarette. When his parents allowed him to go up on cold winter evenings while Jelal was still living here with Uncle Melih's family before he got himself kicked out, Galip really went to watch Aunt Suzan and the beautiful Rüya who was every bit as incredible as her mom, as he'd come to discover, rather than listen to Uncle Melih's tales of Africa. It was in this chair that he sat across from Jelal who kept making light of Uncle Melih's stories using his eyes and eyebrows. During the following months, when Jelal suddenly disappeared and the altercations between Grandma and Uncle Melih made Grandma cry, and the rest of them fought in Grandma's apartment over flats, property, estate, and inheritance, it was here in this chair that Rüya sat dangling her legs when, somebody having said, "Send the kids upstairs," the two of them were left alone among the silent objects, with Galip watching her with awe. That was twenty-five years ago.

Galip quietly sat in the chair for a long time. Then, in order to gather evidence concerning the location where Rüya and Jelal were hiding out, he began a painstaking search through the other rooms in the phantom apartment, where Jelal had re-created the memorabilia of his own childhood and youth. Yet after two hours of walking around the rooms and the hallways in the phantom apartment, and going through the closets with curiosity, more like an aficionado thrilled, enamored, and awed to be visiting the first museum devoted to his pet subject than the reluctant detective looking for his absconded wife's tracks, these were the conclusions he came to after his initial search:

From the pair of coffee cups on the end table he had knocked over in the dark, Galip deduced that Jelal had people visit here. Since the fragile cups had been broken, tasting the thin layer of grounds in the bottom (Rüya took her coffee with a lot of sugar) had not yielded any conclusion. The date on the earliest edition of the *Milliyet* which had piled up behind the door indicated that Jelal had been to the flat on the day Rüya had disappeared. The text of the column entitled "The Day the Bosphorus Dries Up" had been corrected with a green ballpoint pen in Jelal's usual angry scrawl and placed next to the Remington typewriter. Neither in the bedroom closet nor in the coat closet next to the door was there any evidence that Jelal had gone on a trip, or that he no longer lived here, or that he did. Considering his blue-striped pajamas, the fresh mud on his shoes, the navy-blue overcoat he wore during the current season, his cold-weather vests, the exorbitant quantity of underwear he owned (Jelal had confessed in one of his old columns that, like many a man who comes into money in middle age after going through childhood and youth in privation, he had contracted the disease of buying more undershirts and shorts than he could possibly use), the place looked like it belonged to someone who might momentarily return from work and immediately resume his usual life.

Perhaps it was difficult to tell to what extent the decor of the old place had been simulated by considering details like bedsheets and towels, but, obviously, the design in the other rooms was also dependent on the "phantom abode" theme carried out in the living room. So, what got reproduced was the same child's blue bedroom walls that remained from Rüya's childhood, and the skeleton of the replica of the bed that had once been covered under Jelal's mother's sewing materials, the dress patterns and imported European fabrics brought over by Şişli and Nişantaşı socialites along with fashion magazines and clipped photographs. If smells had pooled in some corners replete with their associative powers which could reproduce the past, it was easy to understand that what gave them totality was always the presence of some visual material on the scene. Galip came to the realization that smells can only come back to life in the presence of the objects that surround them when he approached the nifty daybed that had once been Rüya's, and he smelled the scent of the old Puro soap mixed with the now defunct Yorgi Tomatis brand cologne once used by Uncle Melih. In reality, nowhere in the room was there the drawer in which pencils and coloring books were kept as well as the brightly illustrated books sent to Rüya from Izmir or bought in the Beyoğlu stores and at Aladdin's, nor any soap around Rüya's bed to give off the familiar smell, nor any fake bottles of Pe-Re-Ja brand cologne, nor any mint-flavored chewing gum.

It was difficult figuring out to what extent Jelal frequented or inhabited this place by studying the phantom decor. One could imagine that the number of the slim Gelincik or the thick Yeni Harman butts in the worn ashtrays that seemed placed here and there at random, or the cleanliness of the plates in the kitchen cabinets, or the relative freshness of the toothpaste on the end of the tube of Ipana which had been throttled at the neck with the same anger that had precipitated a column denouncing this same brand years ago were all part of the permanent fixtures under constant supervision in this museum arranged with a meticulousness that was sick. One might even go further and imagine that the dust in the globe lamps, the shadows that filtered through this dust to fall on the faded walls, and these shadows which were reminiscent of the faded shapes in the imagination of two Istanbul kids twenty-five years ago of African forests and Central Asian deserts, and the ghosts of the weasels and wolves in the witch and demon stories they heard from their aunt and grandmother were all part of the unique reproductions in this museum. (Galip mused, having, in the meantime, a hard time swallowing.) Consequently, it was impossible to deduce to what extent this place was lived in by examining marks left by the rain that had dried along balcony doors that hadn't been shut all the way, or the gray dust balls that curled up like silk along the walls, or, under the weight of the initial footstep, the brittle squeak of the pieces of parquet which had given from all the central heating. The showy wall clock that was hung across from the kitchen door, a replica of which kept ticking and chiming away with the same joyousness at Cevdet Bey's—who had old money, as Aunt Halé so often mentioned with pride—had been stopped with its hands at 9:35. The place made Galip think of the Atatürk museums, arranged with the same sick obsessiveness, with their clocks stopped at the hour of Atatürk's death

(9:05 a.m., November 10, 1938). But it didn't occur to Galip what 9:35 it referred to or the hour of whose death.

After having suffered the ghostly weight of the past, which rode him silly thanks to the sense of vengeance and sorrow exacted by his thoughts of the original pieces of furniture, hapless and forlorn, that he had known twenty-five years before, which had been sold to a junk dealer when they'd run out of space and then had traveled jiggling around on the dealer's horse cart in order to be forgotten in God knew what distant lands, Galip returned to the corridor to go through the papers in the glass-front elm cabinet that ran the length of the wide wall between the kitchen and the bathroom, which was the only piece of furniture that Galip considered "new" in the place. After conducting a search that didn't last too long, he found these articles that had been arranged on the shelves with the same sick obsession:

Clippings of news stories and interviews from Jelal's cub reporter period; clippings of all the articles written in praise or to the detriment of one Jelal Salik; all the columns and anecdotes Jelal had published under his pseudonyms; all the columns Jelal had published under his own name; all the columns of "Believe It or Not," "Interpreting Your Horoscope," "Today in Retrospect," "Incredible Incidents," "Interpreting Your Signature," "Your Face, Your Personality," "Puzzles and Crosswords," and the like, all of which Jelal had researched and penned; clippings of all the interviews done on Jelal; rough drafts of columns that had not seen print for various reasons; special notes; tens of thousands of news stories and photographs he'd clipped and saved all these years; notebooks in which he'd jotted his dreams, his fantasies, details that must not be forgotten; pieces of reader mail by the thousands kept in dried fruit, candied chestnut, and shoe boxes; clippings of serial novels published under his pen name which he had either done in their entirety or picked up halfway through; copies of hundreds of letters Jelal had written; hundreds of weird magazines, pamphlets, books, brochures, and school and military service yearbooks; boxes of pictures of people that had been cut out of newspapers and magazines; pornographic photographs; pictures of odd animals and insects; two big boxes of articles and publications on Hurufism and the science of letters; stubs of old bus, soccer game, and movie tickets with signs, letters, and symbols drawn on them; photos that had been pasted into albums, or not; awards received from journalism associations; old Turkish and Czarist Russian currency; telephone and address books.

Upon finding the three address books, Galip returned to the chair in the living room and read through all the pages. He concluded, after forty minutes of research, that the people in the address books had figured in Jelal's life during the fifties and the sixties, and that he was not going to be able to find Rüya and Jelal at any of the numbers where the addresses had been exchanged for those that belonged to houses that had most probably been torn down. Following a short investigation among the bits and pieces in the glass-front cabinet, he began reading Jelal's columns from the early seventies and the letters he received during the same time period in order to find the letter allegedly sent by Mahir Ikinci that concerned the trunk murder.

Some people he knew from high school had been involved in the incident, so Galip had been interested in the politically motivated murder, referred to as the "trunk murder" in the news. The ingenious young people who had organized themselves into the political faction found responsible for the murder had unintentionally imitated one of Dostoevsky's novels (*The Devils*) down to the last detail, and now as Galip went through the letters he remembered the couple of evenings when Jelal, who always maintained that in our country everything was in imitation of something else, had discussed the subject. Those were sunless, cold, and distasteful days, which were forgotten as they ought to be: Rüya was married to that "nice guy" whose name kept slipping Galip's mind as he went back and forth between being impressed and feeling contemptuous. That was when Galip, defeated by his own curiosity which he always regretted later, listened to gossip and poked around, and ended up getting more political information than any cogent details concerning the newlyweds' conjugal bliss or the lack thereof. One winter's eve while Vasıf contentedly fed his Japanese fish (red *wakins* and *watonais* whose ruffled tail fins had degenerated from intermarriage within the family) and Aunt Halé did the crossword puzzle in *Milliyet* glancing up at the TV now and then, Grandma had just died staring at the cold ceiling in her cold room. Rüya had come to the funeral alone ("Better this way," said Uncle Melih who openly despised his son-in-law whose background was provincial, thereby giving voice to Galip's secret thoughts), wearing a faded coat and an even more faded kerchief, and had taken off soon after. One night when they got together in one of the flats after the funeral, Jelal had asked Galip if he had any information on the subject of the trunk murder but had been unable to find out what he was really curious to know: by any chance had any of the young people Galip said he knew read that book by the Russian author?

"All the murders," Jelal had said that very night, "like all the books, are all imitations. That's why I could never publish a book under my own name." Next evening they'd gathered at the deceased's flat again, and the two of them were having a late night tête-à-tête when Jelal had gone on, saying, "Even so, in the worst murders there is an original aspect that does not exist in the worst of books." In the following years, Jelal would descend step by step deep into these speculations, which gave Galip a pleasure akin to going on a journey whenever he witnessed it. "So, the total travesties are not murders but books. Since they are concerned with imitations of imitations —exactly the kind of thing that thrills us the most—murders that explain books and books that explain murders appeal to a sensibility common to us all; it goes without saying that one can only bring down the bludgeon on the victim's head if he can put himself in someone else's place (since no one can bear to see himself as the murderer). Creativity mostly lies in anger, anger that renders us insensible, but anger can prod us into action only through methods that we have previously learned from others: knives, guns, poisons, narrative tricks, forms of fiction, verse meters, etc. When a notorious Public Enemy says, 'Your Honor, I was not myself,' he is only expressing this well-known fact: Murder, in all its details and ceremonies, is a business that one learns from others, that is, from legends, stories, recollections, newspapers—in short, from literature. The purest act of murder, a crime of passion committed by mistake, for example, is still an unconscious act of travesty, an imitation of literature. Should I write a column on the subject? What do you say?" He hadn't written it.

Way past midnight, while Galip was busy reading the columns he'd taken out of the cabinet, first the lights in the living room went down like the footlights on a stage, then the motor in the fridge moaned with the sad weariness of an old, overloaded truck changing gears upgrade on a steep and muddy slope, and the place went pitch-dark. Like all Istanbulites who are accustomed to power failures, Galip sat for a long while in the chair without moving, the folder with the news clippings on his lap, entertaining the hope that "it will soon be back on." He sat listening to the internal noises of the building he'd forgotten all these years, the clacking in the radiator, the silence of the walls, the parquet floor stretching out, the moaning in the taps and the plumbing, the muffled tick-tocks of the clock he couldn't place, and the roar from the air shaft that gave him the willies. By the time he groped his way into Jelal's bedroom, it was really late. He was putting on Jelal's pajamas when he thought of the protagonist stretching out on his double's bed in the historical novel by the sad writer he'd met last night at the nightclub. He got in bed but couldn't fall asleep right away.

Chapter Twenty-one

ARE YOU UNABLE
TO SLEEP?

Our dreams are a second life. —GÉRARD DE NERVAL, *Aurélia*

You get into bed. You settle down among familiar things, sheets and blankets redolent with your own smells and memories, your head finds the familiar softness of your pillow, you turn on your side, pulling up your legs, you bend your neck forward, the cold side of the pillow cools your cheek: soon, very soon, you will fall asleep, and in the dark you will forget all, everything.

You will forget it all: the merciless power of your superiors, words that were heedlessly spoken, stupidities, work you didn't get done on time, lack of consideration, disloyalty, injustice, indifference, people who blame you or will end up blaming you, your financial embarrassment, the fast flow of time, time that is heavy on your hands, people you miss, your loneliness, your shame, your defeats, your wretchedness, your misery, the disasters, all the disasters; you will soon forget it all. You're pleased that you will be forgetting. You wait.

Waiting with you are objects that surround you in the dark or the half-light: commonplace wardrobes that are all too familiar, drawers, radiators, tables, stools, chairs, closed curtains, the clothes you've taken off and tossed, your pack of cigarettes, the matches and your wallet in your coat pocket, your watch that you still hear ticking.

You are acquainted with the sounds you hear as you wait: a car going over the familiar pavement stones or over the water standing in the gutter, a door being closed somewhere nearby, the motor of an elderly refrigerator, dogs barking in the distance, the foghorn that can be heard all the way from the sea, the storefront shutter of the pudding shop suddenly getting rolled shut. The sounds, which are full of associations of sleep and dreaming as well as the memories of a renewed world of blissful oblivion, assure you that all is well, reminding you that soon you will forget them, along with the objects that surround you and your dear bed, and you will enter another realm. You are ready.

You are ready; it is as if you are taking leave of your body, your dear legs and hips, even your hands and arms. You are ready and so pleased to be ready, you no longer feel the necessity for your body and your limbs that are so close to you, and you know that you will forget them too as your eyes close.

A soft muscular movement makes you aware that under your eyelids your pupils are well shaded from light. Aware that all is well through the associations of familiar sounds and smells, it is as if your pupils present to you not the tenuous light in the room but the light in your mind which, as it gradually relaxes into repose, bursts into a fireworks display of colors: you see blue stains, blue lightning jolts, purple smoke, purple domes; shivering waves of dark blue, the shadows of lavender waterfalls, the meandering of magenta lava that flows out of the mouths of volcanoes, and the Prussian blue of the stars twinkling silently. You watch the colors in your mind as the colors and the shapes repeat each other quietly, appearing and disappearing, and they gradually change, manifesting memories and scenes that have been forgotten or else have never taken place.

But you're still not asleep.

Isn't it still too early to confess the truth? Recall the things you think when you sleep peacefully: No, not what you did today and what you're going to do tomorrow, but think of those sweet moments that united you unconsciously to the oblivion of sleep: They've all been waiting for your return when you finally show up, making them happy; no, you don't show up at all, you are on a train, which is running between two rows of snow-covered telegraph poles, with all the things you love most packed in your case; you come back with something smart and apropos, and they all realize their mistake and shut up, feeling some sort of admiration for you, albeit secretly;

you embrace a beautiful body that you love and the body embraces you back; you return to an orchard you've been unable to forget where you pick ripe cherries off the boughs; it's summer, it's winter, it's spring; it's morning, a blue morning, a beautiful morning, a sunny morning, a properly delightful morning . . . But no, you cannot sleep.

In that case, do what I do: turn gently in your bed without disturbing your arms and legs in the slightest so that your head can find a cool spot on your pillow. That's when you begin to think about Princess Maria Palaeologina who was sent from Byzantium seven hundred years ago to become the bride of Hulagu, the Khan of the Moguls. She made the trip from Constantinople all the way to Iran to marry Hulagu, but when Hulagu gave up the ghost even before she got there, she married instead his son Abaka who rose to the throne; she lived in the Mogul palace in Iran for fifteen years, and when her husband was murdered, she returned back to these hills where you presently wish to sleep peacefully. Well, put yourself in place of Princess Maria and imagine her sorrow when she set out on the road, then imagine the rest of her days upon her return, spent shut up in the church she had built on the shores of the Golden Horn. Think of the dwarves kept by the Sultana called Handan, the mother of Ahmet the First, who had a dwarf house built in Scutari for her dear friends so that she could make them happy; then, a galleon having been built for them with the support of the Sultan himself, these friends of hers had sailed away from Istanbul to a paradise the location of which couldn't be found even on the map. Imagine the sorrow of Handan Sultana separated from her friends on the morn of the voyage, and the sorrow of the dwarves on board the galleon waving goodbye, as if you yourself were soon leaving Istanbul and your loved ones.

If all this does not put me to sleep, my dear readers, I imagine a troubled man walking up and down a railway platform in a desolate station in the middle of a desolate night, waiting for a train that does not arrive; when I figure out the man's destination, it turns out that I've become that man. I think about the workers digging the underground passage at Silivri Gate which provided access to the Greeks who occupied the city seven hundred years ago. I imagine the bewilderment of the first fellow who stumbled on the secondary meaning of objects. I dream of a parallel universe within the manifested one, imagining my intoxication with new meanings in this new realm as the secondary meanings of things are gradually revealed to me. I think of the blissful confusion of the man who has lost his memory. I imagine being abandoned in a ghost town I don't recognize at all; the neighborhoods once inhabited by millions, the streets, the mosques, the bridges, the ships are all completely deserted, and as I walk through the ghostly emptiness, I weep to remember my own past and my own hometown, walking slowly to my own neighborhood, my own house, to my own bed where I am trying to fall asleep. I think of myself as Jean-François Champollion, who rises out of his bed to decipher the hieroglyphics on the Rosetta stone, and having taken dead-end streets where he comes across exhausted remembrances, he stumbles around absentmindedly like a somnambulist through the dark passages of my memory banks. Imagining myself as Murat the Fourth putting on a disguise at night to check out personally how Prohibition is going, privately assured that I would come to no harm in the company of my armed guard also in disguise, I fondly observe the lives of my subjects idling around in mosques, in the occasional shops still open for business, and in the dens of lassitude concealed in passageways.

Then, at midnight, I've become a quilt maker's apprentice, whispering the first and the last syllables of a cipher to the tradesmen in anticipation of one of the last Janissary rebellions in the nineteenth century. Or else I am the messenger from the seminary who awakens the dormant dervishes of an outlawed order out of their lethargy and silence.

If I am still not asleep, dear readers, then I become the unhappy lover seeking the replica of his sweetheart whose memory traces he keeps losing, and I open doors all over the city, looking for my own past and my sweetheart's trail in every room where opium is smoked, in every company where stories are told, and in every house where songs are sung. If my memory, my power of imagination, and my bedraggled dreams have still not said uncle out of exhaustion, then in a blissfully vague moment between sleep and wakefulness, I enter the first familiar abode I come across, say, the home of a slight acquaintance or the uninhabited mansion of a close relative, and, opening door after door as if going through the forgotten corners of my memory, I find the last room, put out the candle, stretch out on the bed and, among the remote, alien, and outlandish things, I fall asleep.

Chapter Twenty-two

WHO KILLED SHAMS
OF TABRIZ?

How much longer do I seek you, house by house, door to door?
How much longer, corner to corner, street by street? —RUMI

When Galip awoke from a long sleep in the morning, feeling peaceful, the fifty-year-old light fixture hanging from the ceiling was still on, giving off light the color of old parchment. Still in Jelal's pajamas, he turned off all the lights that had been left on, got the *Milliyet* that had already been slipped under the door, sat at Jelal's desk, and began to read. Seeing the same error he'd come across in the column when he was at the newspaper offices on Saturday afternoon ("being yourselves" had been transcribed as "being ourselves"), he let his hand find its way into the drawer and locate a green ball-point pen, and began correcting the piece. When he was done, he remembered Jelal also sitting at this desk wearing the same blue-striped pajamas and smoking while he made corrections with the same pen.

He trusted the feeling that things were going well. He ate his breakfast optimistically like someone who having slept well begins the day confidently, feeling full of himself—as if there was no need for him to be anybody else, either.

After making coffee, he placed on the desk some boxes of columns, letters, and news clippings that he'd taken out of the hallway cabinet. He had no doubt that if he read the papers in front of him with faith and care, he'd find what he was looking for in the end.

Galip tapped into his prerequisite resources of patience and care, reading Jelal's columns about the feral existence of the children who lived in the pontoons on the Galata Bridge, about monstrous orphanage directors who stuttered, about the aerial competition of winged multitalented persons who dived off Galata Tower and into the air as if diving into water, about the history of pederasty in the Levant and "modern" merchants engaged in this business. He hung on to the same goodwill and confidence reading the stories concerning the reminiscences of an auto mechanic in Beşiktaş who'd chauffeured the first Model T in Istanbul, the reasons why chiming clock towers needed to be put up in every neighborhood in "our city," the historical significance of the Egyptian ban on assignation scenes between harem ladies and black slaves in the *Thousand and One Nights*, the benefits of being able to board old-style horse-drawn streetcars on the move, the reasons why parrots fled Istanbul while black crows infested it, causing the first fall of snow as a consequence.

As he read, he remembered the days when he first read these pieces; he took notes on pieces of paper, sometimes reading a sentence, a paragraph, or a word over again; and when he finished reading a column, he fondly pulled a fresh one out of the box.

Sunlight hit only the window ledges without coming into the room. The curtains were open. Water dripped off the tips of the icicles hanging down the eaves of the apartment building across the street and out of the snow- and dirt-filled gutters. A piece of bright blue sky showed in between the triangle of the roof, which was the color of red tiles and dirty snow, and the square of the tall chimney that blew lignite smoke through its dark teeth. When his eyes got tired from reading, Galip focused them on the space between this triangle and the square, observing the crows whose fleet wings cut across the blue, and then as he returned to the sheet of paper in front of him he realized that Jelal also looked up from his work whenever he was tired and looked at the same space to watch the flight of the same crows.

Much later, when the sun now shone on the drawn curtains of the dark windows in the apartment building opposite, Galip's optimism began to give out. It was possible that things, words, meanings were all in their proper places, but the more Galip read, the more he was painfully aware that the profound reality that held them together was long gone. He was reading what Jelal had written on Messiahs, false prophets, pretenders to the throne, and what he said on the subject of the relationship between Rumi and Shams of Tabriz, and on the jeweler called Saladdin with whom "the great Sufi poet" became intimate after the death of Shams, and Çelebi Hüsameddin who took Saladdin's place upon the latter's death. Hoping to shake off the feeling of distaste that welled up inside him, he began to read through the "Believe It or Not" columns, but he was unable to divert himself with the story about the poet called Figani who was strapped on a donkey to be paraded all around Istanbul because he had written an insulting couplet about Sultan Ibrahim's prime vizier, nor with the story about Sheikh Eflaki who married all his sisters in turn and had inadvertently brought about every one of their deaths. Reading the letters he took out of the other box, he realized, with the same astonishment as in his childhood, the great number and the diversity of people who had become interested in Jelal; and yet, the letters were not good for anything besides feeding the feeling of mistrust that increased in Galip's heart, be they letters from people asking for money, or accusing each other, or disclosing the easy virtue of the wives of other columnists with whom he was engaged in controversy, or reporting on some secret sect's conspiracy and the bribes taken by local monopoly directors, or proclaiming their intense love or hate.

He knew everything was connected to the gradual change of Jelal's image that had been in his mind when he first sat down at the desk. Just as things and objects had been extensions of a comprehensible world in the morning, Jelal had been someone whose work he'd read for many years, whose unknown attributes he'd understood and identified at a distance as "unknown attributes." In the afternoon, during the hours when the elevator began transporting a steady stream of sick or pregnant women to the gynecologist's office below, and when Galip understood that Jelal's image in his mind was turning in some strange way into a "deficient" image, he realized that the whole room and the things around him had also changed. Things did not seem at all friendly now; they were the threatening signs from a world which was not bound to yield its secrets easily.

Having come to understand that the transformation was closely connected to what Jelal had written on Rumi, he decided to pursue the subject directly. He soon located a considerable number of pieces Jelal had written about Rumi and began to read rapidly through them.

What attracted Jelal to the most influential mystical poet of all time was neither the poems in Persian written in Konya in the thirteenth century, nor the stock lines chosen out of these poems to provide examples for the virtues taught in the ethics courses in middle school. Jelal was no more interested in the "choice pearls" that ornamented the first page of many a mediocre writer's book than he was in the Mevlevi whirling-dervish ceremonies with the bare feet and the skirts which the tourists and the postcard business were so crazy about. Rumi, who had been in the last seven hundred years the subject of volumes of commentary by the tens of thousands, and his order which had caught on after his death, concerned Jelal only as a locus of interest that a columnist ought to utilize and benefit from. What interested Jelal most about Rumi was his "sexual and mystical" intimacy with certain men.

When he was around forty, Rumi, who had taken over the position of spiritual leader—the sheikhood—in Konya after the death of his father, and who was loved and admired not only by his devoted disciples but by the whole town, had fallen under the spell of an itinerant dervish from Tabriz called Shams who possessed neither Rumi's wisdom nor his values. According to Jelal, Rumi's conduct was totally incomprehensible. The apologias that were penned by commentators for the next seven hundred years, with the object of making some sense of the relationship, also proved this. After Shams disappeared or was killed, Rumi, despite his other disciples' reactions against it, had appointed as Shams's successor a totally ignorant jewelry-store keeper who had nothing to recommend him. According to Jelal, this choice was a sign that Rumi was in sad shape rather than that he had found again the "extremely powerful mystical attraction" Shams of Tabriz supposedly provided, which all the commentators had undertaken to prove. In just the same way, after the death of this successor, the next successor Rumi elected as his "soul mate" was as devoid of attributes and brilliance as was the previous one.

According to Jelal, putting various handles on these three relationships that seemed totally incomprehensible with the object of making them comprehensible, as had been the practice for centuries—inventing for each successor unreal virtues they couldn't possibly carry off and, what's more, faking lineage, as some had done, that proved these men had descended from Muhammad or Ali—was to miss the point concerning Rumi's most cogent attribute. On a Sunday afternoon that coincided with the memorial ceremony celebrated in Konya every year, Jelal had expounded on this attribute which he said was also reflected in Rumi's work. Once more, Galip had the feeling that things around him had changed as he reread, twenty-two years later, the same piece which, like all religious writing, had bored him stiff in his childhood, and he remembered its publication only in conjunction with the Rumi stamp series that were out specially that year (the fifteen-*kuruş* ones were pale pink, the thirties forget-me-not blue, and the rare sixties Rüya was keen on were pistachio green).

According to Jelal, as commentators had related it thousands of times by placing the fact in the crowning spot in their books, it was true that Rumi had produced an effect on and was in turn affected by the itinerant dervish, Shams of Tabriz, the moment he saw him. But it didn't happen because Rumi had intuited that this man was a sage, as it is commonly surmised, following the famous "dialogue" between them occasioned by the question posed by Shams of Tabriz. The conversation between them was based on an ordinary "parable on modesty," variations of which can be read even in the most insipid Sufi books sold in mosque courtyards. If Rumi were the enlightened person that he was supposed to be, he wouldn't have been influenced by such a commonplace parable; at most, he must've pretended he was impressed.

And that was what he did exactly; he behaved as if he had encountered in Shams a profound person, a potent soul. According to Jelal, what Rumi, then in his mid-thirties, really needed on that rainy day was to come across a "soul mate" such as this, someone in whose face he could see the reflection of his own face. Therefore, the moment he saw Shams, he'd convinced himself that this was the person he was seeking, and, naturally, it hadn't been too hard for him to convince this Shams that the truly elevated personality was Shams himself. Following the meeting on October 23, 1244, they had closeted themselves in a cell at the seminary from which they did not emerge for the next six months. As to the question of what had gone on in the seminary cell for six months, the "secular" question on which members of the Mevlevi order that he founded touch only lightly, Jelal had tinkered with it, taking care not to irritate his readers overmuch, and had gone on to his real topic.

All his life, Rumi had sought the "other" who could move and enflame him, the mirror that could reflect his countenance and his soul. Consequently, what they said and did in the cell, like all of Rumi's work, was to be understood as the deeds, words, and voices of many persons masquerading as one person, or else, of one person who'd taken on the personality of many. In order to endure the suffocating atmosphere of a thirteenth-century Anatolian town and the devotion of his blockheaded disciples (whom he just couldn't give up), the poet needed to keep around other identities, just like the tools of disguise the poet always hid in his closet, which he might assume at appropriate times for a little respite. Jelal had reinforced the idea of this profound desire with images he had borrowed from another one of his pieces: "Just the way the ruler of some dumb country, who cannot stand ruling among the sycophants, the cruel, and the poor, might keep peasant's clothes in his closet to wear out in the streets where he finds comfort."

A month after the publication of this piece which, just as Galip might expect, was received with death threats and insults from his most pious readers, and letters of adulation from the hardheaded secular republicans, Jelal had returned to this topic which his boss had requested he keep his hands off of.

In the new piece, Jelal first surveyed some basic facts known to all Mevlevis: the other disciples, who were jealous of Rumi's intimacy with some fly-by-night dervish, had put pressure on Shams and threatened him with death. Following this, on the snowy winter day of February 15, 1246 (Galip cherished Jelal's obsession with chronologic precision, like that in those school history books full of chronological mistakes), Shams disappeared from Konya. Rumi, who could not bear the absence of his beloved, of his other self, having learned from a letter that Shams was in Damascus summoned back his "love" (Jelal had put the word in quotation marks in order not to arouse his readers' suspicions even more) and had him marry one of his foster daughters. Yet, soon after, the circle of jealousy would begin to tighten around Shams once more, and he would be ambushed and "knifed to death on the fifth day of the month of December in 1247, on a Thursday," by a mob that included Rumi's son, Aladdin; and that very night, under a cold and nasty rain, his body would be dumped into a well on the property next to Rumi's house.

Galip came across some material that didn't seem at all unfamiliar in the next lines describing the well where Shams's corpse was disposed of. What Jelal had written about the well, the corpse in it, the corpse's loneliness and sorrow, not only managed to freak Galip out, but hit him with the feeling that he had personally seen with his own eyes the seven-hundred-year-old well with the corpse, recognized the stone wall itself and the Khorasan-style plaster work. After reading the piece a couple times more, and scanning through other articles that he picked up instinctively, he discovered that not only had Jelal lifted some sentences word for word from a column describing the apartment building air shaft as the dark void, he had also managed to keep the style in the two articles consistent.

Later, making too much of a small trick to which he would not have paid any attention had he seen it after being engrossed in what Jelal had written on Hurufism, Galip began reading through the material he had piled on the desk with this new perspective. That was when he understood why reading Jelal's pieces had changed the things around him, why the goodwill and that profound sense of peace, which related the tables, the worn-out curtains and all-too-familiar ashtrays, the chairs, the scissors on the radiator, and the rest of the paraphernalia to each other, had absconded.

Jelal spoke about Rumi as if he were speaking of himself; taking advantage of a magic transposition in the lines and the words, which was not immediately obvious, he put himself in Rumi's place. Galip became certain about the transposition when he noticed that Jelal employed the same sentences, paragraphs, and even the same sorrowful voice both in the pieces where Jelal spoke about himself and in the "historical" pieces where he spoke about Rumi. What made this grotesque game frightening was the fact that he supported it with stuff that he'd penned in his private journals, his unpublished rough drafts, his historical chats, the essays he'd written on another Mevlevi poet (Şeyh Galip, the author of *Beauty and Love*), his dream interpretations, his Istanbul memoirs, and in a great many of his columns.

In his "Believe It or Not" column Jelal had related hundreds of times the stories of kings who thought they were someone else, Chinese emperors who torched their palaces so that they could assume the identity of someone else, and sultans who made going among their subjects in disguise into an obsession, staying away for days on end from affairs of state and the palace. In a journal where Jelal wrote accounts that were something like reminiscences, Galip read that on a plain old summer's day Jelal had thought he was, in order of appearance, Leibniz, the celebrated plutocrat Cevdet Bey, Muhammad, a newspaper mogul, Anatole France, a triumphant chef, an imam famous for his sermons, Robinson Crusoe, Balzac, and six other personages whose names had been crossed out in embarrassment. He glanced at the caricatures inspired by Rumi's likeness on commemorative postage stamps and posters, and he came across a clumsily drawn picture of a casket with the inscription of "Jelal Rumi" on it. Conversely, one of the unpublished columns began with this sentence: "Rumi's *Mathnawi*, which is considered his greatest work, is nothing but plagiarism from beginning to end."

According to Jelal, like all those people who cannot endure being themselves for long and find solace only in assuming another person's identity, Rumi too, in narrating a story, could only tell what someone else had already told. Besides, for such unhappy souls, storytelling was a trick devised to escape from their own tedious bodies and spirits. The *Mathnawi* was an odd and messy "composition" just like the *Thousand and One Nights*, where a second story begins when the first has not yet ended, a third is taken up before the second is done—endless stories, always left behind. Poking through the volumes of the *Mathnawi*, Galip saw that lines had been drawn on the margin to mark stories that were pornographic in nature, and that some pages had been subjected to angry green question marks, exclamation marks, and to being downright crossed out. After hurriedly reading through the stories told on the pages that were rife with dirt and ink, Galip realized that many a column he had supposed was original when he read it in his teenage years was in fact a story Jelal had lifted from the *Mathnawi* and adapted to our present-day Istanbul.

He remembered evenings when Jelal carried on for hours about the courtly art of *nazire*, poems modeled after other poems, divulging that it was his only skill. While Rüya scarfed up the pastries they got on the way, Jelal would say that he wrote many of his columns, perhaps all, with the help of others; he claimed that he took all his columns from other sources, adding that the crucial thing was not "creating" something new but taking something astonishingly wonderful that had been worked on by thousands of intellects over thousands of years, elegantly changing it here and there, and transforming it into something new. What unnerved Galip, making him lose his optimistic faith in the ordinary reality of the things in the room and the papers on the desk, was not learning that the stories he had taken to be Jelal's all these years had actually come from somewhere else, but that this fact pointed to other probabilities.

It occurred to him that, aside from this room in this flat which was a replica of itself as it was twenty-five years ago, there could be another room in a flat that replicated this place in another part of Istanbul. If there did not exist a Jelal sitting at an identical desk telling a story and a Rüya listening to him happily, then there was an unfortunate look-alike of Galip's sitting at an identical desk who assumed that reading an assortment of old columns might enable him to find the trail of his lost wife. It also occurred to him that just as objects, pictures, symbols on plastic bags, were signs of things other than themselves, and just as Jelal's columns signified something different with each reading, his life too might have a different meaning each time he considered it, and that he might get lost between these interpretations that followed each other inexorably like wagons in a train. It was dark outside, and the room had filled with the sort of murky light that was palpable, reminiscent of the smell of mold and death in a dismal cellar covered with spiders. In an effort to free himself of the netherworld nightmare into which he had been plunged unwillingly and get out of this ghostly realm, Galip turned on the desk lamp, realizing he had no other recourse than to make his tired eyes go on reading.

That's how he returned to the place he'd left off, the spider-filled well where Shams's body had been plunged. In the rest of the story, the poet was beside himself sorrowing over the loss of his "friend," his "love." He could not make himself believe that Shams had been murdered and thrown down a well; what's more, he was furious with those who wanted to show him the well which was right under his nose, inventing pretexts to look for his "beloved" in other places: couldn't Shams have gone to Damascus as he had done before, the last time he was lost?

That's how Rumi had gone to Damascus and begun searching for his beloved in the streets. He looked for him in the streets, on street corners, in rooms and taverns, leaving no stone unturned; he looked up his lover's old friends, acquaintances they had in common, his favorite places where he'd hung out, in mosques and seminaries, so much so that, after a while, seeking became more important than finding. At this point in the column, the reader found himself immersed in clouds of opium, bats, and attar of roses that belong to a mystical and pantheistic realm where the seeker and the sought change places, where it is not finding that is essential but keeping on the path, not the beloved but Love, for which the beloved is a pretext. The various adventures that befell the poet in the streets, equivalent to the stages that a traveler on the Sufi path must overcome in order to reach enlightenment, had been briefly outlined: Following the scene of confusion upon realizing that the lover has vanished, if embarking on his trail is the appropriate stage of "Denial, or Subversion of Natural Order," then meetings with the beloved's former friends and enemies, investigating the places frequented by the beloved as well as going through his heartrending belongings were equivalent to the various stages of ascetic "ordeals." If the scene in the whorehouse stood for "Dissolving into Love," then pseudonyms such as those in the ciphered letters found in al-Hallaj Mansur's house after his death, literary devices, and texts adorned with word games stood for being lost in heaven and hell or, as it was also pointed out by Attar, being lost in the valley of mystery. As the storytellers in a tavern each narrating a "love story" in the middle of the night came straight out of Attar's *Conference of the Birds*, so did the poet's wanderings around the streets, shops, and windows rife with mystery which "intoxicate" him into realizing that he is seeking himself on Mount Kaf—and this was an example of "Absolute State of Union with God," or Nothingness, also lifted from the same book.

Jelal's column had been embellished with snazzy lines which were versified in the classical mode, concerning the identification of the seeker with the sought from other Sufi writers, and the well-known verse spoken by Rumi, exhausted from his month-long search in Damascus, which was tacked on in prose by Jelal who hated verse translations: "If I am He," said the poet one day, dissolved in the city's mystery, "then why am I still searching?" Jelal concluded the climactic point with the literary fact that the Mevlevis reiterate with pride. During this stage of the game, Rumi did not sign his own name to the poems he had done such a bang-up job writing but collected them under the name of Shams of Tabriz.

The aspect that interested Galip in this column, just as it had when he first read it in his youth, was its investigative character and the police work involved in the investigation. Here Jelal came to a conclusion which would once more irritate his "religious" readers, whom he'd appeased for a time by writing of Sufi matters, but gratify his "secular" audience: "The person who wanted Shams murdered and thrown down the well was, of course, Rumi himself." Jelal had made this allegation subscribing to a method often employed by the Turkish police and the prosecutor whom he had come to know closely during the early fifties when he reported from the Beyoğlu district court. In the overly confident manner of a small-town prosecutor accustomed to making accusations, Jelal suggested that the person who most benefited from his lover's death was Rumi himself since it gave him a chance to get out of being a humdrum teacher of theology and attain the rank of a Sufi poet, and claimed that, therefore, it was Rumi who had the motivation to get the murder committed. As to the thin line of law between motivation and execution, which is characteristic only of Christian novels, he hurried over it, mentioning odd behaviors—such as obvious guilt feelings, denial that the person is dead which is a ruse common to amateur murderers, going stark raving mad, and refusal to look down the well—and embarked on another topic that plunged Galip thoroughly into deep despair: After the murder was committed, what did the defendant's search in the streets of Damascus signify, the way he combed the city over and over, month after month?

Galip reasoned that Jelal had spent more time on the column than it appeared, based on some notes Jelal had made in his journal and the map of Damascus in the box where he kept ticket stubs from old soccer games (Turkey 3–Hungary 1) and old movies (*Scarlet Street, Going Home*). On the map, the course of Rumi's investigations in Damascus had been traced with a green ballpoint pen.

Long after it got dark, Galip found a map of Cairo and a 1934 City Directory of the Istanbul Municipality in a box where Jelal kept the odds and ends which he'd got hold of during the same time period when he had published a column devoted to the detective stories in the *Thousand and One Nights* ("Mercury Ali," "The Clever Thief," etc.). Just as he expected, a green ballpoint had marked arrows on the Cairo map, working in the *Thousand and One Nights* stories. He saw that the maps in the City Directory had also been marked with arrows, if not with the same pen then in the same green ink. Tracking down the adventures of the green arrows on the confusing maps in the Istanbul directory, he had an impression that he was seeing the map of his own passage throughout the city these past few days. In order to convince himself that he was seeing things, he reminded himself the green arrow had stopped at commercial buildings where he had never set foot, mosques he'd never entered, and steep streets he'd never climbed, but he had in fact stopped off at adjacent commercial buildings, mosques that were nearby, and streets that went up the same hills: Which was to say that all Istanbul, no matter how it was marked on the map, was teeming with folks who were on the same trip!

So, he put the maps of Damascus, Cairo, and Istanbul side by side in the way Jelal had anticipated years ago in a column inspired by Edgar Allan Poe. To do this, he had to cut the bound pages of the City Directory with a razor blade he found in the bathroom on which was the hairy evidence that it had run across Jelal's beard. When he first put the maps together, he couldn't quite figure out what to do with the pieces of lines and signs that weren't the same size. Then he pressed the maps over each other on the glass in the living-room door, just the way he and Rüya had done when they were children to trace a picture out of a magazine, and studied them against the light of the lamp on the other side of the door. The only thing that he could barely make out in the maps spread out on top of one other was the coincidental wrinkle-laden face of a terribly old person.

He stared at the face for such a long time that he began to think he had long been well acquainted with it. The feeling of familiarity and the quietness of the night gave Galip a sense of peace, a feeling of serenity that in turn inspired a sense of self-confidence, self-confidence of long standing that had been carefully prepared for—and that was preordained for someone else. Galip sincerely thought that Jelal was guiding him. Jelal had written extensively about faces, but all that came to Galip's mind was some of his sentences concerning the inner peace Jelal felt looking at the faces of some female foreign movie stars. That's how come he decided to take a look at the box of film criticism Jelal had written as a young man.

In his movie stuff, Jelal talked with pain and longing about some American movie stars' faces as if these were translucent marble sculptures, or the silken surface of the invisible side of a planet, or deft tales from distant lands that are reminiscent of dreams. As he read these lines, Galip felt that the love interest that he and Jelal had in common was not so much Rüya and fiction but the harmony of this longing, reminiscent of barely audible strains of some pleasant music: He loved what he discovered, in concert with Jelal, reading maps, faces, and words; but he also feared it. He wanted to delve further into the pieces on film in order to apprehend the music, but he hesitated and stopped: Jelal never spoke about Turkish actors' faces in the same vein; Turkish actors' faces reminded Jelal of half-century-old telegrams in which the meaning, as well as the code, had been lost and forgotten.

Now he knew all too well why the optimism that had enveloped his whole body while he was eating his breakfast and settling down at the desk had abandoned him. Jelal's image had changed totally in his mind after the eight hours reading, and he himself had also become someone else. In the morning when he had good faith in the world, naïvely thinking that by working patiently he could solve the basic mystery the world kept from him, he had felt no longing to be someone else at all. But now, when the world's mysteries got away from him, when the objects and texts in this room he thought he knew were transformed into incomprehensible signs from an alien world and into the maps of faces he couldn't identify, Galip wanted to break loose from the person who was stuck with this desperate and tiresome outlook. When he began reading the columns relating to some of Jelal's recollections in order to find the final clue which might explain Jelal's relationship to Rumi and the Mevlevi order, it was dinnertime in the city and in the windows the blue light from the TV sets had started to reflect on Teşvikiye Avenue.

Jelal had been interested in the Mevlevi order not only because he knew his readers would themselves be immersed in the subject, prompted by an incomprehensible sense of devotion, but also because his stepfather had been a Mevlevi. Unable to make ends meet as a dressmaker after she was divorced from Uncle Melih who took his own sweet time coming home from Europe and then North Africa, Jelal's mother had married this man who attended a Mevlevi retreat next to a Byzantine cistern, in the district of Yavuz Sultan, and Galip had become aware of the fact through the man's existence as a hunchback lawyer "who speaks through his nose" and goes to a secret ritual, described by Jelal with secular anger and Voltaire-like satire. Reading that during the time he lived under his stepfather's roof Jelal earned money working as an usher at the movies, that he gave and took beatings in fights that often broke out in the dark crowded theaters, that he sold soda pop during the intermission, and that in order to increase the pop sales, he'd made a deal with the *çörek* maker getting him to put lots of salt and pepper in his braided buns, Galip identified with the usher, the brawling audience, the *çörek* maker, and finally—good reader that he was—with Jelal himself.

So, reading a piece containing Jelal's reminiscences of the days after he left his job at the theater in Şehzadebaşı, working for a bookbinder whose shop smelled of glue and paper, a sentence that caught Galip's eye seemed to be a prediction that had been preconceived in relation to his present situation. It was one of those mediocre sentences employed by enthusiastic autobiographers who invent for themselves a sad but praiseworthy past: "I read whatever I could get my hands on," Jelal had written, and that's when Galip realized that Jelal was not speaking about the days he spent at the binder's shop but about Galip himself who read whatever he could lay his hands on concerning Jelal.

Before he went out at midnight, each time Galip thought of that sentence he considered it proof that Jelal knew what he, Galip, was up to at that very moment. So, he considered his past five days of ordeals not as his personal quest on Jelal and Rüya's trail but as part of a game that Jelal (and perhaps also Rüya) had constructed for his benefit. Since this idea fell within the bounds of Jelal's desire to exercise remote control over people tacitly—by setting up small traps, ambiguities, and fictions—Galip had a notion that his investigations in this living museum were signs not of his own freedom but of Jelal's.

He wanted to get out of the place as soon as possible, not only because he could no longer bear this suffocating feeling or his eyes aching from so much reading but because he couldn't find anything to eat in the kitchen. He took Jelal's navy-blue topcoat out of the coat closet and put it on so that Ismail the doorman and his wife Kamer, if they were still up, would sleepily imagine that the topcoat and legs they observed exiting the building belonged to Jelal. He went down the stairs without turning on the light and saw that no light seeped out of the doorman's ground-level window through which he could observe the outside door. Since he didn't have a key for the outside door, he couldn't secure it properly. He was stepping out on the sidewalk when a momentary shiver went through him: he imagined the person he'd been avoiding thinking about, the man on the phone, might just materialize out of some dark corner. He fantasized that it was not the dossier containing proof of the conspiracy for a new military coup that was in the hands of this man, who didn't seem unfamiliar at all, but something more horrible and deadly. But there was no one in the street. He envisioned the man on the phone following him around in the street. No, he was not emulating anyone but himself. "I call it like it is," he said to himself as he went by the police station. The cops on watch in front of the station, carrying machine guns, regarded him suspiciously out of sleepy eyes. In order to avoid reading the letters in the posters on the walls, on billboards with neon lights that sizzled, and in political graffiti, Galip looked down as he walked along. All the restaurants and the short-order counters in Nişantaşı were closed.

Much later, after walking for a long time under the buckeyes, cypresses, and plane trees along the sidewalks where the melting snow still dripped down the spouts making sad sounds, listening to his own footsteps and the racket from local coffeehouses, and after he had stuffed himself full of soup, chicken, and crumpets in syrup at a pudding shop in Karaköy, he bought fruit at an all-night greengrocer's, bread and cheese at a short-order counter, and returned to the Heart-of-the-City Apartments.

Chapter Twenty-three

THE STORY OF THOSE WHO
CANNOT TELL STORIES

*"Aye!" (quoth the delighted reader) "this is sense, this is genius! This I
understand and admire! I have thought the very same a hundred times
myself!" In other words, this man has reminded me of my own cleverness,
and therefore I admire him.* —COLERIDGE, *Essays on His Own Times*

No, my most salient piece on deciphering the mystery in which our entire
lives are buried, without our so much as being aware of it, is not the
investigation in which I revealed, sixteen months ago to date, the incredible
similarities in the maps of Damascus, Cairo, and Istanbul. (Those who wish
can edify themselves, by referring to that particular column, that the Darb-
al Mustakim, the Halili Market, and our Covered Bazaar are each in the
shape of M, and discover the identity of the face that this M calls to mind.)

No, my most "profound" story is not the one I wrote once upon a time
with similar enthusiasm about the two-hundred-and-twenty-year-old remorse
experienced by poor Sheikh Mahmut, who sold the secrets of his order to a
European spy in return for immortality. (Those who wish can check that
particular column to find out how the Sheikh, in an effort to find a hero
willing to relieve him of his immortality, tried to con warriors into assuming
his identity as they lay wounded on battlefields bleeding to death.)

As I recall what I used to write about Beyoğlu thugs, poets who lose their memories, stories of magicians, female singers with double identities, and the mortally stricken lovelorn, I realize that I've always skipped over a subject, failing to hit it or skirting around it with a stiffness that's strange, but which is of great significance to me today. But I am not the sole perpetrator! I've been writing for thirty years, and, if not quite as many, I've devoted nearly the same number of years to reading; but I have never come across any writer, neither in the East nor the West, who drew attention to the truth I am about to tell you.

So, as you read what I am about to write, please visualize the faces as I describe them. (Besides, what is reading but animating the writer's words inside the mind's silent cinema?) On your mind's silver screen, project a sundries store in Eastern Anatolia where herbs, remedies, and notions are sold. On a cold winter afternoon when it gets dark early, seeing how there is not much action downtown, the barber across the street whose apprentice is minding the store, a retired old-timer, the barber's younger brother, and a local customer who's there more for the company than to do his shopping, have all gathered around the stove, making idle conversation. They're talking of their army days, looking through newspapers, gossiping, and at times there is laughter too, but among them there's someone who's upset that he talks very little and has a hard time getting people to listen: the barber's brother. He too has quite a few jokes and stories to tell, but although he's aching for it, he just doesn't have the gift of gab or the knack of making himself shine. The one time all afternoon he's made an attempt to tell a story, the others interrupted him without even being conscious of it. Now, please visualize the expression on the barber's brother's face when his story is interrupted in the middle.

Next, please imagine an engagement party at the home of an Istanbul doctor's family that has become Westernized but is not rich. At some point, several of the guests who have invaded the house gather casually in the room of the girl who's getting engaged, around the bed piled with coats. Among them is a beautiful and charming girl and two fellows who are interested in her. One of the fellows is not much to look at, nor terribly bright, but he's gregarious and talkative. Consequently, the older men in the room as well as the beautiful girl listen to his stories, pay him attention. Now, picture, if you will, the face of the other young man who's brighter and more sensitive than the chatterbox but cannot get people to listen to him.

Now, please imagine three sisters, who have all been married within the past two years, having a get-together at their mother's two months after the wedding of the youngest sister. In the home of a modest merchant where there's the tick-tocking of a huge wall clock and the light clicks of an impatient canary, as the four women are all having their tea sitting in the gray afternoon light, the youngest, who has always been the most vivacious and talkative one, does such a marvelous job in telling about her two months of experimentation with marriage, she has such a way with words and such a sense of comedy, that the oldest and most beautiful sister wistfully considers the possibility, although she's been through similar situations many times by now, that there is perhaps something missing in her husband and her life. Now, picture, if you please, this melancholy face.

Have you done all the visualizing? So, do you see that, in some strange way, these faces resemble one another? Is there not something that makes the faces look alike, just as surely as there is an invisible thread that bonds these persons together in the depths of their souls? Don't you think that there is more meaning and presence in the faces of the quiet ones, the ones who cannot do the narrative, who cannot get themselves heard, who don't seem important, who are mutes, whose stories don't arouse people's curiosity, who think of the perfect comeback only later at home? It seems these faces are suffused with the letters that their stories are composed of, as if they carried the signs of silence, dejection, even defeat. You've managed to think of your own face in the context of these faces, haven't you? What a legion we all are, how touching, how helpless!

But I have no desire to deceive you: I am not one of you. Someone who can pick up a pen, scribble something or other, and do all right in getting others to read the scribbling, has been cured, in some measure, of the ailment. Perhaps that's why I have never come across a writer who is capable of adequately discussing this most significant human condition. Now that whenever I pick up a pen I am well aware there is only one single subject, from this day on I will only attempt penetrating the hidden poetry in a countenance, the terrifying mystery in a gaze. So be prepared.

Chapter Twenty-four

RIDDLES IN FACES

The face is what one goes by, generally.
             —LEWIS CARROLL, *Through the Looking Glass*

On Tuesday morning when Galip sat down at the desk covered with news-paper columns, he wasn't as optimistic as he had been the previous morning. Now that the image of Jelal had changed in his mind after the first day's work, the goal of his investigations seemed unspecified. Since he had no recourse other than reading the columns and the notes he had removed from the hallway cabinet, and constructing hypotheses concerning Jelal and Rüya's hideout, he had a feeling of contentment sitting down and reading that came from doing the only thing possible in face of disaster. Besides, sitting in a room full of happy childhood memories and reading Jelal's work was a lot better than sitting in a dusty office in Sirkeci, reading through contracts drawn up in hopes of protecting tenants against belligerent landlords, and files on steel and rug dealers who'd given each other the shaft. Even if it was the result of a calamity, he felt the enthusiasm of a bureaucrat who's been assigned a more interesting task at a better desk.

As he drank his second cup of coffee, it was with this enthusiasm that he reviewed all the clues at hand. He remembered that the column in the copy of *Milliyet* slipped under the door, entitled "Apologies and Satires," had already been published once before years ago, so it stood to reason that Jelal had not submitted a new column on Sunday. This made it the sixth column the paper had republished: Only one or two more columns remained in the auxiliary file. This meant that if Jelal didn't hurry and get a new piece, his column would soon go blank. Since he'd begun the day with Jelal's column for the last twenty-five years, and Jelal had never defaulted on his column even once under the pretext of illness or time off, every time Galip contemplated the possibility of a blank column on page two, he felt the anxiety of anticipating a catastrophe that was fast approaching. It was a catastrophe that reminded him of the day the Bosphorus dries up.

So that he'd be sure to connect up with any possible clue that might come his way, he plugged in the phone he had disconnected the night he arrived at the flat. He reviewed his phone conversation with the man who introduced himself as Mahir Ikinci. What the man had said about the "trunk murder" and the military coup reminded Galip of some of Jelal's old columns. He took those out of the box, and reading them carefully remembered some of Jelal's bits and pieces on the Messiah. Finding the traces and dates of these bits, which had been sprinkled throughout various columns, took so much of his time that when he sat back down at the desk, he was as tired as if he had put in a whole day's work.

During the early sixties, when Jelal was using his column in an effort to incite a military coup, he must have remembered one of the principles in his Rumi pieces: a columnist who wants to get a large number of readers to accept an idea must have the skill to restore and refloat the sediment of decaying concepts and rusty memories that lie asleep in the readers' memory banks like the corpses of lost galleons that lie at the bottom of the Black Sea. Good reader that he was, Galip expected the sediment in his memory banks to get stirred up reading the stories Jelal had gleaned from historical sources with this end in mind, but it was only his imagination that got activated.

Reading about how the Twelfth Imam, as it is related in the *History of Weaponry*, would strike terror among the keepers of jewelry stores in the Covered Bazaar who employ rigged scales, how the Sheikh who was proclaimed as the Messiah by his own father had mounted attacks on forts leading Kurdish shepherds and master ironsmiths whom he'd attracted to his cause, and how a dishwasher's aide who, after he dreamed of Muhammad going by in a white Cadillac convertible on the mucky paving stones in Beyoğlu, had proclaimed himself as the Messiah in order to incite whores, gypsies, pickpockets, cigarette boys, the shoeshine men, and the homeless

238]   The Black Book

against bigtime gangsters and pimps, Galip visualized what he read in the brick-red and dawn-orange hues of his own life and dreams. He came across stories that jogged his memory as well as his powers of imagination: he was reading about Hunter Ahmet, the pretender who, after he was done proclaiming himself crown prince and sultan, had also claimed to be the Prophet, when he remembered Jelal speculating one evening—as Rüya smiled on, regarding him as usual out of optimistic but sleepy eyes—over what might be involved in grooming an "Impostor Jelal" capable of stepping in to write his column ("Someone capable of acquiring my memory bank," he had said, curiously enough). Galip was suddenly frightened, feeling that he was being dragged into a dangerous game that led to a deadly trap.

He went through the address books again, checking the names and addresses against those in the phone directory. He called a couple of numbers. that didn't jibe: the first one was a plastics concern in Laleli where they made dish-washing basins, pails, laundry baskets; and if the model for a mold was provided, within a week they could produce and deliver any sort of thing in any kind of color by the hundreds. A child answered the second call, and he told Galip that he lived there with his mom, dad, and granny; no, Dad wasn't home, and before Mom could anxiously get hold of the receiver, a big brother, who hadn't been mentioned before, butted in and said they didn't give out their name to strangers. "Who's this? Who's this?" said the mom, careful and frightened. "Wrong number."

By the time Galip was through reading what Jelal had scribbled on bus and theater tickets, it was already noon. On some of them, Jelal had painstakingly put down his opinions on certain films, and on others he'd written the actors' names. Galip tried making sense of the names that had been underlined. There were names and words on some of the bus tickets as well: on one (a fifteen-*kuruş* ticket, which meant it was issued in the sixties), there was a face that had been formed by letters in the Latin alphabet. He read the letters on the ticket, some of the film criticism, some of the earlier interviews (Famous American movie star Mary Marlowe was in town yesterday!), rough drafts of crossword puzzles, some reader mail that he chose at random, and some news clippings about certain Beyoğlu murders that Jelal had planned to write on. Most of these murders seemed to be imitations of each other: only sharp kitchen knives had been used, all had been committed at midnight; they happened because the parties not only were drunk but also were given to the macho instinct, and they'd been written up with a tough-guy sensibility that reflected a morality that says "This is how those who get into shady business meet their end!" Jelal had made use of some newspaper items on "Exceptional Spots in Istanbul" (Cihangir, Taksim,

Laleli, Kurtuluş) in some of his columns where he retold the stories of these murders. Looking at the series called "Firsts in Our History," Galip remembered that the first book in the Latin alphabet had been published in Turkey by Kasım Bey, who owned the Education Library Press, in 1928. The same man had put out for many years the "Educational Calendar with Time Tables" that came in a block of pages; one tore off a page every day on which was printed—aside from daily menus that Rüya loved, aphorisms from Atatürk, or eminent Islamic personages, or foreign notables like Benjamin Franklin or Bottfolio, and nice jokes—a clock dial that showed the times for prayers on that day. When Galip saw that on some of the calendar pages that he had kept Jelal had fiddled with the clock hands on these dials, transforming them into round human faces with either long noses or long mustaches, he convinced himself that he had come across a new clue and made a note of it on a fresh piece of paper. While he ate his lunch (bread, cheese, and apples), he became strangely interested in examining the note he'd made.

On the last pages of a notebook, in which the résumés of two detective novels in translation (*The Golden Scarab* and *The Seventh Letter*) had been entered as well as the secret codes and keys taken out of books concerning German spies and the Maginot Line, he saw the shaky green trail of a ballpoint pen. These traces looked somewhat like the green ink trail on the maps of Cairo, Damascus, and Istanbul, or sometimes like a face perhaps, sometimes like flowers, sometimes like the curves of a narrow river meandering gracefully on a plain. After being subjected to the asymmetrical and meaningless curves in the first four pages, Galip solved the mystery of the trails on the fifth page. He figured out that an ant had been placed in the middle of a blank page, then the haphazard trail of the harried insect had been traced by the ballpoint pen hard on its heels. In the middle of the fifth page, where the exhausted ant had made a trail going in circles indecisively, its dried corpse had been fixed by being pressed into the notebook. Wondering just how long ago the unhappy ant had been executed for its inability to provide any sort of answer, and whether this odd experiment had any connection to the Rumi pieces, Galip began to investigate. In the fourth volume of the *Mathnawi*, Rumi had related the story of an ant's trek over his rough drafts: at first, the insect recognizes that there are narcissi and lilies inherent in Arabic letters, then that a pen has created this garden of words, then that a hand guides the pen, and then that an intelligence operates the hand, "and, finally," Jelal had added in one of his pieces, "it perceived that there was another Intelligence guiding that intelligence." Galip might have been able to establish a reasonable connection between the dates in the journal and the columns, but the very last page contained only the locations of some historic Istanbul fires, their dates, and the number of wood-frame mansions they had managed to turn into ashes.

He read Jelal's piece on the tricks pulled by a secondhand book-monger's apprentice who sold books door to door at the beginning of the century. The apprentice dealer, who went by rowboat to a different district each day to hit mansions that belonged to the wealthy, sold bargain books in his satchel to harem ladies, to shut-ins, to clerks who were buried under work, and to dreamy kids. But his real customers were minister-pashas who were virtually grounded in their ministries and their mansions, thanks to Sultan Abdül-hamit's proscription which he supervised through the agency of his spooks. Galip felt he was gradually becoming someone else, which was what he wanted, reading how the apprentice dealer taught the pashas (whom Jelal had designated "his readers") by letting them in on Hurufi secrets that were necessary to decipher the messages he stuck into the texts of the books he sold. Once Galip understood that these secrets were nothing more than the signs and the key letters given at the end of a simplified version of an American novel that takes place on distant seas, which Jelal had presented to Rüya one Saturday noon when they were children, he knew for sure that he could become someone else through reading. That was when the phone rang; it was, of course, the same guy on the line.

"I'm pleased you hooked up the phone, Jelal Bey!" said the voice, which made Galip think it belonged to someone past middle age. "In view of the terrible developments that are imminent, I wouldn't even want to think that someone like you was disconnected from the city and the nation."

"What page are you on in the phone book?"

"I'm hard at it, but it's going slower than I expected. Reading numbers for hours, a man gets to think stuff he never thinks about. I'm seeing magic formulas, symmetrical arrangements, repetitions, matrices, and shapes in the numerals. They slow me down."

"And faces too?"

"Yes, but those faces of yours appear out of certain arrangements of numbers. The numbers don't always speak, sometimes they are silent. Sometimes I'm under the impression that the fours are telling me something, arriving as they do at each other's heels. They start out two by two, then they've gone and changed columns symmetrically and, what do you know, they've now become sixteen. Then, the sevens have taken over where they've left off, whispering to the tune of the same order. I want to believe that these are nonsensical coincidences, but look, doesn't the fact that Timur Bayazid's number is 140 22 40 remind you that the Battle of Ankara in 1402 was fought between Timur the Lame and Beyazid the Lightning Bolt? And that, following his victory, that barbarian Timur grabbed up Beyazid's wife for his own harem? The phone book is alive with Istanbul and our history! I get drawn into it, missing out on getting to you. Yet I know that you are the only one who can stop this great conspiracy. Since you are the taut bowstring that activated their arrow, Jelal Bey, only you can stop the military coup!"

"Why so?"

"Last time we talked, I didn't tell you that they have misplaced faith in the Messiah and are waiting for Him for nothing. They are just a bunch of soldiers, but they have read some of the pieces you wrote long ago. Like me, they believed it too. Try recalling some of the columns you wrote early in 1961, and reconsider the *nazire* you wrote on "The Grand Inquisitor," and some of your movie reviews, and the conclusion to that snobbish bit in which you went on about why you didn't believe the picture of the happy family on the National Lottery tickets (Mom's knitting, Dad's reading the paper—your column, perhaps—the son's studying, the cat and the granny are by the stove, catching some Zs: if everybody is so damn happy, if they are all like my family, how come so many lottery tickets are sold?). What was the reason you ridiculed domestic films so strenuously back then? In these films, which give so many so much pleasure, and more or less express 'our feelings,' all you manage to see are the settings, the cologne bottles on the bedside commodes, the row of photographs on the piano which has gone to spiders because it doesn't get played, the postcards stuck around mirror frames, the dog figurine sleeping on top of the family radio. Why?"

"I don't know."

"Oh, yes, you do! You point out these things as signs of our misery and collapse. In the same vein you've commented on the pathetic objects thrown down air shafts, close relatives who all live in the same apartment building, and cousins who end up marrying each other due to their close proximity, and about slipcovers placed on armchairs to keep them from wearing out. You do it to present these things as the heartbreaking signs of our descent into banality and our inevitable decay. But soon after, you run away with yourself, hinting in your so-called historical essays that liberation is always possible: even at the darkest hour, a savior might appear to pull us out of our poverty. A savior who'd been here before, perhaps even centuries ago, would come back to life as someone else: this time, He shows up in Istanbul five hundred years later as Jelalettin Rumi or as Şeyh Galip or as some newspaper columnist! While you related this sort of stuff, yammering about the sadness of women in the slums waiting to get water at public water fountains and cries of love inscribed on the backs of wood seats in the old streetcars, there were these officers who took you at your word. They thought that with the coming of the Messiah they believed in, all melancholy and misery would come to an end and everything would be put to right instantly. You took them in! You know who they are! You wrote with them in mind!"

"So, what do you want from me now?"

"Just to see you will be enough."

"What for? There is no dossier-shmossier, is there?"

"If I could just see you, I'd explain everything."

"Your name is obviously assumed too!" Galip said.

"I want to see you," said the voice, which sounded like the pretentious but strangely touching and convincing voice of a dubbing artist saying: I love you. "I want to see you. When you see me, you'll know why I want to see you. No one knows you like I do. But no one. I know you're dreaming all night, drinking the tea you've made yourself, and coffee, smoking those Maltepe cigarettes you've let dry out on the radiator. I know that you type your work and make corrections with a green ballpoint pen, and that you are not happy with yourself or your life. I know that nights when you pace your rooms disconsolately until daybreak, what you want is to be someone other than yourself, but you just cannot settle on the identity of this other you want to become."

"I've written all about that!"

"I also know that you don't love your father, and that when he returned from Africa with his new wife, he kicked you out of the attic flat where you'd taken refuge. I know about the hard times you went through, too, when you moved in with your mother. Ah, brother mine! You invented bogus murders when you were a starving reporter on the Beyoğlu beat. At the Pera Palas Hotel you interviewed the nonexistent stars of American films that had never been shot. You took opium in order to write the confessions of a Turkish opium eater! You were given a beating on the Anatolian trip you took to finish the serial on wrestling you published under an assumed name! You shed tears telling the story of your life in your 'Believe It or Not' column, but people didn't even get it! I know that you have sweaty hands, that you've had two traffic accidents, that you haven't been able to find waterproof shoes to wear, and that you are always alone despite your fear of loneliness. You enjoy climbing minarets, poking around in Aladdin's store, hanging out with your stepsister, and pornography. Who else knows all this besides me?"

"Lots of people," Galip said. "Anybody can read all about it. Are you going to tell me why you really want to see me?"

"The military coup!"

"I'm hanging up now . . ."

"I swear on it!" the voice said anxiously and hopelessly. "If I could just see you, I'd tell you everything."

Galip pulled the plug out. He removed from the hallway cabinet a yearbook that had been on his mind since he first laid eyes on it yesterday, and he sat in the chair where Jelal sat when he returned home in the evening, all tuckered out. It was a 1947 War College yearbook with a good binding job: aside from pictures and aphorisms that belonged to Atatürk, the President, the Chief of Staff, Joint Chiefs of Staff, the Commander and faculty of the War College, the rest of the book was full of nicely done photographs of the student body. Turning the pages with onionskin between them, Galip had no idea exactly why he felt like looking through the yearbook right after the phone conversation, but he thought the faces and the expressions were surprisingly identical, like the hats on the heads and the bars on the collars. For a moment he thought he was poking through an old journal of numismatics, found among cheap or junk books in dusty boxes that secondhand book dealers display in front of their stores, where the pictures of silver coins and the figures stamped on them can only be told apart by an expert. He became aware of the same music that rose inside him when he walked out on the streets or sat in ferryboat waiting rooms: he enjoyed observing faces.

Turning the pages reminded him of the feeling he used to have when he flipped through the pages that smelled of printing ink and paper in a new issue of the comic book for which he'd been waiting for weeks. Of course, as the books said, everything was connected to everything else. He began to perceive in the photographs the same momentary brightness that he'd observed in faces in the street: it was as if these too provided his eyes with as much meaning as did the faces.

Most of the planners of the unsuccessful military coup that was cooked up at the beginning of the sixties—aside from the generals who winked at the young officers without getting into hot water themselves—must have emerged from among the young officers whose photographs had been printed in this yearbook. There was nothing concerning the military coup in what Jelal had scribbled and doodled on the pages, and sometimes on the onionskin that covered them, but the faces in the photographs had been given beards and mustaches such as a child might draw, and some faces had been lightly shaded under the cheekbone or under the nose. The lines on some of the foreheads had been transformed into "fate lines" in which meaningless Latin letters could be discerned, the bags under some of the eyes had been changed into clear round letters that read O or C, and others had been decorated with stars, horns, and spectacles. The young cadets' chin bones, the bones in their foreheads and their noses, had been marked, and proportion scales had been drawn across the width and the length of some of the faces and across the noses, lips, and foreheads. And under some of the photographs there were notes in reference to photographs on other pages. Pimples, moles, discolorations, Aleppo boils, birthmarks, and burn scars had been worked into many of the cadets' faces. Next to the photograph of a face that was too clear and bright to be touched with lines or letters in any way, this sentence had been written: "Retouching a photograph kills its soul."

Galip ran across the same sentence looking through some other yearbooks: he saw that Jelal had put similar lines and markings on the photographs of the student body at the School of Engineering, the faculty of the Medical School, members elected to the parliament in 1950, engineers and administrators who were employed in building the Sivas–Kayseri railroad, the members of the Association for the Beautification of Bursa, and volunteers from the Alsancak district of Izmir who fought in the Korean War. Most of the faces had been divided into two with a perpendicular line down the middle in an effort to make the letters on either side of the face clearer. At times Galip flipped through the pages rapidly, and other times he examined the photographs for a longer period: as if he were retrieving in the nick of time something he recollected with great difficulty before it vanished into the endless chasm of oblivion, as if he were trying to recall the address of a house he'd been taken to in the dark. Some faces did not reveal anything further after the first glance, but the calm and quiet façades of others began a narrative when it was least expected. That's when Galip remembered the colors, the melancholy gaze of a waitress who'd appeared only briefly in a foreign film he had seen many years ago, and the last time a piece of music was played on the radio which he wanted to hear but always missed.

It was getting dark when Galip removed from the hallway cabinet all the yearbooks, the photo albums, the photo clippings, and all the photographs that had accumulated in the boxes from all kinds of sources and, taking them into the study, began going through them like a drunk. He couldn't tell where, when, and why photographs had been taken of some of the faces he saw: of young girls, of gentlemen wearing melon hats, of women wearing head cloths, of honest-faced young men, and of the down-and-out. Yet it was quite obvious where and wherefore the pictures of some sad faces had been taken: under the kindly gaze of the cabinet ministers and the security police, a pair of citizens anxiously watch their alderman present the prime minister with a petition; a mother who was able to save her bedroll and her child from a fire on Dereboyu in Beşiktaş; women waiting in line to buy tickets at the Alhambra for a movie starring the Egyptian actor Abdul-Wahab;

a well-known belly dancer and movie star, having been picked up for pos-
sessing hash, is accompanied by cops at the Beyoğlu precinct station; the
accountant in whose face the meaning went blank the moment he was caught
for embezzlement. The photographs he pulled out of the boxes at random
seemed to explain the reasons for their own being and retention: "What can
be more profound, gratifying, and curious than a photograph, the document
of a person's facial expression?" Galip thought.

He was sad to think that behind even the most "vacant" of faces, robbed
of their meaning and expressiveness by photo retouching and other stock-
in-trade trick photography, there were stories replete with memories, fears,
and concealed mystery that could not be expressed with words but were
present in the sorrow reflected in their eyes, eyebrows, and gazes. There
were tears in Galip's eyes looking at the photographs of the apprentice quilt
maker's happy but bewildered face when he hit the National Lottery jackpot,
the face of the insurance man who knifed his wife, and the face of Miss
Turkey who managed to "represent us in the best possible manner" in Europe
by being selected as the second runner-up in the Miss Europe contest.

He surmised that the traces of sadness he observed throughout Jelal's work
must have been brought on by studying these photographs: the piece about
the laundry hanging in the yards of tenements that overlook factory warehouses must have been inspired by the face of our amateur boxing champion
fighting in the 57 kg. weight class; the piece regarding the notion that the
crooked streets in Galata are crooked only in the eyes of the foreigners must
have been penned by looking at the purple-white face of the hundred-and-
eleven-year-old singer who implied that she had slept with Atatürk. And the
faces of dead pilgrims wearing beanies, who had a traffic accident on their
way back from Mecca, reminded Galip of a piece regarding old maps and
engravings of Istanbul. In that column Jelal had written that there were signs
marking the locations of treasures on some maps as well as signs in some
European engravings showing crazed adversaries who arrived in Istanbul
with the expressed purpose of assassinating the Sultan. Galip thought there
must be a connection between the piece Jelal had written holed up for weeks
in a hideaway somewhere in Istanbul and the maps that had been marked
in green ink.

He began sounding out the syllables in the district names on the Istanbul
map. Since the words had been used thousands of times every day for all
these years, they were so overburdened with associations that, for Galip, they
had no more to offer than words like "this" or "that." Yet the names of
districts that didn't figure ostensibly in his life, when repeated out loud, had
immediate associations for him. Galip remembered Jelal's series of articles

where he described some of the districts in Istanbul. Those he took out of
the cabinet were entitled "Obscure Locations in Istanbul," but as he read
on, he realized the pieces were heavier on Jelal's short fictions than on
obscure spots in Istanbul. Another time, he might have smiled at having
been let down like this, but now he was so put out that he theorized that
Jelal had knowingly deceived all his life not only his readers, but Galip
himself. While he read the narratives of a small altercation that broke out
on the streetcar from Fatih to Harbiye, of the child who never returned to
his home in Feriköy from the grocery store where he'd been sent, of the
musical ticking at a clock shop, Galip kept murmuring to himself, "I will
not fall for it any longer." But only moments later when he couldn't help
thinking that Jelal might be holed up someplace in Harbiye, or Feriköy, or
Tophane, he felt his anger turn away instantly from Jelal, who lured him
into traps, and turn toward his own mental faculties that kept finding clues
in Jelal's writing. He despised the way he couldn't live without narratives in
the same way that he hated the sort of child who constantly seeks entertainment. He concluded instantly that there was no room in this world for signs,
clues, secondary and tertiary meanings, secrets, and mysteries: all signs were
the apprehensions of his own mind and imagination, set on a quest to discover
and understand. He felt a wish to live peacefully in a world where every
object existed only as itself; only then would none of the letters, texts, faces,
streetlights, Jelal's desk, Uncle Melih's erstwhile cabinet, the scissors or the
ballpoint pen with Rüya's fingerprints be the suspect sign of something other
than itself. How might one enter into a realm where the green ballpoint pen
was only a green ballpoint pen, and where one would have no desire to be
anyone other than himself? Like a kid who imagines himself living in a
distant foreign country in the movie he's watching, Galip studied the maps
on the desk, wishing to convince himself that he lived in this other realm:
for a moment he could almost see the wrinkled forehead of an old man;
then a composite of all the sultans' faces appeared before his eyes, to be
followed by the face of an acquaintance—or was it a prince?—but before
he could make it out clearly, it also vanished.

A while later, thinking that he could look through the mug shots that Jelal
had collected for thirty years with the notion that they were images from the
realm where he wanted to live, he sat in the easy chair. He tried looking at
the photographs he pulled out at random, avoiding any recognition of signs
or mystery in the faces. Consequently, every face appeared to be the description of a physical object consisting of eyes, a nose, and a mouth, just
like on identification cards and residence papers. Once in a while he felt
sad when he saw the melancholy in a woman's beautiful and expressive face

in a photograph affixed to an insurance document; then, he pulled himself together and looked at another face that revealed no sorrow or narrative but only itself. In order to avoid getting involved in the faces' stories, he wouldn't read even the inscriptions under them or the letters Jelal had put on and around the photographs. After looking at the pictures for a long time, forcing himself to see them only as the maps of human faces, when the evening traffic in Nişantaşı got heavy and tears began flowing out of his eyes, Galip had managed to go through only a small fraction of the photographs that Jelal had collected for thirty years.

Chapter Twenty-five

THE EXECUTIONER AND
THE WEEPING FACE

Don't weep, don't weep; oh, please don't. —HALIT ZIYA

Why does the sight of a man in tears make us nervous? We perceive a weeping woman as an exceptional but sad and touching part of our lives, accepting her with affection and sincerity. But a weeping man makes us feel helpless. As if he were at the end of his rope, this man either has no other recourse left—as with the death of someone he loved—or some aspect of his world is at odds with ours, an aspect that is bothersome or even terrifying. We all know the terror and confusion occasioned by coming across a territory we have absolutely no knowledge of in the map we call a face with which we assume we are acquainted. I came across a story on the subject in the fourth volume of Naima's *History*, and in Mehmet Halife's *History for Royal Pages*, as well as in the *History of Executioners* by Kadri of Edirne.

A mere three hundred years ago on a spring evening, Black Ömer, the most renowned executioner of his time, was approaching Fort Erzurum on horseback. He had been dispatched twelve days before, having been handed an edict from the Sultan by the Chief of the Palace Guard for the execution of Abdi Pasha, who commanded Fort Erzurum. He was pleased he was making such good time on the Istanbul–Erzurum trip which, in that season, took an ordinary traveler a whole month; the cool spring evening had refreshed him, but still, some kind of heaviness weighed on him which was not how he usually felt prior to doing a job. He felt as if he were under the shadow of a curse, or else the anxiety of an indecision, that would prevent him from discharging his duty properly.

His was indeed a difficult job: he had to enter all alone a garrison full of men loyal to a Pasha who was totally unknown to him, present the edict, impress on the Pasha and his entourage—by virtue of his own intrepid presence and self-confidence—the futility of opposing the Sultan's will; and if, by some remote chance, the Pasha was slow to be impressed that such action would be in vain, he had to kill the man without giving those around him a chance to come up with some culpable intent. He was so experienced with the procedure that the indecision he felt had to be the result of something else. In his thirty-year career, he had executed close to twenty royal princes, two grand viziers, six viziers, twenty-three pashas—more than six hundred persons in all, including honest folk and thieves, innocent and guilty, men and women, old and young, Christian and Moslem; and beginning with the days of his apprenticeship to date, he had put thousands of people to torture.

On that spring morning, the executioner dismounted before entering town, he took a ritual bath listening to the joyful twittering of the birds, and he went down on his knees to pray. Praying and begging God to make things go right for him was something he did very rarely. But, as was always the case, God accepted this diligent mortal's prayer.

So, everything worked like a charm. The Pasha, who instantly knew what manner of man the executioner was from the conical red-felt hat on his shaved head and the greased noose in his cummerbund, realized his fate without fail, but he didn't put up any resistance that could be construed as extraordinary. Perhaps he had become aware of his offense and had already submitted to his fate.

For starters, the Pasha read the edict ten times, each time with the same circumspection. (A characteristic of those who obey the rules.) After he finished reading it, he kissed the edict in an ostentatious manner and touched it to his forehead. (A response that seemed stupid to Black Ömer but one that is still observed in people for whom impressing those around them is a consideration.) He wished to read the Koran and perform his prayers. (A penchant seen both in those who are true believers and those who're playing for time.) After getting through his prayers, he distributed among his company the valuable objects on him, his rings, jewels, decorations, saying "This is to remember me by," thereby assuring himself that these things didn't end up with the executioner. (A response observed in those who are too involved with the world and superficial enough to hold a personal grudge against their executioners.) And before the noose was slipped over his head, like most who display not only a few of these responses but all of them, he made an attempt to fight hand to hand, swearing a blue streak. But as soon as a stiff blow was landed on his chin, he collapsed and began to wait for death. He was in tears.

Weeping was an ordinary response displayed by victims in situations like this, but the executioner observed something else in the Pasha's tearful face which, for the first time in his thirty-year career, made him vacillate. So he did something he had never done before: he covered his victim's face under a piece of cloth before he strangled him. He criticized such behavior in his colleagues, seeing how he believed that, in performing his duty smoothly and flawlessly, an executioner had to be capable of looking his victim right in the eye until the very end.

As soon as he was sure his victim was dead, he severed the head off the body with the aid of a special straight razor called "the cipher," and he plunged the head while it was still fresh in the honey-filled mohair sack that he had brought along: the head had to be preserved so that he could bring it back to Istanbul where those responsible could determine whether he'd performed his job successfully. While trying to place the head carefully into the honey-filled mohair sack, he observed once more with amazement the lachrymose gaze on the Pasha's face, that inexplicable and terrifying expression, which he couldn't forget until the end of his own life which was not too distant.

He mounted his horse at once and left town. While his victim's body was being given a sickeningly sad and tearful funeral, the executioner always wished, what with the head riding on his horse's rump, that he were at least two days' ride away from the site. Consequently, after riding a day and a half, he arrived at Fort Kemah. He ate at the caravanserai and he went in his cell, toting the sack, and fell asleep for a long time.

Just as he began waking from a deep sleep, he was dreaming that he was in Edirne, just as it was in his childhood: as he approached the huge jam jar full of fig preserves which his mom had made, filling not only the house and the garden with the tart fragrance of figs boiling in syrup but the whole neighborhood, he first realized that the small green globes he thought were figs were in fact the eyeballs of a weeping head; then he opened the jar, feeling guilty more for witnessing the inexplicable horror on the weeping face than for doing something forbidden; and when he heard the sound of a mature man's sobs come out of the jar, he became frozen with the feeling of helplessness that immobilized him.

The next night, in the middle of his sleep in a different bed in a different caravanserai, he found himself dreaming of an afternoon in his early youth: just before dark, he was in downtown Edirne, out in an alley. His attention having been called to it by a friend whose identity he couldn't make out, he observed the setting sun at one end of the sky, and the white visage of a pale full moon at the other. Then, as the sun sank and the sky became dark, the moon's gibbous face became more illuminated and more distinct, and soon afterwards it dawned on him that the brilliantly shining face was a weeping face that belonged to a human being. But no, what transformed the streets of Edirne into the disquieting and incomprehensible streets of some other town was not the sadness of the moon's metamorphosis into a weeping face, but its enigma.

The next morning the executioner reflected that the truth he discovered in the middle of his sleep was in agreement with his own recollections. Throughout his career he'd observed the weeping faces of thousands of men, but none of those faces had aroused in him feelings of guilt, ruthlessness, and fear. Contrary to the usual assumption, he felt sad and sorry for his victims, but the feeling was immediately balanced with the logic of justice, necessity, and inevitability. He knew very well that the victims he decapitated, strangled, or whose necks he broke, were always better informed than their executioner about the chain of causes that led to their death. There was nothing unbearable or intolerable in seeing a man go to his death in a flurry of tears, begging through his snot, sobbing and choking. The executioner neither despised tearful men, as do some idiots who expect brave words and flamboyant gestures from the condemned which will go down in history or legends, nor did he become immobilized with a feeling of pity upon seeing them cry as do another class of idiots who have no comprehension at all of life's random and inevitable ruthlessness.

But what was it about his dreams that arrested him? On a bright and sunny morning, riding past deep and rocky chasms with the mohair sack on his horse's rump, the executioner reflected that the feeling of immobility that came over him was connected in some way with the indecisiveness he experienced just before he arrived at Erzurum and the shadow of a vague curse he sensed in his soul. Before he strangled the Pasha, he had seen the mystery that had forced him to cover his head with a coarse cloth, prompting him to consign his victim's face into oblivion. As the day wore on, the executioner no longer thought about the expression on the face he carried behind him on his horse, riding along rocky precipices that had astonishing shapes (a sailboat with a potbellied hull, a lion with a fig-shaped head), along stands of pine and beech trees that were stranger and more surprising than usual, and along the ice-cold rivers over strange-looking pebble stones. It was now the world that was astonishing, a new world that he had become aware of for the first time.

He had just become aware that all trees looked like the dark shadows that stirred on sleepless nights among his recollections. He noticed for the first time that the innocent shepherds who grazed their flocks on the greening slopes carried their heads on their shoulders as if carrying someone else's wares. He realized for the first time that ten-house settlements on the skirts of mountains looked like shoes lined up in front of the entrances to mosques. He had a new apprehension that the purple mountains he rode through a couple of days later in the western provinces, and above them clouds that looked as if they came out of miniature paintings, signified that the world was a bare, butt-naked place. He had just comprehended that all the plants, the objects, and the timid animals were signs of a realm as frightening as nightmares, as plain as helplessness, and as old as memories. As he proceeded westward, and as the lengthening shadows gathered new meanings, the executioner had a feeling that the signs and significances of a mystery which he couldn't fathom were seeping into his environs like blood seeping out of a cracked earthen bowl.

At a caravanserai where he stopped just as it got dark, he had something to eat, but he realized he couldn't sleep in a cell closeted with the head. He knew he couldn't tolerate the fearful dream that would slowly spread out somewhere in the middle of his sleep, like pus draining out of a wound burst open, and the helpless face that kept weeping every night in his dreams under the guise of yet another recollection. For a while he rested, observing with astonishment the human faces in the caravanserai crowd, and then proceeded on his way.

The night was cold and silent. There was no wind or any movement in the trees. His tired horse made its way on its own. He went on his way for quite a while without observing anything, as in the good old days, or dwelling on some irritating question: sometime later, he'd attribute it to the fact that it was dark, considering that when the moon slipped out of the clouds, the trees, the shadows, the rocks were gradually transformed into the signs of an insoluble mystery. What was frightening was neither the pitiful tombstones in the graveyards, nor the solitary cypress trees, nor the howling of the wolves in the desolate night. What made the world so astonishing as to be frightful was his own seeming attempt to extract a story—as if the world wanted to tell him something, to signify some meaning, but the words were lost in a misty uncertainty, as in a dream. Toward daybreak, the executioner began hearing sobs in his ears.

At daybreak, he thought the sobs were an illusion created by the commencement of a wind in the trees; later, he ruled it the result of sleeplessness and fatigue. By noontime, the sobs that came from the sack on the pillion became so definite that, like someone who gets out of his warm bed in the middle of the night to put a stop to the unnerving squeak of a partially closed casement window, he dismounted and tightened as taut as he could the ropes that secured the sack on the pillion. Yet later, under a merciless rain, he would not only hear the sobs but would also feel on his very skin the tears shed by the weeping head.

When the sun came out again, he had understood that the mystery of the world was related to the enigma in the weeping face. It was as if that familiar old world that was comprehensible had been sustained by commonplace meanings and expressions on faces, and after the eerie expression appeared on the weeping face, the meaning of the world had disappeared leaving the executioner stranded, fearful, and alone—just as when an enchanted bowl shatters into smithereens, or a magic crystal vase cracks, things go topsy-turvy. While the wet clothes on him dried in the sun, he realized that for things to go back to normal, he had to change the expression that the head in the sack carried on its face like a mask. Yet, his guild ethics demanded that he bring back to Istanbul the head, which he had pressed into the sack of honey fresh after he cut it off, preserved and intact.

In the morning, following a night spent riding on horseback during which the incessant sobbing that came from the sack had turned into an exasperating music, the executioner found the world so changed that he had a hard time believing his own identity. Pine and plane trees, muddy roads, village fountains where people scattered away in terror when they saw him, all came out of a world he did not know. At noon, in a town whose existence he hadn't been aware of, he had a tough time even recognizing the food he gobbled down out of an animal instinct. When he stretched out under a tree somewhere out of town, so that he could rest his horse, he realized the thing that he had once assumed was the sky was really a strange blue dome he neither had any knowledge of nor had ever seen before. He got back on the horse when the sun began to set, but he had still six days' journey to make. He had finally understood that he was never going to arrive in Istanbul unless he could perform the magic procedure that would restore his familiar world by stopping the sobbing in the sack, and changing the expression on the weeping face.

After dark, when he chanced upon a well in a village where he heard dogs barking, he dismounted. He removed the mohair sack from the horse, he untied the strings, and carefully he lifted the head by the hair out of the honey. He drew pails of water out of the well and washed the head with care as if washing a newborn babe. After drying the head with a piece of cloth, starting with its hair down to its ear canals, he took a look at the face in the light of the full moon: it was weeping. No alteration; the same unbearable and unforgettable expression of helplessness persisted on it.

He placed the head on the wall that circled the well, went to his horse to get some tools of his trade: a pair of special knives and some blunt steel rods for torture. He began with a knife trying to change the mouth gradually by twisting loose the skin from the bone around it. After working like the dickens, he made a mess of the lips but managed to give the mouth something of a smile, albeit crooked and ambiguous. Then he attempted the more delicate operation of opening the eyelids that had been squeezed shut with pain. After the protracted and exhausting effort of giving the whole face a smiling expression, he was tired, but he was relaxed at last. Even so, he was pleased to see the purple mark his fist left on Abdi Pasha's chin just before he'd strangled the man. Childishly pleased to have set things right, he ran and put his tools back in place.

When he turned around, the head was no longer where he left it. At first, he thought the smiling head was playing a trick on him. But when he realized the head had slipped down the well, he had no compunctions running to the nearest house and knocking on the door to wake the people inside. It was enough for the elderly father and the young son to take a look at the executioner for them to comply fearfully with his orders. All three worked until morning to take the head out of the well, which wasn't all that deep. Just as the day began to break, the son, who had been dangled down the well on the greased noose tied to his waist, was brought back up, screaming with horror and holding the head by the hair. The head was a mess but it no longer wept. The executioner calmly dried the head, plunged it back into the honey-filled sack, gladly took off from the village of the father and son, into whose palms he had slipped a couple of coins, and proceeded westward.

The sun was rising and birds were twittering in the spring-flowering trees when the executioner knew, suffused with excitement and a joy of living that was as wide as the sky, that the world had returned back to its familiar old self. There was no sobbing in the sack any longer. Before noon, he got off his horse beside a lake below some hills that were covered with pine trees and lay down blissfully for the deep and untroubled sleep he'd been yearning for all this time. But before falling asleep, he'd risen joyfully from his place to walk to the edge of the lake; observing his own reflection in the water, he had realized once again that all was right with the world.

When he arrived in Istanbul five days later, while witnesses who knew Abdi Pasha well could not identify the head that came out of the mohair sack, claiming that the smiling expression on the face was not anything like the Pasha's at all, the executioner recognized in it his own glad face which he had contentedly seen reflected in the lake. He knew it was no use answering the accusations that he had been bribed by Abdi Pasha to stick in the sack the head of someone else, say, one that belonged to an innocent shepherd he'd murdered which he'd manhandled, disfiguring the face so that the substitution would not be detected: he had already observed the arrival of another executioner who would sever his own head.

Rumor spread quickly that an innocent shepherd's head had been cut off instead of Abdi Pasha's—so quickly, in fact, that the second executioner sent to Erzurum to take his head was anticipated by Abdi Pasha, who was sitting pretty in his garrison, and was himself executed. That's how the insurrection called the Abdi Pasha Revolt started, which lasted twenty years and cost six thousand five hundred heads, although some said the letters they read in the Pasha's face gave him away as an impostor.

Chapter Twenty-six

MYSTERY OF LETTERS AND
LOSS OF MYSTERY

A hundred thousand secrets will be known
When that unveiled, surprising face is shown.
                                    —ATTAR, *The Conference of the Birds*

By dinnertime in the city, when traffic at Nişantaşı Square was unsnarled
and the irascible whistles from the cop at the corner had ceased, Galip had
been staring at photographs for such a long time that he was depleted of all
the pain and sorrow that the faces of his compatriots might have inspired in
him; he had no more tears in his eyes. He was also too exhausted to feel
any elation, joy, or excitement the faces might fetch up; it was as if he no
longer expected anything from life. Looking at the photographs, he only felt
the indifference of someone who had lost his entire memory, his hopes, and
his future; there was the hint of a silence in a corner of his mind which felt
like it might slowly expand to envelop his whole body. Even while drinking
his stale tea and eating the bread and feta cheese he brought from the kitchen,
he kept looking at the photographs now scattered with bread crumbs. The
incredible ambitious bustle of the city had calmed down and night noises
had begun. Now he could hear the fridge motor, the sound of the shutters
being lowered on a store at the end of the street, and the laughter in the

vicinity of Aladdin's store. At times he paid attention to the staccato of high heels rapidly clicking along the sidewalks, and at other times he was oblivious to the silence, when he looked at some visage in a photograph with fear or terror, or with an astonishment which exhausted him.

That's when he began thinking about the relationship between the mystery of letters and the meaning in faces, more with the desire of emulating the sleuths in Rüya's detective novels than with any hope of solving the enigma of the scribbles Jelal had made on the faces in the photographs. "All that's required to be like the heroes of detective novels who are constantly seeing clues in things," Galip thought wearily, "is to believe that the objects in the periphery are keeping some secret from you." Taking the box with the books, treatises, clippings from papers and magazines, and the thousands of photos and pictures connected with Hurufism out of the cabinet in the hallway, he went to work.

He came across faces that had been constructed with letters in the Arabic alphabet, eyes out of *wâws* and *'ayns*, the eyebrows of *zâys* and *râs*, and noses of *alifs*; Jelal had marked the letters one by one with the fastidiousness of a good-natured student learning the old alphabet. On the pages of a lithographed book he saw weeping eyes made of *wâws* and *jîms*, the dot in the *jîms* forming the teardrops that fell down the page. He observed in an old unretouched black-and-white photograph that the same letters could easily be read in the eyes, eyebrows, lips, and noses; under the photograph, Jelal had written the Bektaşi master's name in legible letters. He saw inscriptions of "Ah, sigh of love!" and galleons rocking in storms, lightning bolts that came down from the sky in the shape of eyes, expressions of terror, visages tangled in tree branches—all fashioned of letters—and beards that were each a different letter. He saw pale faces whose eyes had been dug out of the photograph, innocents around whose lips signs of guilt had been worked in letters, and sinners whose terrifying destinies had been tucked in the lines on their foreheads. He noted the absentminded expressions on hanged bandits' and prime ministers' faces, their eyes on the ground where their feet did not reach, wearing their white robes of execution and the record of their sentences hanging on their chests; and he saw the faded color photos sent by those who'd read in a famous movie star's painted eyes that she was a whore, and photos of wannabes and look-alikes of sultans, pashas, Rudolph Valentino, and Mussolini on which they themselves had inscribed letters. He came upon the signs of secret word games that Jelal had discovered in long letters from readers who had deciphered the message Jelal put out for them in a column pointing out the special meaning and the placement of the letter "h" as in the last letter of *Allah*, and from those who explicated the symmetries he delineated in the words "morning," "face," "sun" for a whole week, month, and year, and from those who maintained that monkeying with letters was no better than worshipping idols. He saw pictures of the founder of Hurufism, Fazlallah of Astarabad, copied from old miniatures on which letters in both Latin and Arabic alphabets had been intruded; the letters and words written on the pictures of soccer players and movie actors that came with the chocolate wafers and the colored bubble gum hard as the sole of your shoe that were sold at Aladdin's; and the photos of murderers, sinners, and Sufi masters that his readers had sent Jelal. He saw the pictures of "fellow citizens" by the hundreds, thousands, tens of thousands, which swarmed with letters; he saw photographs of a thousand compatriots sent to Jelal from all parts of Anatolia in the last thirty years, from dusty little towns, from distant burgs where the soil cracks under the sun in summer and where on account of heavy snow for four months in winter nobody visits aside from hungry wolves, from smugglers' villages on the Syrian border where half of the men go lame from having stepped on mines, from villages where they've been waiting to get a road for the last forty years, from bars and casinos in big cities, from slaughterhouses set up in caves, from drug and cigarette traffickers' dens and from stationmaster's offices at desolate railroad stations, from the lobbies of hotels where cattle drovers spend the night and from whorehouses in Soğukoluk. He saw the thousands of pictures taken with old Leicas by street photographers who set up their cameras with tripods and evil-eye beads next to government offices, municipal buildings, and the folding tables where petition writers type out documents for the illiterate, and, disappearing under black sheets like alchemists or fortune-tellers, work the pumps and bellows, the black lens cover, the chemically treated glass plates. It wasn't hard to imagine these fellow citizens as they looked into the camera, gripped by a vague apprehension of death and the wish for immortality. Galip could see immediately that this deep wish was related to the collapse, death, and defeat whose signs he had come to recognize in faces and on maps. It was as if years of happiness followed by a great defeat had been covered over with the dust and ash spewed out by an exploding volcano, and Galip now had to decipher and read in hundreds of compromised signs the lost secret meaning of deeply buried recollections.

The information on the backs of the photographs revealed that some of them had been sent to the "Your Face, Your Personality" column that Jelal had taken over in the early fifties along with puzzles, movie reviews, and "Believe It or Not." Others had arrived in response to Jelal's summons (We'd like to see our readers' photographs and publish some of them in these columns), and still others in response to some letters whose contents Galip couldn't quite make out. They had looked into the camera as if remembering something from their distant past, or as if watching a greenish lightning bolt flash and strike over an indistinct land mass on the horizon, as if their eyes were accustomed to observing their own destinies gradually sink into a dark swamp, as if they were amnesiacs who have no doubt that they will never regain their memory. Feeling the silence in the expressions in the photographs take over his mind, Galip sensed clearly why Jelal might have been inscribing all these letters on pictures, clippings, faces, and expressions; but when he wanted to use the reason as a key to the story of his own life's links to Jelal's and Rüya's, of leaving this phantom abode, of his own future, he immediately became subdued like the faces he saw in the photographs; his mind, which was supposed to make connections between events, merely vanished into the fog of meanings stuck in between letters and faces. This is how he began to approach the terror which he'd read in faces and into which he'd gradually enter.

He read in lithographed books and treatises full of spelling errors about the life of Fazlallah, the founder and prophet of the Hurufi sect, who was born in 1339 in Khorosan, in a town called Astarabad which is near the Caspian Sea. When he was eighteen, he took up Sufism, went on pilgrimage, and became a disciple to a master called Sheikh Hasan. As Galip read about how Fazlallah increased his experience traveling from town to town in Azerbaijan and Iran and what he discussed with masters in Tabriz, Shirvan, and Baku, he felt an irrepressible desire "to begin a new life," as that gets described in this kind of inspirational book. The predictions Fazlallah made concerning his own destiny and his death, which later came true, seemed to Galip like ordinary events that might befall someone who wanted to begin living the new life he desired. Initially, Fazlallah had become known for his dream interpretations. On one occasion, he'd dreamed of a pair of hudhud birds, of Prophet Solomon, and himself, and as the birds on the tree under which Solomon and Fazlallah slept watched, the dreams of the two men had merged, and so, the two hudhud birds on the tree had also merged into one bird. On another occasion, he'd dreamed of a dervish who'd come to visit him in a cave where he'd secluded himself, and then later, when the same dervish actually came to visit, Fazlallah learned that the dervish had dreamed of him; when they leafed through a book together in the cave, they saw their own faces in the letters, and when they looked up at each other, they saw the letters of the book in each other's faces.

According to Fazlallah, since everything that crossed over from nothingness into the material world produced a sound, sound was the demarcation line between Being and Nothingness: striking "the most soundless" objects against each other was enough for us to discern this. The most developed form of sound was, of course, the "word," the exalted thing called "speech," the magic known as "words" which were made up of Letters. The origin of Being, its Meaning, and the material aspect of God were distinguishable in Letters that were clearly written in the faces of men. We were all born with the native characteristic of two brow lines, four eyelash lines, and one hairline—seven strokes in all. At puberty, with the addition of the late-blooming nose dividing our faces, this figure was increased to fourteen, and doubled again when we took into account the imaginary and real numbers which were even more poetic, which all went to show that the twenty-eight letters of the language Muhammad spoke were not accidental in bringing the Koran into existence. When Galip read that in order to jack up the count to thirty-two, which was the number of letters in Persian (the language Fazlallah spoke and wrote his *Book of Eternal Life* in), it was necessary to examine the hair and chin lines more attentively, divide them down the middle—thereby finding two more lines, times two which made four—he realized why the hair had been parted in the middle (as actors in American films had done to their brilliantined hair in the thirties) in some of the photographs he'd found in the boxes. All this was so straightforward that, momentarily pleased with its childlike simplicity, Galip felt he understood once again what it was that attracted Jelal to these letter games.

Fazlallah proclaimed himself to be the deliverer, the prophet: the Messiah of the Jews, the Saviour whose second coming is anticipated by the Christians, the Mahdi whom Muhammad has heralded—the long-awaited figure, in short, who appeared in Jelal's piece about "Him." Surrounding himself in Ispahan with seven believers, Fazlallah began promoting his faith. It gave Galip a feeling of inner peace to read that Fazlallah went from town to town preaching that the world was not a place that yielded up its secrets right off, that it swarmed with secrets, and that in order to penetrate these secrets it was necessary to comprehend the mystery of letters. For Galip, it seemed now to be clearly proved that his world also swarmed with secrets, as he had always anticipated and desired. He sensed that the inner peace he felt was related to the simplicity of this demonstration; if it was true that the world was a place swarming with secrets, then it was also true that the coffee cup on the table, the ashtray, the letter opener, even his own hand that rested like a hesitant crab next to the letter opener, all pointed to and were a part of the existence of a hidden world. Rüya was in this world. Galip was at its threshold. Soon, the secret of letters would let him in.

That's why he had to read more carefully. He read of Fazlallah's life and death once more. He understood that Fazlallah had dreamed of his own death and had approached his death as if in a dream. He had been accused of heresy for worshipping letters, mankind, and idols instead of God, for proclaiming himself as the Messiah, and for believing his own fantasies, which he claimed to be the secret and invisible meaning of the Koran, instead of its real and visible significance. He was caught, tried, and hanged.

Hurufis, for whom it became difficult to hang on in Iran after the execution of Fazlallah and his associates, crossed over into Anatolia, thanks to the poet Nesimi who was one of Fazlallah's successors. The poet, loading Fazlallah's books and manuscripts on Hurufism in a green trunk which would achieve legendary status among Hurufis, traveled throughout Anatolia, hitting each and every town to find fresh adherents in remote seminaries where even the spiders took naps in lazarettos and tekkes for the lazy that teemed with lizards, and in order to illustrate for his trainees that not only the Koran but the whole world swarmed with secrets, he resorted to letter and word games inspired by the game of chess which he loved. Poet Nesimi—who, in two lines of verse, likened a feature and a beauty spot on his sweetheart's face to a letter and a period, the letter and the period to a sponge and pearl in the bottom of the sea, himself to a diver who dies for the sake of the pearl, the diver who voluntarily dives into death to a lover seeking God, and so, coming full circle, likened his sweetheart to God—was arrested in Aleppo, subjected to a long trial, and flayed to death: After his body was strung up and exhibited in the city, the corpse was cut into seven parts, and each part was buried, as an object lesson, in one of the seven cities where he had found himself adherents and where his poems were recited.

Under Poet Nesimi's influence, Hurufism had spread rapidly among the Bektaşis in the land of the Ottomans, and had even turned on Sultan Mehmet the Conqueror some fifteen years after his conquest of Constantinople. When the theologians around him realized that the Sultan carried Fazlallah's treatises around, holding forth on the mystery of the world, the enigma of letters, the secrets of Byzantium, which he observed from his palace where he had moved in recently, and that he investigated how each and every chimney, dome, and tree that he pointed out individually could provide the key for penetrating into the mystery of another realm that existed underground, they had schemed against those Hurufis who managed to get close to the Sultan and had them burned alive.

In a little book which had a handwritten note appended to its last page, informing (or misinforming) that it was printed covertly in Horasan, near Erzurum, at the beginning of World War II, Galip came across pictures of Hurufis being beheaded and burned after an assassination attempt on the Conqueror's son, Bayazit II. On another page, Hurufis who'd been burned to death for not obeying Süleyman the Magnificent's order for their deportation had been depicted with a childlike execution and an expression of horror. In the undulating flames that lapped up the bodies, the *alif*s and *lam*s of the word *Allah* were legible, but what was stranger was that the bodies, which burned furiously in the Arabic alphabet, emitted from their eyes tears that were adorned with O's, U's, and C's of the Latin alphabet. This constituted the first Hurufi interpretation that Galip had run across of the 1928 Alphabet Reform—the transition from Arabic characters to the Latin alphabet—but since his mind was on the formula for the solution to a riddle, he continued reading what he found in the box without evaluating what he'd seen.

He read a great many pages attesting that God's essential attribute was a "hidden treasure" (a *kenz-ı mahfi*), a mystery. The question was to find a way to get to it. The question was to realize that the mystery was reflected in the world. The question was to comprehend that the mystery was present in everything, every object, every person. The world was an ocean of clues, every one of its drops had the salt taste that led to the mystery behind it. The more Galip's tired and inflamed eyes read on, the more he knew that he would penetrate into the ocean's secrets.

Since the signs were everywhere and in everything, the mystery was also everywhere and in everything. Like the beloved's face in poems, the pearls, roses, wine goblets, nightingales, golden hair, night, and flames that Galip kept reading about, the objects around him were both signs of themselves and of the mystery that he was slowly approaching. The curtain lit by the weak light of the lamp, the old armchairs teeming with memories of Rüya, the shadows on the walls, the ominous phone receiver, the very fact that they were so replete with stories and allusions, gave Galip the feeling that he was being sucked into a game unawares, as he had sometimes felt when he was in his childhood. He continued to go ahead, feeling only slightly mistrustful on account of his conviction that he could get out of the scary game (where everyone impersonated someone else and every object simulated something other than itself) by becoming, as he did when he was a child, still another someone else. "If you're afraid, I'll turn the light on," he used to tell Rüya, realizing that she was just as scared as he was when they played the game in the dark. "Don't turn it on," said undaunted Rüya, who liked being scared. Galip went on reading.

At the beginning of the seventeenth century, some Hurufis had settled in remote villages that had been abandoned by the peasantry who had fled from pashas, judges, bandits, and imams during the Jelali uprisings that had left Anatolia in shambles. Galip was trying to make sense of the lines in a longish poem describing the felicitous and meaningful lifestyle that once prevailed in these Hurufi villages, when he recalled the happy memories of his own childhood spent with Rüya.

In those distant felicitous times, significance and action had been identical. In that Golden Age, things in our houses and our dreams of them were the same. Back in those years of happiness, everyone knew that daggers and pens, tools and such that we held in our hands, were extensions not only of our bodies but also of our souls. Back then, when a poet said "tree," everyone could visualize that tree exactly, and everyone knew that in order for the word and the tree in the poem to signify whatever else was in the garden and life as well as the tree, there was no necessity to display undue skill enumerating the leaves and the branches. Everyone knew very well back then that words and what they described were so close that on mornings when fog descended on the phantom villages in the mountains, the words and what they described were intermingled. People who woke from their sleep on foggy mornings could not tell apart their dreams from reality, poems from life, and names from human beings. Back then, stories and lives were so real that nobody even conceived of asking which was the original life or which was the original story. Dreams were lived through and lives were thoroughly interpreted. As was everything else, people's faces too were so meaningful back then that even those who weren't literate, who couldn't tell their *alpha* from an apple, their *a* from a hat, and their *alif* from a stick, began spontaneously reading the letters that reveal the meaning in our faces.

In those distant happy days people were not even conscious of time, the poet wrote that the orange sun stood still in the evening sky, and galleons whose sails were filled with a wind that did not blow made voyages without motion on a still ocean that was the color of glass and ash, and as Galip read he realized, having come across the image of white mosques and even whiter minarets rising like a mirage that would never vanish beside this sea, that the Hurufi imagination and life which had remained concealed since the seventeenth century had nonetheless encompassed Istanbul. When Galip read how the storks, albatrosses, simurghs, and the phoenix taking wing against the three-tiered white minarets toward the horizon swayed for centuries as if suspended in the sky above the domes of Istanbul; how every outing in the streets of Istanbul, none of which crossed each other at right angles nor according to some plan, was as heady and recreative as a holiday trip to eternity; and how on warm moonlit nights in summer, when it was possible to draw from wells not only ice-cold water but also pailfuls of mysterious signs and stars, everyone recited poems all night long that bespoke the meaning of the signs and the signs of the meaning, he understood not only that an unadulterated golden age of Hurufism had once existed in Istanbul, but that his own happy days with Rüya were long gone.

This felicitous age must have been short-lived. Galip read that soon after the golden age during which the secrets of the mystery became notorious, secrets had become more confusing—that in an effort to conceal their mysteries all the more, some people had resorted to elixirs made of blood, eggs, hair, and shit, mixtures like those concocted by the Hurufis in the phantom villages; others had dug passageways under their houses in Istanbul's secret locations in order to bury their mysteries. He read that there were those not as lucky as the ones who had dug passageways, men caught for joining the Janissary rebellions and hanged on trees, whose facial letters got deformed by the greased noose tightened around their necks like neckties, and also that bards who took their lutes to dervish lodges in the slums to whisper Hurufi secrets were met with walls of incomprehension. All this evidence confirmed that the golden age, which was lived as much in secret locales and mysterious streets in Istanbul as in remote phantom villages, had been abruptly brought to an end.

When Galip reached the last page of the book of poetry that mice had gnawed along the edges and on the corners of which glass-green and turquoise mildew had flowered with the pleasant smell of paper and dampness, he came across a note that more elaborate information on the subject had been undertaken in another treatise. According to the long, ungrammatical sentence stuck in by the typesetter from Horasan in small print between the last lines of the poem and the addresses of the printers, the publishers, dates of composition and publication, the seventh book of the same series published by the same outfit in Horasan near Erzurum was a work penned by F. M. Üçüncü, called *Mystery of Letters and Loss of Mystery*, which had rated praise from the Istanbul journalist Selim Kaçmaz.

Galip, fogged out with dreams of Rüya and fantasies of words and letters, weary and sleepless, recalled Jelal's early years in journalism. Back in those days, Jelal's involvement with word and letter games did not go beyond sending coded messages to his lovers, family, and friends in the "Your Horoscope Today" and "Believe It or Not" columns. He searched furiously for the treatise among the wads of paper, magazines, and newsprint. After turning the place completely upside down, when he finally came across the book among the news clips from the early sixties that Jelal had saved, unpublished polemics, and some weird photographs in a box he was going through without any hope, it was way past midnight, and the sort of disheartening stillness that sends cold chills down your spine, characteristic of the curfew when the country was under martial law, had fallen on the streets.

Like many a "work" of this sort, the publication or the near-publication of which is announced prematurely, *Mystery of Letters and Loss of Mystery* had managed to see publication only many years later, in 1967, in another town, Gördes—it surprised Galip that the place even had a printing press back then—as a book of two hundred and twenty-two pages. On the yellowed cover was a dark picture which had been printed from a poorly made plate with cheap ink: in the crude perspective drawing, a road bordered with chestnut trees stretched out to the vanishing point. Beside each tree were letters, terrifying, blood-curdling letters.

At first glance, it looked like one of those books written some years back by "idealist" military officers, in the genre of "Why Have We Not Caught Up with the West in the Past Two Hundred Years? How Do We Make Progress?" It began with the sort of dedication seen in books printed in some out-of-the-way town in Anatolia at the writer's expense: "War College cadet! You are the one who will save this country!" But when Galip began turning the pages, he realized he was in the presence of an entirely different kind of "work." He got up from the chair and went to Jelal's desk; placing his elbows on either side of the book, he began to read attentively.

Mystery of Letters and Loss of Mystery was comprised of three main sections, the first two appearing in the book's title. The first section, "Mystery of Letters (that is, of *Huruf*)," began with the biography of Fazlallah, the founder of Hurufism. F. M. Üçüncü added a secular dimension to the story, introducing Fazlallah more as a rationalist, philosopher, mathematician, and linguist than as a Sufi and a mystic. As much as Fazlallah was a prophet, a messiah, a martyr and saint—or more than he was these—he was a subtle philosopher and a genius, but one "unique to us." Attempting to explain his thought as Pantheism, or through Plotinus, Pythagoras, or the Cabala, as some Orientalists in the West had done, was nothing more than stabbing Fazlallah by using Western thought, which he had opposed all his life. Fazlallah was an unadulterated man of the East.

According to F. M. Üçüncü, East and West shared the two halves of the world: they were total opposites, rejecting, contradicting each other—like good and bad, black and white, angel and devil. Contrary to the optimistic assumptions of those who live in a dream world, it was not at all possible for the two realms to come to terms and live in peace. One or the other of the two had always dominated, one world playing the master and the other the slave. To illustrate this endless war of twins, the writer reviewed a progression of historical events loaded with special significance, starting with Alexander cutting the Gordian knot ("that is, the cipher," the writer comments), the Crusades, the double meanings of the characters and numbers on the magic clock Haroun al-Rashid sent Charlemagne, Hannibal crossing the Alps, the Islamic victory in Andalusia (there was a whole page devoted to the number of columns in the Mosque in Cordova), the conquest of Byzantium and Constantinople by Mehmet the Conqueror who himself was a Hurufi, the collapse of the Khazars, and ending with the defeat of the Ottomans laying siege first to Doppio (*The White Castle*) and then to Venice.

According to F. M. Üçüncü, all these historical facts signified a salient point to which Fazlallah had made veiled allusions in his work. The periods during which either the East or the West dominated over its opposite number were not random but logical. Whichever realm was successful in seeing the world as an equivocal, mysterious place that swarmed with secrets "during the particular historic period" that realm got the better of the other and dominated it. Those who saw the world as a simple, unambiguous, unmysterious place were condemned to defeat and its attendant result, which was slavery.

F. M. Üçüncü reserved the second section for a detailed discussion of the loss of mystery. No matter what it was, be it in reference to ancient Greek philosophy's "idea," Neoplatonic Christianity's "Deity," the Hindu's "Nirvana," Attar's "simurgh," Rumi's "beloved," the Hurufi's "secret treasure," Kant's "noumenon," or the culprit in a detective novel, mystery meant, each time, the "center" that remained hidden in the world. In which case, commented F. M. Üçüncü, observing a culture's loss of the concept of "mystery," one had to deduce that its ideas, being bereft of the "center," had also gone out of kilter.

Galip went on to read lines he couldn't get the hang of, related to the necessity for Rumi to have his "beloved" Shams of Tabriz murdered, his journey to Damascus to protect the mystery that he had "installed,". the insufficiency of his wanderings and searches through that city to support the idea of "mystery," and the locales where Rumi stopped during his wanderings in order to relocate the "center" of his thoughts, which was going off-center. The writer maintained that committing the perfect murder, or disappearing without a trace, were good methods of reestablishing the lost mystery.

Later on, F. M. Üçüncü embarked upon the relationship of "letters and faces," which was Hurufism's most important topic. As Fazlallah had done in his *Book of Eternal Life*, he revealed that God, who was concealed, was manifest in human faces, he examined the lines in human faces at length, and he established the relationship between these lines and the Arabic characters. Following the pages of long, childlike discussions of lines in the poetry of Hurufi poets, such as Nesimi, Rafii, Misali, Ruhi of Baghdad, and Rose Baba, a certain logic was tabulated. During periods of felicity and success, all our faces had meaning, as did the inhabited world. We owed the meaning to the Hurufis, who saw mystery in the world and letters in our faces. Due to the disappearance of Hurufism, then, the letters in our faces, as well as the mystery in our world, had also disappeared. Our faces were, therefore, vacant; there was no longer any rationale to read anything in them; our eyebrows, our eyes, our noses, our gazes and expressions were empty, and our faces meaningless. Although Galip felt like getting up to look at himself in the mirror, he kept on reading carefully.

The horrifyingly dark results of the art of photography, as it got directed toward people as subjects, were related to this emptiness in our faces, just as was the odd topography seen in the faces of Turkish, Arab, and Indian movie stars that reminded one of the invisible face of the moon. That the throngs of people in the streets of Istanbul, Damascus, and Cairo were as alike as restless ghosts moaning at midnight; that the scowling faces of the men all wore the same mustaches; and that all the women wearing the same sort of head cloth always stared identically, were the consequences of this emptiness. Therefore, it was necessary to construct a new system of observing letters in the Latin alphabet which would imbue our vacant faces with a renewed meaning. The second section of the book was concluded with the good news that that very operation would be performed in the third section titled "Discovery of Mystery."

Galip had taken a liking to F. M. Üçüncü, who used words with double meanings and displayed a childlike innocence playing with words. Something about him was reminiscent of Jelal.

Chapter Twenty-seven

A LENGTHY CHESS GAME

Haroun al-Rashid would at times go around Baghdad in disguise, wishing to find out what his subjects thought about him and his rule. So, yet another night . . . —The Thousand and One Nights

A letter that sheds light on a dark juncture in our recent history known as the years of "democratization" fell into the hands of a reader who does not wish his name divulged or, with good reason, the coincidental, compelling, and treacherous circumstances under which the letter was obtained. I am publishing it in these columns as is, without touching the language (the idiom of a Pasha), written by our erstwhile military dictator to one of his sons, or daughters, who was apparently residing abroad.

"Six weeks ago, on that night in August, it was so hot and suffocating in the room where the founder of our Republic had died that one imagined all motion, thought, and time had developed rigor mortis in the terrible heat, and that not only had time come to a standstill for the ormulu clock which had been stopped to show always Atatürk's moment of death at 9:05—a source of amusement for you children inasmuch as it was a source of confusion to your dear departed mother—but all the clocks in Dolmabahçe Palace, as well as those in all Istanbul, had stopped dead in their tracks.

There was no motion at the windows overlooking the Bosphorus, where the curtains usually billowed, and it seemed as if the sentries along the waterfront were standing still as mannequins in the dark night not because I had issued the order but because time had come to a stop. Feeling that I might now undertake something I had wanted to do all these years without ever being able to take the decisive step, I put on the peasant's attire I had in my closet. I slipped out of the palace through the Harem Door which was no longer in use, bolstering my courage by reminding myself that before me, in the past five hundred years, many a sultan, after sneaking out of this side door (as well as out the back doors of other palaces in Istanbul—Topkapı, Beylerbeyi, and Yıldız) and disappearing into the night in the city they longed for, had managed to return safe and sound.

"How Istanbul had changed! It was not only bullets that could not penetrate the windows of the bulletproof Chevrolet limousine, I soon discovered, but also real life in my beloved city! Once outside the palace walls, on my way afoot to Karaköy, I bought some *helva* from a vendor which had a burnt-sugar aftertaste. I stopped at outdoor cafés to talk to the men who sat playing backgammon and cards, listening to the radio. I observed prostitutes waiting for customers in pudding shops, and children panhandling by pointing at kebabs in restaurant windows. I went into mosque courtyards in an attempt to mingle with the crowds that came out of evening prayers, and I sat in family-style tea gardens in back quarters, drinking tea like everybody else and eating roasted seeds. In an alley paved with large flagstones, I saw a pair of young parents returning home from the neighbors'; the mother's head was covered and the father carried their drowsing son on his shoulders: if you could have only seen the devotion with which she leaned into her husband's arm! Tears welled up in my eyes.

"Nay, my concern was not for the happiness or unhappiness of my fellow citizens. Witnessing the real lives of my compatriots, broken and worn out as they were, had rekindled the sorrow and the fear that emerges from dreams, that feeling of having stepped outside of reality, even on this night of my freedom and fantasy. I tried to shake this fear and this sense of unreality by beholding Istanbul. My eyes teared again and again with sadness as I looked through the windows of pastry shops at those gathered inside or watched the crowds disembark from the Municipal Lines ferries with the pretty smokestacks which had made their final trip for the night.

"It was almost time for the curfew I had imposed. Hoping to enjoy the coolness of the water on my way back, I approached a boatman in Eminönü, telling him to take me on a fifty-*kuruş* rowboat ride to the opposite side and drop me off in Karaköy or Kabataş. 'You have your brains for breakfast, fella?' he said to me. 'Don't you know that this is the hour when our President-Pasha takes a ride on his powerboat? And that anyone he sees on the water is arrested and thrown into the dungeons?' I took out a roll of pink banknotes—the ones with the portrait of me on them which, as I know very well, made my enemies' tongues wag when they were first printed—and I offered them to him in the dark. 'If we row out in your boat, would you show me the President-Pasha's powerboat then?' 'Get under that tarp and don't you dare move!' he said, indicating the prow with the same hand he'd snatched the money with. 'God save us!' He began to row.

"I couldn't say what direction we took in the dark. The Bosphorus? Into the Golden Horn? Or out to Marmara? The becalmed water was silent as a city in a blackout. From where I lay, I could smell the thin layer of fog misting over the water. There was the distant sound of a motor when the boatman whispered, 'There he comes now! He comes down every night!' Once our boat was hidden behind harbor pontoons encrusted with mussels, I couldn't help looking into the searchlight that ran mercilessly over the city, the harbor, the water, and the mosques, revolving left and right as if interrogating the surroundings. Then I saw a large white craft approach slowly; on board was a row of bodyguards with life jackets and guns; above them the bridge, where a group of people stood, and on a platform even higher, all by himself, the False President-Pasha! In the half-light, I could only barely perceive him as he went by in his craft, even so, despite the darkness and the thin fog, I had been able to observe that his clothes were identical to mine. I asked the boatman to follow him, but it was in vain. Telling me that the hour of curfew was upon us, he dropped me off at Kabataş. The streets were almost deserted when I returned back to the palace without making a sound.

"I thought about him that night—my look-alike, the False Pasha—but not about who he was and what business he had on the water. I thought about him because through his mediation I could think about myself. In the morning, I issued an order to the commanders who enforced the martial law that the curfew be imposed one hour later, so that I would have more time to observe him. It was immediately announced on the radio, followed by my address to the nation. I also ordered that some of the detainees be set free in order to provide an atmosphere of relaxation, and it was done.

"Was Istanbul any gayer the following evening? Not at all! It went to show that my subjects' interminable sadness does not arise out of political repression, as claimed by my superficial opponents, but is fed by a source that is deeper and cannot be denied. That evening they still smoked, ate roasted seeds and ice cream, drank coffee. And they were as sad and as lost in thought as before, listening to my address on coffeehouse radios announcing the shortened curfew. But they were so 'real'! When I was among them, I felt the pain of a somnambulist who cannot wake up and rejoin reality. For some reason, the boatman in Eminönü was waiting for me. We set out at once.

"It was a rough and windy night this time; we had to wait for the False President-Pasha, who was late—as if some sign had given him cause to be apprehensive. Out on the water, away from Kabataş and tucked behind another pontoon, I was regarding the boat and then the False President-Pasha himself, when I thought to myself that he seemed to be real and that he was beautiful—if these two words can exist together: beautiful and real. Was that possible? Raised above the heads of the crowd on the bridge, he seemed to have fixed his eyes like two searchlights on Istanbul, the populace, and history. What did he see?

"I slipped a pack of pink banknotes into the boatman's pocket, and he pulled on the oars. Rocking and bouncing in the waves, we caught up with them in Kasımpaşa near the boatyards, but we could only watch them from a distance. They got into black and navy limousines, among which was my Chevrolet, and vanished into the night in Galata. The boatman kept complaining that we were late, that the hour of curfew was at hand.

"When I stepped ashore after having rocked so long on the rough sea, at first I thought the irreal sensation I felt was a difficulty with getting my balance, but it was not. Walking late on streets deserted due to my curfew, I was gripped with such a feeling of irreality that an apparition I had thought belonged only in dreams appeared before my eyes. On the avenue between Fındıklı and Dolmabahçe, there was no one but packs of dogs—that is, aside from the roasted-corn vendor who was rapidly pushing his cart twenty paces ahead and who kept turning around to look at me. I surmised from his look that he was afraid of me and was trying to get away, and I wanted to tell him that what he ought to be really afraid of was hidden behind the rows of large chestnut trees on either side of the avenue. And yet, just as in a dream, I couldn't tell it to him; and as it is in dreams, I was afraid because I couldn't speak, or I couldn't speak because I was afraid. I was afraid of what was behind the trees that flowed alongside of us as the roasted-corn vendor sped up on account of me having sped up; but I didn't know what it was and, what was worse, I knew this was not a dream.

"Next morning, not wishing to experience the same terror again, I asked that the curfew be shortened even further and another group of detainees be set free. I didn't make any explanations on the subject; the radio broadcast one of my previous addresses.

"Armed with the experience of age that nothing ever changes in life, I had a good idea that I would only see the same sights in the city streets. And I was not mistaken. Some outdoor movie theaters had extended their hours; that was all. The pink-dyed hands of the pink cotton candy vendors were still the same color, and so were the white faces of tourists from the West, who had dared to venture on the street thanks to their guides.

"I found my boatman waiting for me at the same place. I could say the same thing for the False Pasha, too. Soon after embarking on the water, we encountered him. The weather was as calm as it was on our first night out, but there was no hint of a fog. In the dark mirror of the sea, I could behold the Pasha standing in the same place high above the bridge, as clearly as I could see the domes and the city lights reflected there. He was real. What is more, he had also seen us, as could anyone on a night that was as well-lit as this.

"Our boat pulled up to the Kasımpaşa dock in his wake. I had quietly stepped ashore when his men, who looked more like nightclub goons than soldiers, jumped me and grabbed me by the arms: What was I doing here, at this hour? Anxiously, I tried explaining that there was still time before the curfew, I was a poor peasant staying at a hotel in Sirkeci, that I had ventured on a boat ride on my last night here before I returned to my village: I had no knowledge of the Pasha's curfew . . . But the frightened boatman confessed everything to the President-Pasha who had approached us with his men. Even though he was in mufti, the Pasha looked more like me, and I looked more like a peasant. After hearing us out once more, he gave his orders: the boatman was free to leave, but I had to go with the Pasha.

"As we drove away from the harbor, the Pasha and I were alone on the backseat of the bulletproof Chevrolet. The sensation of our being alone with each other was increased, rather than diminished, by the presence of the driver who was as quiet as the limousine itself where he sat driving in the front seat, separated from us by a glass partition—a feature that was not available in my Chevrolet.

" 'We have both been waiting for this all these years!' said the False Pasha, whose voice I didn't think sounded at all like mine. 'I waited knowing that I was waiting, and you waited without knowing it. But neither one of us knew we would meet like this.'

"He began to tell his story haltingly and halfheartedly, equipped with the serenity of being able finally to finish his story rather than with the excitement of being able to tell it at last. Apparently we were in the same class at War College. We had taken the same courses with the same teachers. We were both out on night training on the same cold nights in winter, both of us waited for water to come out of the tap in our stone barracks on the same hot summer days, and when we were given leave, together we went out on the town in Istanbul which we dearly loved. That was when he had an inkling that things would turn out as they had, although not exactly as it was now.

"Back then he had known that I would be more successful than him even as we competed secretly for the best grade in math, for twelve o'clock on the practice target, for being the most popular among the cadets, for the best record, and for being first in class, and that I would be the one who lived in the palace where the stopped clocks would confuse your dear departed mother. I reminded him that it must have indeed been a 'secret' competition; I neither remembered competing against a fellow cadet at the War College—as I have often advised you children—nor remembered him as a friend. He was not at all surprised. He had withdrawn from the competition anyway, having realized that I had too much self-confidence to be aware of our 'secret' competition; and that I had already gone beyond classmates and upperclassmen, beyond lieutenants and even captains; he had not wished to stand behind me as a pale imitation, nor to be the second-class shadow to success. He wanted to be 'real,' not a shadow. As he went on explaining, I kept looking out the window of the Chevrolet, which I had begun to think didn't look too much like mine, and watching the deserted streets in Istanbul, glancing now and then at our knees and legs which remained motionless before us in identical positions.

"Later, he said that this coincidence had not figured in his calculations. One didn't have to be an oracle to predict back then that our destitute nation would go under the yoke of yet another dictator forty years later, that Istanbul would be handed over to him, and that this dictator would be a career soldier about our age; nor to predict that the 'soldier' would end up being me. So, it was back at War College that he had imagined the future through simple reasoning. He would either be a ghostly shadow traveling back and forth between authenticity and nondescriptness like everyone else—between the damnation of the present and the fantasies of the past or the future in a phantom Istanbul where I'd become the President-Pasha—or he'd devote his life to finding a way of becoming 'real.' I remembered this nondescript cadet for the first time when he admitted that, in order to find his way, he had committed a crime serious enough to get himself expelled from the army, but not serious enough to land him in jail, describing how he had been successful in getting caught inspecting the night-watch corps, impersonating the Commander of the War College. After his expulsion, he'd gone into business. 'Everyone knows how easy it is to become rich in our land,' he said with pride. Antithetically, the reason there was so much poverty was that our people were taught not how to be rich but how to be poor. After a silence, he added that it was me who had taught him how to be authentic. 'You!' he said familiarly, stressing the word. 'After all these years, I realized with astonishment that you are less real than I. You poor peasant!'

"There was a long, a very long, silence. Inside the garb that my aide had put together as an authentic peasant costume, I felt not so much ridiculous as inauthentic, being obliged as I was to take part in a fantasy in a way that was totally undesirable to me. It was during this silence that I understood that the fantasy had been built on the images of Istanbul I saw out of the limousine window flowing by like a slow-motion film: deserted streets, sidewalks, desolate squares. The hour of my curfew had arrived, making the city appear uninhabited.

"I now knew that what my vainglorious classmate had showed me was nothing but this dream city that I had created. We drove past wood-frame houses which seemed all the smaller and more lost under the huge chestnut trees, and past slums that had encroached upon graveyards, arriving at the threshold of the land of dreams. We went downhill on paved streets that had been relinquished to packs of quarreling dogs, up hard streets where streetlamps made it darker instead of shedding light. Going through phantom streets where fountains had gone dry, where the walls were in ruins and chimneys broken, viewing with a strange apprehension mosques that drowsed like storybook giants, driving past public squares where the pools were empty, the statuary neglected, and the clocks stopped, which made me believe that time was at a standstill not only in the Palace but in all Istanbul, I paid no attention to my imitator's narrative of his success in business, nor to the stories he told thinking they were appropriate to the situation in which we found ourselves (the story of an old shepherd who caught his wife with her lover, as well as the tale in the *Thousand and One Nights* in which Haroun al-Rashid gets lost). Toward daybreak, the avenue that bears your last name and mine had become, like all the other avenues, streets, and public squares, an extension of a dream rather than a reality.

"He was narrating the dream that Rumi calls 'The Contest of the Two Painters' when toward morning I composed the proclamation (the same one our Western allies questioned you about behind the scenes) which I later had announced on the airwaves, concerning the lifting of the curfew and martial law. Trying to fall asleep in my own bed after that sleepless night, I daydreamed that the empty squares would be inhabited throughout the night, the stopped clocks would start running, and that an authentic life more real than phantoms and fantasies would ensue on bridges, at the foyers of movie theaters, and in coffeehouses where roasted seeds are consumed. I don't know to what extent my dreams have come true, giving Istanbul a landscape in which I could be real, but I hear from my aides that freedom, as is always the case, inspires my opponents more than it does mere dreamers. Once again, they are beginning to organize in teahouses, in hotel rooms, and under bridges to hatch plots against us; already I hear that opportunists are plastering the palace walls with slogans the meaning of which cannot be deciphered; but none of this is important. The time when sultans went among the populace in disguise is long gone; it exists only in books.

"The other day I read in one of these books, Hammer's *History of the Ottoman Empire*, that Selim the Grim went to Tabriz where he went around in disguise when he was a mere prince. He had quite a reputation as a great chess player, which occasioned Shah Ismail, who was a chess enthusiast, to invite the youth in dervish garb to the palace. After a lengthy game, Selim beat the Shah of Persia. Many years later, when Shah Ismail realized that the man who beat him in the game of chess was not a dervish but the Ottoman Emperor Selim the Grim, who would take the city of Tabriz from him after the Battle of Chalderan, I wondered if he remembered the moves in the game they had played. My vainglorious impersonator must surely remember all the moves in our game. By the way, the subscription to the chess journal, *King and Pawn*, must have run out; it's no longer being sent; I am transferring funds to your account at the Embassy, so that you can get it renewed."

Chapter Twenty-eight

THE DISCOVERY OF
THE MYSTERY

. . . the section you are reading interprets the text of your face.
                                                    —NIYAZI OF EGYPT

Before starting to read the third section in *Mystery of Letters and Loss of Mystery*, Galip made himself some strong coffee. He went into the bathroom to splash cold water on his face, hoping it would keep him awake, and somehow managed to keep himself from looking in the mirror. When he sat down at Jelal's desk with the coffee, he was as keen as a high-school kid getting ready to solve a math problem that had needed solving for quite some time.

According to F. M. Üçüncü, since it was on Turkish soil, in Anatolia, that the imminent advent of the Messiah who would save all the East was to take place, the first step in rediscovering the lost mystery was to firmly establish the correspondences between the lines on the human face and the twenty-nine letter Latin alphabet adopted by the Turkish language after 1928. To this end, extrapolating from obscure Hurufi treatises, Bektaşi poems, Anatolian folk art, phantom ruins of pristine Hurufi villages, figures drawn on dervish lodges and pasha's mansions, and thousands of calligraphic inscriptions, he had illustrated with examples the "values" some sounds had received as they were being transposed from Arabic and Persian into Turkish; then, displaying a certitude that was awesome, he had identified and marked these letters individually on people's photographs. When Galip looked at these faces in which, as the writer pointed out, you didn't need to find the Latin letters in order to read the meaning clearly and precisely, he got the willies just as he had when he was looking at the photographs in Jelal's cabinet. He was turning pages with some badly printed pictures—the captions said that they were of Fazlallah, his two successors, "the portrait of Rumi copied from a miniature," and our gold-medalist Olympic wrestler Hamit Kaplan—when he came across a photo of Jelal taken in the late nineteen fifties which gave him a good turn. Letters had also been marked on this photograph, the placement of which, as it had been in others, was indicated by arrows. In this photograph of Jelal, taken when he was around thirty-five, F. M. Uçüncü had detected the letter U on the nose, Z around the eyes, and the letter N sideways on his entire face. Flipping quickly through the pages of the book, Galip saw that there were additional photos belonging to Hurufi masters, famous imams, persons who had had near-death experiences, and to American film actors who had "profoundly meaningful faces," such as Greta Garbo, Humphrey Bogart, Edward G. Robinson, and Bette Davis, as well as to famous executioners and some of those Beyoğlu hoods whose adventures Jelal had related in his youth. Later, the writer divulged that each letter established by marking it on the face had two discrete meanings: the plain meaning as written and the secret meaning as derived from the face.

Once we accepted that every letter in a face had a hidden meaning that pointed to a concept, F. M. Uçüncü argued, it necessarily followed that every word made up of those letters also had to contain a second, hidden meaning. If one considered that these second meanings could be expressed in other sentences and other words—that is to say, in other letters—then a third meaning could be discovered "through interpretation" to succeed the second, and a fourth could succeed the third and so on ad infinitum, revealing an infinite series of hidden meanings. One could compare this to a network of streets leading into one another: maps that resembled human faces. The reader who attempted to solve the mystery of the letters in human faces in his own way, using his own yardstick, was no different from a traveler who slowly discovers the mystery of a city as he wanders through streets he has seen on a map (a mystery which gets more diffused as it is discovered and is revealed all the more as it gets more diffused), finding the mystery in the streets and paths that he has chosen to walk on, in the flights of steps that he has chosen to climb during his passage through the city and through his life. He, the awaited Saviour, the Messiah, would become manifest at the locus where wistful readers, the downtrodden, the story addicts lose themselves as they become more deeply immersed in the mystery. Somewhere in the middle of life and the text—at the point where faces and maps interfaced—the traveler, armed with keys and ciphers, on receiving the long-awaited signal from the Messiah in the city and in the signs (much like the mystic on the Sufi path), will begin to find his way. He is like someone finding his way with the aid of signposts, as F. M. Üçüncü commented with childlike glee. So the problem, according to F. M. Üçüncü, came down to this: one had to be able to see the signs in life and in the text reposited there by the Messiah. According to him, solving the problem required that we put ourselves in the Messiah's place, foreseeing how He might behave. Like a chess player, we had to anticipate His moves. Saying that he wished to make this prediction in concert with the reader, F. M. Üçüncü requested that his reader visualize a single individual who had the means to appeal to a large readership at any given time and in any circumstances. "For example," he added immediately, "a columnist." A columnist who was read by hundreds of thousands of people on ferries, buses, *dolmuşes*, in coffee shops and barber shops all over the country was a good example of someone who had the wherewithal to propagate the Messiah's hidden messages to show us the way. For those who had no inkling of the mystery, this columnist's texts would carry only a single meaning: the apparent surface meaning. On the other hand, those who awaited the Messiah, and were aware of ciphers and formulas, would be able to read hidden meanings as well, having taken off from the secondary meanings of letters. Let's say the Messiah included a sentence such as, "Those were the things on my mind as I observed myself from the outside": while ordinary readers considered the oddness of the apparent meaning, those who were aware of the mystery of letters would immediately surmise that the sentence was the special message they'd been expecting and, armed with their ciphers, they would embark on an adventure that would take them on a brand-new journey and into a brand-new life.

As the title of the third part of F. M. Üçüncü's book, "The Discovery of the Mystery," implied, what was being revealed was not only the rediscovery of the *idea* of mystery, the loss of which had forced the East into slavery vis-à-vis the West, but how to discover the sentences the Messiah reposited in his texts.

Then F. M. Üçüncü surveyed Edgar Allan Poe's "A Few Words on Secret Writing," and discussed the cipher formulas proposed in the essay. After pointing out that the method of the reshuffled alphabet was closest to the one employed in the coded correspondence of the Sufi mystic al-Hallaj and was the one which the Messiah would use as well, he had suddenly proclaimed at the end of his book this important conclusion: The starting point of all ciphers and formulas had to be the letters to be found in each traveler's own face. Anyone who wished to set forth on the road and establish a new universe must begin by discovering the letters in his own face. The modest book the reader held in his hands was a directory for finding these letters, but it was no more than an introduction to the study of the ciphers and formulas that would lead the way to the mystery. Repositing them in the text was, naturally, work reserved for the Messiah who would soon rise like the sun.

No, Galip thought, the word "sun" here signified Rumi's murdered beloved, Shams of Tabriz, for Shams meant "sun" in Arabic. He flung the book down, ready to go into the bathroom for a good look in the mirror. The thought that had been barely flickering in his mind had now turned into a conspicuous fear: "Jelal must've seen the meaning in my face for ages!" He had the same feeling of doom that would come upon him at times in his childhood and first youth, an apprehension that everything was all over, finished, and could never be fixed—when he felt he had done something wrong, turned into someone else, got contaminated by some mystery. "From now on, I am someone else!" Galip thought to himself now, like a child playing a game he knew, but also like someone who has set forth on a road that has no return.

It was twelve past three in the morning; the flat and the city were under the enchanting silence that can only be felt at that hour—not mere silence, but the feeling of silence, for there was a faint whirring that went through his ears like a twinge, coming from a furnace nearby or the generator on a distant ship. Though he had decided that the time was ripe for him to start on this new road, he would manage to hold off a little longer before he made the move.

Then the thought he'd been trying to forget for the past three days hit him: if Jelal hadn't managed to send in a new piece, his column would soon be blank. Galip didn't want to imagine the empty space in place of the column that had never been absent from the second page in all these years—as if the emptiness would mean Rüya and Jelal could no longer be hiding out somewhere in the city, laughing and chatting while they waited for him. Reading a column he pulled out of the cabinet at random, he thought: "I too could write this!" He had a recipe in hand, after all. No, it wasn't the formula that the old columnist had given him in the editorial rooms three days ago, it was something else: "I know all your work, everything about you; I've read and read." He almost spoke the last word out loud. He went on to read another article he'd pulled out at random. Though it couldn't be called reading; he was going through the text sounding out the words silently, but his mind was on the secondary meanings in some of the words and letters, and he sensed that the more closely he read, the more closely he was approaching Jelal. What was reading someone's work, after all, but gradually acquiring the writer's memory?

He was now ready to look in the mirror and read the letters in his face. He went in the bathroom and took a look. After that, everything happened quickly.

Much later, after months had gone by, each time Galip sat down at the desk to write, surrounded by objects that silently and reassuringly simulated the past of thirty years ago, he would remember the moment he had first looked in the mirror and the same word would come to his mind: terror. Yet when he first looked in the mirror with playful excitement, he had not yet felt the fearful associations of the word. At that moment, he had had a feeling of emptiness, forgetfulness, and inertia. At that moment, he had looked into his own face reflected in the mirror under the light of a bare bulb as if he were looking at the faces of prime ministers and movie stars he was inured to seeing in the papers. He'd looked into his own face not as if he were solving a mystery, breaking the code of a secret message that he'd been trying to decipher for days, but as if it were an overcoat grown familiar with long wear or an ordinary drab winter morning he'd come to accept, or as if it were an old umbrella he was looking at without really seeing it. "Back then I was so used to living with myself, I wasn't aware of my face," he'd think much later on. But the indifference hadn't lasted long. As soon as he was able to see his face in the mirror in the same way that he saw the faces in F. M. Üçüncü's book, he instantly began to perceive the shadows of the letters.

The first odd thing he noticed was the fact that he could look in his own face as if looking at a piece of paper with writing on it—as if his face were an inscription that presented signs for the benefit of other eyes and faces; at first he hadn't dwelled too much on that since he could at last discern the letters that appeared definitively between his eyes and eyebrows. Not too long afterward, the letters became clear enough for him to wonder why he hadn't been aware of them before. Of course, it had occurred to him that what he was seeing was an aberration produced by looking too long at photographs marked with letters—an optical illusion, or part of a game of illusion played for real—but every time he turned his eyes away and then looked back in the mirror, he saw the letters exactly where he had left them.

They did not switch back and forth like the figure-and-ground pictures in kids' magazines which at first glance appear to show the branches of a tree and then reveal thieves hiding in the branches; there they were, in the topography of the face he shaved absentmindedly every morning—in the eyes, the eyebrows, in the nose where all Hurufis insisted on placing the *alif*, and in the round surface they termed the facial orbit. It no longer seemed difficult now to read the letters. The hard thing would be not to read them. Galip tried to ignore them in order to liberate himself from the unnerving mask on his face, summoning up the disparaging thoughts he'd prudently kept in readiness in some corner of his mind while he was reviewing Hurufi art and literature, in the hope now of reanimating his skepticism about everything connected with this business of letters and faces—of dismissing all of it as ridiculous, arbitrary, and childish. But the lines and curves in his face signified certain letters so conspicuously that he couldn't tear himself away from the mirror.

That was when he was seized by the feeling which he later called terror. But everything had happened so quickly, and he'd so readily perceived the letters in his face, and the word signified by those letters, that he would never clearly figure out whether he was first seized by terror because his face had turned into a mask marked with signs, or because he found the meaning the letters implied was so fearful. The letters revealed the mystery that Galip would remember through entirely different words when he wanted to write down the truth he had always known but had struggled to forget, had remembered but assumed he did not, had studied but not taken in. But as soon as he read them definitively in his face without any shadow of a doubt, he had also thought everything was simple and comprehensible; he already knew what he read there, and that he needn't be astonished. Perhaps what he would later call terror was the surprising nature of plain and simple truth. It was somehow like the unnerving double vision intrinsic to the human mind, which is capable of perceiving with supernal insight the slim-waisted tea glass on the table as an incredible phenomenon while the eye simultaneously takes in the same glass as it has always been.

When Galip decided that what the letters on his face signified was not wide of the mark but right on target, he pulled himself away from the mirror and went out in the hallway. Now he could see that this frightening sensation of his had more to do with what the letters themselves signified—what the signpost that had been placed there pointed to—than with his visage turning into a mask, into someone else's face, or into a signpost. After all, according to the rules of this fine game, such letters appeared in everyone's face. As he stooped to look in the shelves of the cabinet in the hallway he felt such profound pain inside him, and he longed for Rüya and Jelal so terribly, that he had a hard time standing up. It was as if his body and soul had abandoned him to suffer for crimes he hadn't committed; it was as if his memory contained only the mystery of defeat and destruction; it was as if all sorrow and recollection of the past, which everyone else had happily forgotten, were retained in his memory and on his shoulders.

Later, when he wanted to recall what he had done in the first three to five minutes after he'd looked in the mirror—since everything had happened so fast—he would remember the moment when he was standing halfway between the cabinet in the hallway and the window that opened on the shaft of darkness. In the bathroom, when he first felt the "terror," he had had difficulty breathing; he turned off the light and got away from the mirror in the dark, cold perspiration beading on his forehead. For a moment, there in the hallway, he had imagined that he could go back and plant himself in front of the mirror again, switch the light on, and pull away that thin mask, removing it as if scratching a scab off a wound; he thought that then he would no more be able to find hidden significance in any letters in the face revealed underneath than he could in the letters and signs he saw in ordinary streets, on commonplace billboards, or on plastic bags. Next, he pulled one of Jelal's pieces out of the cabinet and tried reading it in an effort to overcome his pain, but he already knew everything; he knew everything Jelal had written as if he'd done it himself. He tried imagining, as he would often do later, that he was blind or that, instead of pupils, he had hollowed-out marble holes, instead of a mouth an oven door, and instead of nostrils bolt holes that had rusted. Each time he thought of his face, he realized that Jelal had also seen the letters that appeared in his mind's eye, that Jelal had known Galip would someday see them too, and that they had been in collusion playing this game. But he would never know for sure whether he'd been able to think all this through clearly at that moment. He felt as if he couldn't breathe, nor could he weep, although he wanted to. A moan of pain escaped his throat; his hand automatically reached for the window pull; he wanted to look there, into that shaft of darkness, the void where the well had once existed. He felt like a child impersonating someone whose identity he didn't know.

He opened the window, leaned into the darkness and, his elbows on the window ledge, pushed his face into the bottomless well of the air shaft: a bad odor rose up, the smell of pigeon droppings that had been accumulating over half a century, of all the crap that had been tossed down, of the building's grime, of smog, mud, tar, and hopelessness. They'd thrown down here all the things they'd wanted to forget. He had an impulse to jump into the void from which there was no return, into the recollections that had disappeared without a trace from the memories of those who'd once lived here, into the darkness that Jelal had patiently built up in his writing over the years, weaving into it, as in the elaborations of the old courtly poetry, the motifs of wells, mystery, and fear. But he merely stared into the darkness like a drunk trying to remember. The recollections of the childhood he and Rüya had spent together in this apartment building were closely related to this smell; the innocent kid that he had once been, the well-meaning young man, the husband content with his wife, and the ordinary citizen who lived at the edge of mystery were also created by this smell. The desire to be with Jelal and Rüya arose so powerfully inside him that he felt like crying out; it was as if half his body had been ripped from him and taken away to some distant and dark place, as in a dream, and if only he could raise a hue and cry he'd escape from this trap. But he merely stared into the bottomless dark, feeling on his face the damp cold of the winter night and snow. So long as he exposed his face to the dry well of darkness, he sensed that the pain he'd been carrying around alone all these days was being shared, that what was terrifying had become comprehensible, and what he would later come to call the mystery of defeat, misery, and ruin had become manifest like Jelal's life, the details of which Jelal had prepared long ago like a bait to pull Galip into this trap. There, hanging out the window, he gazed down into the bottomless well for a long time. It was much later, when he became sharply aware of the raw cold on his face, neck, and forehead, that he pulled himself in and closed the window.

What followed was unobstructed, comprehensible, and illuminated. Going from the hallway into the living room, he sank into one of the easy chairs and rested. Then he straightened up Jelal's desk, replaced the papers, news clippings, and photographs in their boxes and put the boxes back in the cabinet. He picked up not only the mess he'd made in the last couple of days but also the clutter that Jelal had sloppily tossed around the place. He emptied the ashtrays, washed the glassware and cups, cracked the windows open, and aired out the apartment. He washed his face, made himself another cup of strong coffee, placed Jelal's heavy old Remington on the desk he'd already cleared and tidied, and sat down. The copy paper that Jelal always used was in the desk drawer; taking out a sheet, he stuck it into the machine and immediately began writing.

Later on, when Galip recalled what he had accomplished by daybreak, not only would he find everything he had done logical, necessary, and appropriate but he'd also remember the clarity and precision with which he'd acted. He wrote for almost two hours without getting up. Feeling that everything had now fallen into place, he wrote with an excitement that the clean, blank pages produced in him. Every time he hit the keys of the typewriter, which moved in concert with an old and familiar piece of music in his head, he realized that he had known and contemplated what he was writing a long time ago. He had to slow down once in a while and momentarily think of the right word, but he wrote with the flow of the sentences and thoughts— as Jelal put it, "without being forced."

He began the first piece with the sentence, "I looked in the mirror and read my face." The second: "I dreamed that I had finally become the person I wanted to be all these years"; and in the third, he narrated old Beyoğlu stories. He wrote effortlessly after the first one and with a sorrow and hope that was even more profound. He was confident that his pieces would settle into Jelal's column exactly as he wished and anticipated. He signed the three pieces with Jelal's own signature, which he had imitated thousands of times on the backs of his notebooks during his high-school years.

At daybreak, as the garbage truck went by with the clang of cans getting banged on the sides, Galip examined Jelal's picture in F. M. Üçüncü's book. Since there was no identification under one of the indistinct, faded photographs on another page, he thought it must belong to the author himself. He read the autobiographical foreword carefully, and calculated the author's age when he was implicated in the thwarted military coup in 1962. Considering that he was a lieutenant when he set off for Anatolia and that he had the opportunity to watch Hamit Kaplan's initial years in wrestling, F. M. Üçüncü had to be close to Jelal's age. Once more, Galip combed through the '44 and '45 graduates in the War College yearbooks. He came across several faces that could belong to the unidentified face in *Mystery of Letters and Loss of Mystery* as a young man, but the most salient feature in the faded photograph, baldness, had been hidden under a military hat in the yearbook photographs of the young cadets.

At eight-thirty, wearing his overcoat with the three columns folded up in the inside pocket, Galip emerged hastily out of the Heart-of-the-City Apartments like a hurried dad going to work and crossed the street to the other sidewalk. Either no one had seen him or else whoever had hadn't bothered calling out to him. The air was clear and the sky winter blue; the sidewalks were covered with snow, ice, and mud. He stopped at the arcade where the barber who came by to shave Grandpa every morning had a barbershop called Venus, which he and Jelal used to patronize later on, and dropped off the keys to Jelal's apartment at the locksmith's shop located at the very end. He bought a copy of *Milliyet* at the news vendor's on the corner. He went in the Milk Company pudding shop where Jelal used to breakfast some mornings and ordered potted eggs, cream, honey, and tea. While he had his breakfast reading Jelal's column, he thought about the sleuths in Rüya's mystery novels who must feel as he now felt when they were able to derive a significant hypothesis out of a bunch of clues. He felt like a detective who, having found a significant key to unlock the mystery, was now looking forward to opening new doors.

Jelal's column was the last one he had seen in the *Milliyet* offices available for publication in the folder on Saturday and, like the others, it too had already been printed once before. Galip didn't even attempt solving the secondary meanings of the letters. After breakfast, waiting in line for the *dolmuş*, he remembered the person he used to be and the life that person had led until recently: In the mornings, he used to read the newspaper on the *dolmuş*, thinking about returning home in the evening, and dreaming about his wife at home sleeping in their bed. Tears welled up in his eyes.

"As it turns out," he thought to himself as the *dolmuş* went by the Dolmabahçe Palace, "the apprehension that one is someone else is all that one needs to believe that the world has changed from top to bottom." What he saw out of the *dolmuş* window was not the Istanbul he'd known all along but another Istanbul whose mystery he had just cracked and would eventually set down on paper.

At the newspaper, the editor was in a meeting with the department heads. After tapping on the door and waiting briefly, Galip entered Jelal's office. Nothing had changed on the desk or elsewhere in the room since Galip had last been here. He sat down at the desk and quickly rifled through the drawers. Old cocktail invitations to openings, bulletins sent by various left- and right-wing political factions, news clippings he'd seen the last time, buttons, the necktie, watch, empty ink bottles, pills, and a pair of dark glasses he hadn't noticed before . . . He put the dark glasses on and left Jelal's office. When he went into the newsroom, he saw the old polemicist Neşati working at the desk. The chair next to him was vacant, where the magazine writer had sat the last time. Galip walked over and sat down. "Do you remember me?" he asked the old man after a while.

"I do!" Neşati said without raising his head. "You are a flower in my garden of memory. 'Memory is a garden.' Whose words are those?"

"Jelal Salik's."

"Nope, they belong to Bottfolio," said the old columnist, looking up. "As translated by Ibn Zerhani in his classical version. Jelal Salik pinched it from there as usual. Just as you've pinched his dark glasses."

"Those are my glasses," Galip said.

"Which goes to show that glasses, like people, are created in each other's image. Give them here!"

Galip took off the glasses and handed them over. When the old man put on the dark glasses after inspecting them briefly, he resembled one of the legendary fifties Beyoğlu hoods Jelal had written about in his columns: the boss of the casino-cum-whorehouse-cum-nightclub who had vanished in his Cadillac. Smiling mysteriously, he turned to Galip.

"No wonder they say that you ought to look at the world through someone else's eyes once in a while. Only then can you really comprehend the mystery of the world and mankind. Have you figured out who said that?"

"F. M. Üçüncü."

"Not in the least," said the old man. "He's as stupid as they come. He's one of those poor slobs. Where'd you come across his name?"

"Jelal once told me it was one of the pseudonyms he'd used for many years."

"Goes to show that when a man grows really senile, not only does he deny his own past and work, he claims to be other people as well. But I can't imagine our shrewd Mister Jelal getting that demented. He must've been up to something, lying out-and-out like that. F. M. Üçüncü happens to be a real-life person who exists flesh-and-blood. Twenty years ago he was an officer in the army who bombarded our offices with mail. When one or two of his letters were printed out of kindness in the reader-mail columns, he turned up at the offices swaggering as if he were on the regular staff. Then, suddenly, he quit showing up; he was nowhere to be seen for the next twenty years. Only a week ago, he turns up again, his head bald as a melon, tells me he's a fan, saying that he came all the way to the paper just to see me. He was pitiful, carrying on about omens that were becoming manifest."

"What omens?"

"Come, come, now. You know very well what omens. Or doesn't Jelal clue you in? Time is ripe, don't you know! All that crap about manifested omens! Out in the street: Day of Judgment, Revolution, Liberation of the East, etc."

"The other day Jelal and I were talking about you in connection with that subject."

"Where's he hiding out?"

"Slips my mind."

"They're closeted in the editorial offices," said the old columnist. "They're going to give your Uncle Jelal the boot for not coming up with any new work. Tell him from me that they will offer his space in the second page to me, but I am going to turn it down."

"Jelal brought your name up with affection the other day when he was talking about the military coup you both got implicated in during the early sixties."

"All lies. He betrayed the coup, which is the reason why he hates me, and the rest of us," said the old columnist in the dark glasses that didn't seem out of place on him, who now looked more like a "maestro" than a Beyoğlu gangster. "He sold out the coup. Naturally, he wouldn't tell you how it was, claiming instead that he was the one who organized everything. But, as usual, your Uncle Jelal joined in only when everyone began believing that it was going to be successful. Before that, while networks of readers were being organized from one end of Anatolia to the other, while pyramids, minarets, freemason symbols, Cyclopes, mysterious compasses, pictures of lizards, Seljuk domes, marked White Russian bank notes, wolves' heads were being passed around, Jelal was collecting photographs of readers like children collect pictures of movie stars. One day he invented the house of mannequins, next he began blathering about an 'eye' that observed him on narrow streets in the dark of the night. We figured he wanted to join us, so we consented. We imagined he'd put his column at the service of the cause; maybe he could even attract some of the officers. Some attraction! Back then, there were a lot of crazies and freeloaders around, men of your F. M. Üçüncü's ilk; first thing Jelal did was to put the headlock on them. Then, using ciphers, formulas, acrostics, he worked up a liaison with another shady bunch. After he got his fill of these liaisons he considered victories, he'd show up to haggle over what cabinet chair he fancied after the revolution. In order to increase his bargaining power, he insisted that he was in contact with the dregs of dervish orders, folks who awaited the Messiah, and people who said they got messages from Ottoman princes loafing around in either Portugal or France; he claimed that he received letters from phantom persons which he promised to show us, that the heirs of pashas and sheikhs who called on him at his place had left him manuscripts and testaments full of secrets, and that weird persons arrived at the newspaper in the middle of the night to see him. He invented all these persons himself. During that same time period, I attempted to burst this guy's bubble who'd put out the word that he was slated to become the foreign minister after the revolution, when he didn't even have any French to speak of. Back then, he was running a commentary about stories which he claimed were the testament of an obscure legendary personage, penning nonsense full of prophets, Messiahs, the Apoc-

alypse, concerning a conspiracy which would reveal an unknown truth regarding our history. I sat down and wrote a column that included Ibn Zerhani
and Bottfolio which revealed the facts. What a coward! Immediately, he
pulled away from us and joined other factions. There's some talk about him
disguising himself after dark and impersonating his heroes in order to prove
the actual existence of his invented personages to his new friends who had
even closer ties to young officers. He appeared at the entrance of some
Beyoğlu movie theater one night, dressed either as the Messiah or Mehmet
the Conqueror, sermonizing at the surprised crowd waiting to see the movie
about how the whole nation needed to take on other guises and lead other
lives: seeing how American films had become just as hopeless as our domestic
films, we no longer had half a chance getting anywhere imitating them.
Apparently, he attempted to turn the movie crowd against the movie pro-
ducers on Yeşilçam Street, trying to get them to follow his lead. It was not
only the 'miserable petite bourgeoisie' he often brought up in his columns,
who lived in rundown wood-frame houses in the slums and on muddy
Istanbul streets, but back in those days too, it was the whole Turkish nation
that was waiting for, just as they do today, a 'savior.' They believed with all
their usual sincerity and optimism that if a military coup took place, bread
would get cheaper; if sinners were put to torture, then the doors to Paradise
would be opened. But thanks to Mister Jelal's passion and greed for keeping
people in his thrall, factions of coup planners got into scraps with each other;
the military coup was off; tanks that were mobilized that night didn't roll up
to the radio station but beat it back to the barracks. Conclusion: You can
see for yourself that we are still being driven from pillar to post. Shamed by
the Europeans, we manage to cast a few votes now and then, so that we can
tell visiting foreign newsmen with impunity that we are just like them now.
But it doesn't mean we have no hope for salvation, either. We do have a
way out. If British TV had wished to talk to me instead of to this Jelal of
yours, I could have told them the secret of how the East can remain itself
quite felicitously for tens of thousands of years yet. Mister Galip, my son,
your cousin Jelal is a pitiful, defective human being. In order to be ourselves,
we don't need to stock our closets, as he does, with wigs, fake beards, historical
costumes, and strange outfits. Mahmut the First went around in disguise
every evening, but guess what he put on? Instead of his sultan's turban, he
wore a fez, and he carried a walking stick. That's it! There is no necessity
to put on all that makeup for hours every night, getting into strange, gaudy
costumes or tattered beggar's rags. Our world is a whole in itself, not a world
where things fall apart. Within this realm, there exists another realm, but
this is not a world that's concealed behind appearances and stage sets, as in

the Western world; so there's no need to pull away the covers to behold victoriously the hidden truth. Our modest universe is everywhere, it has no center, it's not on the maps. But that *is* our mystery, given that comprehending it is so extremely difficult. It requires an ordeal. I ask you, how many of our guys with true grit know that you yourself are the whole universe whose mystery you are seeking? And that the whole universe is yourself who is seeking the mystery? Only when you achieve this enlightenment do you deserve to disguise yourself and become someone else. Your Uncle Jelal and I share only one emotion: Like him I too pity our poor movie stars who can neither be themselves nor anyone else. What's worse, I pity our nation that identifies with these stars! This nation could've been saved, even the entire East could have. But your uncle, your uncle's son Jelal, sold us out for his own gain. Now, freaked out by his own handiwork, he's hiding from the whole nation, him with his weird wardrobe. Why is he hiding out?"

"You know very well," said Galip, "that ten to fifteen politically motivated murders are committed every day out on the street."

"Those are not politically but spiritually motivated assassinations. Besides, what's it to Jelal if pseudo-Sufis, pseudo-Marxists, and pseudo-fascists waste each other? No one is interested in him anymore. By hiding out, he's put out an invitation for death, just so that we're led to believe he's someone who's important enough to assassinate. During the heyday of the Democratic Party, we used to have this nice, polite, but yellow writer who has since passed away; he used pseudonyms to write letters to the press prosecutor every day, denouncing himself, so that he could get prosecuted and attract attention. If that weren't enough, he'd claim that we were the ones who wrote the incriminating letters. You get it? Along with his memory, Mister Jelal has purloined his past, which was the only tie he had to his country. It is no wonder he can no longer write anything."

"He was the one who sent me here," Galip said. He produced the articles out of his pocket. "He asked me to hand in his new columns."

"Let's see them."

While the old columnist read the three articles without taking off the dark glasses, Galip noticed that the volume in Arabic script that stood open on the desk was a translation of Chateaubriand's *Mémoires d'outre-tombe*. The old writer gestured to summon a tall person who walked out of the editor's office.

"Mister Jelal's new columns," he told him. "Still the same interest in showing off, still the same . . ."

"Let's send them down to be typeset immediately," the tall man said. "We'd been considering running an old column."

"I'm going to be delivering his new pieces for a while," Galip said.

"What's the idea of disappearing?" said the tall man. "He has lots of people looking for him these days."

"Apparently, the two of them put on disguises at night," the old writer said, pointing toward Galip with his nose. After the tall man left smiling, he turned to Galip. "You go back in the haunted streets, don't you? In mosques with broken minarets, ruins, vacant houses, abandoned dervish lodges, wearing strange costumes, masks, these glasses, looking for dirty deals, weird mysteries, and ghosts among swindlers and dope fiends, right? Mister Galip, my son, you've changed a great deal since I saw you last. Your face is pale; your eyes are sunk; you've become someone else. Istanbul nights are endless . . . A ghost whose guilty transgressions prevent sleep . . . Say what?"

"I'll just take those glasses, sir, and run along."

Chapter Twenty-nine

I TURNED OUT TO BE
THE HERO

*On personal style: writing necessarily begins by imitating other writing. Don't
children also begin speech by virtue of imitating others?* —TAHIR-ÜL MEVLEVI

I looked in the mirror and read my face. The mirror was a tranquil ocean
and my face sallow paper inscribed with an ink that was sea-green. Back
then, whenever I had a blank look on my face, "My darling," your mother
used to say—your beautiful mother, that is to say, my aunt—"your face is
white as a sheet." I had a blank look because I was fearful of what was written
on my face without me knowing it; I had a blank look because I feared not
finding you where I took my leave of you—at the same place where I left
you among old tables, tired chairs, faded lamps, newspapers, curtains, cigarettes. In winter, evening fell as quickly as the dark. Once it was dark and
doors were closed and lights went on, I'd imagine the corner where you sat
back behind our door: on different floors when we were young, behind the
same door when we grew up.

Reader, dear reader, the reader who has understood that I'm talking about
a girl who was related to me and lived under the same roof: when you read
this, make sure to put yourself in my place and pick up on my signals. For

I know when I talk about myself, I am also talking about you, and you too know that I am bringing my own recollections to bear when I tell your story.

I looked in the mirror and read my face. My face was the Rosetta stone I had deciphered in my dream. My face was a broken tombstone minus the carved turban that was once required on a proper Moslem headstone. My face was a mirror made of skin where the reader beheld himself; we breathed through the pores in unison: the two of us, you and I, our cigarette smoke thick in our living room full of the novels you devoured, the motor of the fridge droning woefully in the dark kitchen, light from the lampshade the color of a paperback cover and your skin falling on my guilty fingers and your long legs.

I was the resourceful and melancholic hero in the book you read; I was the explorer who in the company of his guide speeds along marble stones, tall columns and dark rocks, climbing up stairs that lead up the seven heavens replete with stars, toward those condemned to a fretful life underground; I was the hard-boiled detective who calls out to his sweetheart on the other end of the bridge across the abyss, "I am you!" and who, thanks to the writer's nepotism, detects the trace of poison in the ashtray . . . And you, Rüya, my dream, impatiently and wordlessly, would turn the page. I committed murders of passion, I crossed the Euphrates River on my horse, I got buried under pyramids, I bumped off cardinals: "So tell me, what's the book about?" You were a settled-down housewife and I the husband who comes home in the evening: "Oh, nothing." As the last bus of the night went by in all its emptiness, the easy chairs we sat in jiggled across from each other. You held the paperback book, and I the newspaper I couldn't manage to read, asking you: "If I were the hero, would you love me then?" "Don't talk nonsense!" The books you read talked about night's merciless silence; I knew all about the mercilessness of silence.

I thought to myself, her mother was right; my face has remained white: with five letters on it. On the large horse in the alphabet book it said HORSE, B for Branch, two D's for Dad. Papa in French. Mom, uncle, aunt, kin. It turns out, there was no mountain called Kaf, nor a snake encircling it. I sped along the commas, stopped at periods, expressed surprise at exclamation marks! The world of books and maps was so amazing! The ranger called Tom Mix lived in Nevada. Here's one about the Texas hero, Pecos Bill, in Boston; Black-Boy swashbuckles in Central Asia; Thousand and One Faces, Rummy, Roddy, Batman. Aladdin, please Aladdin, is the 125th issue of *Texas* out yet? Wait a minute, Grandma would say, snatching the comics out of our hands. Wait! If the last issue of that nasty comic book isn't out yet, I'll tell you a story myself. She'd tell it, her cigarette between her lips. The two of us, you and I, climbed Mount Kaf, plucked the apple off the tree, slid down the beanstalk, went down chimneys, went sleuthing. Besides us, Sherlock Holmes was the next best sleuth, then came White Feather who was Pecos Bill's sidekick, then Hawk Mehmet's friend Lame Ali. Reader, dear reader, are you tracking down my letters? I knew nothing about it, I had no idea, but it turns out my face was a map all along. What happened then? you asked, sitting in the chair across from Grandma, dangling your feet that didn't quite reach the floor. And then what, Grandma? What then?

Then, much later, years later, when I was the husband who came home tired from work, I took out of my briefcase the magazine I'd just bought at Aladdin's, and you snatched it and sat in the same chair, deliberately as always, dangling—my God!—your legs. I'd wear my usual blank look, asking myself fearfully: What goes on in her mind? What is the hidden mystery in the secret garden of her mind which is forbidden to me? Taking clues from your shoulder, where your long hair flowed down, and from the color-illustrated magazine, I'd attempt solving the secret that made you dangle your legs, that mystery in the garden of your mind: skyscrapers in New York, fireworks in Paris, handsome revolutionaries, determined millionaires (turn the page). Airplanes with swimming pools, superstars wearing pink ties, universal geniuses, the latest bulletins (turn the page). Hollywood starlets, rebellious singers, international princes and princesses (turn the page). Local news: two poets and three critics hold a discussion on the benefits of reading. I'd still be unable to solve the mystery, but you, after many pages and hours, past the time when hungry packs of dogs went by our place late at night, you would have completed the crossword puzzle: Sumerian goddess of health: Bo; a valley in Italy: Po; symbol of tellurium: Te; a musical note: Re; a river that flows up: Alphabet, I think; a mountain that doesn't exist in the valley of letters: Kaf; a magical word: Listen; theater of the mind: Rüya, a dream, my dream, my Rüya, whom I see before I sleep and dream of as I sleep; the handsome hero in the picture: you always came up with it, I'd never do. "Shall I get my hair cut?" you'd ask, raising your head from the magazine in the stillness of the night, half of your face in the light, the other half a dark mirror, but I'd never know whether you were asking me, or the handsome, famous hero in the center of the puzzle. For a moment, dear reader, I'd go blank again, very blank!

I could never convince you why I believed in a world without heroes. I could never convince you why those pitiful writers who invent the heroes are themselves no heroes. I could never convince you that the people whose photos you saw in the magazines are of a different breed. I could never convince you that you had to be content with an ordinary life. I could never convince you that it was necessary for me to have a place in that ordinary life.

Chapter Thirty

BROTHER MINE

Of all the monarchs of whom I have ever heard, the one who comes to my mind, nearest to the true spirit of God was the Caliph Haroun of Baghdad, who as you know had a taste for disguise.
    —ISAK DINESEN, "The Deluge at Norderney," *Seven Gothic Tales*

When Galip came out of the *Milliyet* building wearing the dark glasses, he didn't start out for his office but for the Covered Bazaar. Going past stores that sold tourist articles and walking across the courtyard at the Mosque of Divine-Radiance-of-the-Ottomans, he suddenly felt so sleepy that Istanbul appeared to be an entirely different city. The leather handbags, meerschaum pipes, coffee grinders he saw in the Covered Bazaar didn't seem like stuff that belonged to a city that mirrored the denizens who'd lived there thousands of years; they were frightening signs of an incomprehensible country where millions of people had been temporarily exiled. "The odd thing is," Galip thought to himself, getting lost in the Bazaar's haphazard arcades, "having read the letters in my face, I can believe in all optimism that I can now be totally myself."

In the row of slipper shops, he was ready to believe what had changed was not the city but himself; yet after reading the letters in his face, he'd become so convinced he comprehended the city's mystery that he just couldn't believe the city was still the one he had known. Looking in the window of a rug store, he experienced a feeling that he'd seen the rugs on display before, that he had stepped on them with his own muddy shoes and worn slippers, that he was well acquainted with the rug dealer who eyed him suspiciously as he sat sipping his coffee in front of the store, and that he knew, as he did his own life, the store's history full of shell games and small-time swindles as well as the stories it could tell, which smelled like dust. He had the same experience looking in the showcases of a jeweler, and at the antique and shoe stores. After hastily skipping a couple more arcades, he imagined that he knew all the stuff sold in the Covered Bazaar down to the copper ewers and the balance scales with pans, and that he was familiar with all the salesclerks waiting for customers as well as all the people walking in the arcades. Istanbul was all too familiar; the city held no secrets from Galip.

Feeling at ease, he walked around the arcades as in a dream. For the first time in his life, the gewgaws Galip saw in the windows and the faces he came across seemed as strange as his dreams and, at the same time, as familiar and reassuring as a noisy family dinner. He went by the brilliantly lit jewelry store windows, thinking that the peace he felt was related to the secret signified by the letters he'd read on his face in terror, yet he didn't want to think about the poor sad sack he was in his former life whom he'd left behind after reading the letters. What made the world a mysterious place was the presence of a second person one sheltered inside oneself, with whom one lived together like a twin. When, after going past the Cobblers' Venue where idle salesclerks loafed in the doorways, Galip saw bright postcards of Istanbul displayed in the entrance of a small shop, he decided he'd left his twin behind long ago: these postcards were so inundated with the familiar, stale, and clichéd images of Istanbul that, studying the common and well-known scenes of Municipal Lines ferries docking at the Galata Bridge, chimneys of the Topkapı Palace, the Tower of Leander, and the Bosphorus Bridge, Galip felt assured that the city could hold no mystery from him. But he lost the feeling as soon as he entered the narrow streets of the Bedesten, the heart of the old market, where the bottle-green windows of the stores reflected each other. "Someone is following me," he thought apprehensively.

There was no one in the vicinity to arouse his suspicion, but soon Galip was taken over by the premonition of an impending catastrophe. He walked briskly. At the Calpac-Makers' Venue, he made a right, walked along the length of the street and left the bazaar. He was about to go through the secondhand bookstores at full steam but when he got to the Alif Bookstore, the name he'd never given a second thought to all these years suddenly seemed like a sign. What was surprising was not the fact that the store's name was "alif," which was the first letter in *Allah* and, according to the Hurufis, the origin of the alphabet and the universe, but that the letter "alif" above the door had been written in Latin letters as F. M. Üçüncü had prescribed. Trying to view this not as a meaningful sign but as a common occurrence, Galip caught sight of Master Sheikh Muammer's store. The fact that the Zamani sheikh's bookstore was closed—a store which had once been frequented by poor pitiful widows from remote neighborhoods and miserable American billionaires—struck Galip as the sign of a mystery still hidden in the city rather than as a consequence of commonplace facts like the venerable sheikh not wanting to go out on such a cold day or his being dead. "If I'm still seeing signs in the city," he thought, going past piles and piles of translated detective novels and interpretations of the Koran which the book dealers left in front of the stores, "it means that I still haven't learned what the letters on my face have taught me." But it wasn't the real reason: every time he thought about being followed, his legs speeded up on their own, and the city was transformed from a tranquil place full of familiar signs and objects into a dreadful realm rife with unknown dangers and mysteries. Galip realized that if he walked faster, he'd shake whoever was shadowing him and shed the disquieting feeling of mystery.

At Beyazit Square, he turned into Tentmakers' Avenue and then into Samovar Street since he liked the name. Then he took Narghile Street, which was parallel to it, and went on down to the Golden Horn; then, taking Brass Mortar Street, he backtracked up the hill. He went past plastics ateliers, soup kitchens, coppersmith and locksmith stores. "It goes to show I was meant to come across these shops as I begin my new life," he thought with childlike innocence. He saw shops that sold pails, basins, beads, shiny sequins, uniforms for the police and the military. For a while, he walked toward Beyazit Tower, which he'd chosen as his destination, then he backtracked and, going past trucks, orange vendors, horse carts, old refrigerators, and political slogans on the walls of the university, he went all the way up to the Mosque of Süleyman the Magnificent. He went into the mosque courtyard and walked along beside the cypress trees; when his shoes got all muddy, he went out in the street by the seminary to walk past the unpainted wood-frame houses that leaned against each other. To his chagrin, he kept thinking that the stovepipes placed through the first-floor windows of the dilapidated houses poked out into the street *like* sawed-off shotguns or *like* rusty periscopes or else *like* the horrifying maws of cannons, but he didn't want to relate anything to something else, and he didn't want the word *like* to linger on in his mind.

In order to quit Youngblood Street, he took Dwarf Fountain Street, where his mind got stuck again on the street name, which led him to think it might be a sign. He concluded that the old stone-paved streets were rife with traps involving signs, and he went up to Prince Avenue. There he observed vendors hawking crisp sesame rings, minibus drivers having tea, and college kids eating pizza while they studied the showcases in front of a movie theater which had three features on its bill. Two were Bruce Lee karate flicks; the other, shown in torn posters and faded photographs, had Cüneyt Arkın playing a Seljuk march-lord who beat up Byzantine Greeks and slept with their women. Fearing he'd go blind if he stared into the actors' orange faces in the publicity stills any longer, Galip took off. He went by the Prince Mosque, trying not to think of the Story of the Prince that sprang into his mind. He passed traffic signs rusting along the edges, jumbled graffiti, plastic signs just overhead that advertised filthy restaurants and hotels, posters advertising pop singers and detergent companies. Even though he was successful, with great difficulty, in taking his mind off the hidden significance of all these, he couldn't help thinking, as he walked along beside the Aqueduct of Valens, about the red-bearded Byzantine priests in a movie he'd seen when he was very young; as he went by the famous Vefa fermented-beverage store, he couldn't help remembering how Uncle Melih, drunk on the cordials he'd tossed down one holiday evening, had brought the whole family here in a taxi to treat them to drinks made of mildly fermented grains; and these images were immediately transformed into the signs of a mystery that remained in the past.

He was crossing Atatürk Boulevard almost at a run when he concluded once more that if he walked fast, very fast, he'd see the pictures and letters the city presented to him as he wanted them: not as aspects of a mystery but as they really were. He went into Weavers' Street briskly and turned into Lumber Market Street, and for a long time he walked without registering the names of any streets, past trashy row houses with rusty balcony railings built interspersed with wood-frames, long-nosed '50s model trucks, tires that had become toys, bent electric posts, sidewalks that had been torn up and abandoned, cats going through garbage pails, headscarved women smoking in windows, itinerant yogurt vendors, sewer diggers and quilt makers.

As he was going down Rug Dealers' Avenue toward Homeland, he suddenly made a sharp left turn then changed sidewalks a couple of times; in the grocery store where he had a glass of yogurt drink, he considered that he must have learned the idea of "being followed" from the detective novels Rüya read, knowing full well that he could no more rid his mind of this idea than he could of the incomprehensible mystery that permeated the city.

He turned into Pair-of-Doves Street, making another left at the next intersection, and he almost ran along Literate Man Street. Crossing Fevzi Pasha Avenue as the traffic light went red, he darted in between the minibuses. When he read the street sign and realized he was on Lion's Den Street, he was momentarily terrified: if the mysterious hand whose presence he'd felt three days ago on the Galata Bridge were still placing signs all around the city, then the mystery that he knew existed must still be quite distant from him.

He went through the crowded marketplace, past fish stalls that sold mackerel, lamprey, and turbot, into the courtyard at the Mosque of the Conqueror where all streets converged. Aside from a black-bearded man who wore a black overcoat and walked like a crow in the snow, the spacious courtyard was deserted. There was no one in the small cemetery either. Mehmet the Conqueror's tomb was locked up; looking in the windows, Galip listened to the city's roar: the din of the marketplace, car horns, children's voices in a distant schoolyard, sounds of hammering and running engines, the screeches of sparrows and crows in the courtyard trees, the racket of the minibuses and motorbikes, the banging of the doors and windows nearby, the noise of construction sites, houses, streets, trees, parks, the sea, ships, neighborhoods, the whole city. The man he longed to be, Mehmet the Conqueror, whose sarcophagus he viewed through the dusty windowpanes, had intuited with the aid of Hurufi tracts the mystery of the city he'd conquered five hundred years before Galip's birth, and he'd undertaken to decipher slowly the realm in which every door, every chimney, every street, every aqueduct, every plane tree was the sign of something else beside itself.

"If only Hurufi tracts and the Hurufis themselves hadn't been immolated as the result of a conspiracy," Galip thought as he took Calligrapher İzzet Street to Mother Wit, "and if the Sultan had been able to attain the city's mystery, what insight might he have come up with walking on the Byzantine streets he'd conquered if he were looking, as I am, at broken walls, centenarian plane trees, dusty roads, and empty lots?" When Galip arrived at the tobacco warehouses and the terrifying old buildings in Temperance, he gave himself the answer he'd known ever since he'd read the letters in his face: "He'd have known the city he'd seen for the first time as if he'd been through it thousands of times." And the astonishing thing was that Istanbul still remained a newly conquered city. Galip had no sense that he'd ever seen or known the muddy streets before, the fractured sidewalks, broken walls, pitiful lead-colored trees, ramshackle cars and buses that were even worse, sad faces that looked alike, and dogs that were skin and bones.

He had realized by now that he wasn't going to be able to shake the tail he didn't know for sure was for real but he kept on walking, past manufacturing plants along the banks of the Golden Horn, empty industrial barrels, ruined Byzantine aqueducts, workmen who were eating bread and meatballs for lunch and playing soccer in the muddy fields, until the desire to see the city as a tranquil place full of familiar scenes became so strong that he tried imagining himself as someone else—as Mehmet the Conqueror. For quite a while, he walked hanging onto this childish fantasy, which seemed neither crazy nor ridiculous to him; then he remembered Jelal saying in one of his columns, written many years ago on some anniversary of the Conquest, that among the hundred and twenty-four rulers of Istanbul in the one thousand six hundred and fifty years from the first Constantine's time to the present, Mehmet the Conqueror was the only emperor who had felt no need to go incognito in the middle of the night. "Our readers know the reasons all too well," Jelal had written in the article Galip recalled as he bobbed along with the other passengers on the Sirkeci–Eyüp bus. He caught the bus to Taksim in Unkapanı, amazed that the person on his tail could change buses so fast: he felt the eye was even closer—on his neck. After once more changing buses in Taksim, he thought that if he talked to the old man next to him, he might be transformed into someone else, thereby getting rid of the shadow behind him.

"Do you suppose it's going to continue snowing?" Galip said, looking out the window.

"Who knows," said the old man who might have said more but Galip interrupted him.

"What does this snow signify?" Galip said. "What does it herald? Do you know the great Rumi's story about the key? Last night I was granted a dream about the same thing. It was white everywhere, snow white, as white as this snow. Suddenly I awoke with a cold, ice-cold, sharp pain in my chest. I thought there was a snowball on my heart, a ball of ice, or a crystal ball, but it wasn't: it was Poet Rumi's diamond key that lay on my heart. I took it into my hand and rose from my bed, thinking it might open my bedroom door; it did. But I was in another room where, sleeping in the bed, there was someone who looked like me but was not me; he had a diamond key lying on his heart. Putting down the key that I held in my hand, I took the second key, opened the door out of this room, and entered yet another room. The same thing in that room too . . . and in the next room, and the next one that opened into the next. Images of myself, much handsomer than I am, with keys placed on their hearts. What's more, I saw that there were others besides myself in the rooms, shadows like myself, ghostly somnambulists with keys in their hands. A bed in every room, and a dreaming man like me on every bed! That's when I realized I was in the marketplace in Paradise. Here there was no commerce, no money, no tariffs; only faces and images. Whatever you liked, you simulated; you pulled on a face like a mask and began a new life. I knew the face I was looking for was in the last of the thousand and one rooms, yet the final key I had in my hand would not open the final door. That's when I realized the ice-cold key I initially saw on my heart was the only key that would open the last door. Yet where was that key now, and in whose hand? I had no idea where among the thousand and one rooms was the room and bed I'd left, and so, beset by confounding regret and tears, I realized I was fated to rush from room to room and door to door along with the other hopeless creatures, exchanging one key for another, astonished by each sleeping face, until the very end of time . . ."

"Look," the old man said. "Look!"

Galip shut up and looked through the dark glasses at the spot where the old man was pointing. On the sidewalk in front of the radio station, there was a dead body; a couple of people were ranting and raving around it, and a curious crowd had quickly congregated. And then, when they got caught in the snarled traffic, passengers who had seats on the bus, as well as those who stood hanging on, leaned toward the windows to observe the dead body in silent terror.

Even after traffic was cleared, the silence in the bus continued for quite some time. Galip got off across from the Palace Theater; he bought salted bonito, fish-roe spread, sliced tongue, bananas, and apples at the Ankara Market on Nişantaşı Corner and walked briskly toward the Heart-of-the-City Apartments. By now, he felt too much like someone else to wish to be someone else. He went down to the doorman's flat right away; Ismail and Kamer were having a supper of chopped meat and potatoes with their little grandchildren, sitting at the dinner table covered with its blue oilcloth in a convivial family gathering that seemed so distant to Galip that it might have been a scene from centuries ago.

"Eat in good health," Galip said and added after a pause: "You didn't manage to deliver the envelope for Jelal."

"We rang and rang," the doorman's wife said, "but he wasn't home."

"He's upstairs now," Galip said. "So where's the envelope?"

"Jelal's upstairs?" Ismail said. "If you're going up, will you take him his electric bill?"

He'd risen from the table and was inspecting the bills on the television set, bringing them close to his shortsighted eyes one by one. It took Galip a moment to sneak the key he took out of his pocket on the nail on the shelf. They didn't catch him doing it. He took the envelope and the bill, and he left.

"Tell Jelal not to worry," Kamer called out after him with a gaiety that was suspect. "I've told no one!"

For the first time in years, Galip took some pleasure in riding the Heart-of-the-City Apartments' old elevator; it still smelled of wood polish and machine oil, moaning like an old person suffering from lumbago as it started up. The mirror in which he and Rüya used to check their height against each other was still in place, but he avoided looking in his own face, fearful at that moment of succumbing once more to the terror brought on by the letters.

After going into the apartment, he'd just taken off his coat and jacket and had just hung them up when the phone rang. Before picking up the receiver, he ran into the bathroom to prepare himself for any eventuality and looked into the mirror for several seconds with desire, valor, and determination: No, it was not coincidental, the letters, everything, the whole universe and its mystery were all in place. "I know," he reflected as he picked up the receiver, "I know." He'd already known the voice on the phone would be the same one who heralded the military coup.

"Hello."

"What should your name be this time?" Galip said. "There are so many pseudonyms around, I'm all confused."

"An intelligent beginning," the voice said; it possessed a self-confidence Galip hadn't expected. "You give me a name, Mister Jelal."

"Mehmet."

"As in Mehmet the Conqueror?"

"Yes."

"Good. This is Mehmet. I couldn't find your name in the phone book. Let me have your address so I can come."

"Why should I give you my address when I keep it a secret?"

"Because I am an ordinary citizen with good intentions who wants to bring a famous journalist the evidence of an impending military coup, that's why."

"You know too much about me to be an ordinary citizen," Galip said.

"I met this fellow six years ago at the train station in Kars," said the voice named Mehmet, "an ordinary citizen. He was an attar, a simple sundries-store owner, and just like the poet Farıd od-Dın Attar, eight hundred years before him, he was passing his years in one of those small shops that smelled of drugs and perfume. He was making a business trip to Erzurum. All through the trip we talked about you. He made comments about the meaning of your family name, Salik, 'the traveler on the Sufi Road.' He knew the significance of your having begun the first column you published under your own name with the word 'listen,' which translates the Persian word *bishnov* with which Rumi had begun his *Mathnawi*. When you wrote a piece in July of 1956 in which you likened life to serial novels and then, exactly a year later, one in which you likened serial novels to life, he was on to your cryptic symmetry and utilitarianism because he'd figured out from the style that it was you who had, under a pseudonym, resumed the series of pieces on wrestlers, the original writer having abandoned it on account of getting sore at the publisher. In another piece around the same time, which you began by saying that your male readers oughtn't to cast scowls at beautiful women on the street but instead smile with affection like Europeans, he knew that the beautiful woman you described with affection, admiration, and tenderness was your stepmother, exemplifying the woman disaffected by such masculine scowls. In the piece where you satirized an extended family who lived in a dusty Istanbul apartment building, comparing them to unfortunate Japanese goldfish who lived in an aquarium, he knew that the aforementioned fish belonged to a deaf-mute uncle and also that the family was your family. This man who hadn't set foot anywhere west of Erzurum, let alone visit Istanbul, knew all your unnamed relatives, the Nişantaşı flats you lived in, the streets, the police station at the corner, Aladdin's store across from it, the Teşvikiye Mosque courtyard with the reflecting pool, autumn gardens, the Milk Company pudding shop, the linden and chestnut trees along the sidewalks, as well as he knew his own shop on the outskirts of Kars where he sold, like Aladdin, all sorts of odds and ends from perfume to shoelaces, from tobacco to needle and thread. He knew in the years when we still lacked a unified accent on our national air waves that only three weeks after you lampooned Ipana toothpaste's Eleven Question Quiz on Radio Istanbul, in order to flatter you into shutting up, they'd made your name the answer to the two-thousand-lira question. Just as he'd expected, you hadn't accepted this small bribe but had advised your readers in your next column not to use American-made toothpaste, and to rub their teeth with mint soap made at home with their own hygienic hands. You wouldn't know, of course, that our well-intentioned attar had rubbed his teeth, which would later fall out one by one, with the hokey formula you gave out. On the other hand, the sundries man and I even put together a quiz game called 'Subject: our columnist Jelal Salik' which took up the rest of the train trip. I was hard put defeating this man whose main fear was missing his stop at Erzurum. Yes, he was an ordinary citizen, one who'd gone to seed quickly, one who didn't have enough money to get his teeth fixed, whose only pleasure, aside from your columns, was spending time in his garden with the various birds he kept in cages and telling stories about birds. Get it, Mister Jelal? An ordinary citizen is also capable of knowing you, so don't you dare sell him short! But I happen to know you even better than the ordinary citizen. That's why we'll be at it all night, talking."

"Four months after the second column on toothpaste," Galip began, "I did one more on the subject. What was that about?"

"You'd spoken about pretty little girls and boys giving their fathers, uncles, aunts, and stepbrothers 'goodnight kisses' before going to bed, their pretty mouths fragrant with minty toothpaste. Wasn't much of a column, to say the least."

"Other examples where I talked about Japanese goldfish?"

"Six years ago in an article where you longed for silence and death. A month later you brought back the goldfish when this time you said you sought order and harmony. You often compared aquariums to the TV sets in our houses. You provided us with information ripped off from the Encyclopaedia Britannica on the catastrophes that befell the Wakin goldfish for interbreeding. Who translated the stuff for you? Your sister or your nephew?"

"What about the police station?"

"It reminds you of dark blue, darkness, birth certificates, the woes of being a citizen, rusty water pipes, black shoes, starless nights, scowling faces, the metaphysical feeling of motionlessness, misfortune, being a Turk, leaky roofs and, naturally, death."

"Did the attar, your sundries man, know all that?"

"That and more."

"And what did the attar ask you?"

"This man, who'd never seen a streetcar and probably would never see one, asked me right off what a horse-drawn Istanbul streetcar smelled like, as opposed to a horseless one. I told him that the real difference was beyond the smell of sweat and horses; it was the smell of motors, oil, and electricity. He asked me if Istanbul electricity had a distinct odor. You hadn't mentioned it, but he'd read it between the lines. He asked me to describe the smell of newsprint hot off the presses. The answer was, according to your column in winter of 1958: a mixture of quinine, cellar dankness, sulphur, and wine;

that is, a heady mixture. Apparently, newsprint loses its smell in the three days it takes to arrive in Kars. The attar's most difficult question was one on the smell of lilacs. I couldn't remember you singling out this flower. According to the attar, whose eyes twinkled like an old man recalling sweet memories, you had mentioned the smell of lilacs three times in twenty-five years: One time, in connection with the story of a strange prince who terrorized those around him while he waited to ascend to the throne, you'd said his sweetheart smelled like lilacs. Another time—and this bore repeating—inspired in all likelihood by the daughter of a close relative, you'd written about a little girl who went back to grade school at the end of summer vacation on a sunny but dolorous day in the fall, wearing a freshly ironed smock and a bright ribbon in her hair, saying that it was her *hair* that smelled like lilacs one year, and that her *head* smelled like lilacs the next. Was this a real-life recurrence or a case of the writer cribbing from himself?"

Galip was silent for a while. "I don't remember," he finally said, as if waking from a dream. "I remember contemplating the story about the prince, but I don't remember writing it."

"The attar remembered. Aside from having a well-developed sense of smell, he was also good at places. Taking off from your columns, not only had he imagined Istanbul as a glut of smells, he knew all the quarters of the city you haunted, loved, cherished cryptically, and deemed mysterious. But he had no idea how close or distant these quarters were to one another. At times I've kept an eye out for you at these locations I also know well, thanks to you, but I haven't bothered to do so lately since your phone number tells me you're holed up somewhere in the Nişantaşı or Şişli area. I know this will interest you: I told the attar to write to you. But it turns out his nephew who reads your columns aloud to him does not know how to write. The attar could neither read nor write, of course. You'd once written that recognizing the letters only stunted the memory. Shall I tell you how I finally managed drubbing the man, whose knowledge of your work came from listening to it, as our choo-choo train pulled into Erzurum?"

"Don't tell me."

"Although he remembered all the abstract concepts in your work, he couldn't visualize their significances at all. For example, he had no idea what the concept of plagiarism or literary appropriation meant. His nephew read him only your column in the paper, and he wasn't at all curious about the rest. You'd think he imagined that all the writing in the world was done by one person simultaneously. I asked him why you kept harping on the poet Rumi. He had no answer. I asked him, concerning your 1961 column entitled "Mystery of Secret Writing," how much of it was you and how much of it was Poe. He had an answer: he said all of it was you. I quizzed him on the dilemma of 'the source of the story and the story of the source,' which was the turning point in the controversy—the sundries man called it a scrap—you and Neşati got into concerning Bottfolio versus Ibn Zerhani. He said with conviction that the source of everything was letters. He had comprehended nothing. I trounced him."

"In that scrap," Galip said, "the argument I put forth to contradict Neşati rested on the notion that letters are the source for everything."

"But that was Fazlallah's notion, not Ibn Zerhani's. After you wrote that *nazire* on 'The Grand Inquisitor,' you were forced to grab onto Ibn Zerhani to save your bacon. I just happen to know just what you were up to when you wrote those pieces, which was nothing more than making Neşati look bad to his boss and get him kicked off his paper. Initially, after the debate on 'Is it translation or plagiarism,' you trapped Neşati, who was green with envy, by irritating him into calling it 'plagiarism.' Then you made him appear as if he put Turks down by implying that the East could not create anything original because his argument stemmed from the fact that you plagiarized from Ibn Zerhani and Ibn Zerhani from Bottfolio, and you suddenly went for defending our glorious history and 'our culture' and put your readers up to writing to his publisher. And when the miserable Turkish reader, who's always vigilant for all kinds of New Crusades against the sort of perverts who claim that the 'great Turkish architect' Sinan was in fact an Armenian from Kayseri, didn't lose a moment in deluging the publisher with letters against this degenerate, then poor Neşati, who was drunk with the pleasure of catching your plagiarism, lost his job and his column. He ended up being employed at the same paper as you, although as a lesser writer, where, I hear tell, he's dug a well of gossip on you. Did you know that?"

"What have I written on wells?"

"That's a subject that's so clear and so endlessly extensive that quizzing a loyal reader like me on it isn't cricket. I won't mention the literary wells in courtly poetry, or the well where Rumi's beloved Shams was dumped, or the wells with genies, witches, and ogres from the *Thousand and One Nights* to which you've always helped yourself freely, or air shafts in apartment buildings and the bottomless darkness where you tell us we lost our souls. You've belabored these themes. How about this? Fall of 1957, you wrote a careful, angry, and sorrowful piece on those sad concrete minarets (you didn't have much quarrel with stonework minarets) that besiege our cities and our brand-new suburbs like forests of hostile lances. In the last few inconspicuous lines of this piece which went unnoticed—as it goes for all articles that go beyond daily politics and scandal—you mentioned a mosque in the slums with a squat minaret which had a dark and silent dry well in the yard infested with asymmetrical thorns and symmetrical ferns. I realized immediately that what you adroitly implied by your description of the actual well was that, instead of raising our eyes to the heights of concrete minarets, it behooves us to look down into our past's dark dry wells teeming with snakes and souls, submerged in our collective unconscious. Ten years later, in an article inspired by the Cyclopes and your own pitiful past, you wrote that on an unfortunate night when you were alone, all alone, grappling with the ghosts of the sins on your conscience, it was not accidental but necessary that you had written, in describing the 'eye' that belonged to the guilt feelings that hounded you pitilessly for years, that this visual organ stood 'like a dark well in the middle of the forehead.' "

Was the voice, which Galip imagined belonging to someone with a white collar, worn jacket, and a phantom face, forming these sentences impromptu by virtue of an overactive memory, or was it reading it off a prompter? Galip thought it over. The voice took Galip's silence as a sign and gave a victorious laugh. Sharing the ends of the same phone cable which went by way of who knew what underground passages and below what hills teeming with Ottoman skulls and Byzantine coins, clinging like black ivy to the walls of old apartment buildings where the plaster was falling off, strung tight like clotheslines between rusty poles and along plane and chestnut trees, he whispered as if confiding a secret with brotherly love instilled by sharing the umbilical cord attached to the same mother: he had much love for Jelal; he had much respect for Jelal; he had much knowledge of Jelal. Jelal didn't have any doubt on any of this anymore, did he?

"I wouldn't know," Galip said.

"In that case, let's get rid of these black telephones between us," said the voice. Because the bell on the phone which sometimes rang on its own accord alarmed rather than alerted; because the pitch-black receiver was heavy as a little dumbbell, and when dialed, it grumbled with the squeaky melody of the old turnstiles at the Karaköy–Kadıköy ferryboat dock; because sometimes it connected with numbers at random rather than the numbers dialed. "Get it, Mister Jelal? Give me your address and I'll be right over."

Galip hesitated at first like a teacher struck dumb by the wonders performed by a wonder student, and then—astonished that the man's garden of memory

seemed to have no bounds, astonished as well by the flowers that bloomed
in the garden of his own memory, and aware of the trap he was gradually
falling into—he asked:

"What about nylon stockings?"

"In a piece you wrote in 1958, two years after the time when you were
obliged to publish your column not under your own name but under some
hapless pseudonyms you came up with, on a hot summer day when you
were stressed out with work and loneliness, watching a movie which was
halfway through in a Beyoğlu movie theater (the Rüya) where you took refuge
from the noonday sun, you wrote that you were startled by a sound you
heard nearby through the laughter of Chicago gangsters dubbed into Turkish
by pitiful Beyoğlu dubbers, the report of machine guns, and the crash of
bottles and glass: somewhere not too far off the long fingernails of a woman
were scratching her legs through her nylons. When the first feature was over
and the houselights went on, you saw, sitting two rows in front of you, a
beautiful stylish mother and her well-behaved eleven-year-old son talking to
each other like chums. For a long while you observed their camaraderie,
how they carefully listened to each other. In another piece two years later,
you'd write that, watching the second feature, you were not listening to the
clash of steel blades and storms on the high seas that roared out of the sound
system but to the buzz produced by the restless hand with long fingernails
traveling on legs that would feed Istanbul's mosquitoes on summer nights,
and that your mind was not on the pirates' dirty deals on the screen, but on
the friendship between the mother and the son. As you revealed in a column
you wrote twelve years after that, your publisher had scolded you soon after
the publication of the piece with the nylons: Had you no idea that it was
dangerous, a very dangerous practice, to focus on the sexuality of a wife and
mother? That the Turkish reader would not tolerate it? And that if you
wished to survive as a columnist, you had to be careful what you said about
married women as well as your writing style?"

"On style? Make it brief, please."

"For you, style was life. Style, for you, was voice. Style was your thoughts.
Style was your real persona you created within it, but this was not one, not
two, but three personas . . ."

"These are?"

"The first voice is what you call 'my simple persona': the voice that you
reveal to anyone, the one with which you sit down at family dinners and
gossip through billows of smoke after dinner. You owe this persona the details
of your everyday life. The second voice belongs to the person you wish to
be: a mask that you appropriated from admirable personages who, having

found no peace in this one, live in another world and are suffused with its mystery. You'd written that you would have holed up in a corner, unable to face life, waiting for death like many an unhappy person if it hadn't been for your habit of whispering with this 'hero' whom you initially wanted to imitate and then become, if it hadn't been for your habit of repeating, like a senile person reciting the refrains stuck in his mind, the acrostics, the puzzles, parodies, and banter that this hero whispered in your ear. I was in tears reading it. What took you—and me, naturally—into realms unavailable to the first two personas you call 'the objective and subjective styles' is the third voice: the dark persona, the dark style! I know even better than you what it was that you wrote on nights when you were too unhappy to be satisfied with imitation and masks; but you know better what it was that you perpetrated, brother mine! We're meant to understand each other, find one another, and put on disguises together; give me your address."

"Addresses?"

"Cities are composed of addresses, addresses of letters, just as faces of letters. On Monday, October 12, 1963, you described Kurtuluş, called Tatavla in the old days, an Armenian quarter, as one of your most beloved spots in Istanbul. I read it with pleasure."

"Reading?"

"On one occasion, in February of 1962, should you require a date, during the tense days when you were preparing for a military coup that would save the nation from poverty, on one of the dark streets in Beyoğlu, you'd seen a gilt-framed large mirror being carried, goodness knows for what strange reason, from one nightclub where belly dancers and jugglers operate to another, which had first cracked, perhaps due to the cold, and then had burst into smithereens right before your eyes; that's when you'd realized it wasn't for nothing that the word in our language for the stuff that turns glass into mirror is the same as the word for 'secret.' After divulging this moment of insight in one of your columns, you'd said this: Reading is looking in the mirror; those who know the 'secret' behind the glass manage to go through the looking glass; and those who have no knowledge of letters will find nothing more in the world other than their own dull faces."

"What's the secret?"

"I'm the only one besides you who knows the secret. You know very well it's not something that can be discussed over the phone. Give me your address."

"What's the secret?"

"Don't you realize a reader has to devote his whole life to you to get to the secret? That's what I've done. Shaking with the cold in unheated state libraries, an overcoat on my back, hat on my head, and woolen gloves on my hands, I've read everything I suspected you might've written, the stuff you knocked off when you didn't publish under your own name, the serials you wrote passing for someone else, the puzzles, the portraits, the politically and emotionally charged interviews, just to figure out what that secret might be. Given that you have produced without fail eight pages a day on the average, in thirty-some years your output would be a hundred thousand pages, or three hundred volumes, each three-hundred-thirty-three pages. This nation ought to erect your statue just for that!"

"Yours too, for having read it all," Galip said. "What about statues?"

"On one of my Anatolian trips, in a small town the name of which I've forgotten, I was waiting in the town square park until it was time for my bus when a youngish person sat beside me and we began to talk. We started by mentioning the statue of Atatürk pointing at the bus terminal as if the only viable thing to do in this pitiful town was to leave it. Then, at my instigation, we talked about a column of yours on the subject of Atatürk statues which number over ten thousand throughout our country. You'd written that on the day of the apocalypse, when lightning and lightning bolts tore through the dark sky and quakes moved the firmament, all those terrifying Atatürk statues would come to life. According to what you wrote, some of the statues wearing pigeon droppings and European garb, some in the field marshal's uniform and decorations, some riding rearing stallions with large male organs, some in top hats and phantom-like capes, they would all start moving slowly in place; then they would get down from their bases which are covered under flowers and wreaths, and around which dusty old buses and horse carts have circled for years, and where soldiers whose uniforms smell of sweat and high-school girls whose uniforms smell of mothballs have gathered to sing the national anthem, and all these statues would vanish into the dark. The obsessive young man had read the piece where you described the night of the apocalypse when the ground quaked and the sky was rent, how our poor citizens listening to the roar outside through their closed windows would hearken with abject fear to the sounds of bronze and marble boots and hooves on the slum sidewalks; and the young man had become so overwhelmed that he had immediately written you a letter impatiently inquiring when the day of the apocalypse would come. If what he said was true, then you'd sent him a short answer asking him for a document-size photo; and after you got it, you'd given him the secret 'omen of the impending Day.' Don't get me wrong, the secret you gave the young man was not 'The Secret.' Disappointed after waiting for years at the park where the pool had gone dry and the grass had become patchy, the young man had divulged to me your secret that must have been, perforce, personal. You'd explained to him the secondary meanings of some letters and told him to consider a sentence he'd someday run across in your writing as a sign. Reading that sentence, our young man would decipher the encoded column and get to work."

"What was the sentence?"

" 'My entire life was full of these sorts of horrible memories.' There, that was the sentence. I can't figure out if he'd made it up or if you'd actually written it to him, but the coincidence is that, these days when you complain that your memory has been stunted or even completely erased, I've read this sentence, as well as others, in an old piece that's recently been rerun. Give me your address and I'll give you an instant explanation of what it means."

"What about other sentences?"

"Give me your address! Give it. I happen to know that you aren't curious about any other sentences or stories. You've given up on this country so thoroughly that you're not curious about anything. Your screws are getting loose from loneliness in that rat's nest where you're hiding out hatefully, without friends, comrades, anybody . . . Give me your address so that I can tell you in just which secondhand bookstore you might find students from the Religious High School who trade your autographed pictures, and wrestling umpires who fancy young boys. Give me your address so I can show you the etchings depicting eighteen Ottoman sultans who had assignations in secret places around Istanbul with their own harem wives whom they had masquerading as European whores. Did you know that in high-class haberdasheries and whorehouses in Paris this disease which requires wearing lots of dressy clothes and jewelry is called 'the Turk's disease'? Did you know of the etching that shows Mahmut the Second, who copulated in disguise on some dark street in Istanbul, wearing on his naked legs the boots Napoleon wore on his campaign to Egypt? And that his favorite wife, Bezm-i Alem, the Queen Mother—that is, the grandmother of the prince whose story you like so much and the godmother of an Ottoman ship—is shown in the same picture nonchalantly wearing a diamond-and-ruby cross?"

"What about crosses?" Galip said with some sort of joy, aware that he was getting some pleasure in life for the first time since his wife left him six days and four hours ago.

"I know it was no coincidence that under your January 18, 1958, column, right below your lines harping on Egyptian geometry, Arab algebra, and Syriac Neoplatonism in order to prove that the cross as a form was the opposite of the crescent—its repudiation and negation—appeared the news concerning the marriage of Edward G. Robinson, whom I really love as the 'cigar-chomping tough guy of the cinema and the stage,' to the New York clothes designer Jane Adler, showing a photograph of the newlyweds under the shadow of a crucifix. Give me your address. A week later, you'd proposed that instilling a phobia for the cross and zealotry for the crescent in our children resulted in stunting them into adults incapable of deciphering Hollywood's magical faces, leading them to sexual disorientation such as imagining all moonfaced women to be either mothers or aunts; and in order to prove your point, you'd claimed that if state boarding schools for the poor were to be raided on the nights after the kids studied the Crusades in history class, hundreds of them would be discovered having peed in their beds. These are just bits and pieces; give me your address, and I'll bring you all the stories about crosses that you want, all the stuff I came across in provincial newspapers, scratching around in libraries for your work. 'Having escaped the gallows when the oiled noose around his neck snapped, a convict tells about the crosses he saw on his short trip to Hell upon returning from the realm of the dead.' *The Erciyaş Post*, Kayseri, 1962. 'Our edicor-in-chief has wired che Presidenc, poincing ouc chac using this symbol inscead of che obviously cross-shaped leccer is more in keeping wich curkish culcure.' *Green Konya*, Konya, 1951. If you give me your address I'll rush you many more . . . I'm not suggesting that these are material for your writing; I know that you hate columnists who regard life as grist for the mill. I can bring the stuff that sits in boxes in front of me right over; we'd read it together, laughing and weeping. Come on, give me the address, I'll bring you stories serialized in İskenderun papers about local men who could only stop stuttering when they were telling hookers at nightclubs how much they hated their fathers. Give me your address and I'll bring you love and death predictions made by a waiter who was not only illiterate, he couldn't even speak proper Turkish, let alone Persian, but who could recite Omar Khayyam's undiscovered poems on account of their souls being twins; give me your address. I'll bring you the dreams of a journalist-printer from Bayburt who, upon finding out he was losing his memory, serialized on the last page of his newspaper everything he knew as well as his life and memories. In the last dream where faded roses, fallen leaves, and the dry well in the extensive garden are described, I know that you will find your own story, brother mine! I know you take blood-thinning medication to keep your memory from drying up, and that you spend hours everyday lying down with your feet up on the wall in order to force the blood into your brain, pulling out your recollections one by one out of that dry and dismal well. 'March 16, 1957,' you say to yourself, your head blood-red from hanging down the side of the sofa or a bed . . . 'On March 16, 1957,' you force yourself to remember, 'I was having lunch with colleagues at the City Grill, when I spoke about the masks that jealousy compels us to wear!' Then, 'Yes, yes,' you say, pushing yourself, 'in May of 1962, after an incredible bout of love at noon, waking up in a house on a backstreet in Kurtuluş, I told the naked woman lying beside me that the large beauty spots on her skin looked like my stepmother's.' Then you're gripped by a doubt that you will later call 'merciless': Had you said it to her? Or was it to that ivory-skinned woman in the stone house where the interminable noise of Beşiktaş Market came in through the windows that didn't close snugly? Or to the misty-eyed woman who, daring to return home late to her husband and children, left the one-room house overlooking Cihangir Park where the trees were naked, and trekked all the way to Beyoğlu, just because she loved you so much, to get you the lighter which, as you would later write, you didn't know why you demanded so capriciously? Give me your address and I'll bring you the latest European drug called Mnemonics which opens slam-bam brain vessels clogged with nicotine and horrible memories, taking us back instantly to our lives in the paradise which we have lost. After you start taking twenty drops of the lavender liquid in your tea in the morning, not ten as instructed in the package insert, you will remember a lot of your memories which you'd forgotten forever, and which you had even forgotten that you'd forgotten, as if finding your childhood's colored pencils, combs, and lavender-colored marbles which suddenly turn up behind an old cupboard. If you let me have your address, you will remember your column, as well as why you wrote it, regarding maps that can be read on all our faces, teeming with signs of compelling locations in the city where we live. If you give me your address, you will remember why you were forced to tell in your column Rumi's story about the competition between two ambitious painters. If you give me your address, you will remember why you wrote that incomprehensible column saying that there can be no hopeless solitude since even when we are the loneliest, the women of our daydreams keep us company; what's more, that these women who are always intuitively aware of our fantasies wait for us, look for us, and some of them even find us. Give me your address, and let me remind you of what you cannot remember; brother mine, you are now slowly losing the Heaven and Hell that you've lived and dreamed. Give me your address, I'll hurry and save you before your memory sinks into oblivion's bottomless well. I know everything about you, I've read all that you've written: there's no one besides me who can re-create that world so that you can write those magical texts again which glide like predatory eagles over the country by day, and like cunning ghosts at night. When I come to you, you will resume writing pieces which kindle the hearts of young men reading in coffeehouses in the most forlorn places in Anatolia, which make tears flow like rain down the cheeks of primary-school teachers and the students they teach in the boondocks, which awaken the joy of living in young mothers who live on backstreets in small towns reading photonovels and waiting for death. Give me your address: We'll talk all night and you will regain your tender love for this land and for this people, as well as for your lost past. Think of the downtrodden who write you letters from snow-covered mountain towns where the mail cart stops only once every two weeks; think of the bewildered who write you asking your advice before leaving their fiancées, before going on pilgrimage, before casting their votes in general elections; think of the unhappy students who read you sitting in the last row in geography class, the pitiful dispatch clerks glancing at your column sitting in a desk in some obscure corner while they wait for their retirement, the hapless who'd have nothing to talk about besides what's on the radio, were it not for your columns. Think of all those reading you at unsheltered bus stops, in the sad, dirty foyers of movie theaters, in remote train stations. They're all waiting for you to perform a miracle, all of them! You have no choice but to provide them with their miracle. Give me your address; two heads are better than one at this. Write, telling them the day of redemption is at hand, telling them the days of waiting in line with plastic cans in their hands to get water at the neighborhood fountain will soon be over, telling them it's possible for runaway high-school girls to avoid Galata whorehouses and become movie stars, telling them post-miracle National Lottery tickets will all carry prizes, telling them when husbands come home dead drunk they won't beat their wives, telling them extra carriages will be put on the commuter trains following the day of the miracle, telling them that bands will play in all town squares as in those in Europe; write that one day everyone will be a famous hero, and that one day, soon, aside from everyone getting to sleep with any woman he wants including his own mother, everyone will be able to resume considering—magically—the woman with whom he has slept an angelic virgin and a sister. Write and tell them the code of the secret documents unraveling the historic mystery which has led us into misery for centuries has finally been cracked; tell them that a popular movement networked all over Anatolia is about to take action, and that the homos, priests, bankers, and whores who've organized the international conspiracy condemning us to poverty, and their local collaborators, have been named. Point out their enemies to them, so they can be comforted by knowing who to blame for their desperate lot; let them sense what they can do to rid themselves of their foes, so they can imagine, even as they tremble with rage and sorrow, that one of these days they can accomplish something great; explain it thoroughly to them that the cause of their lifelong misery is these repulsive enemies, so they can feel the peace of mind that comes from dumping their sins on others. Brother mine, I know your pen is mighty enough to realize not only all these dreams but even more unbelievable tales and the most unlikely miracles. You will bring the dreams to life with wonderful words and incredible recollections that you'll pull out of the bottomless well of your memory. If our attar from Kars has been able to know the colors of the streets where you spent your childhood, it's only because he could perceive these dreams in between your lines; give him back his dreams. Once upon a time you'd written lines that sent chills down the spines of the unfortunate people in this land, making their hair stand on end, stirring their memories and giving them a taste of the marvelous times to come by reminding them of festival days of yore with their swings and merry-go-rounds. Give me your address and you can do it again. In this wretched country, what can someone like you do besides write? I know you write out of helplessness because you are unable to do anything else. Ah, how often I've contemplated your helpless moments! You felt excruciated seeing pictures of pashas and fruit hanging in green groceries; you felt saddened seeing fierce-eyed but pitiful brothers playing cards in coffeehouses with decks pasty from sweat. Whenever I saw a mother and son get in line in front of the State Meat and Fish Foundation at the crack of dawn hoping to do their shopping on the cheap, or whenever my train went by small clearings in the morning where workers' markets had been set up, or whenever my eye caught fathers who sat on Sunday afternoons with their wives and children in treeless parks without a blade of green, smoking and waiting for the end of the eternal hour of boredom, I often wondered what you *thought* about these people. Had you seen all the scenes I observed? I knew you would've written their stories on white paper that absorbed the ink when you returned home to your tiny room in the evening to sit at your timeworn desk which was totally appropriate to this pitiful, forgotten land. I'd imagine your head bending over the paper and conjure up the image of you rising from your desk around midnight feeling sick at heart to open the refrigerator, as you had once written, and look in absentmindedly without touching or seeing anything, and then how you walked around the rooms and the desk like a somnambulist. Ah, my brother, you were alone, you were pitiful, you were sad. How I loved you! I thought of you, only you, when I read all you'd written all these years. Please, give me your address; at least give me an answer. I'll tell you how I saw letters that were stuck like large dead spiders on the faces of some cadets from the War College whom I'd come across on the Yalova boat, and when I got those robust cadets alone in the filthy head on board how they were beset by a sweet childlike dread. I'll tell you how the blind lottery-man who, after drinking a shot of *rakı*, had his tavern companions read the letters he got from you that he carried in his pocket, proudly pointing out the mystery in between the lines which you'd divulged to him, and how he had his son read him *Milliyet* every morning to find the sentence which would clinch the mystery. His letters carried the stamp of the Teşvikiye Post Office. Hello, are you listening to me? At least, say something; let me know you're there. Oh my God! I hear you breathe, I hear your breathing. Listen: I've taken great pains composing these sentences, so listen carefully: When you wrote that the narrow smokestacks on old harbor ferryboats letting out melancholic trails of smoke seemed so delicate and breakable, I understood you. When you wrote that you suddenly couldn't breathe at provincial weddings where women danced with women and the men with the men, I understood you. When you wrote that the depression you felt walking along past wasted wood-frame houses in the slums turned into tears when you returned home, I understood you. About that movie featuring Hercules, Samson, or Roman history which you saw at the sort of theater where small children sell secondhand *Texas* and *Tom Mix* comics at the door, when you wrote that you were so confounded by the silence that fell over the theater pulsating with men as soon as a third-class American movie star with a dolorous face and long legs put in an appearance on the screen that you wanted to die, I understood you. How about that? Do you understand me? Answer me, you· wretch! I am that incredible reader any writer would consider himself lucky for running across even if only once in his lifetime! Give me your address and I'll bring you photos of high-school girls who adore you, all hundred and twenty-seven of them, some with their addresses on the back and others with their adulation as quoted in their journals. Thirty-two of them wear glasses, eleven have braces on their teeth, six have long swanlike necks, twenty-four of them sport ponytails just as you fancy. They're all crazy about you, they think you're to die for. I swear it. Give me your address and I'll bring you a list of women each of whom was wholeheartedly convinced that you meant her in a conversational column you wrote in the early sixties, saying, 'Listen to the radio last night? Well, listening to "Lovers' Hour," I myself could only think of one thing.' You have as many admirers in high-society circles as you do among army wives and infatuated highstrung students in their provincial or white-collar homes. Did you know that? If you let me have your address, I'd bring you photos of women in disguise, masquerading not only for those sad society balls but in their daily private lives. You'd once written, rightly so, that we have no private lives, that we don't even have any real comprehension of the concept of 'private life' which we appropriated from translated novels and foreign publications, but if you could just see these photos taken in high-heeled boots and devil's masks, well . . . Oh, come on, give me that address, I beg you. I'll quick bring you my incredible collection of human faces I've been saving up for the last twenty years. I have pictures of jealous lovers taken immediately after they've destroyed each other's faces with nitric acid. I have bewildered-looking mug shots of bearded or clean-shaven fundamentalists caught conducting secret rites for which they'd painted Arabic letters on their faces, of Kurdish rebels where the letters on their faces had been burned away by napalm, execution photos of rapists who get hanged hush-hush in provincial towns which I got by bribing my way into their official files. Contrary to the depictions in cartoons, when the greased noose snaps the neck, the tongue doesn't stick out. But the letters become more legible. Now I know what secret compulsion drove you to write in an old column that you preferred old-style executions and executioners. Just as I know you go in for ciphers, acrostics, cryptograms, I also know you walk among us in the middle of the night wearing just the sort of costume to reestablish the lost mystery. I'm onto what shenanigans you pull on the lawyer husband to get your half sister alone and trash everything all night for the sake of telling the simplest story that makes us who we are. In response to lawyers' wives who wrote angry letters about your bits ridiculing lawyers, when you said the lawyer in question didn't happen to be their husband, I knew you were telling the truth. It's high time you gave me your address. I know all the individual significances of those dogs, skulls, horses, and witches whooping it up in your dreams, and I also know which love missives you were inspired into writing by the tiny pictures of women, guns, skulls, soccer players, flags, flowers that cab drivers stick in the corner of their rearview mirrors. I know quite a lot of the code sentences you dole out to your pitiful admirers just to get rid of them; and I also know you never part with the notebook in which those key sentences are written, nor with your historical costumes . . ."

Much later, long after Galip had pulled the phone cord out of the jack and searched through Jelal's notebooks, old costumes, closets, and worked like a somnambulist looking for his memories, lying in Jelal's bed wearing his pajamas and listening to night noises in Nişantaşı, he understood once more, as he fell into a long and deep sleep, that the capital aspect of sleep was—aside from forgetting the heartbreaking distance between who a person was and who he believed he could someday become—peacefully scrambling together all that he'd heard and all that he hadn't, all that he'd seen and all that he hadn't, all that he knew and all that he did not.

Chapter Thirty-one

THE STORY GOES THROUGH
THE LOOKING GLASS

The two of them being together,
Reflection of the reflection entered the mirror. —ŞEYH GALIP

I dreamed I had finally become the person I wished to be all these years. I was sleeping with the weariness of sorrow in the middle of the journey of our life we call a dream, *rüya*, in a dark wood of high-rises in a muddy city where the faces are even gloomier than the gloomy streets, when I came upon you. For the duration of this dream, or some other story, it seemed as if you'd love me even if I didn't manage becoming someone else; it seemed as if it was necessary that I accept myself just as I am with the same resignation I feel looking at my passport picture; it seemed like it was useless struggling to be in someone else's shoes. It seemed as if the dark streets and terrifying buildings which stooped over us parted as we walked by, that our passage gave meaning to shops and sidewalks along our way.

How many years has it been since you and I were startled to discover the magical game we would so often come across in our lives? It was the day before a religious holiday when our mothers led us to the children's wear section at a clothing store (back in those wonderful times when we didn't yet have to go to separate women's and men's departments); there, in a semilit corner of the store which was more boring than the most boring religion class, we found ourselves caught in between two full-length mirrors and observed how our reflections multiplied and got smaller and smaller as they went on into infinity.

Two years after that, we were making fun of the kids we knew who'd sent in their pictures to the page called "Friends of Animals Club" in *Children's Week*, where each week we would read the columns on "Great Inventors" quietly to ourselves, when we noticed on the back cover the picture of a girl reading the magazine we were holding in our hands; and, when we examined the magazine the girl held in her hand, we realized the pictures had multiplied inside each other: the girl on the cover of the magazine that we held was holding the magazine on the cover of which the girl held the magazine on the cover of which the girl was holding the magazine who was the same redheaded girl and the same *Children's Week* that got incrementally smaller and smaller.

Later, when we were even taller and had drifted away from each other, I saw the same thing on a jar of black-olive paste that had recently come on the market, which, since it didn't get served in our flat, was available to me only at your breakfast table on Sunday mornings. The label on the jar, promos for which ran on the radio—"Wow, I see you're having caviar!" "Oh no, it's Exceptional Brand black-olive paste"—showed a perfect happy family where the mother, father, son, and daughter were sitting at their breakfast table. I showed you the jar that sat on the table pictured on the label of the jar, on the label of which was pictured yet another jar, and you realized that the pictures of jars of olive paste and the happy families got smaller and smaller inside each other; that was when we both knew the beginning of the fairy tale I am about to tell, but not how it ends.

The boy and the girl were cousins. They grew up in the same apartment building, climbed up the same staircase, gobbled together Turkish delights and coconut candy which bore the molded relief of a lion. They did their homework together, they came down with the same bug, they scared each other playing hide-and-seek. They were the same age. They went to the same school, the same movies, listened to the same radio shows, records, they read the same *Children's Week* magazine, the same books, and went through the same closets and trunks where they found the same fezzes, the same silk covers, and the same boots. One day when their adult cousin whose stories they adored dropped by for a visit, they grabbed the book he was carrying and began reading it.

The book first amused the girl and the boy with its old words, highfalutin language and Persian expressions, then it bored them into throwing it down; and yet, thinking perhaps it had an illustration of a torture scene, a naked body, or a submarine, they riffled through the book curiously and ended up actually reading it. It turned out the book was terribly long. But near the beginning there was such a love scene between the hero and the heroine that the boy wished to be in the hero's shoes. Love had been described so beautifully that the boy wanted to be in love like the hero in the book. So, when he realized he showed the same symptoms of love as the ones later on in the book which he'd fantasized about (impatience with food, inventing reasons to go see the girl, not being able to drink a whole glass of water even when thirsty), the boy realized he'd fallen in love with the girl at that magic moment they held the book together, each fingering the corners of opposing pages.

So what was this story they read fingering the corners of opposing pages? The story, which happened long ago, was about a boy and girl who'd been born into the same tribe. The girl and the boy, named Beauty and Love, who lived at the edge of a desert, were born on the same night, studied with the same teacher (Professor Madness), walked around the same fountain, and fell in love with each other. When the boy asked for the girl's hand many years later, the elders of the tribe stipulated that he go to the Land of Hearts and bring back a certain alchemical formula. The boy who set out on the road met with a great many difficulties: he fell down a well and was enslaved by a painted witch; he got inebriated looking at the thousands of faces and images he saw in another well; he fell for the daughter of the Emperor of China because she resembled his beloved; he climbed out of the wells and got locked up in castles; he followed and was followed, struggled through winter, traveled great distances, went after clues and signs; he delved into the mystery of letters, telling and listening to stories. Finally, Poetry, who followed him in disguise and helped him get through his ordeals, said to him: "You are your beloved, and your beloved is you; do you still not understand?" That is when the boy in the story remembered how he fell in love with the girl reading the same book when they were studying with the same teacher.

The book *they* had read together told the story of a king called King Jubilant and a beautiful young man called Eternal with whom he had fallen in love; the bewildered king had no idea what was going on, but you'd already caught on that the lovers in this story would've fallen in love reading together a third love story. The lovers in that love story too would've fallen in love reading yet another love story in a book, and the lovers in that story would've fallen for one another reading still another love story.

Many years after we'd gone to the clothing store, read *Children's Week* together, and studied the jar of black-olive paste, I'd discovered that our memories' gardens also led into each other like these love stories, forming an infinite string of stories that were tied together like a series of doors to rooms that led into one another; that was when you'd run away from home and I'd taken up fiction and my own story. All love stories were sad, touching, pathetic, whether they were set in Damascus in the Arabian Desert, or in Khorosan on the steppes of Asia, or in Verona at the foot of the Alps, or in Baghdad on the River Tigris. Even more pathetic was how easily these stories stuck in one's mind, making it very simple to identify with the most ingenuous, long-suffering, and sorrowful hero.

If someday someone (perhaps me) ends up writing our story, the ending of which I still cannot figure out, I don't know if the reader can immediately identify with one of us as I've done reading those love stories, or if our story can stick in the reader's mind, but I intend to do my homework since I'm aware that certain kinds of passages are always present which set the heroes and the stories apart from each other:

On a visit we paid together, you were listening carefully to a long story whose narrator sat close by in a room where the heavy air had turned blue with cigarette smoke, when sometime past midnight the expression in your face gradually began saying "I'm not here"; I loved you then. You were listlessly looking for a belt among your slips, your green sweaters, and your old nightgowns you couldn't bring yourself to discard, when you became aware of the incredible mess that was revealed through your closet's open door and a daunted expression appeared on your face; I loved you then. Back when you had a passing fancy to become an artist when you grew up, you were sitting with Grandpa at a table learning to draw a tree, and when Grandpa teased you gratuitously you didn't get angry at him but laughed; I loved you then. You'd slammed the *dolmuş* door on the hem of your purple coat, when the five-lira piece fell out of your hand and rolled prettily defining a perfect arc into the grate in the gutter, and I loved the playfully surprised expression on your face; I loved you. On a brilliant April day, seeing how the hankie you'd put out on our tiny balcony to dry in the morning was still wet, you realized the bright sun had fooled you, and immediately afterwards you were listening to twittering in a vacant lot out back when your face took on a wistful look; I loved you then. I'd realized apprehensively how different your memory and recollections were than mine when I overheard you tell a third person about a movie we'd seen together, and I loved you then; I loved you. When you sneaked off into a corner to read some professor's pearls of wisdom in a richly illustrated newspaper article, haranguing on intermarriage among close relatives, I didn't care what it was that you read but loved seeing you read with your upper lip slightly pursed like some Tolstoyan character; I loved the way you checked yourself in the elevator mirror as if looking at someone else and then, for some reason, the way you anxiously rifled through your purse as if looking for something you'd just remembered; I loved the way you hurriedly slipped into the pair of high-heeled pumps you kept waiting side-by-side for hours, one on its side like a narrow sailboat and the other like a hunchbacked cat, and when you returned home hours later, I loved watching the skillful movements your hips, your legs and feet spontaneously performed before you abandoned the pair of muddied pumps to their asymmetrical retirement; I loved you when your melancholic thoughts went who knew where as you regarded the mound of cigarette butts and burned-out matches with their black heads bent forlornly in the ashtray; I loved you on our usual walks when we came across a scene or light so brand new that it seemed for a moment that the sun might have risen in the west that morning; it was not the street I loved but you. On a winter day when a sudden south wind cleared Istanbul of snow and dirty clouds, it wasn't Mount Uludağ appearing in the horizon behind antennas, minarets, and the islands which you pointed out but you shivering with your head tucked into your shoulders that I loved; I loved your wistful gaze at the water vendor's tired old horse pulling the heavy cart loaded with enameled containers; I loved the way you poked fun at people who say don't hand out money to beggars because actually beggars happen to be quite rich, and the way you laughed joyously when you found a shortcut to get us out in the street before all the others who were slowly winding their way up through labyrinthine stairways out of the movie theater. After we ripped another page off the educational calendar with schedules for prayer, an activity which took us a day closer to our death, I loved your voice reading, seriously and sorrowfully as if reading the signs of our impending death, the suggested daily menu consisting of meat and chickpeas, pilav, pickles, and mixed fruit compote; and when you taught me patiently how one opens the tube of Eagle brand anchovy paste by first removing the flat perforated disk and then turning the cap all the way, I loved the way you recited from the label, "submitted with the respects of the manufacturer, Monsieur Trellidis"; I loved you anxiously when I noticed that your face on winter mornings was the same color as the pale white sky, or when in our childhood I watched you cross the street running wildly among the stream of vehicles that flowed down past our apartment house; I loved you when you observed carefully, and with a smile on your lips, the crow that landed on the coffin that was laid on the catafalque in the mosque courtyard; I loved you when you acted out our parents' fights using your imitation radio-theater voice; I loved you when I held your face between my hands and I fearfully saw in your eyes where our lives were taking us; I hadn't understood why you'd left your ring lying next to the vase in the first place, but when I saw it there again several days later, I loved you; I loved you when I realized that you had also joined the solemn festival with your jokes and inventiveness toward the end of prolonged lovemaking that was reminiscent of the slow flight of mythical birds; when you pointed out the perfect star in the heart of the apple you cut crosswise instead of top to bottom, I loved you; in the middle of the day when I found a strand of your hair on my desk and couldn't figure out how it got there, and on a ride we took together when I realized how little alike our hands looked grasping the bar on the crowded municipal bus, side-by-side among all the other hands, I loved you as I loved my own body, as if I were looking for my absconded soul, as if I comprehended with pain and joy that I'd become someone else. I loved you. When that mysterious expression appeared on your face as you watched a train go by to an unknown destination, and when its exact dolorous replica reappeared at the hour when screaming flocks of crows flew insanely, and when the electricity suddenly went out in early evening and the darkness inside and the light outside slowly replaced each other, I loved you with all the helplessness, the pain and jealousy that gripped me whenever I saw your mysteriously dolorous face.

Chapter Thirty-two

I AM NOT A MENTAL CASE,
JUST ONE OF YOUR LOYAL READERS

I made your person my mirror. —SÜLEYMAN ÇELEBI

Galip woke, if it could be called waking, at seven in the morning after having gone to sleep the previous night for the first time in two days. As he would later remember when he tried comprehending all that had happened and all that had gone through his mind during the period between the time he got up at four in the morning and the time he went back to sleep after listening to the call to morning prayer to wake up again an hour later, he was experiencing "the wonders of the mythic land between sleep and wakefulness" that Jelal so often mentioned in his writing.

Like people who wake up in the middle of a deep sleep after a long period of sleeplessness and exhaustion, and many a worn-out unfortunate who finds himself waking in a bed other than his own, when he woke at four he had trouble remembering the bed, the room, the apartment, and how he got there, but he didn't press himself too much to come out of his memory's enchanting bewilderment.

So when Galip saw Jelal's box of disguise paraphernalia next to the desk where he'd left it before going to bed, he began taking out the familiar objects inside it without registering any surprise: a melon hat, sultan's turbans, caftans, canes, boots, stained silk shirts, fake beards that came in various sizes and colors, wigs, pocket watches, eyeglass frames, headgear, fezzes, silk cummerbunds, daggers, Janissary decorations, wristbands, a pile of other odds and ends that are available at Mr. Erol's famous shop in Beyoğlu which supplies costumes and equipment to Turkish filmmakers who make historic films. Then, as if remembering a recollection that had been pushed into a corner in his mind, Galip tried visualizing Jelal going around Beyoğlu at night masquerading in these costumes. But like the blue-tinged roofs, modest streets, and phantom-like persons in the dream he'd been having just moments ago, which were still stirring in his mind, the scenes of going incognito seemed to Galip like one of the myths of "the land between sleep and wakefulness": wonders that were neither mysterious nor real, neither comprehensible nor totally incomprehensible. In his dream he had tried locating an address which existed in districts of Damascus and Istanbul, as well as in the outskirts of the Fort of Kars, and he found what he was looking for as easily as coming up with the simpler words in the crossword puzzles in newspaper magazine supplements.

Since Galip was still under the spell of the dream, when he saw the large book of names and addresses on the desk he was gripped by an impression of coincidence which made him feel joyous, as if he'd come across signs left there by a hidden hand or intimations of a sportive god who played hide-and-seek like a child. Pleased to be living in such a world, he grinned as he read the addresses in the book and the sentences across from them. Who knew how many fans and enthusiasts all over Istanbul and Anatolia awaited the day when they'd come across these sentences in Jelal's columns; some of them might've already done so. Galip tried remembering through the fog of sleep and dreams. Had he ever seen these sentences before in Jelal's work? Had he read them years ago? Even if he didn't remember having read some of the sentences, he knew he'd heard them straight out of Jelal's mouth—such as, "What makes the marvelous is its peculiar way of being ordinary; what makes the ordinary is its peculiar way of being marvelous."

And even if he couldn't place some of the sentences in Jelal's work or discourse, he remembered noticing them in other places, such as Şeyh Galip's admonition written two centuries ago in connection with the school years of the two children named Beauty and Love.

"Mystery is sovereign, so treat it gently with respect."

There were still others he couldn't remember seeing in Jelal's work or anyplace else, yet they felt familiar, as if he'd read them both in Jelal and elsewhere. Such as the sentence that would be the signal for a Fahrettin Dalkıran who resided on Serencebey in Beşiktaş. "The gentleman, being someone with enough sense to imagine that his twin sister, whom he'd been dying to meet all these years, could only appear to him in the guise of death on the Day of Judgment and liberation—which for many people fetches up images of themselves beating their teachers to an inch of their lives, or to put it more simply, of taking pleasure in bumping off their fathers—had made himself scarce for quite some time and hadn't stirred out of his place, the location of which was known to no one." Who might "the gentleman" be?

Just as it began to grow light, Galip had an impulse to plug in the telephone; he washed, helped himself to whatever was in the fridge, and soon after the call to morning prayer went back to Jelal's bed. As he was about to fall asleep, in the realm closer to dreams than to daydreams, in the state between sleep and wakefulness, he and Rüya were children taking a boatride on the Bosphorus. There were no aunts, no mothers, nor any boatmen anywhere around: being all alone with Rüya made Galip feel insecure.

The phone was ringing when he woke up. By the time he reached it, he'd made up his mind that it must be the usual voice on the phone and not Rüya. He was startled to hear a woman's voice.

"Jelal? Jelal, is that you?"

Not a young voice and certainly not at all familiar.

"Yes."

"Darling, darling, where have you been? For days I've been calling and calling, trying to find you, ah!"

The last syllable became a sob, the sob turned into weeping.

"I can't place your voice," Galip said.

"Can't place my voice!" said the woman, imitating Galip's voice. "He tells me he can't place my voice. He's so formal with me." After a pause, she laid down her cards like a player confident of her hand, somewhat conspiratorial and somewhat haughty: "This is Emine."

Her name had no associations for Galip.

"Yes."

"Yes? That's all you have to say?"

"After so many years . . ." Galip murmured.

"Darling, at last, after so many, many years. Can you imagine how I felt reading you call out to me in your column? I'd been waiting for the day for twenty years. Can you imagine how I felt reading the sentence I'd been anticipating for twenty years? I wanted to shout it out for all the world to hear. I almost went crazy; I had a time containing myself; I wept. As you know, they retired Mehmet for getting involved in all that revolution business. But he's out and about, always busy with stuff. Soon as he left, I hit the street. I ran all the way to Kurtuluş. But there was nothing, but nothing, left on our street. Everything had changed, all torn down, nothing left standing. Our place was nowhere to be found. I began crying right in the middle of the street. People took pity on me and gave me a glass of water. I returned home at once, packed my suitcase, and left before Mehmet got home. My darling, my Jelal, now tell me how I find you? For the last seven days, I've been on the road, staying in hotel rooms and with distant relatives, feeling unwanted and unable to hide my shame. I called the paper so many times only to hear them say "We don't know." I called your relatives, the same answer. I called this number, no answer. I took nothing with me aside from a few small things, I don't want anything. I hear Mehmet has been looking for me like a madman. I left him a short letter that explained nothing. He has no idea why I left. No one does, I haven't told anything to anyone. I didn't divulge our love, the pride of my life, to anyone, my darling. What's going to happen now? I'm afraid. I am on my own now. I have no responsibilities anymore. You no longer have to fret that your plump bunny has to return home to her husband before supper. The kids have grown up, one is in Germany, the other in the army. My time, my life, everything that belongs to me, are all yours. I'll do your ironing for you, I'll straighten your desk, your dear writings; I'll change your pillowcases; I never saw you anywhere but in that bare love nest where we met; I'm so curious about your real place, your things, your books. Where are you, my darling? How am I to find you? How come you didn't signal your address in secret code in your column? Give me your address. You too kept thinking back, didn't you, thinking back all these years? We will be alone once more, in the afternoon, back in our one-room stone house, sunlight pouring through the linden leaves on our faces, tea glasses, and our hands that knew each other so well. But Jelal, that house no longer exists! It's been torn down, vanished; no Armenians either, nor any old-style shops . . . Were you aware of that? Or did you want me to go there and cry my eyes out? How come you didn't mention it in your column? You can write anything, you could've written this too. It's high time you talked to me! Say something after twenty years! Do your hands still sweat when you're embarrassed? Does a childlike expression still appear on your face when you sleep? Tell me. Call me 'my darling' . . . How am I to see you?"

"My dear lady," Galip said carefully. "Dear lady, I've forgotten everything. There must be some mistake, I haven't submitted anything to the paper for days. They've been running my old columns from twenty or thirty years ago. Do you understand?"

"No."

"I had no intention of sending you or anyone else encoded sentences or anything. I no longer write. The editors have been reprinting my old columns one more time. That sentence must have been in a twenty-year-old piece."

"That's a lie!" the woman shouted. "It's a lie. You do too love me. You loved me madly. You always talked about me in your writing. When you wrote about the most beautiful spots in Istanbul, you described the street on which stood the house where you made love to me; you described our Kurtuluş, our tiny spot, not some commonplace bachelor's pad. What you saw in the garden were our linden trees. When you mentioned Rumi's moonfaced beauty, you weren't writing purple prose but describing your own moonfaced one: me . . . You mentioned my cherry lips, the crescents of my eyebrows . . . it was me who inspired you with all that. When the Americans went to the moon, I knew you weren't just writing about the dark spots on the face of the moon but about the beauty spots on my cheeks. My darling, don't you ever deny it again! 'The terrifying unfathomableness of dark wells' was a reference to my eyes, for which I thank you; it made me weep at the time. When you said, 'I returned to that apartment,' you naturally meant our little house, but not wanting to have anybody guess our forbidden secret trysts, I know that you were forced to describe a certain six-story apartment building in Nişantaşı with an elevator. We got together at that house in Kurtuluş eighteen years ago. Exactly five times. Please don't deny it, I know you love me."

"My dear lady, as you have said, it all happened long ago," Galip said. "I no longer remember anything. I gradually forget everything."

"My darling Jelal, this couldn't be you. I just can't believe it. Are you being kept hostage there, is someone making you say these things? Are you alone? Just tell me the truth, tell me you've loved me all these years, that will be enough. I waited for eighteen years, I can wait for another eighteen. Just once, tell me you love me just once. All right, tell me at least that you loved me back then. Say I loved you back then, and I'll hang up for all eternity."

"I loved you."

"Call me darling . . ."

"Darling."

"Oh, no, not like that; say it sincerely!"

"Dear lady, please! Let bygones be bygones. I've aged, perhaps you too are no longer young yourself. I'm not the person in your imagination. I beg you, let's go ahead and forget this unpleasant joke played on us through carelessness due to a publishing error."

"Oh, my God! What's going to happen to me now?"

"Go back home to your husband. If he loves you, he'll forgive you. Make up some story, he'll believe it if he loves you. Return home without delay, before you break your faithful husband's heart."

"I wish I could see you once more after eighteen years."

"Lady, I'm not the man I was eighteen years ago."

"Yes, you are too that man. I read what you write. I know all about you. My mind has been on you so much, so very much. Tell me: the day of Salvation is at hand, isn't it? Who's the savior? I too am waiting for Him. I know He is you. A lot of others know it too. The whole mystery resides in you. You won't be arriving on a white horse but in a white Cadillac. Everyone is having this same dream. My Jelal, how I've loved you. Let me see you just once, even if at a distance. I could stand off and watch you in a park, say, the park in Maçka. Come to Maçka Park at five."

"My dear lady, I apologize for hanging up. But before I do, please forgive this aged recluse for presuming on your undeserved love and requesting something of you. Tell me, please, how'd you get hold of my phone number? Do you have any of my addresses? These are very important to me."

"If I tell you, will you let me see you just once?"

Pause.

"I will," Galip said.

"But you will have to give me your address first," the woman said cunningly. "To put it plainly, I no longer trust you after eighteen years."

Galip thought it over. He could hear the woman breathing nervously like a tired steam engine—he had a feeling it might even be two women—as well as the sound of a radio in the background, the sort of music that reminded Galip of the last years of Grandma and Grandpa and their cigarettes rather than the love, abandonment, and pain of the "Turkish folk music" on the radio. Galip tried imagining a room with a large old radio sitting in one corner, and in the other, a weeping, breathless older woman in a worn armchair holding a telephone receiver, but all that he could visualize was the room two floors below where Grandma and Grandpa once sat smoking: it was there that he and Rüya used to play "Didn't See."

After the pause, Galip had started saying, "The addresses . . ." when the woman shouted with all her might: "Don't, don't tell them! He's listening in! He's here too. He's making me talk. Jelal, darling, don't give your address, he's going to find and kill you. Ah . . . oh . . . ah!"

After hearing the last moans Galip heard strange, horrible metallic sounds and unintelligible clattering in the receiver which he pressed hard on his ear; he imagined a scuffle. Then there was a huge ruckus: it was either a gunshot or else the receiver that was being fought over had fallen down. It was immediately followed by silence, but it wasn't a real silence either; Galip could hear Behiye Aksoy singing "Philanderer, philanderer, you philanderer!" on the radio that was still playing in the background, as well as the sobs of the woman crying in another far corner. Although there was heavy breathing on the line, whoever had got hold of the receiver wasn't saying anything. These audio effects went on for a very long time. Another song came on the radio; the breathing and the woman's monotonous sobbing persisted.

"Hello!" Galip said, unnerved. "Hello! Hello?"

"Me, it's me," a man's voice said finally; it was the same voice he'd been listening to for days, the usual voice. He spoke maturely, coolheadedly, even as if to mollify Galip and close an unpleasant subject. "Emine confessed everything yesterday. I found her and brought her back. Mister, you make me sick! I'll put you in your grave!" Then, like an umpire proclaiming the end of a dull game that has gone on much too long and turned everyone off, he added in an impartial voice: "I'm going to kill you."

There was a silence.

"Perhaps you could hear me out," Galip said out of professional habit. "The column was published by mistake. It happens to be an old column."

"Give it a rest," said Mehmet. What was his family name? "I've heard it already, I'm done hearing all the stories. That's not why I'm going to kill you, even though you also deserve death for that extra. You know why I'm going to kill you?" But he wasn't expecting an answer from Jelal—or Galip; he already seemed to have the answer down pat. Galip listened out of habit: "Not because you betrayed the military action that would have made something of this lazy country, not for ridiculing afterwards the undaunted officers and other stalwart people who were driven from pillar to post, having embarked on patriotic work only to fall into disgrace thanks to you, and not for having insidious and ignominious daydreams sitting in your easy chair while they took their lives into their hands embarking on the adventure your writing provoked them into, presenting to you their plans for the coup and their homes with respect and admiration, not even for having been able to carry out your dreams insidiously among these modest patriotic people whom you conned into taking you into their homes, and not for having seduced my poor wife—I'll be brief—who was having a breakdown during the days when we were all swept away by revolutionary zeal, no. I will kill you for having seduced all of us, the whole country, and for having conned us with your ignominious dreams, your absurd apprehensions, your heedless lies under the guise of cute antics, suggestive refinements, hard-hitting prose, and for having been able to palm it off year after year on the whole nation and especially on yours truly. I know what's what now. Time that others knew it too. Remember the sundries man, the attar, whose story you listened to mockingly? Well, I will also be avenging this man whom you've shrugged off with a laugh. While I was covering the city inch by inch this whole week, looking for your trail, I figured out that this is the only course of action: This nation and I must forget all that we have learned. You were the one who wrote that we eventually abandon all our writers, after the first fall following their funerals, to their eternal sleep in the bottomless well of oblivion."

"I agree with everything wholeheartedly," Galip said. "I'd told you I'm going to give up this business completely once I write the last few bits, just to get rid of the last crumbs in my memory that keeps emptying itself out, hadn't I? By the way, what did you think of today's column?"

"You rotten bastard, have you no sense of responsibility? Any idea about devotion? Honesty? Altruism? Don't these words remind you of anything other than pulling your readers' legs or putting out an amusing message for some boob who's been seduced? You know what brotherhood means?"

Galip was about to say, "I do!" not to defend Jelal but because the question appealed to him. But Mehmet on the other end of the line—which Mehmet was this Muhammad?—was swearing a blue streak executed with massive and pathetic zeal.

"Shut up!" he said, having finally exhausted his swear words. "Enough!" Galip realized he was speaking to his wife who was still weeping in one corner in the ensuing silence. He heard the woman's voice explain something and the radio being turned off.

"You knew she's my cousin, so you wrote smart-aleck articles belittling family romance," continued the voice claiming to be Mehmet. "Even though you know full well half the young people in this country marry their aunts' sons, the other half their uncles' daughters, you nonchalantly penned scandalous pieces mocking marriage between close relatives. No, Mister Jelal, I didn't marry her because I had no opportunity to meet another girl in my life, nor because I feared women who aren't my relatives, nor because I was unable to believe that any woman aside from my mother or my aunts and their daughters could either love me sincerely or patiently put up with me; I married this woman because I loved her. Can you imagine what it is like to love a girl who's been your playmate since your childhood? Can you imagine what it is like to love only one woman all your life? For fifty years, I loved this woman who's now weeping on your behalf. I loved her since my childhood, do you understand? I still love her. You have any idea what love means? You have any idea what it is like to look longingly at someone who complements you like the awareness of your own body in a dream? You have any idea what love is? Have these words ever served you other than as material for the disgraceful literary sleights of hand you produce for your retarded readers who're all too ready to believe your fairy tales? I pity you. I despise you. I feel sorry for you. What else have you done with your life aside from turning a phrase and diddling with words? Answer me!"

"My dear friend," Galip said, "it's my profession."

"His profession!" cried the voice on the other end. "You seduced, deceived, degraded us all! I used to believe in you so much, I agreed with your pompous essays which proved mercilessly that my whole life was nothing but a parade of misery, a series of stupidities and delusions, a hell of nightmares, and a masterpiece of mediocrity based on pitifulness, pettiness, and vulgarity. What's more, instead of realizing I was being debased and despised, I used to be proud of having met someone who possessed such lofty ideas and a mighty pen, and of having talked to him and once served with him in the military coup whose boat was stove in the moment it was launched. You damn crook, I admired you so much that when you pointed out not only my cowardice as the author of all the misery in my life, but this nation's cowardice as a whole, I used to wonder what error in my ways had made cowardice a way of life, imagining you, who I now know to be a bigger coward than I, as the paragon of valor. I worshipped you so much that I read every one of your columns, even those discussing the remembrances of your youth which were no different from anyone else's, but you wouldn't know that since you weren't interested in the slightest in the rest of us. I read those columns on the smell of fried onions in the dark stairwell of the apartment building where you spent your childhood; I read the ones on your dreams with ghosts and witches as well as the nonsense concerning your metaphysical experiments; not only did I read them, hundreds of times, to detect the miracle they might contain but I had my wife read them, and after discussing them for hours in the evening I used to imagine that the only thing worth believing was the secret meaning signified therein and ended up convincing myself that I understood the secret meaning, which turns out to be devoid of meaning."

"I never wanted to foster that kind of admiration," Galip ventured to say.

"What a lie! You spent your literary career looking to sucker in people like me. You wrote back, you asked for their pictures, you examined their handwriting, you pretended to divulge secrets, sentences, magic words . . ."

"All in the interest of the revolution, the Day of Judgment, the coming of the Messiah, the hour of liberation . . ."

"And then what? What happens when you give it up?"

"Well, at least the readership could believe in something after all."

"They believed in you and that's what turned you on . . . Listen, I admired you so greatly that when I read a particularly brilliant essay of yours I'd jump up and down in my chair, tears pouring down my eyes; I couldn't sit still but paced up and down in the room and out in the street, dreaming of you. And that is not all, I thought so much about you that, after a certain point, the distinction between our two persons would disappear in the mist and smoke of my imagination. No, I was never too far gone to imagine I was the author of the work. Remember, I am not a mental case, just one of your loyal readers. But it seemed to me as if I had some share, in some strange fashion, in ways too complicated to be readily demonstrated, in the creation of your brilliant sentences, your clever inventions and ideas. As if it weren't for me, you wouldn't be hatching those ideas. Don't get me wrong, I'm not talking about the stuff you cribbed from me, stealing without even once considering to ask for my permission. I am not speaking of all that Hurufism has inspired in me, nor about my discoveries at the end of my book which I had such difficulty publishing. They were yours anyway. What I'm trying to explain is the feeling of having thought the same thing conjointly, the feeling as if I too had my share in your success. You know what I'm saying?"

"I do," Galip said. "I'd also written something along the same lines."

"Yes, in that notorious piece that was run again due to a mishap, but you don't really understand me; if you had, you'd have immediately joined in. That's why I'm going to kill you, exactly why! For feigning to understand although you never have, for having the temerity to insinuate yourself into our souls and showing up in our dreams at night, even though you have never been with any of us. All those years when I read all your work as if devouring it, having convinced myself that I too had a share in those brilliant pieces, I used to try recalling that in happier times when we were friends we had talked about, or might have talked about, and come up with something similar. I was so involved in thinking about this and dreaming about you that whenever I came across one of your fans, the incredible praise spoken about you seemed to be about me; it was as if I were as famous as you. The gossip about your mysterious secret life seemed to prove that I was not just another person but someone who had become partially infected by your godlike thrall, as if I too were a legendary figure like you. I'd get all worked up; on account of you, I'd become someone else. During the initial years, whenever I overheard a couple of citizens discuss you over their paper on the Municipal Lines ferry, I had an urge to shout out with all my might, 'I happen to know Jelal Salik, and quite well, too!' and to divulge secrets you and I shared in common, taking pleasure in their surprise and admiration. Later on, this urge became even stronger; should I happen to come across a couple of people reading or talking about you, I immediately wanted to announce, 'Gentlemen, you are very close to Jelal Salik, so close, in fact that I happen to be Jelal Salik himself!' The idea seemed so intoxicating and cataclysmic that every time I thought of speaking out, my heart began to pound, drops of sweat stood on my forehead, and I came close to passing out imagining the admiration in those astonished people's faces. The reason I never shouted out that sentence victoriously and joyfully was not because I thought it was silly or exaggerated, but because it was enough that it flashed across my mind. You know what I'm saying?"

"I do."

"I used to read what you wrote victoriously, feeling that I was as intelligent as you. They weren't applauding only you but also me, I was sure of it. We were together, far from the crowds. I understood you all too well. Like you, I too now hated those crowds who went to the movies, soccer games, fairs, and festivals. You thought they'd never amount to anything, coming up, as they do, with the same old stupidities and falling for the same old stories; not only were they the victims in their most heartbreaking tear-jerking moment of misery and destitution when they seemed at their most innocent, they were at the same time also the culprits or at least collaborators in crime. I am sick and tired of their false saviors, their most recent prime ministers and their latest stupidities, their military coups, their democracy, their torture, their movies. That's why I loved you. As I thrilled to think every time I finished reading another piece of your work, I'd say, gripped by an entirely new excitement, tears streaming down my eyes, 'That's why I love Jelal Salik!' Until yesterday when I sang like a mockingbird, proving to you that I remembered all your old pieces text and paragraph, would you have ever imagined that you'd have such a reader as me?"

"Perhaps, somewhat . . ."

"Listen, in that case . . . In a remote point of my own pitiful life, during a tasteless, commonplace moment of our ignominious world when one of my fingers was mashed by a *dolmuş* door slammed on it by some crude beast, having to endure a worthless wise guy while I was trying to put together the

necessary papers with the object of securing a small increment on my retirement pay—that is, smack dab in the middle of my destitution—I'd suddenly get hold of this thought as if grabbing onto a life buoy: 'What would
Jelal Salik have done in this situation? What would he have said? I wonder
if I'm acting like him?' Last twenty years, the question became like a sickness.
Getting in the circle to dance the *halay* with the other guests just to be
accommodating at a relative's wedding, or laughing with pleasure upon
winning the round of gin rummy at the neighborhood coffeehouse where I
go to kill time playing cards, it would suddenly occur to me: 'Would Jelal
do this?' This was enough to ruin my whole evening, my whole life. I spent
my entire life asking myself, What would Jelal Salik do now, What's Jelal
Salik doing now, What's Jelal Salik thinking of now. If that were all, it
would be fine and dandy. As if that weren't enough, another question would
hook into my mind: 'I wonder what Jelal Salik thinks about me?' When I
reasoned that you would never ever remember me, nor think of me, that I
would never even cross your mind, the question would take another form:
'What would Jelal Salik think of me if he saw me now?' What would Jelal
Salik say if he saw me still in my pajamas after breakfast, smoking away?
What would Jelal Salik think if he'd witnessed me scold the creep who
bothered the miniskirted married lady who sat next to him on the ferryboat?
How would Jelal Salik feel if he knew I clip all his columns and file them
in ONKA brand binders? What would Jelal Salik say if he came to know all
my thoughts about him and about life?"

"My dear reader and friend," Galip said, "tell me, why haven't you looked
me up all these years?"

"Can you imagine I didn't think of it? I was scared. Don't get me wrong,
I wasn't afraid of being misunderstood, of being unable to help myself
toadying up which goes with the territory, of brownnosing you as if your
most ordinary statements were great marvels, or imagining that's what you
wanted, of laughing out of place in a way that was not all right with you.
I'd gone much beyond all the possible scenarios I'd imagined a thousand
times."

"You are smarter than what those scenarios suggest," Galip said kindly.

"I was afraid that once we met and I, in all sincerity, delivered myself of
the sort of flattery and adulation I just mentioned, we'd have nothing further
to say."

"But, see, it didn't turn out like that at all," Galip said. "See, we ended
up having a good time chewing the fat."

There was a silence.

"I'm going to kill you," said the voice. "I will kill you. You are the reason why I could never be myself."

"No one is ever himself."

"You've written that a lot, but you could never feel it like me; you could have never understood that fact as I do . . . What you call 'mystery' was your knowing it without understanding it, writing the truth without getting it. No one could ever discover this truth without first being at one with himself. If he does discover it, then it also means that he hasn't managed to become himself. Are you into the paradox?"

"I am both myself and also another," Galip said.

"No dice, you don't say it as if you mean it," said the man on the other end of the line. "That's why you'll have to die. Just as in your writing, you convince without having the conviction yourself, and you succeed in making others believe because you yourself don't believe. But people you've managed to deceive are gripped by terror when they realize you can convince but have no conviction."

"Terror of what?"

"Of what you call 'mystery.' Don't you get it? I'm afraid of that ambiguity, of that game of dissimulation called writing, of the obscure faces of letters. Reading you all those years, I felt that I was both there, where I read at my desk or in my chair, and also somewhere entirely different with the author of the narrative. Do you have any idea what it means to be deceived by disbelievers? Knowing that those who persuade you aren't persuaded themselves? I am not complaining because you are the reason why I could never be myself. My poor pathetic life was enriched; I became you, thereby escaping the dreariness of my own tiresome inanity, but I am not at all certain about the magical entity I call 'you.' I don't know, but I know without knowing it. Can that be called knowing? Apparently I did know where my wife of thirty years vanished after leaving me a goodbye letter that explained nothing on the dining table, but I hadn't known that I knew it. It was because I didn't know that I went through the city with a fine-tooth comb, not searching for you but for her. But as I was looking for her, I was also, without being aware of it, looking for you, given that I had this terrible thought in my head even on the first day I began trying to solve the mystery of Istanbul going at it street by street: 'I wonder what Jelal Salik would say if he knew my wife suddenly left me?' I'd come to think the situation was 'a predicament that was pure Jelal Salik.' I wanted to tell you everything. I thought the subject was the perfect subject to discuss with you that I'd been looking for but didn't manage to come up with all these years. I was so excited that I had the nerve for the first time to get in touch with you, but I couldn't find you anywhere; you were nowhere. I knew it, but I did not know it. I had several phone numbers for you that I'd acquired just in case I might call you someday. I called all those, but you weren't there. I called your relatives, the aunt who's fond of you, your stepmother who adores you, your father who cannot control his feelings for you, and your uncle; they are all very concerned but you weren't there. I went to the *Milliyet* offices, you weren't there either. Others were looking for you at the paper, like your cousin and your sister's husband, Galip, who wanted to arrange for British TV people to interview you. I followed him around on an impulse, thinking that this dreamy kid, this somnambulist, might just know Jelal's whereabouts. Not only would he know, I said to myself, he'd also know that he knows. I followed him all over Istanbul like a shadow. He in the lead and I following him at a distance, we hit the streets, went in brownstone business buildings, old shops, glass arcades, grungy movie theaters, we went all over the Covered Bazaar, out to slums without sidewalks, over bridges, to dark places and obscure districts in Istanbul, wading through dust, mud, and filth. We never reached the destination but still kept going. We walked on as if we knew Istanbul well but didn't recognize it. I lost him, then found him, only to lose him again: I found him once more, then lost him again. Once, when I lost him again, he was the one who found me in a ramshackle nightclub. There, sitting around the table, each of us told a story to the group. I like telling stories but I can never find an audience. But they were listening this time. In the middle of my story, as my audience's curious and impatient eyes tried reading the end of the story in my face, and, as is always the case, fearful that my face might give away the ending, as I went back and forth between the story and such thoughts, I realized that my wife had left me for you. 'I'd known she'd gone to Jelal,' I thought. I knew it but hadn't known that I knew it. What I was looking for must have been this state of mind. I'd finally succeeded in going through a door in my psyche to enter a new realm. For the first time after all these years, I'd managed simultaneously being both someone else and also myself as I'd always wanted. On one hand, I felt like saying something phony like, 'I took this story from a newspaper column'; on the other hand, I felt I'd finally relaxed into the peace of mind that I'd been seeking all these years. I read your old columns in order to locate where I might find you, ending up going through Istanbul street by street, beating the jumble of sidewalks, muddy landings in front of stores, and watching the sorrow in the faces of our compatriots. But I'd concluded my story and figured out where my wife had gone. What's more, while I listened to the stories told by the waiter and the tall writer, I'd foreseen the terrible denouement that I just mentioned: I'd been deceived all my life, I'd always been taken in! My God! My God! Does any of this make sense to you?"

"It does."

"Listen, in that case. I've concluded that the truth you had us all running after all these years under the guise of 'mystery,' the truth that you knew without knowing it and wrote without understanding it, was this: No one can ever be himself in this land! In the land of the defeated and oppressed, to be is to be someone else. I am someone else; therefore, I am. All right, so what if the person with whom I want to trade places happens to be someone else? That's why I say I've been seduced and deceived. The person I read and trusted could not have stolen the wife of someone who idolized him. I wanted to shout out to the whores, waiters, photographers, and cuckolded husbands around the table telling stories in the middle of the night, saying: 'Hey you defeated! Hey you wretches! Hey you accursed! Hey you neglected! Hey you inconsequential! Don't be afraid, no one is himself, but no one! Not even the kings, the privileged, the sultans, the stars, the rich and the famous with whom you want to trade places. Liberate yourselves of them! It's in their absence that you will find the story they tell you as if it were a secret. Kill them off! Establish your own secret yourselves, find your own secret!' You know what I'm saying? I will kill you, not out of a cuckolded husband's brute outrage and vengeance but because I don't want to be roped into your new world. That's when all of Istanbul, all the letters, the signs, and the faces you arranged into your writing will regain their true mystery. 'Jelal Salik Has Been Shot!' the headlines will read: 'A Mysterious Murder.' And the 'Mysterious Murder' will never be solved. Our world's dubious meaning will perhaps be completely lost and, just before the Messiah you keep talking about shows up in Istanbul, there will be anarchy; but for me and many others that will be the rediscovery of mystery that has been lost; that is, no one will be able to solve the secret behind this business. What else could it be but the rediscovery of the mystery you know all too well? The same mystery I talked about in my modest book which I was able to get published through your help."

"Not so," Galip said. "You go ahead and commit the most mysterious of murders, but they—the privileged and the downtrodden, the stupid and the neglected—would all get together and make up a story proving that there is no mystery involved. Their hoked-up story which they'll readily fall for will transform my death into a colorless piece about conspiracy of the garden variety. Even before my funeral is over, everyone will have decided that my death was the result of a conspiracy that endangered our national integrity, or else of an intrigue that went on for years involving love and jealousy. They'll end up saying the murderer turns out to be an agent of drug traffickers or one of the organizers of a coup d'état; it turns out the murder was instigated by the Nakşibendi order or an organization of politicized pimps; it turns out the dirty deed was arranged by the grandsons of the deposed sultan or flag burners; it turns out the trick was the work of persons who have designs against the Republic and democracy or persons who are hatching up the Crusade to End All Crusades aimed against the whole Islamic world!

"The corpse of the columnist is mysteriously found in the middle of an Istanbul garbage dump among vegetable peelings, carcasses of dogs, and lottery tickets, or out on a muddy sidewalk . . . How else can you get it through to these losers that the mystery on the shore of oblivion still walks incognito among us? Somewhere way down deep, buried in our past, among the dregs of our memories, lost among words and sentences. And that we need to discover this mystery?

"I say this on the strength of thirty years of experience writing," Galip said. "They don't remember anything, not a single thing. Besides, it's not a foregone conclusion that you'll manage to find me and pull off the job. At best, you'll manage hitting me in a nonlethal spot and wounding me needlessly. What's worse, while they beat the living daylights out of you at the police station—to say nothing of torture—I'll become the hero you didn't intend, one who has to put up with the prime minister's stupidities paying his get-well visit. Rest assured, it ain't worth it. They no longer have any desire to believe that there is an unattainable secret behind the visible."

"Who's going to prove to me that my whole life was not just a hoax, a bad joke?"

"Me!" Galip said. "Listen . . ."

"*Bishnov*," he said in Persian. "No, I won't stand for it."

"Believe me, I too fell for it like you."

"I'll believe it," Mehmet cried with ardor. "I'll believe it so that I can rescue the meaning of my own life. But what about the apprentice quilt makers trying to spell out the lost meaning of their lives on the strength of the codes you've stuck into their hands? What about the dreamy virgins who imagine the furniture, the orange-juice machines, the fish-shaped lamps, and the lacy linens they'll have in Paradise as you promised, waiting in vain for their fiancés who will neither return from Germany nor ever send for them? And what's to become of the retired bus-ticket collectors who, using the procedure they've learned in your columns, have managed to see in their own faces the floor plans of the condos they'll own outright in Paradise? What about the land surveyors, the gas-bill collectors, the *simit* vendors, the beggars (see, how I can't get rid of your words?) who, inspired by the numerical values of letters as given in your columns, calculate the day of the Messiah's advent in the cobblestone streets, who will save us all in this miserable land? And our sundries man, the attar, from Kars, and your readers, your pathetic readers, who've figured out, thanks to you, that the mythical bird that they seek is in fact themselves?"

"Forget it," Galip said, fearful that the voice on the phone might, out of habit, keep going on with the list. "Forget them, forget it all, don't think of any of them. Consider instead the last Ottoman sultans going around incognito. Consider the traditional methods of Beyoğlu hoods who routinely torture their victims before killing them just in case they have gold or secrets stashed away. Consider why the color touch-up artists always paint the sky Prussian blue, and our muddy land the color of English lawns on the black-and-white pictures of mosques, dancers, bridges, beauty queens, and soccer players cut out from magazines, such as *Life, Sound, Sunday, Post, 7-Days, Fan, Girls, Review, Week,* that hang on the walls of two-thousand-five-hundred barber shops. Consider all the Turkish dictionaries you have to plow through to find the hundreds of thousands of words describing the thousands of smells, their origins, and the ten thousands of their mixtures that fill our dark and narrow stairwells."

"You bastard writer, you!"

"Consider the mysterious reason why the first steamboat the Turks ever bought from England had been christened *Swift.* Consider the left-handed calligrapher's obsession with order and symmetry who, being a student of telling fortunes by reading coffee grounds, reproduced the bottoms of the thousands of cups of coffee he drank in his lifetime, showing the pictorial representations of his fortune which he then appended with his beautiful calligraphy and produced a three-hundred-page handwritten masterpiece."

"You aren't deceiving me anymore."

"Consider that when all the wells dug in the gardens in the city for hundreds of thousands of years were filled with cement and stone in order to build foundations for high-rises, the scorpions, frogs, grasshoppers, and all manner of bright Ligurian, Phrigian, Roman, Byzantine, and Ottoman gold coins, the rubies, diamonds, crosses, representational paintings, and forbidden icons, books and treatises, maps for buried treasure, and unfortunate skulls of murder victims whose killers remain unknown . . ."

"Here comes the corpse of Shams of Tabriz again, huh? Tossed down the well."

". . . the concrete that they support, the steel, all the apartments, the doors, the elderly doormen, the parquet floors where the cracks in between turn black like dirty fingernails, the troubled mothers, the angry fathers, the refrigerator doors that won't stay shut, the sisters, the half sisters . . ."

"Do you get to play Shams of Tabriz? Or the Dadjdjal? The Messiah?"

". . . the cousin who's married the half sister, the hydraulic elevator, the mirror in the elevator . . ."

"Enough already, you've already written all that."

". . . the secret corners the children discover to play in, the bedspreads saved for trousseaus, the length of silk that grandfather's grandfather bought from a Chinese merchant when he was the governor of Damascus which no one has been able to bring herself to cut . . ."

"You're handing me a line, right?"

". . . consider the very mystery of our lives. Consider the sharp straight razor called 'the cipher,' which old-time executioners used to lop the heads off their hanged victims' bodies in order to display them on pedestals as a deterrent. Consider the vision of the retired colonel who renamed chess pieces, calling the king 'mother,' the queen 'father,' the rook 'uncle,' the knight 'aunt,' and the pawns 'jackals' and not 'children.' "

"You know, after you betrayed us, I saw you only once in all those years, masquerading as Mehmet the Conqueror, perhaps, in a strange Hurufi getup."

"Consider the immutable serenity of the man who on an ordinary evening sits down at the table to solve enigmas in divan poems, and crossword puzzles in the paper. Consider that everything in the room, aside from the papers and letters lit by the lamp on the table, remains in the dark, all the ashtrays, the curtains, clocks, time, memories, pain, sorrow, deception, anger, defeat—ah, defeat! Consider that you can only compare the freedom from gravity you feel while you are in the mysterious vacuum created by the movements down and across of a crossword puzzle's letters to the unappeasable fascination with going incognito."

"Look here, friend," said the voice on the other end of the line, assuming a know-how tone which surprised Galip, "let's put aside for now all the fascinations and the games, as well as the letters and their twins; we've gone past all that, we're beyond that stuff. Yes, I tried setting you up, but it didn't work. You already know it, but let me spell it out for you. Not only was your name not in the phone book; there never was a military coup or any file on it! We love you, we think about you all the time, both of us are your admirers, real fans. Our lives were always devoted to you and will remain so. Let us now forget all that needs to be forgotten. Tonight, Emine and I can come and see you. We'll pretend nothing has happened, we'll talk as if nothing ever had. You can go on and on for hours just as you've been doing. Please, say yes! Trust us, I'll do anything you want, bring you anything you wish!"

Galip thought it over for quite a while. Then he said, "Let's hear these telephone numbers and addresses you've got on me!"

"Sure enough, but I won't be able to erase them out of my mind."

"Just go ahead and give them to me."

When the man went to get his book, his wife got on the phone.

"Trust him," she said in a whisper. "He's really contrite this time, in all sincerity. He loves you very much. He was going to do something crazy, but he's already given it up. He'll take it all out on me; he won't go after you; he's a coward, I guarantee it. I thank God for having put everything right. Tonight I'll wear the blue-checkered skirt that you liked so much. My darling, we'll do whatever you want, both him and me! Let me just tell you this, though: Not only does he try to emulate you in the Hurufi Mehmet the Conqueror costume but he also tries to read the letters on the faces of your whole family . . ." She fell silent as her husband's footsteps approached.

When the husband got back on the phone, Galip began to write down the phone numbers and addresses, which he had the voice on the other end of the line repeat many times, in the last page of a book (*Les Caractères*, La Bruyère) he pulled out of the shelf next to him. He planned to tell them that he'd changed his mind and didn't want to see them, that he didn't have much time to waste on persistent readers. He was thinking of something else. Much later, recalling approximately all that happened that night, he'd say, "I think I was curious. I was curious to take a look at the pair from a distance. Perhaps my motivation was being able to tell Jelal and Rüya, after having located them through these phone numbers and addresses, not only this incredible story and the phone conversations but also what this strange husband and wife looked like, how they walked, what they were wearing."

"I won't give my home address," he said. "But we could meet somewhere else. Nine o'clock tonight, say, in front of Aladdin's store."

Even this bit pleased the husband and wife so much that Galip was made uncomfortable by the gratitude on the other end of the line. Would Jelal Bey prefer that they bring an almond cake or else petit fours from the Lifespan Cake Shop? Seeing how they'd be sitting down for a long chat, how about nuts and stuff and a large bottle of cognac?

When the weary husband cried, "I'll bring along my photograph collection, the mug shots, and the pictures of the high-school girls too!" and gave a frightening laugh, Galip realized an open bottle of cognac must have been sitting between the husband and wife for quite a while. They repeated the time and the place of the meeting enthusiastically and hung up.

Chapter Thirty-three

MYSTERIOUS PAINTINGS

I appropriated the mystery from the Mathnawi. —ŞEYH GALIP

The grandest of all dens of iniquity, not only in Istanbul and all of Turkey but in all the Balkans and the Middle East, was opened in the summer of 1952, on the first Saturday in June to be exact, on one of the narrow streets off the red-light district in Beyoğlu which go up to the British Consulate. The happy occasion fell on the same date as the outcome of a hotly contested painting competition that had lasted six months. The famous Beyoğlu mobster who owned the place, a fellow who would eventually become legendary by virtue of having disappeared into the waters of the Bosphorus in his Cadillac, had set his heart on getting scenes of Istanbul painted on the walls of his establishment's spacious lobby.

The mobster hadn't commissioned these paintings in order to become a patron of this art form, which remained terribly undeveloped in our culture thanks to the prohibition against it in Islam (I mean painting, not prostitution), but for the purpose of supplying his distinguished clients, who came to his pleasure palace from all sectors in the city and the country, with the enchantments of Istanbul along with music, drugs, alcohol, and girls. When our mobster was turned down by academic painters who would only accept commissions for bank buildings (armed as these painters are with protractors and triangles in order to represent our village damsels in the shape of rhomboids in imitation of Western cubist art), he'd called for the artisans, sign painters, and craftsmen who ornament the ceilings of provincial mansions, the walls of outdoor movie theaters, and gussy up vans, carts, and snakeswallower's tents at local fairs. And when the only two artisans to come forth after many months both claimed, as do real artists, to be the better craftsman, our racketeer, taking his cue from bank presidents, put up a large sum of prize money and set up a contest between the competing artisans for the "Best Painting of Istanbul," offering the two ambitious contestants opposite walls in the lobby of his pleasure palace.

Right off, the two artists, being suspicious of each other, had put up a thick curtain between them. One hundred and eighty days later, on the night the pleasure palace was inaugurated, the same patched curtain was still in place in the lobby, now full of gilt chairs upholstered in crimson waled velvet, Holbein rugs, silver candelabras, crystal vases, portraits of Atatürk, porcelain plates, and stands inlaid with mother-of-pearl. When the boss pulled the sackcloth curtain aside for the distinguished crowd among whom even the governor was present in his official capacity (after all, the joint was formally registered as the Preservation of Classical Turkish Arts Club), the guests beheld a splendid view of Istanbul on one wall and on the wall directly opposite it a mirror that made the painting, in the light of the silver candelabras, appear even finer, more brilliant, and more attractive than the original.

Naturally, the prize went to the artist who'd installed the mirror. Yet for years afterward many of the customers who found themselves in the clutches of the vice joint were so bewitched by the incredible images on the walls that, experiencing various delights in either masterpiece, they'd walk up and down between the two walls, viewing both works for hours on end, trying to figure out the mystery of the pleasure they felt.

The scrawny, miserable mongrel eyeing the lunch stand in a market scene on the first wall was transformed into a sad but cunning beast when you looked at the reflection in the mirror opposite, yet when you went back to the painting on the first wall, you perceived not only the dog's cunningness, which must have been there all along in the original, but also a suggestion of movement that aroused your further suspicions; crossing the room once more for a confirming glance in the mirror, you saw strange stirrings that might explain the nature of that movement, and now, completely bewildered, you found it difficult to hold yourself back from running over to look again at the original painting on the first wall.

A nervous old customer had once detected that the dry fountain in the painting, located on the square that hooked up with the street patrolled by the sad dog, ran like crazy in the mirror. When he went back to the painting again, flustered like an absentminded dotard who suddenly remembers that he's left the water tap on back home, he realized that the fountain was in fact dry; yet, when he witnessed water gush even more abundantly in the mirror this time, he sought to share his revelation with the women who worked there, but meeting with indifference on their part, for they were sick and tired of hearing about the mirror's tricks, he pulled back into his solitary life, the essence of which is, and has always been, not being understood.

Yet in fact the women who worked for the joint were not indifferent; on snowy winter nights when they lolled around telling each other the same old fairy tales, they made use of the painting's tricks, and those of the mirror opposite it, as an amusing touchstone to gauge the personalities of their clients. There were the hasty, insensitive, anxious ones who did not notice in the slightest the mysterious discrepancies between the painting and its reflection. These were men who either kept going on and on about their own problems or else expected to get pronto the only thing men want from bordello girls whom they can't even tell apart. There were others who were totally wise to the play between the mirror and the painting but didn't make anything of it; these were men who'd already been through too much to be perturbed by anything, fearless men who were to be feared. Then there were others who bedeviled the B-girls, the waiters, and the gangsters with their apprehensions, and who, as if they were suffering from some obsession with symmetry, childishly demanded that the discrepancy between the painting and the mirror be corrected as soon as possible. These were tightfisted, penurious individuals who could never let go of the world either drinking or making love; being stuck on bringing order into everything made them poor lovers and miserable friends.

Some time later, when the inmates of the pleasure palace had become inured to the dalliance of the mirror with the painting, the police chief, who frequently honored the joint with the kindness of his protective wings rather than the powers of his purse, came face-to-face in the mirror with a shady looking baldheaded fellow who was depicted toting a gun in a dark alley; that's when he had a hunch that this was the very perpetrator of the infamous "Şişli Square Murder" and, asserting that the artist who'd installed the mirror on the wall knew the mystery surrounding the murder, he'd launched an investigation into the artist's identity.

On another occasion, one sticky humid night in summer when the filthy water running down the sidewalks couldn't make it to the grate on the street corner before turning into steam, the son of a land baron, who'd left his father's Mercedes parked in front of a NO PARKING sign, seeing in the mirror the image of a good homemaker who wove rugs in her home in the slums, had concluded that she was the love of his life he'd been looking for; yet when he turned to the painting, he was only confronted by one of those sad colorless girls who inhabit his father's villages.

As far as the boss was concerned—himself slated to discover the other world within this one by driving his Cadillac into the waters of the Bosphorus as if it were his stallion—all the pleasant jokes, the pleasant coincidences, and the world's mystery were tricks perpetrated neither by the painting nor the mirror; customers high on drugs and booze, flying on clouds of woe and melancholy, rediscovered the golden age in their imaginations and, full of the joy of solving the mystery of that lost world, they confused the enigmas in their minds with the replica before their eyes. Despite his hardnosed realism, the famous gangster had been observed on Sunday mornings cheerfully joining in a game of "find the seven differences between the two pictures" with the children of the B-girls, the girls and boys waiting for their weary mothers to take them to the kids' matinee in Beyoğlu.

But the differences, the significances, and the mind-boggling transformations on the two walls were not merely seven, but endless. The representation of Istanbul on the first wall, although its technique was reminiscent of scenes painted on horse carts and on tents at local fairs, fetched up, in the mirror's treatment of its subject matter, unnerving associations with dark and creepy engravings. The mirror opposite showed the large bird floating in one corner of the fresco on the opposite wall as if it were beating its wings languorously like a mythic creature; the unpainted façades of ancient woodframe mansions in the fresco were transformed in the mirror into terrifying faces; fairgrounds and merry-go-rounds became livelier and more colorful in the mirror; old-fashioned streetcars, horse carts, minarets, bridges, murderers, pudding shops, parks, seaside cafés, Municipal Lines ferryboats, inscriptions, trunks were all transformed into signs of a realm that was altogether different. A black book the artist had prankishly stuck into the hand of a blind beggar turned into a two-part book in the mirror, a book with two meanings and two stories; yet, looking at the painting, one realized the book was of uniform consistency and that its mystery was lost in itself. Our domestic movie star with the red lips, bedroom eyes, and long lashes, whom the artist had depicted on the wall in the manner of fairground art, was transformed in the mirror into the poverty-stricken, big-breasted national mother figure;

then, casting another clouded glance back to the first wall, you recognized with horror and pleasure that the mother figure wasn't who she appeared to be but your wedded wife you'd been sleeping with all these years.

But what was most deeply disturbing at the pleasure palace were the new significances, the strange signs, the unknown worlds that appeared in the faces reflected in the mirror, the ones that belonged to the interminable multitudes on the bridges and in the streets, faces that appeared everywhere in the artist's creation. Looking first at the painting and then at the mirror, the befuddled customer could perceive that someone's visage (someone who appeared to be just an ordinary fellow or a happy-go-lucky guy wearing a melon hat) when reflected in the mirror was crawling with signs, with letters, that became transformed into a map or the traces of a missing story, giving certain viewers, who were now also contained in the mirror as they paced up and down among the velvet chairs, the impression that they were privy to a secret known only to an elite few. Everyone knew that such persons, whom the bordello girls treated like pashas, would not rest until they discovered the secret involving the painting and the mirror, and would be ready to set forth on all sorts of journeys, adventures, and free-for-alls for the sake of finding the solution to the enigma.

Many years later, long after the boss disappeared into the enigma of the Bosphorus and the pleasure palace fell into disrepute, the aging bordello girls took a look at the sorrow-laden visage of the police chief who'd dropped in, and they realized that he was one of the aforementioned restless souls. As it turned out, the chief had wanted to consult the mirror before reopening the case of the infamous Şişli Square Murder. But he discovered that during a brawl that broke out, more out of boredom than over a dispute involving women or money, the colossal mirror had come down on the rowdies and broken into smithereens. Thus, standing among shards of glass, the police chief, himself on the verge of retirement, could neither apprehend the perpetrator of the murder nor discover the secret of the mirror.

Chapter Thirty-four

NOT THE STORYTELLER,
THE STORY

*My way of writing is rather to think aloud, and follow my own humours,
than much to inquire who is listening to me.*
　　　　—THOMAS DE QUINCEY, *Confessions of an English Opium Eater*

The voice on the phone had given Galip seven different numbers just before
making the arrangement to meet in front of Aladdin's store. Galip was so
confident he'd reach Jelal and Rüya at one of those numbers that he could
visualize the streets, the doorsteps, and the apartment where he'd once more
get together with them. He knew that as soon as he saw them, he'd find the
reasons Jelal and Rüya would give for hiding out completely logical and
justifiable from beginning to end. He was certain Jelal and Rüya would say:
"Galip, we've been looking for you, but you were neither home nor at the
office. No one answered the phone. Where were you?"

Galip rose from the chair where he'd been sitting for hours, took off Jelal's
pajamas, washed, shaved, and got dressed. The letters he made out in his
face as he looked in the mirror didn't seem now like extensions of a mysterious
plot or a crazy game, nor a visual error that might lead to uncertainty about
his own identity. Like the bar of pink Lux soap endorsed by Silvana Mangano

or the old razor blade in front of the mirror, the letters too were part of the real world.

He read his own sentences as if they were someone else's in the piece which appeared in Jelal's usual place in the copy of *Milliyet* that had been slipped under the door. Considering that they'd been published under Jelal's picture, they had to be Jelal's sentences. On the other hand, Galip also knew he'd written the sentences himself. The situation didn't seem at all contradictory to him; on the contrary, it seemed no more than the extension of a known, comprehensible world. He imagined Jelal sitting in one of the apartments he had addresses for, reading someone else's work in his own column, but he guessed that Jelal wouldn't consider this as a personal attack on himself or an imposture. There was a good chance he wouldn't even be able to figure out that it wasn't one of his old pieces.

After feeding himself on bread, fish-roe spread, sliced tongue, and bananas, he wanted to strengthen his ties to the real world even more by bringing some order into business affairs of his that he'd neglected. He looked up a colleague with whom he collaborated on some political cases. The fellow had suddenly been called out of town, he was told. A certain case was progressing slowly, as usual, but in another a decision had been reached, and that the clients they represented had each been sentenced to six years for having harbored the founders of a clandestine Communist organization. When he remembered having glanced at the news item in the paper he'd just finished reading without connecting the story to himself, he got angry. He wasn't quite clear why he felt angry, or against whom. As if it were the only natural thing to do, he called home. "If Rüya picks it up," he thought, "I'm going to play a trick on her, too." He was going to disguise his voice and say he was someone looking for Galip, but there was no answer.

He called İskender. He was going to tell him that he was about to get hold of Jelal and ask how much longer the British television people were going to be in town. "This is their last night," İskender said. "They're leaving for London early in the morning." Galip explained he was about to track Jelal down, that Jelal wanted to see the Brits to set them straight on certain subjects; he too thought this was an important interview. "In that case, I'd better get in touch with them this evening," İskender said. "They are also keen on it." Galip said he was going to be "here for the time being" and read off the number on the receiver for Iskender.

He decided to call Aunt Halé. It had occurred to him that his relatives might have gone to the police because they hadn't heard from Jelal or Rüya. Or were all the family still waiting for his and Rüya's return from the Izmir trip he made up and told Aunt Halé about, saying that Rüya was sitting in a cab, waiting for him to finish the phone call he is making from a grocery store? Or had Rüya stopped by and told them everything? In the meantime, had there been any word from Jelal? He dialed Aunt Halé's number and, disguising his voice by lowering it, explained that he was a loyal reader and admirer who wanted to congratulate Jelal on today's column. Aunt Halé's sober response telling him no more than that Jelal wasn't there and referring him to the newspaper offices did not provide him with any explanation. At two-twenty, he began to call, one by one, the seven numbers he'd written on the last page of *Les Caractères*.

By the time he found out that of these seven numbers one belonged to a family he didn't know at all, one to the sort of mouthy kid everyone knows, one to a brusque, shrill old geezer, one to a kebab shop, one to a know-it-all realtor who hadn't been so much as curious about the people who previously had the same number, one to a seamstress who said she had had the same number for the last forty years, and the last to newlyweds who had got home late, it was seven in the evening. At some point during the time he struggled with the phone, he'd found ten snapshots in the bottom of a box full of postcards which he hadn't been previously interested in going through at all.

This was an eleven-year-old Rüya curiously staring into the camera which had to have been in Jelal's hands, taken on an excursion on the Bosphorus, at the café under the famed elm tree, with Uncle Melih wearing a coat and tie, beautiful Aunt Suzan who looked like Rüya when she was younger, and a weird sidekick of Jelal's or else someone who could have been the imam at the Emirgan Mosque . . . Rüya in the strapped dress she wore the summer between second and third grades, and Vasıf, who is showing Aunt Halé's then two-month-old kitten Coals the aquarium, with Mrs. Esma laughing with her eyes narrowed because of the cigarette between her lips and at the same time trying to shield herself from the camera by straightening her scarf although she isn't quite sure she is in the camera's field of vision . . . Rüya sleeping like a baby on Grandma's bed, her knees pulled up to her stomach and her head stuck straight into the pillow, in the same pose Galip had seen her last seven days and ten hours ago, tired after stuffing herself on the communal Ramadan holiday lunch which she's made it to unexpectedly on a winter's day, although alone, during the first year of her first marriage when the revolutionary and unkempt Rüya didn't have much truck with her mother, uncles, and aunts . . . The whole family and the doorman Ismail and his wife Kamer posing in front of the Heart-of-the-City Apartments, looking into the camera while a beribboned Rüya on Jelal's lap watches a street dog on the sidewalk who must be long dead . . . Aunt Suzan, Mrs.

Esma, and Rüya observing the passage of De Gaulle, who doesn't make it into the photograph other than the nose of his limo, through the crowd that has lined up on Teşvikiye Avenue along both sidewalks all the way from the girls' lycée to Aladdin's store . . . Rüya, sitting at her mother's vanity covered with powder pots, tubes of Pertev's cold cream, vials of rosewater and cologne, perfume atomizers, nail files and bobby pins, having stuck her head with its bobbed hair between the two side panels of the mirror becomes three, five, nine, seventeen, and thirty-three Rüyas . . . Fifteen-year-old Rüya in a printed cotton sleeveless dress, unaware that her picture is being snapped, leans over a newspaper on which sunshine spills through the window, doing the crossword puzzle, a bowl of roasted chickpeas next to her, wearing the expression on her face which makes Galip realize with fear that he's being excluded, tugging her hair and chewing on the eraser of her pencil . . . Rüya five months ago at most, seeing that she's wearing the Hittite Sun medallion Galip had given her on her last birthday, laughing happily in this very room where Galip had been pacing for hours, sitting in the chair in which Galip presently sat, next to the phone on which he'd just finished talking . . . Rüya pulling a long face at some country café Galip couldn't place, saddened on account of parents' fights that get terribly intense on excursions . . . Rüya, trying to look happy but wearing the wistful, dolorous smile the mystery of which her husband, looking at photographs, has never been able to fathom, on Kilyos beach where she went the year she graduated from high school, the ocean breaking behind her, her beautiful arm resting proprietorially on the carrier of a bicycle that's not hers, wearing a bikini which exposes her appendicitis scar, the twin moles the size of lentils halfway between the scar and her navel, and the barely perceptible shadows of her rib cage on her silken skin, holding a magazine the title of which Galip couldn't make out not because the photograph isn't focused but because of the tears in his eyes.

Now Galip was weeping inside the mystery. It was as if he were someplace he knew but didn't know he knew, as if he were immersed in a book he'd read before but which still excited him because he didn't remember having read it. He knew that he had felt the sense of doom and deprivation before and yet, at the same time, that this pain was so powerful that it could be felt only once in a lifetime. He considered the pain of having been deceived, of his illusion and loss, too specific to happen to anyone else, yet he felt that it was the outcome of a trap someone had set up as if setting up a game of chess.

He didn't wipe off the tears that fell on Rüya's photographs, he had a hard time breathing through his nose, and he sat in his chair without moving.

Friday-night noises on Nişantaşı Square came into the room; the sound of the tired motors on overloaded buses, car horns that got blown willy-nilly in the snarled traffic, whistles of the traffic cop hot under the collar, the ebb and flow of pop tunes from the loudspeakers set up by music shops at the arcade's entrances, and the steady hum of the crowds on the sidewalks reverberated not only in the windowpanes but also ever so slightly in the objects in the room. As he focused on the reverberations in the room, Galip remembered that furniture and objects had their own private world that remained outside of the daily environment shared by everyone. "Getting deceived is getting deceived," he said to himself. He repeated this expression so many times that the words were emptied of both meaning and pain as they were transformed into sounds and letters that signified nothing.

He constructed fantasies: He was not here in this room but with Rüya at their own place on a Friday night; and after getting a bite somewhere, they were going to the Palace Theater. Afterwards, they'd get night-owl editions of the morning papers and settle down back home with their papers and books. In another story he dreamed up, someone, a phantom-faced person, was saying: "I've known for years who you are, but you didn't even recognize me." When he remembered the phantom man who said this, he realized that this person had been keeping an eye on him all these years. Then, it also followed that the man had been watching not Galip but Rüya. Galip had secretly watched Rüya and Jelal once, and he was freaked out in a way he hadn't expected. "It was as if I'd died and were watching life continue at a distance after my demise." He sat down at Jelal's desk and immediately wrote a column that began with this sentence and signed Jelal's name to it. He was certain that someone was watching him. If not someone, at least an eye.

The noise of Nişantaşı Square was gradually being replaced by the roar of the TV sets in the buildings next door. He heard the signal music for the eight o'clock news, realizing that six million Istanbulites had gathered around their dining room tables to watch TV. He felt like whacking off. But he was distracted by the continual presence of the eye. He had such a strong desire to be himself, only himself, that he felt like smashing up all the stuff in the room and killing those who'd brought him to this pass. He was considering pulling the phone off the wall and tossing it out the window when the contraption rang.

It was İskender. He'd talked to the BBC-TV people; they were excited and were expecting Jelal tonight at the Pera Palas, in a hotel room that had been set up for the taping. Had Galip got hold of Jelal?

"Yes, yes, yes!" said Galip, surprised by his own fury. "Jelal's ready. He has some important revelations to make. We'll be at the Pera Palas at ten."

After he hung up, he was seized by an excitement that vacillated between fear and happiness, calmness and anxiety, feelings of vengeance and the joy of brotherhood. Hastily, he searched through notebooks, papers, old articles, and news clippings, looking for something or other, but he didn't know what he was looking for, either. Some sign that would prove the existence of the letters on his face? But the letters and their meaning were too obvious to necessitate any proof. Some logic to help him choose the stories he had to tell? But he wasn't in any condition to trust in anything else but his own anger and excitement. Some example to reveal the beauty of the mystery? He knew the task required that he only tell his stories believing in what he said. He went through the cabinets, read quickly through the address books, he spelled out the "key sentences," looked at the maps, quickly glanced through the mug shots. He was poking through the box of costumery when, suffering the damning regret for being late on purpose, at three minutes to nine he dashed out of the house.

At two minutes after nine, he'd ducked into the dark entrance of the building opposite Aladdin's store, but nobody like his bald-headed interlocutor or the man's wife was anywhere on the sidewalk across the street. Galip tried to visualize the bald man's face, the way he told his story at the nightclub. He was angry at the man and the wife because the numbers they gave him turned out to be wrong: Who was deceiving who? Who was putting one over on who?

Only a small section of Aladdin's well-lit store could be seen through the window that was chock-full of stuff. Galip could make out Aladdin's head and body bending up and down among toy guns hanging on strings, rubber balls in net bags, orangutan and Frankenstein masks, boxes of parlor games, *rakı* and cordial bottles, sports and entertainment magazines in living color, and dolls in see-through boxes: he was counting the newspapers packed to be returned. There was no one else in the store. Aladdin's wife who worked behind the counter during the day must now be home in the kitchen, waiting for her husband. Someone went in the store, and Aladdin stepped behind the counter; soon after, an elderly couple who made Galip's heart skip showed up. Following the oddly dressed man who first went into the store, the elderly couple came out carrying a large bottle and walked off arm in arm; Galip knew instantly they weren't the ones because they seemed all too self-absorbed. A gentleman in a fur-collared overcoat went in and he and Aladdin began to talk. Galip couldn't help imagining their conversation.

Now there was no one that attracted attention, neither on the Nişantaşı Square sidewalk nor on the one next to the mosque, nor on the street off

Ihlamur: only absentminded people, salespersons without overcoats walking by briskly, the lonely who were overly lost in the dark-blue night. For the moment, the streets and the sidewalks were deserted; Galip thought he could hear the hum of the neon light advertising the store across the street that sold sewing machines. There was no one around besides the cop with a machine gun in his hand, keeping watch in front of the station. Galip felt frightened looking at the branches of the chestnut tree on the trunk of which Aladdin attached illustrated magazines with underwear elastic and clothespins. It was a feeling of being under surveillance, of being found out or being in danger. Then there was a noise. A '54 Dodge that came up Ihlamur and an old Skoda bus going up to Nişantaşı almost collided on the corner. When the bus braked hard and came to a stop, Galip observed the passengers pull themselves up and turn their heads toward the other side of the street. In the dim lights provided by the bus, not more than three feet from where he was standing, his eyes met the eyes in a tired face that didn't show any interest in the event: a sixtyish, exhausted man; his eyes were odd, full of pain and sorrow. Had he come across this man before? A retired lawyer, or a teacher waiting to die? Perhaps both were thinking of similar things when they stared at each other daringly thanks to a chance moment city life had afforded them. Once the bus tore off, they parted perhaps never to see each other again. Through the purple exhaust fumes, Galip observed some sort of movement commence on the other sidewalk. A couple of young men stood in front of Aladdin's store, lighting each other's cigarettes: two university students waiting for a third before going on to the Friday-night movies. Aladdin's store had become crowded, three people browsing through the magazines and a night watchman. An orange vendor with a huge mustache had arrived at the corner within an eyeblink, pushing his cart, but perhaps he'd been there for some time without Galip becoming aware of him. A couple walked up the sidewalk next to the mosque, carrying packages. Then Galip saw that a child was also being carried in the young father's arms. At the same moment, the elderly Greek lady who was the proprietress of the small cake shop right next door turned off the lights inside the shop and wrapping herself in her worn coat went out in the street. Smiling politely at Galip, she made a racket pulling down the metal rolling shutters with a hook. Aladdin's store and the sidewalks were suddenly deserted. The neighborhood lunatic from the upper district who imagined he was a famous soccer player came from the direction of the girls' lycée, wearing a blue and yellow soccer uniform, and passed by slowly pushing a baby carriage; he sold newspapers out of the baby carriage at the entrance of the Pearl

Theater at Pangaltı. As the wheels of the carriage turned they made music that Galip liked.

A light wind was blowing. Galip felt cold. It was twenty after nine. "I'll wait for three more people to go by," he thought. Now he could no longer see either Aladdin inside the store or the cop who should be in front of the station. The door to a narrow balcony in the apartment building across the street was opened, Galip saw the red tip of a lit cigarette; then the guy tossed the cigarette out and went in. Aside from the slight moisture on the sidewalk reflecting the metallic light from the neon lights and the billboards, there were bits of paper, refuse, cigarette butts, plastic bags . . . For a moment Galip felt the street he'd lived on since his childhood and which he'd observed with all its changing details, the neighborhood, and the chimneys of distant apartment buildings that were visible in the drab dark-blue of the night were as alien and as distant from him as the dinosaurs pictured in a children's book. Then he felt like the man with X-ray vision who he'd always wanted to be in his childhood: the world's secret meaning was visible to him. The letters in the billboards for the rug dealer, the restaurant, and the cake shop, the cakes in the display case, the croissants, sewing machines, and newspapers all really pointed to this secondary meaning, but the unfortunate people who beat the sidewalks like somnambulists, having forgotten the memories from the realm whose mystery was once known to them, eked out a living from the mere primary meaning that remained to them—like those who've forgotten about love, brotherhood, heroism and make do with what they see in the movies on the subject. He walked to Teşvikiye Square and took a cab.

As the taxi went by Aladdin's store, Galip imagined the bald-headed man was also hiding in a dark corner, just as he himself had, waiting for Jelal. Was he just imagining it? Or had he seen a scary, oddly dressed shadow among the enchanted scary bodies of frozen mannequins lit by neon lights, sewing on the machines in the window of the store where sewing machines were being displayed? For a moment he wasn't sure. At Nişantaşı Square, he stopped the cab and bought the night-owl edition of *Milliyet*. He read his own piece with surprise, playfulness, and curiosity as if he were reading Jelal, imagining at the same time Jelal reading someone else's piece published under his own name and picture; but he couldn't zero in on Jelal's reaction. He felt anger rise inside him against Jelal and Rüya: "You'll get what's coming to you!" he felt like saying. But he couldn't figure out exactly what it was in his mind that was coming to them: was it retribution or a reward? What's more, somewhere in his mind he had an image of running into them at the Pera Palas. The cab was going up the crooked streets in Tarlabaşı, past dark hotels and miserable coffeehouses with bare walls brimming over with men, when Galip had a feeling all Istanbul was anticipating something. Then he was surprised by how dilapidated the cars, the buses, and the trucks were that he saw in the streets, as if he'd become aware of this for the first time.

The lobby of the Pera Palas Hotel was warm and bright. In the large reception room on the right, İskender was sitting on one of the old divans and had joined some tourists in watching some sort of a crowd. It was a domestic film crew shooting the hotel's nineteenth-century decor to make a historical film. In the brightly lit room there was a feeling of fun, camaraderie, and cheer.

"Jelal isn't here, he couldn't come," Galip began explaining to İskender. "Something very important came up. He's been hiding out because of this mysterious business. He wanted me to do the interview in his place, again due to the same mystery. I've got the story down pat. I'll stand in for him."

"I don't know if these people will go along with that!"

"Just tell them I'm Jelal Salik," Galip said with rage which surprised even him.

"But why?"

"Because it's the story that's important, not the storyteller. We have a story to tell now."

"They know you," İskender said. "You even told a story at the club that night."

"Know me?" Galip said, sitting down. "You're using the word loosely. They've seen me is all. What's more, today I am someone else. They know neither the person they saw that time nor me whom they'll be seeing now. I bet they think all Turks look alike."

"Even if we tell them the man they saw that night was someone else," said İskender, "they'd certainly expect Jelal Salik to be someone older in any case."

"What do they know about Jelal?" Galip said. "Someone must have said, do an interview with such and such a famous columnist, he'd be super for your program on Turkey. And they would have written his name on a piece of paper. They'd probably not have asked his age or his description."

Just then, they heard laughter in the corner where the historical film was being shot. They turned around where they sat on the divan and looked.

"What are they laughing at?" Galip said.

"I didn't catch it," İskender said, but he was smiling as if he had.

"None of us is himself," said Galip, whispering as if he were imparting a secret. "None of us can be. Don't you suspect that others might see you as someone else? Are you quite so certain that you are you? If you are, then are you certain that the person you are certain you are is you? What do these people want anyway? Isn't the person they are looking for some foreigner whose stories will affect British viewers watching TV after supper, whose troubles will trouble them, whose sorrow will make them feel sad? I have just the story to fit the bill! No one need see my face even. They could keep my face in the dark during the shooting. A mysterious and well-known Turkish journalist—and don't forget my being a Moslem which is most interesting—fearing the repressive government, politically motivated assassinations, and juntaists, grants the BBC an interview, provided that his identity is kept secret. Isn't that even better?"

"Okay," said İskender. "I'll buzz them upstairs, they must be waiting."

Galip watched the shooting at the other end of the large salon. A bearded and fezzed Ottoman pasha, wearing a crisp uniform resplendent with medals, orders, and sashes, was talking to his dutiful daughter who was listening to her darling father, yet her face wasn't turned to him but to the busy camera that the waiters and bellboys observed in respectful silence.

"We have no help, no might, no hope!" the pasha was saying. "We have nothing! And everyone, but everyone—the whole world—is against the Turk! God knows, the government is probably being forced to relinquish this fort too . . ."

"But, my dearest father, regard what we still have . . ." the daughter started speaking, holding out the book in her hand for the benefit of the audience rather than her father, but Galip couldn't make out what it was. When the take was repeated, he still didn't get the book's title, which made him more curious once he figured out it wasn't the Koran.

Later, having ridden up on the old elevator to enter Room 212 where İskender took him, he had the same feeling of deficiency as when he couldn't recall a name that he knew only too well.

All three British journalists he'd seen at the nightclub in Beyoğlu were in the room. The men had drinks of *rakı* in their hands while they attended to the camera and the lights. The woman looked up from the magazine she was reading.

"Our famous journalist, Jelal Salik, the columnist, is here in person," İskender said in English which seemed stilted to Galip and which, good student that he was, was translated simultaneously into Turkish in his mind.

"Very pleased to meet you!" said the woman, with the two men chiming in together like a pair of twins in a comic book. "But haven't we met you before?" added the woman.

"She says, but haven't they met you before," İskender said to Galip.

"Where?" Galip said to İskender.

İskender then told the woman that Galip had asked, "Where?"

"At that nightclub," the woman said.

"I haven't been in a nightclub in years, and I won't be going anytime soon, either," Galip said with conviction. "I don't think I've ever been in a nightclub in all my life. I find that sort of social intercourse, that kind of mob scene, anathema to my psychological health and the solitude that I need in order to pen my works. The intensity of my literary life which reaches tremendous proportions and the politically motivated murders and repression, which reach even more incredible proportions, have always kept me from that sort of life anyway. On the other hand, I am well aware that I have compatriots not only all over Istanbul but all over the country who think of themselves as Jelal Salik, who introduce themselves as Jelal Salik for very righteous and appropriate reasons. What is more, some nights when I go around incognito in the city, I'm startled to run into some of them in dives located in slum districts, somewhere in our dark, incomprehensible lives, in the center of the mystery; I've even made friends with these unhappy persons who are capable of being 'me' enough to terrify me. Istanbul is a grand place, an incomprehensible place."

When İskender began to translate, Galip looked out the open window at the Golden Horn and the dim lights of Istanbul. Obviously they had meant to light the Mosque of Selım the Grim to make it attractive to tourists, but, as is always the case, some of the lights had been stolen, turning the mosque into an odd and scary pile of stone, making it look like the dark mouth of an old geezer who had but a single tooth in his head. As soon as İskender was through translating, the woman courteously made an apology about having been mistaken, which wasn't lacking in humor and playfulness, saying that she had confused Mr. Salik with a tall, bespectacled novelist who'd told a story there that night, but she did not appear to be convinced of what she was saying. It looked as if she'd decided to accept Galip and the odd situation as an interesting Turkish eccentricity, having assumed the "I don't understand it but I respect it" attitude adopted by tolerant intellectuals up against a different culture. Galip felt affectionate toward this sensitive woman who was a good sport, not calling off the game even though she sensed that the cards were rigged. Wasn't she somewhat reminiscent of Rüya?

When Galip sat in the back-lit seat that was a bit like a modern execution chair with the black power cables, the mike and camera lines placed next to it, they noticed that he was uneasy. One of the men stuck a glass in Galip's hand and smiling politely filled it with *rakı* and water to Galip's taste. The woman, exercising the same sense of play—they kept smiling, anyway—hastily put a cassette into the player, and when she pushed the button provocatively like someone slipping a pornographic tape into the video machine in the twinkling of an eye the sights of Turkey they'd been recording for the last eight days appeared on the small portable screen. They watched quietly as if watching a porno film, with a vague sense of humor but without being totally disinterested: an acrobatic beggar who merrily exhibited his maimed arms and his unhinged legs; a fervent political demonstration and a fervent leader making a statement afterwards; two old coots playing a game of backgammon; scenes from taverns and nightclubs; a rug dealer priding himself on his display window; a nomadic tribe going up a hill on their camels; a train locomoting with its steam engine puffing out clouds; kids waving at the camera in shantytown districts; veiled women considering oranges at the greengrocer's; the victim of a politically motivated murder and its aftermath covered under newspapers; an old porter transporting a grand piano on a horse cart.

"I happen to know that porter," Galip said suddenly. "That's the porter who moved us from the Heart-of-the-City Apartments to the place on the side street."

They all had a sense of being game as well as serious, watching the old porter, who was also smiling with an identical sense of being game as well as serious, while he pulled his cart loaded with the piano into the front yard of an old apartment building.

"The Prince's piano has come back," Galip said. He had no clear idea of whose voice he was helping himself to, who in the hell he was, but he was sure everything was going well. "A Prince once lived in a hunting lodge that stood exactly on the same grounds as that apartment building. I'll tell the story of the Prince!"

They set things up very quickly. İskender reiterated that the famous columnist was here to make a very significant historical statement. The woman prefaced the segment enthusiastically to her audience by placing it adroitly into a wide framework that covered the last Ottoman sultans, the clandestine Turkish Communist Party, Atatürk's mysterious, concealed legacy, Islamic fundamentalism in Turkey, the politically motivated assassinations, and the risk of a military coup.

"Once upon a time, a Prince lived here in this city who had discovered that the most important question in life was whether or not one could be oneself," Galip began narrating. As he told the story, he felt the Prince's rage inside him so strongly, he experienced himself as someone else. Who was this person? He was narrating the Prince's childhood when he sensed that the new person whose identity he'd assumed had once been a kid called Galip. When he told how the Prince struggled with his books, he felt like the authors of these books. When he told about the days of solitude the Prince spent at his lodge, he felt like the heroes in the Prince's stories. When he told how the Prince dictated his thoughts to his scribe, he felt as if he were the person enjoying these thoughts. When he told the Prince's story as if telling Jelal's stories, he felt himself to be the protagonist in a story told by Jelal. When he told of the final period in the Prince's life, he thought, "Jelal used to tell it like this," and felt angry toward the others in the hotel room for not catching on. He was empowered with such rage that the English crew listened to him as if they understood Turkish. As soon as he came to the end of the Prince's days, he began to tell the same story over without coming to a stop. "Once upon a time, a Prince lived here in this city who had discovered that the most important question in life was whether or not one could be oneself," he began with the same conviction. When he returned to the Heart-of-the-City Apartments four hours later, and considered the difference between the first time he told it and the second time, he would conclude that Jelal had been alive the first time, and that the second time he was lying dead right across from the police station, just a little way from Aladdin's store, his body covered with newspapers. He'd stressed parts of the story to which he hadn't paid attention when he'd first told it, and when he told it the third time, he understood clearly that each time he told it he could become a new person. "Like the Prince, I too narrate in order to become myself," he felt like saying. Enraged against those who would not permit him to feel like himself, convinced that the mystery in life and the city could only be solved by telling stories, experiencing the inner sense of death and whiteness at the end, he'd finished his third narration when there was complete silence. Then the British journalists and İskender briskly applauded Galip, displaying the sincerity of an audience applauding a master player after one heck of a performance.

Chapter Thirty-five

THE STORY OF THE PRINCE

How nice were the former streetcars! —AHMET RASIM

Once upon a time, a Prince lived here in this city who had discovered that the most important question in life was whether or not one could be oneself. His discovery was his entire life and his entire life was his discovery. It was his short statement on the subject of his short life which he dictated to his scribe whom he retained toward the end of his life for the purpose of having his discovery penned. The Prince spoke and the Scribe wrote.

Once, a hundred years ago, our city wasn't yet a place where millions of unemployed traipsed around like bewildered chickens, not yet a place where garbage flowed down the streets and sewers underneath bridges, where chimneys spewed up tar-colored smoke and people waiting at bus stops elbowed each other mercilessly. Back then, horse-drawn streetcars went by so slowly, you could hop on them while they were in progress; the ferries sailed so leisurely that some passengers would disembark and walk talking and laughing under the lindens, the chestnuts, and the planes to the next ferry station, and after having tea at the station teahouse, they'd get back on the same ferryboat that had finally caught up with them and continue on their way. Back then, the chestnut and walnut trees hadn't yet been felled to be transformed into electric poles which would end up becoming places to stick handbills advertising tailors and circumcisers. Outside the city limits, it wasn't bald garbage hills bristling with electric and telephone poles that met the eye, but woods, groves, and meadows where once wistful and insouciant sultans had hunted game. The Prince had lived twenty-two years and three months at the hunting lodge on one of these green hills that would eventually be riddled with sewage tiles, pavement stones, apartment buildings.

Where the Prince was concerned, dictating was a way of being himself. The Prince was convinced that he was himself only when he was in the process of dictating to the Scribe who sat at a mahogany desk. It was only when he dictated to his Scribe that he could prevail over other people's voices which he heard in his ears all day long, their stories that stuck in his mind as he walked up and down in his lodge and their ideas he couldn't shake off no matter what he did as he enjoyed his garden that was surrounded by high walls. "In order to be oneself, it is necessary that one apprehends only one's own voice, one's own stories, and one's own thoughts," the Prince said, and the Scribe wrote it down.

But that didn't mean that the Prince heard only his own voice as he dictated. On the contrary, the Prince was fully aware that whenever he began to narrate, he was thinking of someone else's story, that just as he was about to develop his own idea, he got involved with an idea someone else put forth, that just as he surrendered to his own anger, he also apprehended someone else's anger. Yet he also knew that one could only find one's own voice by producing a voice that contended against all the voices inside one's head, or as the Prince put it, "by going at other snarling throats." Dictation, he thought, was a battlefield where he had the upperhand in this melee.

The Prince gave battle against ideas, stories, and words as he walked up and down the rooms in the lodge, changing a sentence going down a twin staircase that he'd uttered as he went up the other that met its twin at the same landing; then, he'd have the Scribe read back the sentence he'd dictated as he went up the first staircase, or else sitting or lying down on the sofa directly across from the Scribe's desk. "Read it back to me then," the Prince would say and the Scribe would read in a monotone the last few sentences that his master had dictated.

"Prince Honorable Osman Jelalettin knew that unless the question of being oneself was properly addressed as being paramount, all of us in this land, in this accursed land, were condemned to destruction, defeat, and slavery. According to Prince Honorable Osman Jelalettin, peoples who had not discovered a way of being themselves were condemned to slavery, races to degeneracy, nations to nonexistence, to nothingness, nothingness."

"Nothingness must be repeated three times," the Prince said, either going up the staircase or coming down, or else circling the Scribe's desk, "not merely twice!" He'd say this in such a voice and manner that, as soon as he said it, he'd be convinced he was imitating Monsieur François, who had taught him French in his early youth, down to mannerisms he used in *dictée* exercises, including his angry stride and even the pedagogic tone in his voice, and the Prince would be overcome by a crisis that would suddenly "interrupt his intellectual activity" and "bleach all the color out of his imaginative powers." The Scribe, who was accustomed to all these fits, thanks to his years of experience, would drop his pencil and, wearing the frozen, meaningless, blank expression that he pulled on like a mask over his face, wait for the paroxysms and tantrums of "I cannot be myself" to cease.

Prince Osman Jelalettin was ambivalent about his memories of his childhood and youth. The Scribe remembered having once written down recollections of happy scenes from a joyous, entertaining, and active youth that had taken place in royal Ottoman palaces, lodges, and mansions, but these now remained in previous journals. "Since my mother, Honorable Lady Nurcihan, was his favorite, my father Sultan Abdül Mecid Khan loved me the best of all his thirty children," the Prince had once revealed many years ago; and on another occasion of dictating these happy scenes, again many years ago, he had said, "Since my father Sultan Abdül Mecid Khan loved me the best of all his thirty children, my mother Honorable Lady Nurcihan, who was his wife number two, was his favorite in his harem."

The Scribe had written how the Negro chief of harem had fainted when the little Prince had slammed a door in his face while running through the harem quarters of Dolmabahçe Palace opening and closing doors, skipping down the stairs two steps a time, in an effort to get away from his older brother Reşat who was chasing him. The Scribe had written about the night when the Prince's fourteen-year-old sister Princess Münire was given in matrimony to a forty-five-year-old pompous ass of a pasha, how she had taken her sweet little brother on her lap and wept, saying she was sad only, and only, because she could no longer be with him; and that the Prince's white collar had been completely sodden with his older sister's tears. The Scribe had written about an entertainment held in honor of British and French personages who'd arrived in Istanbul on account of the Crimean War, where the Prince, besides getting to dance with an eleven-year-old English girl with his mother's permission, had spent a lot of time together with the same girl, looking through the pages of a book where there were illustrations of locomotives, penguins, and corsairs. The Scribe had written about the time at a ceremony on the occasion of a ship being named after his grandmother, the Queen Mother Bezmi Alem, when the Prince had collected on a bet that he could eat exactly four pounds of Turkish delight, some of the pieces rose-flavored and some with pistachio nuts, by getting to deliver a slap on the nape of his retarded older brother's neck. The Scribe had written about the time when the princes and the princesses had been punished when it got back to the palace that, having ventured out in royal carriages to a Beyoğlu store where all the handkerchiefs, bottles of cologne, fans, gloves, umbrellas in the world were on display, all they'd managed to buy was the apron off the sales boy, which they thought might come in handy for their playacting games. The Scribe had written how the Prince in his childhood and first youth used to imitate anything at all, the physicians, the British Ambassador, the ships that went by the window, prime ministers, the sound of squeaky doors and castrati voices of the harem chiefs, his father, horse-drawn carriages, the sound of rain on the windowpane, all that he read in books, people who wept at his father's funeral, waves, and his Italian piano teacher Guateli Pasha. And later, the Prince would admonish the Scribe that all his recollections, which he reiterated with exactly the same details each time he related them, using words of anger and hate, had to be considered in conjunction with the kisses, all the kisses, presented him by dozens of women and girls, young and old, along with the cakes, confections, mirrors, music boxes, and lots and lots of books and toys.

Later, during this time when he employed a scribe to put down his past and his thoughts, the Prince would refer to his happy years by saying, "The happiness of my childhood lasted a long time. The foolish happiness of my childhood went on for so long that I lived as a foolish happy child until I was twenty-nine years old. An empire that can provide a prince, one who might end up succeeding to the throne, a life of childish foolishness and happiness until the age of twenty-nine is necessarily doomed to collapse, dissolution, and annihilation." Up to his twenty-ninth year, the Prince had helped himself to a swell time, as would any prince fifth in line of succession, made love to women, read books, acquired property and worldly goods, developed a superficial interest in music and painting, and an even more superficial one in military science, married, fathered three children two of whom were boys, and, like everybody else, made friends and enemies. Later the Prince would dictate: "It turns out that I had to turn twenty-nine before I was rid of all that baggage, all those women and possessions, all those friends and foolish ideas." When he was twenty-nine, he had suddenly become third in line for succession, instead of the fifth, due to some entirely unexpected historic developments. Yet, according to the Prince, only fools maintained that events were "entirely unexpected"; no development could be construed as more natural than the sickness and the ensuing death of his uncle Sultan Abdül Aziz, whose soul was just as decrepit as his ideas and his willpower, and the dethronement of his eldest brother on account of his having gone mad soon after ascending his uncle's throne. Upon dictating the last bit, the Prince would go up the staircase saying that his next older brother Abdülhamit, who succeeded to the throne, had been just as crazy as their eldest brother; and as he descended the twin staircase, he would dictate perhaps a thousand times over that the prince who was ahead of him in the order of succession and who awaited at another mansion to ascend the throne, as he himself did, was even crazier than their elder brothers; the Scribe, after taking down these dangerous words for the thousandth time, would patiently write the explications concerning why the Prince's royal brothers had gone mad, why they were obliged to go mad, and why Ottoman princes were incapable of doing anything else besides going mad.

After all, anyone who spent his life waiting to ascend the throne of an empire was condemned to madness; anyone who witnessed his brothers go mad living in wait for their dream had no choice other than going mad, since he too was already caught on the horns of the dilemma of whether to go mad or not to go mad; a person went mad not because he wanted to but because he made it into a problem by trying to avoid going mad; any prince-in-waiting who contemplated even once how his ancestors and forefathers immediately upon ascending the throne had their younger brothers killed by strangling could no longer live without going mad; given that he was obliged to know the history of the realm he was to rule, and given that he could read in any old history book that his ancestor Mehmet the Third, upon becoming the Sultan, had his nineteen brothers executed one by one, some among whom were still at mother's breast, madness was the sentence imposed on any prince who had little choice but to read accounts of sultans putting their kid brothers to death; besides, at some point of the intolerable waiting period which was bound to terminate in getting poisoned, strangled, or murdered under the guise of suicide, madness, since it meant "I give up," was the way out as well the most deep-seated secret wish for all heirs apparent who anticipated ascension as if anticipating death; going crazy was the best chance for escaping from the Sultan's informers who kept him under surveillance, from plots and snares laid by lowlife politicians who sneaked through the network of informers to get to the prince, as well as from his own intolerable dreams of ascending the throne; every time an heir apparent took a look at the map of the empire he dreamed of ruling, he had no choice

but to get on the verge of madness upon realizing how far-flung, how boundless, and how vastly large were the countries for which he would soon be
responsible and which he was to rule all on his own—yes, on his own alone;
any heir apparent who had no apprehension of this boundlessness, and no
comprehension of the immensity of the empire he would one day have to
be responsible for, had to be considered already mad. Right at this point, of
the reasons for going mad that he'd been enumerating, Honorable Prince
Osman Jelalettin would say, "If I am today a more sensible person than all
those fools, lunatics, and retards who have ruled the Ottoman Empire, then
it is due to my comprehension of this maddening boundlessness! Contemplating the boundlessness of the responsibility I would one day shoulder did
not drive me mad like those other wimps, weak sisters, and wretches. On
the contrary, contemplating it carefully brought me to my senses. It was
because I took care to bring this apprehension under control, through my
own willpower and resolution, that I discovered that the most important
question in life was whether or not one could be oneself."

As soon as he went up from fifth place to third in line of succession, he'd
given himself over to reading. He thought it behooved a prince who didn't
consider getting on the throne something of a miracle to develop himself,
and he optimistically believed that this could be achieved through reading.
He extracted "useful ideas" from the books he read arduously as if devouring
the pages, hoping to believe in dreams he grasped at obsessively in order to
fulfill these ideas within a short time in the future of a happier Ottoman
Empire, as well as hang onto his sanity, for the sake of which he had moved
to this hunting lodge where he would live for the next twenty-two years and
three months, having left his wife and children, as well as his previous habits
and things, at his waterfront estate on the Bosphorus, since he wished to rid
himself of everything that reminded him of his erstwhile foolish and childlike
life. The hunting lodge was situated on a hill that would get covered one
hundred years later under pavement over which streetcar rails were laid,
terrifying dark apartment buildings built under the influence of various styles
from the West, boys' and girls' lycée buildings, a police station, a mosque,
haberdashery, florist, rug store, and cleaners. Over the high wall put up so
that the Sultan might keep his hazardous brother under better surveillance,
as well as protect the Prince from the foolishness of the world outside, large
chestnut and plane trees could be seen which would end up sporting, a
century later, black telephone cables wound around their branches and nudie
magazines pinned on their trunks. The only sound heard in the lodge, aside
from the screams from flocks of ravens that wouldn't depart from the hill
even after all the centuries, was the noise of military drills and music that

came from the barracks on the opposite hills on days when wind blew from land to sea. The Prince had dictated innumerable times that the first six years he spent at the lodge were the happiest period in his life.

"For I was only engaged in reading during that period," the Prince used to say. "I only dreamed about what I read. During those six years, I lived only with the ideas and voices of the writers that I read." Then he'd add, "Still, all through those six years, I was unable to be myself at all. I was not myself, and perhaps that was the reason why I managed to be happy. Yet, a Sultan is not in the business of being happy but being himself!" he'd dictate every time he remembered those six happy years with pain and longing; then he would repeat the other sentence he'd already had his Scribe take down maybe a thousand times: "Everybody but everybody is in the business of being himself, not just sultans."

The Prince had dictated that on an evening toward the end of those six years he'd clearly become aware of the perception which he called his life's discovery and its goal. "On one of those happy evenings, I was imagining myself on the Ottoman throne, as I so often did, giving some fool an irate scolding in the course of trying to solve a matter of state. I'd just rebuked the fool in my imagination by saying 'as Voltaire also states,' when I froze up, having suddenly became aware of the strait I was in. It was as if the person I imagined as the thirty-fifth sultan on the Ottoman throne was not me, but Voltaire; as if it was not me but a Voltaire impersonator. It was at that moment that I realized the horror of a sultan's being not himself but someone else—a sultan, that is, who would be determining the lives of millions and millions of subjects and administer lands that seemed boundless on the map."

Later on, the Prince had related other stories concerning the moment when he became aware of this perception, but the Scribe knew full well that the moment of enlightenment always turned on the same quandary: Was it right for a sultan, who'd be determining the course of millions of people's lives, to entertain in his mind other people's sentences? Didn't it behoove a prince who would someday rule one of the world's greatest empires to act only according to his own will? Should a person who kept other people's thoughts in his head like so many nightmares be considered a sultan, or a shadow?

"After I comprehended it was necessary that I be not someone else but myself, not a shadow but a true sultan, I realized I had to be liberated from all the books I'd read not only during those six years but in the course of my entire life," the Prince would say when he began to narrate his account of the next ten years of his existence. "It was necessary for me to free myself from all those books, all those writers, all those stories, all those voices if I wanted to be myself and not someone else. It took ten years of my life."

So, the Prince began to dictate to his Scribe how he liberated himself one by one from all the books that had influenced him. The Scribe would put down that the Prince had burned all the volumes of Voltaire in the lodge because the more the Prince read this writer the more he fell under the impression that he was an intelligent, atheistic, and jocose Frenchman with a ready wit, rather than himself. Then the Scribe would write that volumes of Schopenhauer had been removed from the lodge since the Prince had identified himself with someone who contemplated his own will by the hour and for days on end, which meant that the pessimistic person with whom he identified would end up not being the Prince who'd someday ascend the Ottoman throne but, in essence, the German philosopher. The volumes of Rousseau which had been acquired at great expense had also been removed from the lodge, after first being torn into shreds, since they turned the Prince into a savage trying to apprehend himself red-handed. "I had all the French thinkers put to the fire—Deltour, De Passet, Morelli who gave an account of the world as a rational place, and Brichot who maintained the contrary —because when I read them I didn't see myself as the future sultan but as an argumentative and derisive professor who attempted to disqualify the absurd observations put forth by thinkers who were his precursors," the Prince used to say. He had the *Thousand and One Nights* burned since sultans who went around in disguise, with whom he identified on account of this book, were no longer the sort of sultans it behooved the Prince to become. He had *Macbeth* burned, given that he was made to feel each time he read it like a weakling and a coward who was ready to get blood on his hands for the sake of the crown and, what's worse, to derive a poetic pride from it, instead of being ashamed of being this person. He had Rumi's *Mathnawi* removed from the lodge because every time he was distracted by the stories in this utterly disorganized book, he identified himself with some dervish saint who optimistically believed that disorganized narratives were the essence of life. "I burned Şeyh Galip because I regarded myself as a melancholic lover whenever I read him," the Prince would explain. "I had Bottfolio burned because by reading him I regarded myself as an Occidental who wants to be Oriental, and Ibn Zerhani because reading him made me regard myself as an Oriental who wants to be Occidental. I wanted to regard myself neither as Oriental nor Occidental, nor obsessive, nor mad, nor adventuresome, nor somebody that comes out of some book." And, concluding these words, the Prince would obsessively take up the refrain the Scribe had written down repeatedly innumerable times into so many journals all these six years: "I wanted to be just myself; I wanted to be just myself; I wanted to be just myself."

Yet he knew this was no easy task. After ridding himself of a set of books, and finally of the voices that for years kept repeating the fictions in them, the silence in his mind would seem so intolerable to the Prince that he'd reluctantly send one of his men to town to get some new books. After reading as if devouring them, the books that he tore out of the packages, he would initially make fun of the authors; then he would immolate the books with anger and ceremony, and yet, since he kept on hearing the voices and imitating the authors, he would send his man out to Babıali where the foreign language bookmongers awaited him with bated breath, thinking that he might rid himself of these voices by reading yet other books, although he was painfully aware that it was a case of the hair of the dog that bit him. "Prince Honorable Osman Jelalettin, after resolving to become himself, battled against these books for ten whole years," the Scribe had written one day, but the Prince had corrected him by saying, "Not battled against, write 'went for their throats'!" It was only after ten years of going for the throats of the voices heard broadcast in these books that he had come to understand he could only become himself by raising his voice against those books' voices, and had gone ahead and engaged himself a scribe.

"During these ten years, not only had Prince Honorable Osman Jelalettin gone for the throats of these books and fictions but for the throat of anything that prevented him from becoming himself," the Prince would add, shouting down from the top of the stairs; and the Scribe would write the sentence along with the other sentences that followed it, which the Prince would dictate with equal zeal and with the same conviction and excitement that he had when he first spoke them, although he had repeated them thousands of times. The Scribe had written that during these ten years the Prince had gone for the throats not only of the books but of things in his surroundings that influenced him quite as much as did the books, given that all the furniture—the tables, chairs, stands—took a man outside his inner discourse by virtue of providing him with the necessary or unnecessary means of his comfort or discomfort; given that his eye caught ashtrays or candelabras which made the Prince unable to concentrate on an idea that would allow him to become himself; given that the Prince was drawn into undesirable psychological states by all the paintings on the walls, the vases on the stands, the billowing pillows on the sofas; given that all those clocks, bowls, pens, and antique chairs were loaded with memories and associations that prevented the Prince from becoming himself.

The Scribe had written that aside from the objects that the Prince had removed from his sight by breaking some, by burning others, and by throwing away yet others, all through the ten years he had also gone for the throats of recollections that made him into someone else. The Prince used to say, "I am driven to distraction by suddenly finding in the middle of a train of thought, or of dreams, the simplest and most unimportant small detail from my past which has followed me like a merciless killer who wants to murder me or a lunatic who has been driven for years to exact some unfathomable revenge." After all, it was a terrifying thing for a person who had to consider the lives of millions and millions of people after ascending the Ottoman throne to suddenly find in the middle of a train of thought a bowl of strawberries he'd eaten in his childhood or a stupid remark made by some inconsequential chief of harem. A sultan—nay, not only a sultan but anybody at all—whose duty it was to be himself, in possession of only his own thoughts, will, and resolution, had to go against the grain of haphazard and arbitrary memories which prevented him from becoming himself. On one occasion the Scribe had written, "For the purpose of going at the throats of all the memories that spoiled the purity of his thoughts and his own will, Prince Honorable Osman Jelalettin had eliminated all sources of smell throughout the lodge, disposed of all his familiar clothing and furniture, eschewed any relationship with the anesthetizing art called music, shunned playing his white piano, and had all the rooms in the lodge painted white."

"Yet, worst of all, more unbearable than the memories, objects, and books, are people," the Prince would add after the Scribe read back what he'd dictated from where he lay on the sofa of which he had yet to divest himself. They came in all sorts: they dropped in at the most inopportune moments and inappropriate times, bearing disgusting gossip and worthless rumors. Trying to perform a good deed, they only managed to destroy a person's peace of mind. Their affection was more engulfing than comforting. They kept talking just to prove they had something to say. They told you stories in order to convince you that they were interesting. Just so they could display their affection for you, they made you uncomfortable. Perhaps these were not important things, yet the Prince who was dying to be himself, who wanted to be alone with his own thoughts, sensed that he was unable to be himself for a protracted period each time he was paid a visit by these fools, these unnecessary, disaffected, common gossips. "Prince Honorable Osman Jelalettin was of the opinion that the greatest detriment to a man's being himself is the people around him," the Scribe had written at some point, and at another, "Man's greatest pleasure is to make others look like himself." He'd written that the Prince's greatest fear was that the day he ascended the throne, he would have to establish relations with these people. "A man is affected by his pity for those who are pitiful, miserable, and wretched," the Prince used to say. "We are affected because we end up becoming common and undistinguished ourselves in the company of those who are common and undistinguished," he said. "We are also affected by those who have a distinctive personality and command our respect because we unconsciously begin emulating them and, when all things are considered, these last are the most dangerous of all," said the Prince. "But be sure to write that I have sent them all away, the whole pack of them! Also write that I am not putting up a fight just for myself, in order that I may become myself, but for the liberation of millions of subjects."

It was in the tenth year of the incredible life-and-death battle he waged in avoiding others' influence, on an evening when he struggled against familiar things, scents that he loved, books that affected him, that as he was viewing through the louvers of the "Venetian" blinds the moonlit snow that covered the extensive gardens, the Prince suddenly understood that the battle he waged was in reality not his own battle but the battle of the millions of unfortunates who had staked their lot on the Ottoman Empire which was collapsing. As his Scribe put down in the journals perhaps tens thousand times during the last six years of the Prince's life, "all peoples that are unable to be themselves, civilizations that imitate another, nations that find happiness in the stories that belong to others" were condemned to collapse, annihilation, and oblivion. So, on the sixteenth year of withdrawing to his lodge to await his ascension to the throne, during the days he realized he could only combat the stories he heard in his head by raising the voices of his own stories, he was about to engage him a scribe when the Prince understood that his personal and psychological struggle had been in reality a "historical life-and-death battle," "the last stage of a bout that is observed only once in a thousand years which involves the dilemma of shedding or not shedding the shell," "the most important historical standstill in a development which historians would appropriately evaluate centuries later as a turning point."

Following the night when the snow-covered garden was illuminated by moonlight reminiscent of the vastness and fearfulness of infinite time, during the days when he had begun telling his story and discovery every morning to the elderly, loyal, and patient Scribe sitting at the mahogany desk, the Prince would eventually remember he had actually discovered "the most significant historical dimension" in his story many years ago: Hadn't he observed with his own eyes, prior to secluding himself in his lodge, that Istanbul streets were changing with every passing day in imitation of an imaginary city in a nonexistent foreign country? Didn't he know that the unfortunate underprivileged that crowded the streets transformed their garb by observing Occidental travelers and studying photographs of foreigners that fell in their hands? Hadn't he heard that the sorry folk who gathered in the evening around the stove at coffeehouses in the slums, instead of telling each other their own traditional tales, read for each other's edification the sort of garbage in the papers written by second-rate columnists who pinched material from *The Count of Monte Cristo* or *The Three Musketeers*, in which the names of the heroes had been Moslemized? What's more, with the object of looking for pleasant pastimes, hadn't he himself been in the habit of frequenting Armenian bibliopoles who published collected editions of this odious stuff? Before displaying the decisiveness and the will to seclude himself, had the Prince not felt that his own face had also been gradually losing its former mysterious meaning, just as it happened to the underprivileged, dragged as he was into banality along with the underprivileged, the pitiful, and the unfortunate? "He had, indeed!" wrote the Scribe in response to each question, cognizant of the fact that that was how the Prince wanted it. "Yes, the Prince felt his face was also changing."

Before the end of his first two years working with the Scribe—he called what they were up to "working"—the Prince had the Scribe take down everything: from the various ship horns which he imitated in his childhood, and the Turkish delights he managed to gobble, down to the nightmares that he had and the books he read in his forty-seven years of life, from the clothes he liked best down to the ones he disliked the most, from all the illnesses he survived down to everything he knew in connection with animals; and, as he frequently expressed it, he had done it, "by evaluating each sentence, each word in the light of the immense truth he had discovered." Every morning when the Scribe sat at the mahogany desk and the Prince took up his position either on the sofa across from the desk or else his pacing grounds around it, or on the twin staircases that went up to the floor above and down again, perhaps they both knew that the Prince had no new story to dictate. But they were both in search of this silence, since, as the Prince was wont to say, "It is only when a man has nothing left to tell that he has come close to being completely himself. Only when his narrations have come to an end, when he hears inside him a profound silence because reminiscences, books, stories, and memory itself have all shut down, only then can he hear his own true voice which will make him himself, rising, as it does, from the depths of his own soul and the infinite dark labyrinths of his own being."

On one of the days when they awaited for the voice to rise slowly out of somewhere deep inside a bottomless well of tales, the Prince took up the subject of women and love which, since he considered these "the most dangerous subjects," he had rarely touched upon until that particular oc-casion. For a period that took nearly six months, he spoke of his old flames, affairs that couldn't be considered love, his "intimacy" with some of the harem women whom, aside from a couple of them, he remembered with pity and sorrow, and his wife.

The most horrible aspect of this kind of intimacy, according to the Prince, was that even a commonplace woman who had no special attributes could, unbeknownst to you, invade a considerable portion of your thoughts. During his first youth, his marriage, and the early part of his residence at the lodge after leaving his wife and children at his estate on the Bosphorus—that is, until he turned thirty-five—the Prince had not been too concerned about this situation since he had as yet formed no resolution to become "only himself" and "free of influence." What is more, since this "miserable copycat culture" had taught him, as it did everyone else, that forgetting yourself through love for a woman, a boy, or God—that is, "dissolving into love" —was something to be proud of and esteemed, the Prince too, like the multitudes in the streets, had taken pride in being "in love."

After secluding himself at the lodge, reading continuously for six years, and at last perceiving that the most important question in life was whether or not one could be oneself, the Prince had immediately resolved to be cautious where women were concerned. It was true that he felt incomplete without the presence of women. Yet it was also true that every woman he became intimate with would spoil his thoughts and take up residence in the middle of his dreams, which he now desired to have originate only within himself. He had thought for a while that it was possible to immunize himself against the poison called love by being intimate with as many women as possible, but since he approached it with the utilitarian notion of getting inured to love and getting himself sick on the intoxication of love, he hadn't been too interested in these women. Later, he had begun to see mostly Lady Leyla with whom he didn't believe he could fall in love, given that she was, as he had dictated to the Scribe, "the most nondescript, colorless, blameless, and harmless" among all the women he knew. "Prince Honorable Osman Jelalettin was able to lay his heart bare without fear, believing, as he did, that he would not fall in love with her," the Scribe had written one night, now that they'd begun to work also at night. "Since she was the only woman with whom I could lay bare my heart, I immediately fell in love with her," the Prince had added. "It was one of the most horrifying periods of my life."

The Scribe had written about the days when the Prince and Lady Leyla met at the lodge and quarreled. Lady Leyla would take off by carriage from the mansion of her father, the Pasha, accompanied by her men, and after half a day's travel would arrive at the lodge, and the two of them would sit down at the meal prepared for them, the likes of which they read about in French novels, and eat talking about poetry and music like the delicate, refined characters in the novels, and just after the meal when it was time for her to go back home, they'd set to a quarrel that upset the cooks, the manservants, and coachman who listened behind doors that were partly ajar. "There was no ostensible reason for our quarrels," the Prince had explained on one occasion. "I was merely angry with her since it was on her account that I couldn't manage to be myself, my thoughts lost their purity, I could no longer hear the voice that rose out of the depths of my being. This went on until she died as a result of a mishap for which I will never understand whether or not I was to be blamed."

The Prince had dictated that after Lady Leyla's death, he was grieved but liberated. The Scribe, who was always quiet, respectful, and attentive, had done something he'd never done in his six years with the Prince; that is, he had tried prying into this love and death by broaching the subject several times, but the Prince would only return to it on his own terms and in his own good time.

One night six months before his death, the Prince explained that if he still had not managed to become himself, so to speak, if he were unsuccessful at the end of the fifteen-year battle he had put up at the lodge, then Istanbul streets would also turn into the streets of an unfortunate city that could no longer "be itself," and that the hapless people who walked on the squares, parks, and sidewalks of this city which imitated squares, parks, sidewalks in other cities could never achieve being themselves; and he was saying that he had knowledge of each and every street in his beloved Istanbul and, even though he had not stepped outside even once, beyond the garden at the lodge, had kept every streetlight and shop alive in his imagination, when he abandoned his usual angry voice and dictated hoarsely that, during the period when Lady Leyla came every day to the lodge in her carriage, he'd spent the major portion of his time imagining a horse-drawn carriage trailing through the city streets. "During the days when Prince Honorable Osman Jelalettin struggled with becoming himself, he spent half the day imagining the route from Kuruçeşme to our lodge in a carriage drawn by two horses, one bay and the other black; and after their usual meal and the ensuing quarrel, he'd spend the rest of the day imagining the return trip that took the tearful Lady Leyla back to her Pasha father's mansion in the carriage, going up and down streets that were mostly on the same route," the Scribe had written in his usual painstaking, fastidious hand.

On another occasion, in order to suppress other voices and other stories he'd again begun to hear in his mind one hundred days prior to his death, the Prince was enumerating with anger all the personas he had carried around inside him all his life like a secondary soul, with or without his being aware of it, when he began quietly dictating that among all the personas, which he assumed like the different disguises some unhappy sultan was driven to assume every evening, he had affection for only one, the persona that loved a woman whose hair smelled like lilacs. Since the Scribe fastidiously read over and over again every line the Prince dictated to him, and since in his six years of service he had thus gradually come to know, acquire, and own the Prince's past and his memory banks down to the last detail, the Scribe knew that the woman whose head smelled like lilacs was Lady Leyla because he remembered taking down on another occasion the story of a lover who couldn't achieve becoming himself, this time on account of the smell of lilacs he couldn't forget, when the woman whose head smelled of lilacs was killed due to an accident or mistake for which he would never be certain he was to blame.

The Prince described, with the sort of enthusiasm that precedes illness, the last months he and the Scribe worked together as being a period of "concentrated work, concentrated hope, and concentrated faith." These were the happy days when the Prince strongly heard inside his head the voice with which he dictated all day and which made him more himself the more he dictated and told his own stories. They'd work late at night, and no matter how late it was, the Scribe would get in the carriage which waited for him on the grounds and go home, and he'd return early in the morning to take his place at the mahogany desk.

The Prince would narrate the stories of kingdoms that had collapsed because they couldn't be themselves, races that had been annihilated because they imitated others, peoples in distant and unknown lands who'd fallen into oblivion because they couldn't live their own lives. Illyrians had withdrawn from the world's stage because they couldn't come up with a king who through the sheer strength of his personality could teach them to be themselves. The collapse of Babel was not due to King Nimrod's challenge to God, as it was commonly presumed, but because in an effort to put everything he had into building the tower, he had dried up the sources that could have made Babel be itself. The nomadic people of Lapitia were about to move into a settled economy when they fell under the enchantment of the Aitipal with whom they traded and, having given themselves over to complete emulation, had disappeared. The collapse of the Sassanids, according to Tabari's *History*, was due to the fact that their last three rulers (Hormizd, Khosru, and Yaz-digird) were incapable of being themselves for a single day in their entire lives because they were so fascinated by the Byzantine, Arabian, and Hebrew civilizations. After the Lydians' first temple under Susian influence was built in their capital city of Sardis, it had taken fifty years for the mighty Lydian kingdom to fall and shuffle off the theater of history. Serberians were a race which not even historians could place today, not only because they'd lost their memories but because just as they were about to build a great Asian empire, they'd forgotten the mystery that made them themselves and they all began wearing Sarmatian attire and ornaments, and reciting Sarmatian poems as if the whole population had caught an epidemic disease. "Medes, Paphlagonians, Celts," the Prince would dictate, and the Scribe would beat his master to the punch by adding, "collapsed and disappeared because they could not be themselves." Late at night when they were dead beat and done telling the tales of death and collapse, they'd hear the determined chirping of a cicada in the silence of the summer night outside.

When the Prince caught a cold and took to his bed on a windy fall day, just as crimson chestnut leaves began to drop into the frog and lily pond on the grounds, neither of them had taken it too seriously. During that period, the Prince had been holding forth on what would befall the bewildered people who'd inhabit the degenerated streets of Istanbul, saying that "they would see their lives through the eyes of others, listen to other's tales in favor of their own, and be spellbound with others' faces rather than their own," in case he failed in becoming himself and ascending the Ottoman throne in possession of the full power of being his own man. They made and drank linden blossom tea that came from the lindens on the grounds and proceeded to work until all hours.

Next day when the Scribe went upstairs to get another quilt to put over his feverish master prostrated on the sofa, he realized as if under a strange spell that the lodge, where the tables and chairs had been demolished, the doors pulled out, the furniture eradicated, was bare, so very bare. There was a dreamlike whiteness in the bare rooms, on the walls and the staircases. In one of the bare rooms stood the white Steinway, unique in all of Istanbul, which came from the Prince's childhood; it hadn't been played for years and had been totally forgotten. The Scribe observed the whiteness also in the white light that fell as if on another planet into the lodge through the windows which gave the impression that all recollections had faded, memory had frozen, and all sound, smell, objects having retreated, time itself had come to a stop. Going down the stairs with an unscented white quilt in his arms, he felt that the sofa the Prince lay on, his own mahogany desk where he'd worked all these years, the white paper, the windows, were all breakable, delicate, and unreal like the furnishings of dollhouses. As he laid the quilt over him, the Scribe noticed the white in the growth on his master's face that hadn't been shaved for a couple of days. There was half a glass of water and some white tablets on the table next to his head.

"Last night I dreamed that my mother was waiting for me in a dense, dark wood in a distant land," dictated the Prince from where he lay on the sofa. "Water was pouring out of a large crimson pitcher, but slowly like fermented cereal," dictated the Prince. "That was when I understood that I survived because I had insisted on being myself all my life." The Scribe wrote: "Prince Honorable Osman Jelalettin spent his life waiting for silence so that he might hear his own voice and stories." "To wait for silence," repeated the Prince. "Clocks shouldn't stop in Istanbul," dictated the Prince. "When I looked at the clocks in my dream," the Prince began, and the Scribe wrote, "he was always under the impression that he was telling other people's stories." There was a silence. "I envy stones in the desert for just being themselves, and rocks in mountains where no man has ever set foot, and trees in valleys hidden from human eyes," the Prince dictated with effort and passion. "In my dream, wandering around the garden of my memories," he began, and then added, "nothing at all." "Nothing at all," the Scribe put down with care. There was a long, long silence. Then the Scribe rose from his desk and approached the sofa where the Prince was lying down, took a good look at his master and returned quietly back to his desk. Then he wrote, "Prince Honorable Osman Jelalettin was deceased after dictating his last sentence, on the 7th of Shaban, 1321, Thursday, at 3:15 in the morning, at his hunting lodge on the hills of Teşvikiye." But twenty years later what he wrote in the same hand was this: "The throne which Prince Honorable Osman Jelalettin didn't live to ascend was, seven years later, occupied by Honorable Mehmet Reşat whose neck he had slapped when he was young and during whose administration the Ottoman Empire, having entered the Great War, collapsed."

The notebooks were presented by a relative of the Scribe's to Jelal Salik, among whose papers this article was discovered after our columnist's death.

Chapter Thirty-six

BUT I WHO WRITE

Ye who read are still among the living;
But I who write
shall have long since gone my way
into the region of shadows. —EDGAR ALLAN POE, "Shadow—a Parable"

"Yes, yes, I am myself!" Galip thought when he finished telling the Prince's story. "Yes, I am me!" Now that he had told the story, he was so certain that he was capable of being himself and so pleased for having finally done it, he wanted to tear off for the Heart-of-the-City Apartments, sit down at Jelal's desk, and write brand-new columns.

In the cab he got outside the hotel, the cabby began telling a story. Since he understood that one could only be himself through telling stories, Galip listened tolerantly to the cabby's tale.

It seems that on a hot summer day a century ago, the German and Turkish engineers who built the Haydarpaşa train station across the Bosphorus were working on their computations spread out on a table, when one of the boyishly beautiful divers combing the bottom of the sea nearby for anything of value approached with a coin he'd found. There was a woman's face embossed on the coin, a strange, enchanting face. The diver asked one of the Turkish engineers working under their black umbrellas if he could solve the mystery of the face, which he himself could not solve, by reading the letters on the coin. The young engineer was so deeply affected, not so much by the letters as by the enchanting expression on the face of the Byzantine empress, he was seized by such wonderment and awe, that it surprised even the diver. There was something in the face of the empress that involved not only the Arabic and Latin alphabets, both of which the engineer was busy using, but was also reminiscent of the beloved face of his uncle's daughter whom he had dreamed of marrying someday. The girl was about to be married off to someone else at just about that time.

"Yeah, the street next to the Teşvikiye police station is blocked off," the cabby said in response to Galip's question. "Looks like they've shot someone again."

Galip got out and walked down the short, narrow street that connects Emlak Street to Teşvikiye Avenue. Where the street met the avenue, the reflections on the wet asphalt of the blue lights of the squad cars parked there had the pale, sad color of neon signs. Over the small square in front of Aladdin's store, where the lights were still on, a silence had fallen which Galip had never experienced before in his life and would only encounter again in his dreams.

Traffic had come to a stop. Trees were still. There was no wind. The small square seemed set up with the artificial colors and sounds of a theater stage. The mannequins placed between the Singer sewing machines in the window looked as if they were about to join the cops and the other officials. "Yes, I too am myself!" Galip felt like saying. When some photographer's silver-blue flash went off in the crowd of cops and curiosity seekers, Galip became aware of something—as if it were a memory that came from a moment in a dream, or as if finding a key that had been lost for twenty years, or as if recognizing a face he didn't want to see. A few paces from the window where the Singer machines were displayed, there was a pinkish-white blotch on the sidewalk. A solitary figure: he knew it was Jelal. The body had been covered under newspapers, except for the head. Where was Rüya? Galip got closer.

Clearly visible above the printed paper covering the body like a quilt, the head was resting on the filthy, muddy sidewalk as if resting on a pillow. The eyes were open but distracted as if dreaming; the face wore the expression of someone lost in his own thoughts, peaceful as if observing the stars, as if both resting and dreaming. Where was Rüya? Galip was overcome with the feeling that it was a game, a joke, then with a sensation of regret. There was no sign of blood. How had he known that the corpse was Jelal's even before he'd seen the body? Had you known, he felt like saying, that I didn't know that I knew everything? A well was on Jelal's mind, on my mind, on our minds; the dry well of the air shaft; a button, a purple button: coins, soft-drink bottle caps, buttons discovered behind the cupboard. We are observing the stars, stars as seen in between the branches. There was something about the corpse that seemed to request being covered so as not to get cold. Cover him well, Galip thought, so he won't get chilled. Galip felt chilly. "I am myself!" He realized the newspaper sections which had been folded open in the middle were copies of *Milliyet* and *Tercüman*. Stained with colors of the fuel-oil rainbow. Newspaper sections they used to check out for Jelal's columns: Don't get chilled. It's cold.

He heard on the radio in the police van a metallic voice asking for the inspector. Sir, where's Rüya, where is she, where? Traffic light blinking aimlessly at the corner: Green. Red. Then again: Green. Red. Then on the cake-shop lady's window too: Green, red. I remember, I remember, I remember, Jelal was saying. Lights were on in Aladdin's store, although the shutters had been rolled down. Could that be some sort of a clue? Mr. Inspector, Galip felt like saying; I am writing the first Turkish detective novel, and as you can see, here's the clue: The lights have been left on. On the ground were cigarette butts, pieces of paper, trash. Galip sized up a young cop and went up to question him.

The incident had taken place between nine-thirty and ten. The identity of the assailant was not known. The poor man had been shot and was dead instantly. Yes, he was a famous journalist. No, there was no one with him. No, thank you, he didn't smoke. Yes, police work was difficult. No, there was nobody with the dead man, the officer was certain of it; why did the gentleman ask? What kind of work did the gentleman do? What was the gentleman doing here at this hour? Would the gentleman be so kind as to show some identification?

While his identification was being checked out, Galip studied the quilt of newsprint that covered Jelal's body. It was more noticeable from a distance that the light from the window with the mannequins shed a pinkish light on the newspapers. He thought: Officer, the deceased used to pay attention to such little details. I am the one in the picture, and the face is my face. There, take it. My pleasure. I'd better be going. You know, my wife happens to be waiting up for me at home. Seems like I managed things easy as pie.

He went by the Heart-of-the-City Apartments without stopping, crossed Nişantaşı Square at a running pace, and had just gone into his own street when, first time ever, a stray dog, a mud-colored mongrel, barked at him, snarling as if it meant business. What did it signal? He changed sidewalks.

Were the living-room lights on? He thought in the elevator: How could I have missed it?

There was no one in the place. There was no sign anywhere that Rüya had been here even briefly. Everything in the place was intolerably painful, the furniture he touched, the door knobs, the scissors and spoons strewn about, the ashtrays where Rüya had once stubbed her cigarettes, the dining table where they once sat and ate together, the sad, desolate armchairs where once upon a time they used to sit across from each other, they were all too unbearably pathetic. He couldn't wait to get himself out of there.

He walked the streets for a long time. On the streets that ran from Nişantaşı to Şişli, on sidewalks where he and Rüya excitedly sped toward the City Cinema in their childhood, there was no movement aside from the dogs going through the garbage cans. How many stories had you done on these dogs? How many will I end up doing? After what seemed a very long walk, he went around Teşvikiye Square by way of the street behind the mosque and, just as he anticipated, his feet took him back to the corner where Jelal's body had been lying forty-five minutes ago. But there was no one on the corner. Along with the body, the squad cars, the reporters, and the crowd had all disappeared. In the neon light reflected from the window where the sewing machines graced with mannequins were being displayed, Galip could see no trace on the sidewalk where Jelal's body had been laid out. The newspapers that had covered the body must have been meticulously picked up. A cop in front of the station was, as usual, standing the usual patrol duty with his machine gun. Lights were still on in Aladdin's store.

When he arrived at the Heart-of-the-City Apartments, he felt fatigue that was unusual for him. Jelal's flat, which simulated the past so faithfully, seemed as heartbreaking, surprising, and familiar as home seems to a soldier returning from years of war and adventure. How distant was the past! Although it hadn't been quite four hours since he had left it. The past was as inviting as sleep. Like a guilty child, an innocent child, imagining that he would dream of newspaper columns in the lamplight, photographs, mystery, Rüya, and what it was that he was seeking, he got in Jelal's bed and fell asleep.

When he woke up, he thought: Saturday morning. But it was, in fact, Saturday noon. A day free of the office and court hearings. Without putting on the slippers, he went and got the *Milliyet* that had been slipped under the door: Jelal Salik has been murdered. The headline appeared above the masthead. They had printed a picture of the body before it was covered under newspapers. They'd devoted the whole page to him and had got quotes from the prime minister and other officials as well as from celebrities. They'd put the piece coded "come home," which Galip had written, in a frame and printed it as the "final column." They'd printed a recent picture of Jelal which looked nice. According to the mavens, the bullets had been meant for democracy, freedom of speech, peace, each and every good thing that people mention every chance they get. Measures had been taken to apprehend the perpetrator.

He was sitting and smoking at the desk that overflowed with paper and news clippings. He sat in his pajamas and smoked for a long time. When the doorbell rang, he had a feeling he'd been smoking the same cigarette for the last hour. It was Kamer. She just stood there at first with the key in her hand, looking at Galip as if she'd seen a ghost, then she came in and had hardly made it into the easy chair by the phone before she burst out crying. Everyone had thought Galip was also dead. Everyone had been worried about them for days now. As soon as she read the news in the morning papers, she'd set out running to Aunt Halé's. She'd seen the crowd congregated in front of Aladdin's store. That's when she realized it was morning before Rüya's body had been discovered in there. It was when Aladdin opened the store, it seems, that he'd come upon Rüya's body lying among the dolls, as if sleeping.

Reader, dear reader, at this point in my book, allow me to intervene at least once before I send these lines to the typesetter, given that I've been meticulously trying—that is, exerting much well-meaning effort that perhaps you yourself might have observed—to keep the narrator separate from the protagonist, although not entirely successfully, as well as the newspaper columns from the pages where the action is depicted. There are pages in some books which penetrate us so deeply that we can never forget them, not on account of the writer's skill but because "the stories seem to flow on their own" as if "they have written themselves." Those pages don't remain in our minds, our hearts—or whatever you want to call it—as prodigious creations of a master craftsman but as tender, heartbreaking, and tearful moments that we shall remember for many years like the periods of heaven or hell in our own lives, or like both, or more like something beyond either. So, you see, had I been a top-notch wordsmith instead of the johnny-come-lately columnist that I am, I'd assume with assurance that this is one of those pages in my work called *Rüya and Galip* which might accompany my sensitive and intelligent readers for many years to come. But I don't possess that sort of assurance; I happen to be a realist when it comes to my talent and my work. That's why I wish to leave you, the reader, alone on this page with your own recollections. Best way of going about it might be for me to suggest that the printer cover the pages that follow with black printing ink. So that you might use your own imagination to create what I cannot do justice to with my prose. So that I might depict the color of the black dream I've embarked on at the point where I interrupted my story, I remind you of the silence in my mind as I tell you what happened next like a somnambulist. Consider, then, the following pages, the black pages, as the memoirs of a somnambulist.

It seems Kamer ran from Aladdin's store all the way to Aunt Halé's. There everyone was weeping, they were under the impression that Galip too was dead. Kamer had finally divulged Jelal's secret: She'd told them that Jelal had been hiding out in the flat on the top floor of the Heart-of-the-City Apartments for years, and so had Rüya and Galip for the last week. That's when everybody thought once again that Galip was also dead as well as Rüya. Later, when Kamer returned to the Heart-of-the-City Apartments, Ismail had told her, "Go upstairs and take a look!" When she'd come upstairs with the key, Kamer was gripped by a strange fear before opening the door, which was followed by a premonition that Galip was alive. She had on a pistachio-colored skirt Galip had often seen her wear and a soiled apron.

Later, when he went over, Galip saw that Aunt Halé was wearing a dress made of material with the same pistachio-green background on which purple flowers were blooming. Was it mere chance, or a reminder that the world, like the gardens of remembrance, was magical? Galip told his mother, his dad, Uncle Melih, Aunt Suzan, and everyone else who listened with tears, that he and Rüya had been back from Izmir for the last five days and that they'd spent a great portion of their time, sometimes even overnight, with Jelal at the Heart-of-the-City Apartments: Jelal had bought the top-floor flat years ago but had kept it from everyone. He was hiding out from some people who'd been threatening him.

Late in the afternoon, Galip was giving out the same story to the agent from the National Bureau of Investigation and the prosecutor who wanted to take his deposition, when he brought up the voice on the phone and went on at great length about it. But he couldn't draw the pair, who sat there listening with a know-it-all manner, into his story. He felt helpless, like someone who could neither escape his fantasies nor get anyone involved in them. There was a protracted and deep silence in his mind.

Toward evening he found himself in Vasıf's silent room. Perhaps because it was the only room where no weeping was being done, he could still observe in there the unspoiled signs of a happy family life which now belonged to the past: the Japanese goldfish, degenerated "due to marrying in the family," were gliding peacefully in the aquarium. Coals, Aunt Halé's cat, had stretched out on the edge of the rug and was absentmindedly scrutinizing Vasıf. Vasıf sat on the edge of his bed examining a pile of papers he had in his hands. These were telegrams of condolence sent by hundreds of people from the prime minister down to the most unpretentious reader. Galip observed Vasıf wearing the same surprised and playful expression that appeared on his face when he sat between Galip and Rüya on the same corner of the bed, looking through old news clips. The room was lit by the same weak, low light as it was whenever they met here before the evening meal Grandma, and later Aunt Halé, used to prepare for them. The somniferous light from the low-watt naked bulb, in unerring and definite conjunction with the faded old furniture and wallpaper, reminded Galip of the sorrow associated with the sadness of his life with Rüya which pervaded him like an incurable disease. That sadness and grief had turned into a good memory now. Galip had Vasıf get up from where he sat. He turned off the light. And without removing his clothes he stretched out on the bed, like a child who feels like weeping before going to sleep, and he slept for twelve whole hours.

The next day at the funeral, which was held at the Teşvikiye Mosque, Galip had a moment with the editor-in-chief; he explained that Jelal still had boxes of unpublished pieces, that although he'd turned in only a few new columns last week, he'd been working incessantly; not only had he polished off some of the columns in rough draft he had in his bottom drawer, he'd playfully turned out new pieces on many a novel subject which he had never previously taken in hand. The editor-in-chief said that he wanted to run these pieces for sure in Jelal's usual space. So, this was how the road was paved for Galip to continue a literary career that would go on for years in what had been Jelal's space. When the congregation came out of the Teşvikiye Mosque and proceeded to Nişantaşı Square where the hearse was waiting, Galip saw Aladdin looking on absentmindedly from his store entrance. He held in his hand a doll he was about to wrap up in a piece of newspaper.

It was on the night after Galip took his initial batch of Jelal's new pieces over to the *Milliyet* editorial offices that he first dreamed of Rüya in conjunction with this doll. He'd handed in Jelal's work and listened to words of sympathy and theories on the murder from friends and foes, including the old columnist Neşati, then retreated into Jelal's office and begun reading the last five days' papers which had piled up on the desk. Among all the lachrymose and overly laudatory obituaries and the articles describing similar murders in our recent history—where the inclination was to lay the blame on the Armenians, the Turkish mafia (Galip felt like editing it in green ink to read "Beyoğlu hoods"), Communists, contraband cigarette traffickers, Greeks, religious fundamentalists, right-wingers, Russians, the Nakşibendi order—Galip's attention was attracted by a piece done by a young journalist concerning the modus operandi of the murder. The piece, which had come out in *Cumhuriyet* the day of the funeral, was short and clear, but written in a style that was more than a little rhetorical, the protagonists had not been cited by name but by their designations, which had been capitalized.

The Famous Columnist and his Sister had left the columnist's place in Nişantaşı at seven o'clock Friday evening and gone to the Palace Theater. The movie, which was *Coming Home*, let out at nine twenty-five; the Columnist and the Sister (married to a young Lawyer)—(this was the first time Galip had ever seen himself mentioned in a paper, even if it was in parentheses)—had been in the crowd that came out of the theater. Snow, which had been the order of the day in Istanbul for the last ten days, had subsided, but it was still cold. They had gone past Governor's Road and taken Emlak up to Teşvikiye Avenue. It was when they were right in front of the police station, at nine thirty-five, that death had met up with them. The Killer, who had used a Kırıkkale make gun of the sort issued to retired military personnel, had in all probability aimed at the Famous Columnist but managed to get them both. Perhaps because the trigger was stiff, of the five bullets spent three had hit the Columnist, one the Sister, and one the Teşvikiye Mosque wall. The Columnist had died on the spot since one of the bullets had hit him in the heart. Another bullet had shattered the pen in the left pocket of his jacket—all the journalists had gone wild over this coincidental image—which was the reason why the Columnist's white shirt had been stained more with green ink than with blood. The Sister, wounded badly in her left lung, had managed to get to the attar store across the street which was the same distance from the murder site as the police station. The reporter, as if he were a detective who had a key scene on film rewound and played over and over, had described how the Sister had slowly walked into the attar store known as Aladdin's, and how the Storekeeper hadn't seen her go in, having been prevented by the trunk of the large chestnut tree behind which he had taken cover. The Sister enters the store, walking very slowly, and collapses among the dolls in the corner. The article began to sound to Galip like the account of a ballet being performed under strobe lights. But then the film suddenly went on fast forward and became absurd: the Storekeeper, who had been busy at closing time taking down the papers he had pinned up on the trunk of the chestnut, gets alarmed hearing the shots, and not having noticed the Sister go into the store, rolls down the shutters and leaves the scene in a sweat to beat it home fast.

Even though the lights had been on all night in the store known as Aladdin's, neither the police investigating in the vicinity nor anyone else had thought of going in to discover the young woman dying in agony inside. In the same vein, the authorities considered it odd that let alone not intervene, the policeman on duty on the opposite sidewalk had not even been aware that a second person was involved in the shooting.

The Killer had gotten away. A citizen had volunteered to inform the authorities that he had been out to Aladdin's to get a lottery ticket when he had seen, just moments before the incident, a frightening apparition wearing a strange outfit and strange cape appropriate for historical films ("looked something like Sultan Mehmet the Conqueror") and, what's more, he had been wildly telling his wife and sister-in-law all about it even before he read about the incident in the papers. The young journalist had finished his article wishing with the wish that this last clue would not also fall victim to dereliction and ineptitude as had the young woman who was found in the morning lying dead among the dolls.

That night Galip dreamed of Rüya among the dolls sold at Aladdin's store. She wasn't dead. She was waiting for Galip and breathing lightly in the dark in synch with the other dolls, winking at him, but Galip was late, he just couldn't get to the store no matter what; all he could do was look through his tears, watching out of the window in the Heart-of-the-City Apartments the light from Aladdin's window reflecting on the snow-covered sidewalk.

One sunny morning in early February, Galip's father told him that Uncle Melih had received a response to the inquiry he made at the Şişli Land Deeds Office, and that it had been determined that Jelal owned another flat somewhere in the back streets of Nişantaşı.

The flat Uncle Melih and Galip went to with a hunchback locksmith in tow was on one of Nişantaşı's old streets, on the top floor of one of those three- or four-story buildings where the façade is blackened with soot and smoke, and the paint has peeled off in pieces like the skin of an incurable patient; it was on a street paved with rectangular stone and with sidewalks that had potholes, which had always made Galip wonder, whenever he was on a street like this, why rich people would have ever wanted to live in places that were this miserable, or, conversely, why people who lived in miserable places like this would have ever been considered rich. The locksmith didn't need to sweat it, easily opening the worn lock in the door on which there was no name.

In the back, there were two narrow bedrooms with a bed in each. Up front, they saw a small living room, which was on the street and got sunlight, with a dining table standing in the middle; there were a pair of easy chairs across from each other at the table on which were news clips concerning recent murders, photos, movie and sports magazines, new issues of children's comics from Galip's childhood such as *Tom Mix* and *Texas*, detective novels, and piles of paper and newsprint. The pistachio shells mounded on the large copper ashtray proved to Galip without leaving any doubt in his mind that Rüya had indeed been sitting at this table.

In the room that had to be Jelal's Galip came across packs of memory-boosting medication called Mnemonics, vasodilators, aspirin, and match boxes. What he saw in Rüya's room reminded him that his wife hadn't taken very much with her when she left home: some makeup, her slippers, her lucky key chain that held no keys, and her mirror-backed hairbrush. Galip took such a long look at these articles sitting on the Thonet chair next to the bed in the sparsely furnished room with its bare walls that for a moment he slipped out of the enchantment of illusion, feeling that he had caught on to the secondary meaning the objects signaled to him, to the repressed mystery which was hidden in the world. "They came here to tell each other stories," he thought when he went back to Uncle Melih who was still out of breath after climbing the stairs. The way the papers were placed on the table revealed that Rüya had begun to write down the stories Jelal had been dictating, and that Jelal had sat in the chair on the left where Uncle Melih was now sitting and Rüya had sat and listened to him in the other one that was vacant. Galip pocketed Jelal's stories, which would later come in handy doing the pieces for *Milliyet*, and gave the explanation Uncle Melih felt he was entitled to without getting too pushy:

Jelal had long been suffering from a terrible memory disease which was discovered by the famous English physician, Dr. Cole Ridge, but for which he'd been unable to find a cure. Jelal had hid out in all these apartments in order to keep his affliction a secret from everyone, constantly asking for Rüya and Galip's help. To this end, Rüya sometimes spent the night and sometimes Galip, listening to Jelal's stories and sometimes even transcribing them, in order to help him recall and reconstruct his past. When it snowed outside, Jelal kept telling them his countless stories by the hour.

Uncle Melih fell silent as if he understood everything all too well. Then he wept. He lit a cigarette. He had a light wheezing attack. He said Jelal had always been subject to wrongheadedness. He had developed this odd obsession to get even with the whole family on account of having been kicked out of the Heart-of-the-City Apartments and the bad treatment he and his mother got when his father remarried. Yet his father had loved him at least as much as he did Rüya. Now he had no children left anymore. Well, no, Galip was his only son now.

Tears. Silence. The internal noises of an unfamiliar place. Galip felt like telling Uncle Melih to go and get his bottle of *rakı* at the corner store and go on home. Instead, he asked himself a question that he would not consider again, the same question which those readers who wish to put it to themselves would do best to skip (one paragraph):

On account of what stories, recollections, fairy tales blooming in the garden of remembrance had Rüya and Jelal felt it necessary to exclude Galip? Was it because Galip didn't know how to tell stories? Was it because he wasn't as hip and fun as they were? Was it because he didn't catch on to some stories at all? Was it because he spoiled their fun by his excessive admiration of Jelal? Was it because they fled from the stubborn sadness that he seemed to put out like a contagious disease?

Galip noted that Rüya had slipped a plastic yogurt bowl under the radiator's leaking valve, just the way she had done it at home.

Toward the end of summer, Galip vacated the apartment he and Rüya had rented—what with the furniture seeming to wince with terrible pain, he couldn't stand being around unbearable memories that involved Rüya—and moved into Jelal's place in the Heart-of-the-City Apartments. Just as he had been unable to look at Rüya's body, he hadn't wanted to see their stuff his father sold or gave away. He could no longer entertain fantasies of resuming their lives together, as if going on with a book they'd been interrupted reading halfway through, as he optimistically did in his dreams where Rüya turned up again from someplace or other, just as she had done after her first marriage. Hot, sultry summer days seemed endlessly long.

At the end of the summer, there was a military coup. A new government, composed of cautious patriots who hadn't sunk into the cesspool called politics, announced that all the perpetrators of past politically motivated murders would be apprehended. In response, journalists who didn't have much to report on account of the censorship, pointed out in nice, polite language that even the "Jelal Salik Murder" had yet to be solved. One of the papers, not for some reason *Milliyet* for which Jelal wrote but some other one, promised a sizable reward to any informer who was instrumental in getting the killer caught. The money was enough to buy a truck, or a small flour mill, or a grocery store that would bring in a steady income every month for a lifetime. This was what created the impetus and excitement to bring the mystery of the "Jelal Salik Murder" into light. Martial law commandants in provincial towns had also gone all out in an effort to solve it, so as not to miss their last chance at becoming celebrities.

My prose style probably betrays it to you that it is me again who's narrating all that transpired. It was during those days when the chestnut trees began leafing out once more that I was converted from a melancholic person into an angry one. The angry person I was being transformed into didn't pay much attention to the trial balloons provincial reporters passed on to Istanbul with the claim that "the investigation is being conducted under wraps." One week he read that the killer had been caught in some mountain town he'd previously heard mentioned in connection to an accident that left a bus load of soccer players and their fans crushed in the bottom of a ravine just outside of town; the next week the suspect was supposedly apprehended in a seaside town gazing longingly at the skyline of the neighboring country which had paid him sacks of dough for committing the crime. Since the news not only encouraged citizens who wouldn't have dared otherwise to think of turning stool pigeons, but also spurred on sundry martial law commandants into industrious competition with their successful colleagues, at the start of the summer there was a glut of news claiming that "the killer has been caught." It was during this period that security officials began hauling me out in the middle of the night to their central bureau in the city with the object of getting "information" and "a positive identification."

In addition to imposing the curfew, the authorities now turned the power off from midnight to morning, since the city couldn't afford to run the generators all night, and so our nights in Istanbul became as dark as in those distant small towns where they're big on their religion and their graveyards. Beleaguered as we were in a milieu where a terrifying darkness reigns and illegal butchers furiously slaughter old horses execution-style, the life of all of us in the city and in the entire nation had been cut down the middle into opposing factions as if with a knife. Around midnight I'd slowly emerge from the smoke rising from my desk where I'd written my latest column with inspiration and creativity that was worthy of Jelal's talents, and I'd go down the dark stairs of the Heart-of-the-City Apartments and out on the deserted sidewalk and wait for the police car that would take me to the Bureau of National Investigation built on the heights of Beşiktaş, which looked like a fort surrounded by a high wall. The city lay deserted and motionless, but the fort was hopping, full of action and glitter.

They'd bring out mug shots of sleep-deprived young men with dreamy expressions, deep purple circles under their eyes, and disheveled hair. Some of their eyes were reminiscent of the water-carrier's black-eyed son who used to come in with his dad and whose camera gaze committed to memory all the furniture in Uncle Melih's apartment by the time they finished refilling the water tank. Others recalled the pimply nonchalant "friend of a friend of mine's older brother" who came up to Rüya, not giving two hoots if her male cousin was with her or not, during the five-minute intermission at the movies where we went together when Rüya ate with relish her frozen Penguin bar; others, the salesboy who was the same age as us whose sleepy eyes watched the schoolkids go home through the half-open door of the old haberdashery store, some others—and this was the most horrible—were reminiscent of no one, had no association to anyone or anything at all. Looking at these vacant faces posed against police department walls that were unpainted, dirty, and stained with who knows what, was frightening. When I was about to make out through the fog of my recollections a vague shadow which neither gave itself away completely nor remained entirely indefinite, that is, when I was stumped, the hardboiled agents who stood over me would encourage me, supplying me with provocative information concerning the identity of the phantom expression in the mug shot: this kid had been picked up at a right-wing coffeehouse in Sivas, thanks to a tip, and was responsible for four previous killings; this other one whose mustache hadn't quite come in yet had published a long piece in a journal partisan to Enver Hoxha which identified Jelal as a life-size target; this one with the buttons on his jacket missing was being transferred from Malatya to Istanbul—he was a teacher, but he had persisted in telling his nine-year-old students that Jelal had to be slain for blaspheming against a great religious figure, on account of the piece he'd written on Rumi fifteen years ago; this timid, middle-aged fellow who looked like a family man was a drunk who had held forth at a Beyoğlu tavern on the subject of disinfecting our land of all the microbes, inspiring the citizen at the next table, whose mind was on the reward money offered by the newspaper, to report him to the Beyoğlu Precinct, saying the guy had also mentioned Jelal's name among the microbes. Did Mr. Galip know the hungover drunk, these deadbeats lost in daydreams, these cranks, these wretches? Had Mr. Galip seen in Jelal's company in recent years any one of these visionary or guilty faces whose photos were presented to him one by one?

In midsummer when the new five-thousand-lira notes came out with Rumi's image engraved on them, I read in the papers the obituary of a retired colonel whose name was Fatih Mehmet Üçüncü. During the same hot July nights the imperative midnight visits began to escalate and the mug shots placed before me to multiply. I saw faces that were sadder and more mournful, terrifying, and incredible than those in Jelal's modest collection: bicycle repairmen, archaeology students, serging machine operators, gas station attendants, grocery stock boys, extras at Yeşilçam Films, coffeehouse owners, authors of religious treatises, bus ticket-takers, park attendants, nightclub thugs, young accountants, encyclopedia salesmen . . . They'd all been through torture, roughed up, and given small or large beatings; they'd all looked into the camera with an expression that said, "I am not here" or "I happen to be someone else anyway," obscuring the fear and sorrow on their faces, as if to forget that lost mystery that settled in the bottom of their memory banks, but the existence of which they'd forgotten, and which they didn't miss since it was forgotten, that secret knowledge they wanted to lose in the bottomless well to make sure it would never come back.

Since I no longer want to go back to the predetermined moves I made totally unconsciously, in order to see what pieces are in which places in this old endgame that seems to me (and to my readers) to be a foregone conclusion, I thought I'd not bring in anything about the letters I saw in the faces in the photographs. But during one of those endless nights at the fort (or should I call it "the castle"?) when I rejected with the same certainty all the faces that had been presented to me, the NBI agent who was, as I learned later, a staff colonel asked me a question. "The letters," he said, "can you also make out any letters?" Then he added with seasoned professionalism: "We too know how difficult it is for a man to be himself in this land. But won't you help us out a little?"

One night I'd listened to a chubby major's inferences concerning the belief in the Messiah that still existed among remnants of the Sufi orders in Anatolia which he invoked not as the conclusions of secret intelligence work but as if giving voice to his own dark and tasteless childhood memories: During his clandestine trips into Anatolia Jelal had tried to make contact with these "reactionary dregs" and was successful in meeting a bunch of these somnambulists either at a car mechanic's in the outskirts of Konya or else at a quilt maker's home in Sivas, and he'd told them he would indicate the signals for the Day of Judgment in his columns, all they had to do was wait. The pieces in which he mentioned Cyclopes, the day that the Bosphorus dries up, sultans and pashas in disguise all teemed with these very signals.

When one of the diligent officers, who divulged that he had finally broken the code, said in all seriousness that the acrostic formed by the initial letters of the paragraphs in the piece called "The Kiss" was the key to the enigma, I felt like saying, "I've known that." And when they presented me with the significance in the title of the Ayatollah Khomeini's book, *Discovery of Mystery*, where he narrates his own life and struggles, and the man's photographs taken in dark city streets during the years of his exile in Bursa, I also felt like saying "I know," being quite cognizant of what they were trying to point out. When they had a good old time laughing that Jelal was looking for someone who would kill him in order to "establish" some sort of lost mystery, or, in their words, because "his screws were loose" and he had lapses of memory, or when I came across in the photographs put before me a face that looked like one of those lost, dolorous, mournful persons in the photos I found in the depths of Jelal's elmwood cabinet, again I felt like saying, "Don't I know it!" I wanted to tell them that I knew the identity of the beloved he summons in the piece on the Bosphorus's receding waters, the phantom wife he calls out to in the piece on kissing, the heroes he meets in the twilight of sleep. I still felt like saying, "I know," although I felt skeptical about anything they said, like when they remembered with great amusement that the scalper, whom Jelal mentioned in one of his columns going crazy with love for the pale Greek girl in a movie ticket booth, was in fact a plainclothes cop on their staff, or when I said after staring at it long and hard that I didn't recognize yet another face that had lost its integrity, secrets, and meaning due to torture, beating, and sleeplessness, besides being disconcerted by the presence of the magic two-way mirror through which we could see him but he couldn't see us, and they resorted to explaining to me that Jelal's stuff on faces and maps was in fact an old garden-variety scam that made use of a cheap tactic to make his readers happy by suckering them into thinking he'd send them some sort of a secret, a keepsake, a sign of something held in common.

Perhaps they already knew what I knew or didn't know, but because they wanted to be done with it as soon as possible, they wanted to kill off Jelal's lost, dark mystery, the mystery obscured by the black tar and colorless dregs of our lives, before we had a chance to discover it, or to cut off any doubt budding not only in my mind but in the minds of newspaper readers and compatriots everywhere before it grew and gave off shoots.

Sometimes one of the hardboiled spooks who thought enough was enough already, or a general that I met for the first time, or the skinny prosecutor I got to know some months ago would attempt to narrate a full-blown story like the unconvincing detective who unfolds with the ease of a magician the concealed significances of all the clues and the details for the benefit of the readers of mystery novels. While a scene reminiscent of the last pages of Rüya's mystery novels developed, the other functionaries present listened on, taking notes on paper in front of them that said State Supply Office—just like schoolteachers judging the intramural debates, listening with patience and pride to their best students' pearls of wisdom: The killer was a pawn sent by foreign powers who wanted to "destabilize" our society; the Bektaşi and the Nakşibendi orders who realized their secrets had been made the subject of derision, as well as some poets who wrote classical verse that involved acrostics along with some present-day bards—voluntary Hurufis every one of them—had become the unwitting representatives for the foreign powers in the plot to push us into anarchy or a kind of apocalypse. No, this murder presented no political implications. In order to figure this out, all one had to do was remember that the murdered journalist had been writing nonpolitical nonsense concerning his own private obsessions which he penned in an outmoded manner and a prose style that was unreadable and much too long. The murderer had to be either the Beyoğlu hood who was affronted thinking he was being lampooned by the exaggerated legends Jelal wrote about him, or some other gunman that he had hired. On one of those nights when college kids who turned themselves in for the sake of making a name for themselves were put to torture to change their minds about confessing to the murder, or when innocent people picked up at the mosque were forced into making a confession, a false-toothed professor of Classical Ottoman Literature—he and an NBI big cheese had spent their childhood together in old Istanbul backyards and streets overlooked by trellised balconies—after making a short but boring introduction to Hurufism and the ancient art of word games which was interrupted by jokes, had listened to the story I told unwillingly and then, putting on airs like a slum-district gypsy fortune-teller, explained that "the incidents could very well be placed into the framework of Şeyh Galip's *Beauty and Love* without too much difficulty." During that period, a two-man committee had been busy at the fort, examining informants' letters which had been written to the newspapers and the authorities in the heat of the general frenzy brought on by the promise of the award money; so no attention was paid to the literary solution presented by the professor who pointed out two-hundred-year-old problems in poetry.

It was around the same time when they concluded that the killer was a barber who'd been turned in. After showing me the small thin man in his sixties, and seeing how I still couldn't make an identification, they stopped summoning me to the mad festivals of life and death, mystery and power, that went on at the fort. The newspapers were busy for an entire week with the barber's story down to the last detail; he had initially denied the crime, then confessed to it, then denied it again only to confess once more. Jelal Salik had first mentioned this man years ago in his column titled "I Must be Myself." In that piece, and in others that followed it, he'd written that the barber had come to the paper and put to him questions that would illuminate the profound mystery concerning the East, ourselves and our existence, and that the columnist had responded to the questions by cracking jokes. The barber had been enraged seeing that these jokes, which he considered slander heaped on him in the presence of witnesses, had been brought up not once but repeatedly in the columns. Upon seeing the initial column printed yet again under the very same headline twenty-two years later, only to slander him once more, the barber, prodded by certain figures around him, had decided to get even with the columnist. As to the identities of the provocateurs, not only were they never discovered but their very existence was denied by the barber who characterized his work as "an individual act of terrorism," using language he'd picked up from the police. Not too long after the papers printed the man's tired and beat-up face scoured of any meaning or letters, he was tried and sentenced and then, one morning at an hour when only woebegone packs of dogs wandered through the streets of Istanbul unwary of the martial law curfew, was hanged in order to demonstrate the efficiency of this speedy justice by the speedy execution of the sentence.

Back then, I was busy working on stories I recalled or researched on the subject of Mount Kaf and also listening groggily to theories put forth by people who came to see me at my office for the purpose of shedding light on the "events," but not providing much help. That was the state I was in when listening to the obsessive student from the school of theology who'd figured out from his writings that Jelal had been the Dadjdjal and, explaining at great length and substantiating it by pointing out the letters in the news clippings that were rife with references to executioners, he reasoned that if he had come to this conclusion, so could the killer, who by killing him emulated the Messiah, that is, Him. I also listened to the Nişantaşı tailor who disclosed that he'd been sewing historical costumes for Jelal. Like someone who barely recalls a movie he's seen years ago, I had a hard time even remembering that the tailor was the same one I'd seen working late in his store on the snowy night that Rüya had vanished. I displayed the same reaction to my old friend Saim the archivist who turned up to get the nitty-gritty on just how extensive the NBI archives were, and also to bring the good news that the innocent student had been sprung from jail now that Mehmet Yılmaz had finally been caught. While Saim held forth on "I Must be Myself," referring to the headline of the column assumed to give the motive for the murder, I was so far from being myself that I was becoming a stranger to this black book, as well as to Galip.

There was one period when I devoted myself exclusively to the law and my cases. During another period, I let things slide, looking up old friends and going out to restaurants and taverns with new acquaintances. Sometimes I noticed the clouds over Istanbul take on an incredible shade of yellow or ash; at other times I tried convincing myself that the sky over the city was the same old sky. I'd rise from the desk past midnight, having easily knocked off two or three pieces for that week, as Jelal used to during his productive periods, and I'd sit in the chair next to the phone and stretch my legs out on the footstool, waiting for the things around me to gradually get transformed into things from another world, signs from another universe. It was then that I sensed somewhere deep in my memory a recollection stir like a shadow, and as the shadow advanced through a gate in the garden of remembrance that opened into another garden, only to continue through a second and then a third and fourth gate, I felt all through this familiar process the gates of my own personality open and close as I was being transformed into another person who could become involved and happy with that shadow; it was then that I'd catch myself before I began to speak with that other person's voice.

I kept my life under some sort of control, although not too strictly, so as not to come up against a remembrance of Rüya when I wasn't up to it, carefully avoiding grief I was afraid might descend on me unexpectedly anywhere anytime. When I was at Aunt Halé's for supper three or four times a week, I helped Vasıf feed the Japanese goldfish, but I never sat on the edge of the bed with him to look at the news clippings he brought out. (Even so, that was how I chanced upon Edward G. Robinson's photo in the paper, printed above Jelal's column, and discovered that there was something of a family resemblance between the two of them—more like distant relatives.) Whenever it got very late and either my dad or Aunt Suzan suggested that I go home before I was any later, as if Rüya were waiting for me in her sickbed, "You're right," I'd tell them, "I better leave before it's time for curfew."

Yet I wouldn't take the route that went by Aladdin's store, the one Rüya and I used to take, but would walk through backstreets the roundabout way both to our place and to the Heart-of-the-City Apartments, and would again change my course trying to avoid going into the streets Jelal and Rüya walked through after leaving the Palace Theater, finding myself in Istanbul's strange dark alleys, walking along unfamiliar walls, streetlights, letters, mosque court-yards, and buildings with terrifying faces and windows with curtains pulled shut like blind eyes. Walking along past these dark and dead signs changed me so much into another person that, when I arrived on the sidewalk in front of the Heart-of-the-City Apartments a little before the onset of curfew and I saw the rag still tied on the top floor balcony grillwork, I'd easily take it as the signal that Rüya was home waiting for me.

After walking through the dark deserted streets, seeing the signal Rüya left for me on the grillwork, I'd remember what we talked about at length, the third year of our marriage in the middle of a snowy night, like a pair of old friends who've carried on for years without needling each other, without letting the conversation drop in Rüya's bottomless well of indifference, and without being aware of the profound silence that appeared between us like a phantom. We had imagined, at my instigation and with Rüya's relish in her own powers of imagination, a day we'd spend together when we turned seventy-three.

When we were seventy-three, we'd go up to Beyoğlu together on a winter's day. We'd buy each other presents with the money we'd been saving: a sweater or a pair of gloves. We'd be wearing our heavy old overcoats that smelled like us and which we'd come to like. We'd be window-shopping absentmindedly without looking for anything in particular, talking to each other. We'd be swearing hatefully, complaining about things that kept changing, talking idly about how clothes, store windows, and people used to be so much better and nicer in the old days. While we went through the rigmarole, we'd be conscious that we behaved like this because we were too old to expect much from the future, but we still would carry on without changing any of our behavior. We'd buy a few pounds of marrons glacées making sure they were weighed and packaged right. Then somewhere in the backstreets of Beyoğlu we'd come across an old bookstore which we'd never seen before and, amazed and overjoyed, we'd congratulate each other. Inside, there would be mysteries sold reasonably which Rüya hadn't read before or didn't remember reading. While we poked around for novels, we'd get growled at by an elderly cat stalking around the piles of books, and the sensitive saleslady would smile at us. We'd stop at a pudding shop, pleased with the packages of books we'd come by so cheaply which would take care of Rüya's mystery habit for the next couple of months at least, and while having our tea, we'd have a small altercation. We'd fight because we were seventy-three, and knew that we'd spent our seventy-three years in vain, which was something that happened to all people as it would to us. We'd open the packages upon returning home, we'd take our clothes off without being shy, and we'd put our white, flabby old bodies to work making love at length, accompanied with lots of marrons glacées and sticky syrup. The pale color of our tired old bodies would be the same semitransparent cream color of our childhood skin when we first met sixty-six years ago. Rüya, whose imagination was always more vivid than mine, had said that we'd stop in the middle of this insane lovemaking to have a smoke and a good cry. I was the one who brought the subject up because I had a hunch Rüya would come to love me when we were seventy-three when she was in no condition to yearn for different lives. Whereas Istanbul, as my readers have noticed, would keep on living in its misery.

I still come across something of hers sometimes in one of Jelal's old boxes, or among the stuff in my office, in some room, or at Aunt Halé's, which hasn't been disposed of due to my having overlooked it in some strange way. The purple button from the flowered dress she was wearing when I first saw her, a pair of those "modern" cycglass frames with the pointy corners, the kind that began appearing in the sixties on the faces of sound and able women in European magazines, which Rüya had managed wearing for six months before she cast them off; the small black hairpins one of which she held between her lips while she fastened the other in her hair using both hands; the tail-shaped lid she'd been unhappy about having mislaid for years, which went on a hollow wood duck where she kept her needle and thread; the homework assignment for literature class on the mythical bird called simurgh that lived on Mount Kaf, which had been copied right out of the encyclopedia and got left in Uncle Melih's legal files; strands of her hair stuck on Aunt Suzan's hairbrush; a shopping list made out for me (smoked bonito, a *Silver Screen* magazine, butane for the lighter, Bonibon chocolates with hazelnuts); a picture of a tree drawn with Grandpa's help; the horse in the alphabet book; an odd sock from the green pair I'd seen her wear riding a rented bicycle nineteen years ago.

Before I left one of these articles gently, respectfully, and meticulously in one of the garbage cans in front of some apartment building in Nişantaşı and ran off, I'd carry them around in my grubby pockets for a couple of days, sometimes a week, and even—all right, okay—a couple of months; and even after giving them up painfully, I'd fantasize that these mournful objects would one day return to me along with their memories, just like the articles that came back from the dark void in the apartment building.

Today all that I have of Rüya is merely this text, these dark, black, pitch-black pages. Sometimes when I remember one of the stories in these pages, say the story of the executioner or the first time we heard Jelal tell the tale called "Rüya and Galip" on a snowy winter's night, I end up recalling some other story in which the only way to be oneself is by becoming another or by losing one's way in another's tales; and the tales I want to put together in the black book remind me of a third or fourth tale, just like our love stories and memory gardens that open into one another, and I am thrilled to remember the story of a lover who becomes someone else upon getting lost in the streets of Istanbul, or the story of the man looking for the lost mystery and meaning in his own face, which make me embrace with increasing ardor my newly found work which is nothing more than retelling these old, very old—ancient—tales, ending up with me coming to the end of my book. At the end, Galip hurries to meet the newspaper deadline, writing the last of Jelal's stories which, when you come right down to it, aren't the hottest thing in print anymore. Then toward morning he aches remembering Rüya and gets up from the desk to gaze at the city sleeping in darkness. I remember Rüya and, getting up from the desk, I gaze at the city's darkness. We remember Rüya and gaze at Istanbul's darkness. And, in the middle of the night, we are seized by the sorrow and the thrill that get me anytime between sleep and wakefulness when I think I've come across Rüya's trace on the blue-checkered quilt. After all, nothing can be as astounding as life. Except for writing. Except for writing. Yes, of course, except for writing, the sole consolation.

1985–1989

HARVEST IN TRANSLATION

Stanislaw Benski	*Missing Pieces*
Umberto Eco	*The Name of the Rose*
Bohumil Hrabal	*Too Loud a Solitude*
Pawel Huelle	*Who Was David Weiser?*
	Moving House
Danilo Kiš	*Garden, Ashes*
Pavel Kohout	*I Am Snowing: The Confessions of a Woman of Prague*
George Konrád	*A Feast in the Garden*
Cees Nooteboom	*The Following Story*
	Rituals
Amos Oz	*Fima*
	In the Land of Israel
	A Perfect Peace
	To Know a Woman
Orhan Pamuk	*The Black Book*
Octavio Paz	*The Other Voice: Essays on Modern Poetry*
José Saramago	*The Gospel According to Jesus Christ*
	The Stone Raft
	The Year of the Death of Ricardo Reis
Luis Sepúlveda	*The Old Man Who Read Love Stories*
A. B. Yehoshua	*A Late Divorce*
	The Lover
	Mr. Mani